VOLUME 2

VOLUME 2

JOHNATHAN MCCLAIN
AND
SETH MCDUFFEE

Cover design by GrafitArt

ISBN: 978-1-0394-5542-9

Published in 2025 by Podium Publishing
www.podiumentertainment.com

For anyone reading this . . . thank you for sharing in the journey

VOLUME 2

ACT ONE

(NOT QUITE A) RETURN OF THE KING

PROLOGUE

The expression on her face isn't one of anger. Not exactly. It's something harder to place, like her mind is trying to glue two halves of a myth together and realizing the seam won't hold.

And in this split second, I wonder if I just did the right thing.

Not morally, maybe. Morally, I feel pretty sure I did.

But tactically. Strategically. The way you sometimes do the wrong thing because you know it's the only card that keeps you in the game long enough to matter.

Hell, maybe this was ever the only way forward. Maybe it always had to come to this: The inevitable moment when the story turns itself around and demands of the author rather than the author demanding of it.

I try to tell myself it wouldn't have changed much: That the Guardian still would've shuffled the board. That reality would've cracked somewhere anyway. That the walls would've split open all the same, and everything sharp would've come pouring out.

Still, the part of me that loves fantasies wonders if all of this could've been avoided.

If the splintering, the shock, the fallout breaking through the seams . . .

If it all goes back to one moment. One single, solitary instant . . .

If I should've just come clean way back when Almeister said . . .

CHAPTER ONE

"You're not Carpathian."

A hush overtakes the room, a feeling of suspended animation. For me, it very much resembles the experience I have right at the moment Control becomes active, sans any type of Mezmeric hoo-ha, just the naturally occurring kind of tension-filled moment that people share when they have been collectively taken up short by a sense of "*Whaaaaa?*"

My back is to Brit and Seph, yet I can very much sense the shared tilt in their heads. Almeister stares at me, confused, but in a guileless way. Like a baby in one of those videos I've seen online of people tossing cheese slices onto their infants' heads for some weird reason. I mean, it's funny every time I see it, which is, I suppose, why people do it, but that doesn't diminish the fact that it's a super strange thing to do to a ten-month-old.

The floorboard beneath my chair creaks. I feel my eyes squint and my head nod. I clear my throat. I cluck my tongue. Then, after what feels much longer than only the second or two I know it to be, I ask . . . "Say what now?"

"Father?" Persephone stands and comes over to the bed, stroking her hand across Almeister's brow and looking at him with concern. "It is. It's Carpathian. He came to rescue you."

She twists her head to glance at me with a look that's half concern, half apology. Kind of an eye-rolling, sorry-my-dad's-acting-so-weird look.

"No," Almeister says. "No, Carpathian Einzgear is dead. They told me. They told me he was killed attempting an attack on the Tower."

"Well, yes," Seph admits. "He . . . was. But he is reconstitute. He has returned to set right all that has heretofore been thrashed asunder."

Almeister torques his neck to see around her and look at me again. I give a small wave.

"She's right. You know what they say: Can't keep a good Saviour down."

His eyes narrow. "You do not speak like Carpathian."

Shit. I keep forgetting to . . . Carpathian-up my speech. Partially because there's more than enough to keep track of with all that's happened, and partially because, well, I'm a writer, not an actor. Or a voice . . . accent . . . guy . . . or whatever. I suppose I could attempt to make myself sound more like the audiobook narrator made Carpathian sound, but I feel like I'd just come off like some sort of hacky, amateur dungeon master or something and call even more attention to the disconnection. So, I decide to just go with the same excuse I've been using.

"Yeah, I know. Trust me, Almeister, I was as surprised as anybody when I opened my mouth and heard what the reconstitution had done! But remember, being recarbonified does a kind of hard reset. I mean . . . don't you recall how different I was when you and I first met!"

That much is at least true. When I first started writing the character, he was kind of dopey and puppy doggish and sounded totally different than the version of himself he was when Almeister last knew him. He had grown up. It shouldn't be hard to believe that a remorted Carpathian wouldn't have full Saviour swag just yet.

"Almeister." I lean in to speak softly. "It's me."

It's a difficult thing to own, for what are fairly obvious reasons. I've spent almost the entirety of my time on Meridia rejecting the notion that I am Carpathian, only to finally start accepting that that might actually be my role—or *identity*—here, just to then have this dude reject the very premise I've begun to embrace.

"And," I go on, "I've come back to . . . y'know . . . finish what I started. To, um, repair the Heart Guard? And to, erm, unseat the Ninth Guardian? And . . . stuff?"

I obviously don't volunteer "to find out how in the Steve Winwood to find my way home," but I think it.

It's not lost on me that the band Steve Winwood was in when he recorded "Can't Find My Way Home" was called Blind Faith, and that's ostensibly what I'm supposed to have when it comes to the System and my place here on Meridia, but I think it's probably just a coincidence?

(Unless Steve Winwood *is* the Ninth Guardian. Oh, man, that'd be crazy.)

(And now the song is stuck in my head. Great.)

Almeister's face contorts, clearly wrestling with something that's eating at him.

"Father? What is it? What's wrong? You can speak safely here."

He sucks in a deep breath, which causes him to cough a bit, then says, "Carpathian is no more. We are now to await the arrival of Brucillian."

I don't know who opened a portal that allowed an Antarctic blast into the room which chills my spine and causes me to shudder, but it feels like that's what just happened.

"Father . . ." Seph starts again, looking at me with worry, but I can only shrug in return, shaking my head tightly in what I intend to project as a quintessential expression of "Iunno."

But I need to say something, I suppose, so I try convivially, "Almeister, Almeister, hey, hey. Al? Buddy? Can I call you Al? I know we never really had a nickname-y relationship before, but—"

"Father, how can you believe such heresy?" Seph interjects.

He pauses as if he's trying to understand it himself, then offers, "Because . . . that is what they told me."

"Who?" I ask. "Who told you that?"

". . . The Disciples," he mumbles. "The Disciples of the Ninth Guardian."

"Father, why would you believe anything that DONG has said? Ever?!"

She now looks at me with a very clear, what-have-they-done-to-him? face.

"Because . . . Because . . ." His neck twists, his breathing ramping up. He pops his lips like his dentures have just fallen out. He's stumbling around inside his brain, trying to figure out the answer to a simple question. It's so odd; he's completely unlike the Almeister I wrote about or anticipated finding. He's much more . . . absentminded professor? Sorta nervous. Timid.

Frankly, it's not a great look. I was expecting to rescue Almeister the great and powerful wizard, not Almeister the scared, doddy old guy who feels like he's been getting all of his information from listening to a bunch of questionably intentioned podcasts.

"Al," I say again, putting as much compassion into my tone as possible even though I am all kinds of angsty about the fact that after what we went through to retrieve the guy, the version of him with which I'm being greeted is vastly different than what I had hoped for. "Can you tell us what happened? After you were taken?"

He nods slowly. He looks at me again, his eye twitching. He appears to regard me with skepticism. Then he says, "I . . . can."

I sigh out a breath. "Okay, so—"

"If you can prove to me that you truly are Carpathian Einzgear."

Oh, crap.

"Father—"

"I must be sure!" he erupts. Seph pulls back. That is very un-Almeister-like. "There is too much at risk for an imposter to assume the mantle! I must know that you are he!"

"Okay, okay, no problem," I attempt to assure. "How . . . How would you like me to prove it?"

I'm worried he's going to ask me to do something extra, like fly or move a boulder with my mind or something proto-Carpathian. Fortunately, I can continue to fall back on the old, *I'm just a baby Saviour. I ain't got no fancy superpowers yet. Goo-goo, ga-ga, me need Saviour food.*

But, as not-luck would have it, he doesn't ask for any of that. He asks for something that should be—theoretically—much easier to provide.

"Tell me the last thing Carpathian Einzgear said to me before I was taken."

Damn.

"The last thing . . . that Carpathian . . . that I . . . said . . . before . . ."

I swallow hard and look to Brit with wide eyes. Because there are two people in this room who know damn good and well that I can barely remember what I wrote two sentences ago, much less an entire book's worth of prose back. Brittany stares back at me with eyes equally widened; it appears to me that she knows the answer and is trying to will it into my brain.

The irony is that there is a kind of Heart Guard mind-meld thing we could use in a situation like this, but Carpathian didn't develop that with the Heart Guard until book five, when his Resonance Tier reached Witchmetal. As of my last Pulse Well check-in, I'm still just at Etherflint. Entry Level. I may have jumped up somewhat, but until we hit another Pulse Well, I'm not gonna know for sure, and even then, it's enormously unlikely I would have leapt all the way past Manasteel.

(At least I *think* that's the order? Again, I have an issue with memory retention. Which is my big problem right now in the first place.)

Both Seph and Al are also staring at me; Seph with hope and Al in challenge.

Shit!

Alright, think, Silvert, think.

So . . .

What did Carpathian say to Almeister before he was taken? *Right before* . . .

Goddammit, it's just on the edge of my brain. I do remember it was a real nice scene. Book nine. Almeister and Carpathian were pinned down like Butch and Sundance, and for the first time ever, Almeister showed something like uncertainty. He expressed worry that they might not escape, showed real anxiety. Almeister was the father figure Carpathian always wanted, and that moment was what I thought of as a kind of a passing of the torch, when Carpathian was to become the nominal caretaker as opposed to the one of whom care needed to be taken.

And he saaaaaaaaaiiiiiid . . .?

"Carpathian?" Seph's voice and pleading look snap me back.

"Yeah? Yeah! Uh, yeah . . . Um, no, I know. Yeah, no, yeah, no, I remember what I said. And what I said waaaaasssss . . ."

Thump-thump. Thump-thump.

All of a sudden, it hits me like a switchsaw to the dome. But in a good way. I gasp and . . .

"I said, 'I vow now unto you, Almeister, that we shall prevail! You have my word! And if ever you are imperiled—placed into any type of danger—I will not rest until you are returned to safety! I will roil oceans and overturn mountains if I must, but you shall know peace! This life I have, I owe it to you, and I will not allow yours to be taken, no matter the price!'"

It just spills out; it's like I went into a trance or something. I do worry that I may have written "no matter the cost" instead of "no matter the price," but with luck, he won't word cop me on it.

Almeister twists his neck, side-eyeing me, before finally, *finally* saying, "Carpathian."

A collective sigh leaves all of our lungs.

"Yep. That's me," I say once more.

"Forgive me," he intones. "It's just . . . They told me that . . . And your *Aura* is—"

"Hey, no problem, you don't have to apologize. It's—I get it. Whatever. Easy mistake."

"So . . . you are . . . recarbonified?"

"Uh, yeah. Yeah. I took a bit of a . . . murdering. But then Teleri over here"—I point at Brittany, who waves—"she incanted a little bit and then, y'know, abracadabra, I came back."

"She said . . . *Abra? Ca? Dabra?* I do not know this invocation."

"Not literally, it's just . . . Whatever. I'm here, is the point. And you're here—I kept my word! I got you back! I rescued you just as I said I would!"

I feel an enormous amount of pride at that. It may be unearned—I did try and have Carpathian dip out in book ten, after all—but at the end of the day, Almeister is here because I saved him.

So, yay me.

"But please, Almeister, can you talk me through what happened since I, uh, last saw you? Since you were captured and imprisoned in the Tower? What exactly DONG did? What did DONG do, I mean?" There is simply no way of asking a question like that so that it doesn't undermine the gravity of the situation, but I'm not sure saying "DONG" multiple times was the solution.

"I can," he replies quietly.

I nod and wink at Brit and Seph. Seph smiles, while Brit gives me a good-job-dancing-between-raindrops headshake. The two of them place themselves back into the chairs they were sitting in before softly, gingerly, as though any amount of disturbance could cause the delicate equilibrium we now have going on to tilt on its axis and send us spiraling again.

"Well," Almeister continues, his eyebrows knitting together in a look of consternation as he attempts to recount the precise details of what's happened to him. "The last thing I can recall before my being seized is . . . my own reflection?" He stares at the floor, and the already richly carved lines in his wizened forehead deepen in contemplation.

Yeah, right, that was how the Super Vizier and DONG managed to capture him.

By that point in the series, Almeister's well-documented powers were known to be second only to Carpathian's near god-tier capabilities. So, in a moment of what seemed like divine inspiration at the time—and which I now understand as something real that got shoved inside my brain by whatever force crammed Riftbreaker into my noggin—I wrote that the High Council, using some kind of Dark Mezmer (the name of which I also can't remember at the moment), crafted something called the Mirror of Nullification and used it to bounce a Spell shot forth by Almeister back *at* him, thus knocking him ass over teakettle with his own enchanted boom-bap and laying him out cold to be scooped up by Templars.

Not gonna lie, it was pretty sexy. On the page. Here in Meridia, it is proving to have been a real shitty way for Almeister to get got.

"I recall," I affirm, trying to exude patience and sympathy. "Yes. You were hoist by your own petard. As it were."

"Yes," he mutters, reflecting further on the memory. "And then . . ."

I can feel myself fidgeting as I await the details, the Heart working hard inside me.

Thump-thump. Thump-thump.

"And then," he goes on, "And then . . . I awakened to the sound of screaming."

"Screaming? Who was doing the screaming? Do you know?"

He nods. "I was."

I swallow and issue a small throat clearing. Somehow, I knew that was going to be the answer.

"Wh—Why? Why were you, uh, screaming?" I manage.

"I was . . . being tortured."

Persephone gasps. Brit reaches out and takes Seph's hand, giving it a squeeze of reassurance. Rubbing at my mouth, feeling the beard that's starting to settle in nicely, I hesitate. I don't want to ask about the specifics, but the guy has clearly been "rode hard and put up wet," as a horse trainer I met one time might say, and I need to know exactly what happened. What did they do to the dude that has him so shaken and doubtful?

"What, uh, what kind of torture?" I force the unpleasant question.

He looks up from the floor where he's been staring, lost in his recollection. "All kinds. All manner of torment one might suffer was inflicted upon me, it seemed. Every Spell imaginable. Shatterbone. Poisoned Blood. The Flaying of the Soul."

Flaying of the Soul?! Jesus, that sounds rough.

"Starvation of the Spirit. Mezmeric Disembowelment. The Severing of the Scrotum—"

"Got it! Got it! I got it!" I damn near scream, throwing a hand up to stop the itemization of anguish. That's a lot of foul magic to have been magicked up on the guy. "Why?" I gasp out. "What was the purpose of it all?"

I mean, I get that DONG is notoriously evil, but in my experience—as I wrote about the Disciples of the Ninth Guardian—there was always a reason, no matter how deviant or irrational. Sadism for sadism's sake isn't something I ever imagined them practicing. There has to be some kind of rationale.

The alternative is too grim to consider.

"The purpose?" he repeats. "The purpose was to induce me to divulge the location of the Rebellion, of Garr Haven, and of Carvesend. Obviously."

I feel like I'm gonna throw up.

"But I did not," he says proudly. "I held fast. Or . . . as long as I could."

"As long as you could? What does that mean?"

He couldn't have told them. When Moridius and company showed up at Garr Haven, it was because Waslan (fka "The Ronine") led them there. My arrival (or re-arrival, I suppose) on Meridia set the hunt in motion, and it was seven Lunar Rotations after Almeister got captured before that happened. If he had told them where the Rebellion was housed before then, they would've already sacked everything before I got there. So . . .

"Almeister? Al? Buddy? Hey?" He's gone back to his thousand-yard stare. I snap my fingers to try and get his attention, but . . . nothing. He's tripping on the memories.

Oh! Y'know what? He's a member of the Heart Guard! I bet I can run an inventory and see what's going on!

I pull up the statuses of everyone in the old HG real quick.

Heart Guard Evaluation:

Heart Guard Member [Teleri Nightwind]. Status: Present
Heart Guard Member [Pergamon Slow Bottom]. Status: Present
Heart Guard Member [Persephone Vizardsdottir]. Status: Present
Heart Guard Member [Mael Anderbariach]. Status: Absent
Heart Guard Member [Tavrella Redacted]. Status: Deleted

Do You Wish to Permanently Delete Member?
[Yes] [No]

Seeing Mael come up as "Absent" and Tavrella, especially, as "Deleted" stings quite a bit. My goal was to save and reunite the Heart Guard, not lose one member a second time and add a new member only to have them perish on my watch. Tavrella would probably still be alive if she hadn't chosen to stick with me and come to the Tower. Which is a particularly hard thing to square, given the state in which we have found Almeister. But . . . I dunno. Maybe there was another reason she was there, considering the fact that she was a kind of avatar for Mom.

Whatever, not the time. But I'm not going to delete her permanently. Not yet. Just . . . not yet.

(Side note: Why is her last name redacted? Unless her last name *is* "Redacted"? I don't know what to make of that. It's all very confusing.)

Continuing the check-in . . .

Heart Guard Member [Xanaraxa Caputrukahs]. Status: Missing
Heart Guard Member [Zerastian Teronia]. Status: Missing

"Missing," as opposed to "Absent," like Mael. Subtle distinction, but worthy of note. Finding them needs to be the next order of business, no matter what. Having Almeister's counsel in the matter will be invaluable, so let me see if I can get a full download on . . .

Heart Guard Member [Almeister T. Wizard]. Status: Corrupted

"*Corrupted?*" Corrupted. That doesn't sound awesome. I tap on his name to dig a little deeper.

Access [DENIED]

. . . *The flip?*

Additional information about Heart Guard Member [Almeister T. Wizard] Is Currently [UNAVAILABLE]
It appears that the connection with Almeister T. Wizard, founding member of your Heart Guard, has been corrupted. Further interrogation of the matter is likely to reveal the cause of such a corruption, but that interrogation must be performed manually. Because, you know, it's been corrupted.
A reset may be required to reestablish the connection.
Good luck with that.
{COURTESY MESSAGE #29}

Oh, for the love of—

"Father?" Persephone asks, moving from her chair to crouch beside me and Al on the floor, giving a shot at reaching the old wizard somehow. "Father?" He looks up. His eyes meet hers.

"When you say you 'held on as long as you could'? What do you mean? Held on how?"

Her voice draws Almeister's glassy eyes out of his stupor and back onto his daughter.

"Held on until I could no longer tolerate the punishment I was enduring and acted in such a way as to compel them to cease," he says, as though marveling over the recollection.

"Compel them to cease?" I repeat. He sniffs, sets his jaw, and nods. "How did you compel them? If you didn't give up the information they wanted, what did you do to get them to stop?"

"What did I . . .? I can't . . ." His ruminative countenance holds for another brief beat as he appears to be struggling with recalling the exact details. "I . . . I . . . I . . ."

Then, the memory appears to come to him all at once as, in another abrupt shift of demeanor, his expression softens, an unseen weight seems to fall from his shoulders, a smile works its way onto his lips, and with an almost relieved sigh pushing the sound from his mouth, he says . . .

". . . I died."

CHAPTER TWO

What?! What does he mean, he died? That don't sound right," Perg says.

He, Brit, and I are wandering the streets of Bell's View. Which, on the one hand, seems potentially dangerous, but on the other, given what we've just endured in the Tower, feels like it doesn't really matter and if someone wants to roll up on us out of nowhere and try to pick our pockets or something, they'll get a face full of Blade of the Starfallen.

Right now, I need to walk and get my head straight, so that's what I'm doing.

"I thought he died one time before," Perg goes on. He's small again, perched on Brit's shoulder.

"He did," I acknowledge. "In Riftbreaker book six, *Axes of Fate*, he sacrificed himself to the Tempest of Eternal Damnation—a once in a millennium storm that sweeps over Meridia, blanketing the planet in darkness—because there was only enough space in the shelter they had available at the time for the rest of the crew to hide in."

"Okay," he says.

"I thought that would be a cool, low-key Easter egg homage for anyone who was paying enough attention to clock it."

"Alright."

"Y'know, the wizard himself being swept up in what was essentially a tornado?"

"Yeah, I get it, homeboy, you're dead clever. But my question is: how can he come back from death a second time? I thought, according to the rules, once someone died and came back one time, they couldn't do it again."

"How do you know that?" Brittany asks. Fairly. It's not like Perg read the books. Up until very recently, he lived in a snail habitat without a library, as far as I know.

"I pay attention, *chica*. I may be slow, but I'm not *slow*, you feel me?"

"Normally, you don't," I confirm, regarding the established remorting rules on Meridia. "I mean, to my knowledge, no one has. But in Almeister's case . . ." I pause, because even though Almeister just explained to us what happened, I had a hard time tracking it. And since Brittany is the "keeper of details" and I am not . . . "Brit, can you . . . ?"

She huffs. "Sure. Yes, once someone is dead a second time, they stay dead. Unless they have access to a Spell."

"A Spell?"

"What I said. He called upon a dark rider on a dark horse to ferry him to the noncorporeal plane."

"So, basically, he chose to die," Perg states rather than asks.

"Basically." She nods. "Except that, as he explained it, it's not really so much a Death Spell as it is a Spell that put him into a deep sleep."

"It's like when doctors put a person into a medically induced coma when they have a traumatic brain injury or something," I contribute. "It keeps the body's systems from having to work too hard in an attempt to keep those systems from shutting down permanently. Except, in his case, Almeister did it with Mezmer instead of pentobarbital or whatever a nonmagically endowed person might use."

I can't see Perg's eyes in his snail-size form, but I know they're squinting at me when he says, "Yeah. I get it. A deep sleep. You don't have to overexplain everything, *hombre*. So, instead of continuing to be tortured, he peaced out for a while to escape the pain."

"Yes," Brit replies.

"Which is kind of like what Carpathian did at the end of the last book, right?"

"Yeah," Brittany deadpans. "Kind of."

I can feel her eyes on me, but I pretend to be distracted by some sort of flying ostrich-looking creature that I can make out in the sky off in the distance.

"*Chillero,*" Perg goes on. "Then, how did he pull himself back?"

"Well, the answer to that is what makes this all kinds of complicated."

"Oh, the *answer to that* is what makes this all complicated? As opposed to the simple way shit has been going up to now?" Perg scoffs.

"Don't be a dick," Brit snaps. "Yeah, it makes shit complicated because instead of the Spell playing through on its own like it should have, DONG apparently decided to get all froggy and used a Ritual on the guy to haul him back before he was supposed to be hauled back."

"Ritual . . . ?" Perg mutters, trying to work it out. "Wait. Didn't—?"

"Didn't Persephone use a Ritual when she brought Jameson back from the dead? Comport Familiar? Bingo-bongo, homie, you got it."

Suddenly, Perg hops off Brittany's pauldron and expands to his miniature pony size in the air before he hits the ground. He's gotten good at that really fast. Slow mover, quick learner.

"Okay," he starts, "and correct me if I'm wrong—but you won't have to, because I'm not—when she was breaking down what she did to Jameson, she said it was some heavy, complicated voodoo that transformed him into the way he is now. She said it turned him into, like, part super chill macaque and part something else."

"Exactly," Brit confirms.

"So, does that mean wizard homie is not all himself anymore?"

"Maybe?" I sigh. "A little? Which explains why he's so different from what we—or at least *I*—expected."

"Why would they do that? Bring him back like that? Just to torture him some more? That's some cold-blooded shit, fool."

"I mean, yeah, it is, but that's not entirely why they did it."

"Then why?"

I rub my hands through my hair, which, like my beard, is starting to feel shaggier by the second.

"Seems as though when they couldn't get him to give up the location of Garr Haven, DONG's alternate idea was to just try and force Almeister into supplication by getting him to stand up at his trial and decry Carpathian—me—as a false prophet. They intended to keep brutalizing him until he couldn't take it anymore and agreed to at least that much. But by winking out like he did and them hauling him back to existence, he actually gave them an easier option to get what they wanted. They still broke his spirit, just literally instead of figuratively."

"What are you saying?"

"They used Templar Mezmer," Brittany clarifies. "Ninth Guardian Mezmer."

"Whoa," Perg says, nodding his head and causing his moustache to bounce. "So, Almeister the Wizard, the Sherpa who once led Carpathian up the mountain of Saviourhood and the dude who's supposed to have all the answers to the questions we're seeking, is now . . . infused with DONG Mezmer?"

I cringe. "Can you *not* say *DONG Mezmer*? Something about the sound of it . . . But yes. The Super Vizier didn't just beat Almeister down; she managed to brainwash him into buying into their cult," I say aloud. "To reject Carpathian Einzgear as the Saviour and instead get him to believe that the true Saviour is—"

"Jesus Christ," Perg interrupts.

"No, Lord Brucillian," Brittany corrects. "You're thinking of a different cult."

I continue. "When I was up in his room in the Tower—the place where Almeister was being held—there was a copy of *The Gospel According to Brucillian* there. I noted at the time that it appeared as though some type of ceremony had been taking place . . ."

"That's so fucked up, *ese*! So he's been corrupted by the Ninth Guardian?"

"Oh shit!" That's me, reacting to hearing the word *corrupted* like it's a bag of bricks with ACME printed on the side smashing down on top of Wile E. Coyote.

"What?" Brit asks. "What is it?"

"*Corrupted.* I got a Notification earlier when I tried to get some four-one-one on Almeister from the Heart. It said that it couldn't tell me anything because the connection has been corrupted."

No one says anything for a moment as we all work out what this now means.

Almeister, the sage wizard who plucked Carpathian from his place of obscurity at the bottom of a chasm of municipal anguish and propelled him to celebrity as the World Saviour, standing beside him for nine books worth of adventure and tumult, and who Brit and I thought would be our own individual instrument of salvation and would somehow know the probable secret to why we're here and potentially whisk us away back home . . . is now a brain-scrambled kook who is, ostensibly, a newly recruited minion of the Ninth Guardian and has been told that Carpathian is a false prophet and Brucillian, who in some belief systems is prophesied to be the true Saviour, is set to arrive and lord over the peoples of Meridia in some kind of, I dunno, alternate Saviour reality.

A lot of words in that particularly egregious run-on sentence just to say we're even more screwed than we initially thought. Goddammit.

So, where things stand right now, we have to:

De-corrupt Almeister to ensure he's fully back on our side. And while I'm at it . . .

. . . Find and rescue the *rest* of the Heart Guard while also . . .

. . . attempting to see if Lonnaigh is still alive somewhere so I can . . .

. . . try to repair things with Mael, to get his aid in . . .

. . . discovering the true home of the Nexus Core so that we might . . .

. . . bring down DONG . . .

. . . unmask the Ninth Guardian . . .

. . . and restore the free flow of Mezmer to all the peoples of Meridia in the . . .

. . . hope that that resolves matters sufficiently so we can return home? Maybe?

Or . . . maybe just see if we can figure out a way to throw out this draft of our lives and start the whole damn thing over. A virtual page-one rewrite, as it were. That'd be pretty sweet.

However, since the odds of being able to do that seem fairly well nonexistent, I should probably just pick an objective to tackle first, focus on that, and see where it leads us.

As if reading my mind (which, again, can't actually happen until I hit at least Manasteel), Brit asks, "So? What the fuck do we do now?"

I straighten my spine. "We could try to see if we can track down Mael and square things with him—"

"But he was pretty pissed, and he hadn't even seen the shit that went down at Garr Haven yet, yo," Perg offers helpfully.

"Yes. I know. That is what I was going to say," I respond icily.

"Then why bring it up if we can't do anything about him right now?"

"I'm thinking out loud!" I exclaim, a little more forcefully than usual.

Perg bows his head. "Sor-*ry*. I'm still learning how your brain works. It's a lot."

Ignoring the backhanded apology, I continue. "So, I don't want to do that yet. I feel like we need to give him some space before we try and bring him back in. Maybe find Lonnaigh?"

Brittany avoids my gaze.

"What?" I ask.

"We don't know for sure that Lonnaigh's—"

"We don't know for sure she isn't," I head her off at the pass. "Let's not . . . Doesn't matter. Let's just focus on what's next."

"Okay. And what is that?"

"I don't know. Shit. The plan was to rescue Almeister and then coast off of his Skills and knowledge to get some questions answered and build out the rest of our plan, but now . . ." I blow out my lips. It hangs in the air.

"I mean, this shit with your wizard seems bad, homie."

"Yeah, I know. Thanks for confirming."

"No, but I mean, like *real* bad."

"YES. *I. Know.*"

"How is homegirl Seph feeling about it?"

"She feels great, Perg! Just super. Her dad's been co-opted by forces of evil, and she's also being lied to by all of us about who we are and what's really happening here, so you have to figure she's feeling jake about the world right now."

Once again, I'm being way snarkier than usual, but I've been through a lot.

Thump-thump. Thump-thump.

"Damn. Fine. I don't know why we can't just tell her about us, though. At least take that off the table."

I don't know either, other than I'm concerned on some level that if I open up too much about my true self to her that I'll be placing myself in even greater danger than I'm already facing from the Ninth Guardian, DONG, and the Super Vizier combined.

Thump-THUMP. Thump-THUMP.

Ow. Shit. The Heart is really doing a blast beat right now.

"We could try and find Zerastian. I mean, she's a precog. Precog could be enormously useful," Brit suggests.

". . . Yeah." I consider this option. "The problem is, I don't know if we're adequately powered up to go after her."

"Why not?" Perg asks.

"Because she was lost in the Mokeisan Desert."

"Okay."

"And if we go to the Mokeisan to try and find her, we'll very likely have to do battle with the Giant Serpent of the Mokeisan."

"What? I thought Carpathian, Teleri, and Pergamon defeated it in that last book. Book ten."

"How do you know that?"

"That was the last part you let homegirl hear out loud before you stopped sharing and went all stealth mode and killed off your hero. Or, you. Or whoever."

"You were really paying attention to everything, huh?"

"What else did I have to do, fool? There's only so much burrowing that can happen in an aquarium. So, why would we have to fight it again?"

I glance at Brit. She tightens her lips and shakes her head at me.

"What?" Perg asks. "What is it? I don't like this unspoken, private language bullshit you two pull all the time."

I sigh.

"Well . . . so . . . it's like this . . ."

CHAPTER THREE

Consecration of Destiny, Riftbreaker Book Nine, Chapter Ten

Zerastian squinted against the whirling sand, her teammates vanishing in the billowing ochre storm. The giant serpent's thrashing had kicked up a maelstrom, isolating her from Carpathian and the others. She cursed under her breath, her quick mind racing to assess the situation as grit stung her eyes and skin.

My blasted damn Murmur Spell isn't working, *she thought to herself, finding some sort of disruption blocking her casting.* I can't get any messages to them.

Without communication—one of her primary benefits for being part of the party composition—she was all but useless to her friends.

However, something else lurked in the chaos—a presence she couldn't quite pin down. Zerastian's pale, nimble fingers flew over her gear, touching specific runes and activating a series of Eidolon Drones. The small technomantic devices, no larger than her palm, hummed to life with a soft blue glow before zipping out to scan the perimeter.

As the drones searched, she reached for another device: the inelegantly named Rebuker. She'd crafted it long ago and imbued Pergamon's Hexkeeper energy into it, borrowing some of his considerable power and weaving it within the object to protect herself—and others—when necessary.

The item sparked to life with a crackle of green electricity, projecting a shimmering, opalescent shield around her. The worst of the sandstorm's fury broke against the barrier in a spray of golden particles, giving Zerastian a moment to gather her strength and analyze the data streaming in from her eidolons.

While her heads-up display was not as innately . . . procured and righteous as Carpathian's Mechanical Heart, it was infinitely more customizable to her preferences. The single-eye lens was fastened over her left brow and ear, the thin membrane of Mezmerically enhanced alo-glass swimming with information. She brushed back her black fringe to focus.

Her eyes flicked over the readings flooding before her.

Multiple Mezmer sources pinged on her display, scattered across the maelstrom. Weak flickers, no stronger than Etherflint, dotted the landscape. Ironspark and Steelshard were in the mix as well, along with more substantial spikes—Manasteel level—pulsing rhythmically. Carpathian? The serpent? Both?

Then, a massive surge. Zerastian's breath caught.

That couldn't be right.

She blinked and recalibrated the alo-glass at the touch of a rune. The reading persisted. Something out there radiated power an order of magnitude above Manasteel. It was impossible. Such a level was beyond anything she'd encountered, beyond even theoretical limits.

Zerastian's mind raced, analyzing possibilities. A glitch? The interference from the storm? Something else that was far more dangerous than they'd anticipated?

Suddenly, Zerastian's Oraculborn Omen Ability flared to life. In her mind's eye, she saw a massive shape hurtling toward her, her body splattering across the sand. Without hesitation, she dove to the side, dragging the Rebuker's shield atop her. The tail of the Mokeisan serpent whipped through the space she'd just occupied, stirring up another cloud of sand.

Zerastian laughed, a near-maniacal sound escaping her wind-burnt lips as she climbed to her feet. Not for the first time (nor did she believe the last), she gave thanks to Endershadow of the Deepvoid. Her old mentor had ensured her Omen would remain passively active all those years ago, and it had kept her safe.

If only it had warned me about Mael's fate . . . *she thought. But she couldn't afford those thoughts. Not here, thick amid battle. Even if I can't see the blasted damn battle, she huffed to herself.*

Her eyes darted to an incoming transmission from one of her Eidolon Drones. The source of the disturbance.

That . . . Is that real?

She quickly opened a Mezmeric meld with the drone, accessing its ocular features.

Her breath caught as the data confirmed her suspicions.

It is!

A portal. But not just any portal—the readings indicated it led to another plane entirely.

Zerastian's fingers weaved in the air, summoning more Mezmer from her core and pouring it into the connection between her and the machine. The drone's feed sharpened, revealing the rift in stark detail. It shimmered at the edge of visibility, its edges pulsing with that impossible energy far beyond Manasteel. Whatever lay beyond was entirely new—and potentially catastrophic.

What was this? It was not something she had foretold. Not something that had ever appeared to her in any vision . . .

She needed to warn the others, but her primary communication Spell remained useless. More pressing, however, was the gnawing sensation in her gut. It was a familiar impulse, one that had driven her to countless discoveries and just as many close calls. The hunger, the thirst, the lust to know more.

Zerastian's mind fluttered, weighing the risks against the potential rewards. The serpent still posed a threat, but this portal . . . What could it be?

Having ever had the ability to predict the likeliest outcome to situations made moments like this one—moments of uncertainty, of the unknown—all that much more thrilling.

Her fingers hovered over her gear, ready to push forward or pull back, when her display exploded with energy spikes crackling like lightning bolts as Carpathian's signature flared in response. His Mezmer surged between modes with an intensity that could only be performed by someone of Three-Type distinguishing characteristics.

Well, that settles that, then, doesn't it?

Decision made, she summoned a tether from her closest drone and felt the power as it shot out like a Mezmeric leash, homing in on her location. It took mere moments to reach her, and when it did, she grasped the lead tightly. A heartbeat passed, and the snap of a release, and Zerastian felt the tension pull her across the treacherous sands toward the pulsating portal, reeling her in like a freshly caught sea creature.

As she landed before the shimmering opening, a surge of triumph filled her chest, though it was quickly overshadowed by a wave of wrongness. Stepping into the radius of the portal, she felt a violent influx of foreign Mezmer pour into her own energy reserves. It was like being drained and amplified in the same instant, as if some sort of Mezmeric vampire had latched on to her and was draining her life force.

The sensation was overwhelming and disorienting, causing her to stumble as she tried to push back against the portal's consuming barrier. She could feel the intense energy pulsating against her skin, almost like an electric shock coursing through her body. Her hand outstretched, tugging on the tether . . .

With no time to waste, she hastily threw her leashed Eidolon Drone through the opening. For a moment, the sensation abated. As readings flooded in, she turned to make a run for it—but she froze. Hastily, she switched to control the ocular node of the drone she'd just sacrificed for the greater good, and what she saw clawed at her bones with icy nails.

This . . . This was a behemoth beyond comprehension.

It's . . . It's not just one—

Her Omen activated.

Before she could even process the terror gripping her, it happened. She watched helplessly, her fingers frantically tapping at the runic controls, as her drone's connection was suddenly severed. Panic surged through her veins like wildfire, threatening to consume her entirely. It was only then that she noticed she was still tethered to it, and she was being pulled.

Igniting a Pyrestick, she hurled that into the portal too, watching as the rift lapped it up greedily. She pivoted the Rebuker just as the Pyrestick exploded, sending a forceful shock wave rippling out of the edge of both realms. The immense power sent her rocketing back and away from the foreign-world-spanning yawning maw. The entirety of the sands around her quaked.

This is it.

Accepting the distraction, she charged toward Carpathian's Manasteel signature, fighting against the relentless winds and swirling sand of the raging maelstrom that had shrouded him from view. Each gust felt like a slap to her face, but she refused to let anything stop her from reaching him. He had to know.

Something whizzed by her, and she tapped another rune on her belt.

Depth Charger.

ZHOOM!

A figure, huge and scaly, exploded above her as her Mezmeric missile fired into the obscuring winds and detonated. Pieces of creature rained down in a shower of gore, but it was only a mild inconvenience. Something was coming for her. Powers. Sapience. Something hungry.

It's not one . . .

She kept moving, noticing that one by one, she lost the connection to all but one of her drones, their spark extinguished by whatever she'd done.

She felt the desire to scold herself, but she didn't have the luxury to reprimand; she was almost there, and—

She burst out of the cloud of wailing sands to see Carpathian. There he stood, facing down the monstrous beast. But Zerastian had no time to admire his bravery. This was not an escape. There was no refuge. This was a message. She was still tethered, but she needed him to know.

The vampiric effect intensified, threatening to rip her apart. She tried to shout a warning, to explain the true nature of their foe—but the words caught in her throat as the tether's pull grew stronger, threatening to tear her limb from limb. With her Murmur Spell, she was able to use the last of her strength to utter a single, solitary word and send it.

"Saviour."

Carpathian's head snapped in her direction. His eyes, so serious—so burdened—found hers, and they softened.

He knows. The Saviour knows I won't make it, though he doesn't know why.

"It's not one . . ." she muttered as the winds pulled at her clothing, the tether yanking her backward. "It's five."

She held up five fingers. Hoping. Willing the Saviour to understand.

There are five. Blasted dammit, there are five!

He wouldn't be able to hear her, but if anyone would understand her message, it would be Carpathian Einzgear.

And with that, she was thrust backward, swallowed by the portal into a bleak void that sealed the moment she passed its threshold.

. . . There are five.

CHAPTER FOUR

Perg just stares at me and Brit for a moment, moustache twitching. Then, in a remarkably understated way, he says . . .

"Are you fucking kidding me?"

"No," I tell him.

Then, less understated, he says, "Five?!"

"I—"

"Why would you do that?!"

"I dunno! I just . . . Obstacles! Stakes! Tension!"

"Complicating the simple," Brit offers.

"Because," I soldier on. "Because the giant serpent is a cool villain. A World Boss. A Big Bad who I could keep getting mileage out of. I knew I wanted to keep bringing it back, but I didn't want to just have them battling the same old, same old, time after time. So, I gave it a family."

"A family?!"

"Probably a husband and three kids? I never specified. They could all be siblings. I dunno."

"Fool, are you—?"

"*But*, I didn't want *Carpathian* to know that," I keep going. "I wanted him to misinterpret her indication of five as a wave goodbye. I thought it would be neat for Carpathian to *think* he was killing the same serpent over and over—believing it was coming back Jason Voorhees style—when, in fact, he was fighting different ones each time."

"So you're saying there are four more?"

"Yeah. Had I not had Carpathian die in the last book, he was to have eventually sought and found Zerastian, and she would have explained the whole mix-up, and they'd all have had a laugh about it."

"Well, *hardee-har-har*. Shit is hilarious, homes!"

"It seemed cool when I wrote it in my Notes app! Gimme a break!"

A quiet moment. I feel like I hear the revving of engines somewhere in the distance, but it's probably just my imagination. But since my imagination is now indistinguishable from the truth, it may not matter.

"Regardless," I put forth, "that's the obstacle we likely face if we try to get Zerastian next."

"Well," Brit says, scratching at her neck and looking at the maps, "at least we know where that is. We don't have any idea at all where Xanaraxa was taken, just that she was."

"Right. Okay . . ." I think it over. "Well, then I feel like the first thing we need to do is get hands on the Gauntlet of Sorenthali."

"Why so?"

"Because that's, like, one of the primary tools Carpathian used when he took the serpent out. I mean . . . the Arm of Hearts is what actually, technically, took it down, but I can't get at the Arm of Hearts until I have all the other artifacts, can I?"

"No." Brit shakes her head. "The others are like the keys you have to have before the Arm of Hearts can be unlocked."

"Holy shit, homes, you really wrote yourself into some pickles, huh?"

Ignoring Perg's less-than-helpful observation, I go on. "So, yeah, I mean . . . I feel like maybe, possibly, if we have that, coupled with the added force of Persephone, we might stand a chance against it and be able to find Zerastian wherever she is in the desert."

"Long shot," Brit sighs.

"Everything's a long shot. But this seems to be the shortest blade in a garden of tall weeds."

"Weird, mixed metaphor," she says, "but I get your point. Okay, well," she goes on, pointing at one of the maps, "the Mokeisan is in this direction. Near Elderkeep."

"Which is where the Gauntlet is supposed to be held?"

"In Origin Pass, yeah, exactly."

I look at where she indicates. "Alright. Cool. Then let's get everyone together and—AHHHHH!"

THUMP-THUMP. THUMP-THUMP.

I fall to my knees and feel myself grabbing at my chest.

"Bruce?!" Brit shouts, reaching out to me.

"Big homie!" Perg exclaims. "I'm sorry! Is it my fault? I didn't mean to get shit all stirred up! I take back what I said! You're a good writer, and I think the way you're able to weave together various complex narratives is enviable!"

I try to answer, to say anything, but I can't make words form. I don't know what's going on. It feels like the physical sensation of having the Heart ripped from my chest and the metaphysical version of the same are happening all at once. I roll onto my back, writhing.

"Bruce?! What's happening?!" Brit and Perg lean over me, their faces coming into full view like Kathy Griffin and the other actors in the scene in *Pulp Fiction* after Butch runs over Marsellus Wallace while he's crossing the street with donuts.

But I only see their concerned expressions for a moment before their images are fully obscured by the Notification that appears. It blots out everything and supplants their worried eyes with words that are even more worrisome . . .

ALERT!

Heart Guard Member [Mael Anderbariach] is attempting to extract himself from your Heart Guard.

Do you wish to allow this extraction?

[Yes] [No]

CHAPTER FIVE

"Once Upon a Time in Meridia."
Part 4

Scorching suns beat down mercilessly on the desolate highway, shimmering waves of heat perverting the distant horizon. Towering red rock formations loomed all around, their jagged silhouettes frank against the cloudless azure sky as a Zalexiel serpent slithered on the ground, its scaly belly cascading across the broken terrain in a mocking imitation of flowing water.

Suddenly . . . a quaking. The ground shook as though a chasm deep beneath the land's surface had opened. The serpent stilled, its reptilian senses informing it that danger was near. A predator.

A shadow seemed to fall across the plane, casting the serpent in darkness and, feeling a deep, instinctive compulsion to flee, the Zalexiel burrowed its way under an errant stone, rendering it indistinguishable from the terrain upon which it made its home, just in time to avoid being trampled to dust by a monumental foot. A foot belonging to the colossal figure who trod unerringly in the direction of his home, dark skin glistening with sweat as he labored under the crushing weight of sorrow and regret.

His eyes, once sharp and alert, now held a haunted look. His mind reeled, fragments of memories and nightmarish visions swirling in a toxic cocktail of confusion and pain. The Cavern of Sorrows had left its mark, both physical and mental, etched deep into his very being like the intricate tattoos that adorned his arms and torso.

Mael Anderbariach. Scion of Clan Catarinci. Vanguard of the Valley. The Dark Lion of Hope. Clinging desperately to what fragments of himself still remained.

His dreadlocks, matted and unkempt, hung heavily down his back, swaying with every unsteady movement, the faint glow of the Tri-Venn on the back of his titanic fist the only hope for him that remained. As long as the glow remained, however hazy and weak, it meant that she was still alive. Somewhere. Somewhere, his sister's life force continued to thrum.

Through the fog of his thoughts, one imperative burned bright: Garr Haven. Home to his clan; those upon whom he could depend for aid in the task ahead. The task of retrieving Lonnaigh.

The distance was great. He knew that it would take him many Lunar Rotations to reach Garr Haven on foot even if he was at the peak of his form, which he was most decidedly not.

He needed to find a vehicle, something that would allow him to reach a gateway, a portal, that he might pass through at the precise velocity required to expedite his return to Santus Luminous. And Garr Haven.

The image of Lonnaigh being pulled beneath the waters of the Cavern of Sorrows flashed through his mind. He shook the nightmare away, his dreadlocks brushing against his shoulders. Unfortunately, even as the vision of his sister being drawn under was swept away, another figure appeared in his mind's eye.

Einzgear. Carpathian. The World Saviour.

It was him, wasn't it? Although he did not speak as Mael remembered, nor did his command of self present in the same way it once did, he supposed it could be the reconstitution. The remortification. The man did say he had died and returned, after all.

Died? Carpathian Einzgear? How?

It had ever been Mael's understanding that the only thing that could kill Einzgear . . . was Einzgear. The Saviour himself.

What Black Mezmer could have caused . . . ?

Mael felt the connection to the Saviour's Heart. His place in the Heart Guard remained fast, even if it did feel uncanny. Off. There was only one bearer of the Heart, after all.

No, thought the giant. *No, there was one bearer per* Age.

His own people had spawned previous Saviours to battle against previous Guardians.

And Nightwind . . . He had heard her. She'd called the man with them in the Cavern of Sorrows "Bruce." Even through the tumult and calamity, he had heard her as clear as a crystal bell ringing in the dawn of a new era.

Bruce! She had cried out.

Before he could ruminate on the matter further, he heard a sound. Not in his memories but in the hard, dry present. Intruding into the miasma of his fractured mind, there was a deep rumble from somewhere in the distance.

Squinting against the harsh glare of the suns, he could make out the approaching silhouette of a massive transport freighter filled, no doubt, with precious goods bound for faraway markets. Or, perhaps, with something less temporal.

To be honest, Mael did not care. It was not the cargo that interested him.

As the vehicle drew nearer, its speed gradually decreased. It was rare to encounter anyone out here, especially on foot and under the unrelenting heat of Meridia's blazing suns.

Mael lifted his chin to face the driver head-on, pausing his trudging shamble toward home, and waited. And waited. Unmoving. Broken but unbowed.

On a fundamental level, Mael Anderbariach still understood himself, who he was—and the power he could summon and command.

As expected, the freighter's brakes hissed, and the metal behemoth came to a stop a mere short distance before him. With a Mezmerically pneumatic whoosh, the driver of the transport lowered the window and peeked his head out. His eyes widened as he took in the size, distress, and strange aura that seemed to radiate off the man he could see.

"Hey there," the driver called. "Are you . . . alright?"

Rather than providing a response, Mael walked toward the open window, which the driver—perhaps not unwisely—quickly rolled up before placing his foot on the accelerator and throwing the rig into reverse.

But not quickly enough, as it happened.

For, battered and diminished though he may have been, Mael Anderbariach was still very much Mael Anderbariach. And Mael Anderbariach would not allow something as insignificant as a twenty-ton transport attempting to flee from him interfere with his desire for it to . . . not.

Mael gripped the wheel of the freighter as it hurtled through the shimmering portal, emerging moments later on the other side with a thunderous roar into the city of Santus Luminous. His dreadlocks whipped wildly in the rush of air from the now-broken window, eyes fixed ahead of him where Garr Haven awaited. The truck's engine roared as he pushed it as hard as it could tolerate. His yearning to return to his home ached more with each kilostryde.

Finally, in the near distance, the entrance to Mt. TaumSauk appeared. Mael felt his pained scowl give way to something so minor as to barely be called a smile, but it was closer than anything he had showed in a longer time than could be quantified.

However . . . as the freighter drew closer still, the inconsequential whisper of a smile disappeared as rapidly as it had arrived. Even from afar, Mael could sense that something was terribly wrong.

The entrance—the stone-covered camouflage that kept Garr Haven's location a secret—was open. Flung wide. And the detritus of something like a battle was visible.

Black tire tracks painted the ground leading away from the haven for the Rebellion. Multiple tracks, from multiple types of tires. Magecycles left a particular manner of stain wherever their wheels touched. Mael knew it well.

He brought the truck to a screeching halt just before arriving at the garage and leapt from the cab, his massive frame landing heavy on the ground. Rushing inside to evaluate the scene, he very nearly fell to the ground in the same way he had been brought to his knees by the Cavern of Sorrows. Only, this time, not by a force from without but a pain from within.

Blood.

Everywhere.

Not just "streaking the walls" or "trailing across the floor" but truly everywhere.

The stench of death hung thick in the air.

Mael's chest heaved as grief and disbelief warred within him. He stumbled forward, eyes darting frantically, searching for any sign of life in the midst of the apparent slaughter.

He could find none.

Each step coated the soles of his feet with the remnants of his fallen family.

It took him a moment to process and realize what else there was to see . . .

Templars. All slain, but Templars nonetheless. One particularly unfortunate minion of the Ninth Guardian had been run through with rock, impaled in a half-dozen places, turned into a macabre monument to whatever butchery had taken place.

Moving his head slowly around, Mael spotted the entry to the passageway that led to the Temple of the Body, also demolished, the great doors splintered apart and yet more rock fragments peppering the ground.

Unsure why, he felt pulled to explore in that direction.

He wanted to run; to leave and perhaps find the edge of a canyon off which he might be able to pitch himself so that he could enjoy sweet relief from the ever-mounting anguish that seemed determined to plague this thing he called his life.

But, looking at the back of his fist once again, the light from the Tri-Venn still clung to its determination to pulse with timid light. And as long as the tattoo projected that Lonnaigh was alive, he must remain alive as well.

So, he shuffled along the corridor that led to the temple, leaving bloody footprints with each padding step.

Upon arriving, he saw that the temple, too, was nothing more than a shattered husk. Wrecked. Like the skeleton of a great ship that had been caught in an unexpected storm and dashed upon the rocks.

The Pulse Well—the sacred cradle of the temple—destroyed, twisted and broken, whisps of Mezmer wafting from its severed connection to the magic of the world.

How? How could this have happened? Carpathian said he had been here, had visited the Annex. It was where, he said, he had acquired the garments he was wearing in his recarbonified form. Could he be somehow . . . ?

". . . eeeeeeeeeeeee . . . !"

A sound distracted him from his thoughts. Faint. High-pitched. Coming from somewhere . . . above him?

He looked to the ceiling and saw the temple's shattered skylight. Beyond, up in the atmosphere, a dot. A small, tiny speck, growing larger as it careened toward the ground like a falling comet.

And, as it fell, the sound grew louder . . .

". . . eeeeeeeeeeeeeeEEEEEEEEEE . . . !"

. . . and louder . . .

". . . eeeeeeeeeeeeeeEEEEEEEEEEEEEEEEEEEEEEEEE . . . !"

. . . until . . .

BOOF!

A body hit the floor. A small body, decorated with a long, luxurious beard and wearing ragged, torn Templar gear.

A Dwarf.

A Dwarf Templar.

"Owwwww! Ow! Ow! Owwwwwwwwww!" the Dwarf bellowed, having landed violently onto the metal frame of a broken Smith Press in a grim spectacle of bloodshed.

And, curiously . . . ice.

Mael stared at the small, icy, bloodied Dwarf Templar. He had seen things in his time that no other human could have imagined, and yet, this . . . this was a curiosity that made even the Saviour of Clan Catarinci take pause.

Mael's eyes narrowed, and he knelt down, putting himself close to the Dwarf's mangled face. "Where have you come from? What happened here? Do you know?"

"Einzgear," the Dwarf whispered. "He did this."

Mael blinked, unsure of what he thought he had just heard.

"Again, small menace? What are you saying?"

"Einzgear," the Dwarf worked out. "We came for Einzgear, but . . . he . . . he vaulted me. There. Through the sky."

Mael looked up at the shattered ceiling as he began piecing ideas together.

Carpathian . . . threw the Dwarf? He must have. That must be what the little, crumpled soldier was saying. Besides Mael himself, only the Saviour might be in possession of such power.

It would, Mael supposed, explain the ice, at least. Was it possible that the Dwarf had been cast so hard, so high, that he'd . . . exited the pull of Meridia's gravity itself?

"Einzgear," the Dwarf muttered again. "He did this. This is . . . his . . . fault."

A hiss of air escaped the Dwarf's miniature lungs, and then . . . he was no more. Having survived more than could be reasonably expected for anyone to weather—especially one so petite—he gave himself over to his improbable wounds . . . and died.

But before he expired, he had managed to paint a picture for Mael Anderbariach that, while incomplete, was still enough. Somehow, in some way, Einzgear was the cause of . . . all this. This bloodshed. This destruction. Not only had he failed to honor his word and keep Lonnaigh safe, his mere presence had forfeited the lives of the entirety of Mael's clan.

Bruce. Why did she call him Bruce?

It was a question he could not answer, and it left him with an anxiety he could not separate from himself. The pieces refused to align, forming a maddening puzzle that only fueled Mael's frustration. He had made a promise. Sworn a vow. To stand by the Saviour and fight for this world, fight to steady its frantic spiraling and to ensure that it once again righted itself.

But now . . .

It seemed as if the Saviour himself had failed to honor that vow. And, as a result, everyone and everything that Mael had loved was gone, and the world was an even more wretched and unstable place than the one he had left when he committed his body and spirit to the agony of the Cavern of Sorrows.

He needed answers. Understanding. To somehow get to the primary core of the matter and begin trying to craft together an explanation for all that had happened.

But in order to even begin addressing his mounting questions and resting himself from his disquiet, he realized he must first separate himself in another way. A more essential one.

He stalked toward the ruined Pulse Well, his mind churning with the Templar's final words.

He glared at the wrecked device, its once vibrant energy now nothing more than sporadic sparks and dead Mezmeric channels. Mael's eyes darted around the devastated chamber, settling on a massive cable lying amidst the debris. A basic, unenchanted, entirely pedestrian cable. And an idea—desperate and perhaps foolish—sprang into his thoughts.

With grim determination, Mael grasped the cable. Its weight—easily over one thousand tesiliograms—would have been impossible for any ordinary human to budge.

But Mael was far from ordinary.

Muscles straining, he began to drag the enormous hawser toward the Pulse Well.

He didn't know if it would work, if the remnants of the Well's power could be harnessed in such a crude, thuggish manner. But it was better than inaction, better than doing nothing and wandering blindly in the wilderness, hoping for answers, for some manner of salvation while his kin lay dead and his sister toiled in the unknown void.

As he approached the Well, Mael's determination burned bright.

He would find the answers, he decided.

He would know the truth of what was afoot.

He would unravel the ball of mystery that plagued him now.

He would do it all.

Even if it meant severing the bond he swore to keep the world from spinning completely off its axis . . .

CHAPTER SIX

"Gyaaaaaaaaaaahh!" I screech, grabbing at my chest as the world around me blurs and twists, a kaleidoscope of distorted faces and frantic movements. My body feels like it's caught in a vise grip, the pounding of the Mechanical Heart reaching a deafening crescendo.

THUMP-THUMP! THUMP-THUMP! THUMP-THUMP!

"What's happened to him?! What is it? Carpathian?!"

I can make out a glimpse of Persephone and Jameson running down the street in my direction. My screams appear to have called them toward me. Their voices are distant, like calling to me from the other end of a long tunnel.

"Big Saviour! Wha' be gwan?!"

I gasp for air. The Notification hovers ominously.

ALERT!
Heart Guard Member [Mael Anderbariach] is attempting to extract himself from your Heart Guard.
Do you wish to allow this extraction?
[Yes] [No]

Trying to focus, my vision swims, black spots dancing at the edges.

Mael is trying to leave the Heart Guard? Why?

"Is that a rhetorical question, Bruce? Mael's never been, like, a super chill guy. I know he was always Carpathian's ride or die, but after what he's just been through? What you put him through? I mean . . . would you be?"

Aw, shit, inner Bruce is right. Great. Like I need *this* right now too.

"Bru—Carp!" Brittany's voice is sharp, urgent. She puts her hands on my shoulders. "Talk to us! What's going on?"

I try to speak, but all that comes out is a strangled groan.

The pain is excruciating, like molten lava coursing through my veins where blood should be. The Heart is straining, its rhythm erratic and desperate.

THUMP-THUMP-THUMP. THUMP—THUMP—THUMP.

"Me can hear him heart!" Jameson shouts.

"Oh, shit! He's having an *ataque al corazón*, homies!" Perg yells.

"Let me near him!" Persephone kneels beside me. I can just see her hands glowing softly with Mezmeric energy. "His life force is destabilizing!"

Another surge of agony, and I can't suppress the scream that rips from my throat.

"*Carpathian*, focus!" Brittany shakes me slightly, her face getting close to mine. "What's happening? Do you know? Can you say anything?"

I nod weakly, forcing the words out between ragged breaths. "Mael . . . trying to . . . leave . . . Heart Guard."

"What?" Perg asks, I presume, reflexively. I'm pretty sure he heard me.

"Well, then fucking let him go!" Brit exclaims.

Let him go? Just like that? But Mael is . . . He's a cornerstone of the Heart Guard. If he leaves, if I just let him go, what does that mean for us? For me?

He's Carpathian's best friend.

He's . . . mine?

"Carpathian, please!" Persephone pleads. "You have to release him! I can feel your essence fading!"

I try to respond, but my voice is nothing but a dry whisper.

The cursor on the Notification continues blinking.

Do you wish to allow this extraction?
[Yes] [No]

Another wave of pain, more intense than the last. It's as if the Heart is tearing itself apart, each pulse sending shock waves through my body.

"He's going into arrest!" Perg yells. "Does anyone have those crazy shock paddles?"

"Stand back!" Persephone commands, kneeling down. She places her hands over my chest, her fingers weaving patterns as she channels her Mezmer. "This might hurt," she says.

"He's already hurting," Perg notes.

"More," Seph clarifies.

Her glare bores into me, forcing me to keep eye contact. My vision blurs.

Memories flood in. Mael. Me. Our battles together, the companionship, the trust we built. But also, the recent distance, the confusion, the pain he must be feeling.

"Wait . . . That wasn't me. I wasn't involved in those things. That was Carpathian. These feelings aren't mine, are they?"

"Who gives a shit, Bruce? You're the one who's about to die."

Brain Bruce is right. It doesn't make a difference. It's one and the same.

With a heavy heart (both literal and metaphorical), I select [Yes], and the effect is immediate. The searing pain in my chest dissipates, replaced by a hollow ache.

GASP!

I take in an enormous gulp of air, and . . . the Mechanical Heart resumes a steady, albeit subdued, rhythm.

Thump-thump. Thump-thump. Thump-thump.

[CONFIRMED.]
Heart Guard Member [Mael Anderbariach] has been extracted.

Yeesh! Close one, Saviour! But you're going to be all right! I mean, for the moment. The fact that Mael is likely now your sworn enemy

is sure to present its own set of very bad problems down the line, but at least you're not dead now! Yaaay?
{COURTESY MESSAGE #30}

My body goes limp as the world comes slowly back into focus, the concerned faces of my friends now the only thing hovering above.

"Are you okay?" Brittany asks.

"I think so?" I squelch out.

Persephone lets out a sigh of relief. "Thank Richemerion."

"Is Mael . . . ?" Brittany doesn't finish the sentence.

I don't know if she's asking if he's dead or if he's merely done. With me.

"I don't know," I admit. "I dunno exactly what it is, precisely. What happened. I dunno. But he's no longer part of the Heart Guard."

"Shit," Perg says. "So. What now?"

"Now? Now we need to go find Zerastian and . . . What's happening over there?"

Every head turns to see what I do.

Waslan, the Ronine, bursts out of Seph's workshop and comes stampeding toward us down the street.

"What's that about?" Brit asks.

"No idea," I reply, but I'm awfully concerned because either Waslan has turned heel again and is on his way to eat us alive, or else there's some danger he's coming to warn us about.

Or—and I probably wouldn't have come up with this if I hadn't seen it—a third option.

"Treachery! Slay the villain!"

Almeister, also running forth from the workshop, hobbles along with a fireplace poker in hand, attempting to lance Waslan like some kind of crazy old heretic hunter in the town square.

Seph turns to me with sad, worried eyes.

"Or perhaps we should have a conversation about what's been done to your father and how we can undo it," I tell her as Almeister trips, falls headfirst into a bucket, and continues racing around, poker in hand.

"Flufflepuffens! I am blind! Brucillian! Save us! Slay the heretics!"

". . . Hey, Bruce?"

"Yeah, Bruce?"

"You may want to consider fixing your wizard before you go charging into battle again."

"Thanks, Bruce."

"What I'm here for, Bruce."

"Richemerion," says Seph.

Standing beside Sheila, the light of the now setting suns glistening off the sleek hood of the Panamera, I notice she's got a few dings and scratches she didn't have before, courtesy of our recent escapades. But a little cosmetic damage is to be expected when you're trying to save an entire realm you both knowingly and unknowingly created and then propelled to the brink of global collapse.

The rest of the crew is in front of me. Persephone, Brittany, Perg, Jameson, Almeister—wrestled off the back of Waslan and currently staring intently at a pebble as if it holds the secrets of the universe—and the Ronine itself, eyeing Almeister warily and with great agitation.

"Richemerion?" I repeat.

"Yes, perhaps the Warden of Protection might be able to help Father."

"How?"

"Lord Richemerion is the one who gifted Father your Heart. Lord Richemerion's sole purpose has ever been to offer protection against the threats presented by the Ninth Guardian. They are uniquely versed in the intricate workings of Mezmer and its various applications and idiosyncrasies. Perhaps they have some panacea for what ails Father."

I glance at Brit, who shrugs me a "yeah, sure, why not?" shrug.

I never wrote of an actual encounter with Richemerion in any of the Riftbreaker books. I only established that they are, in fact, the Warden of Protection, one of the Mystic Elders, and the person to whom people will occasionally throw up their prayers and hopes.

After the battle with Azteral the Punisher, a battered Carpathian crawled into an abandoned building to ask Richemerion to save him. And Richemerion did so by transforming the place into a Temple of the Body and the Pulse Well's first appearance. So, the logic tracks. Beyond which, Richemerion will surely have a Pulse Well on hand that we can use to all check in.

And, just maybe, even if they can't get Al's situation sorted out, they might have some answers about this world, what our best path forward might be, how and why I wound up here, and how I can get back home. That all feels like the kind of thing that's in the purview of a "Warden of Protection."

"Have you met Richemerion? Yourself?" I ask her.

"No, but Father has communed with the Warden many times. Father?" she calls out. "You can lead us to Lord Richemerion's haven, can't you?"

Almeister is still staring at the pebble in his hand, turning it over as if it might whisper something profound to him. His brow is furrowed, mouth slightly open, lost in some indecipherable thought.

"Richemerion?" he mutters as though the name has only just now surfaced from some long-buried memory.

Persephone's expression lights up. "Yes, Father. The Warden of Protection. They are the one who gifted you the Heart. You know how to reach the Warden, do you not?"

Almeister hums absently. Then, after a long pause, he adds, "Yes. Yes, I believe . . . I do."

Brittany shakes her head and whispers to me, "We sure this is gonna be worth it?"

"I dunno," I admit. "But we need to try something. I was expecting to have our own Gandalf available to us. If we don't get him sorted out, it feels kind of like we'll end up lugging around Bran Stark through this whole jacked-up odyssey."

And, honestly, even that may be generous. Bran could at least see through the three-eyed raven and stuff, so that was cool and potentially kind of useful. Right now, Almeister is more like Schmendrick. I'm not even sure if the guy could cast a Level One lock-breaking Spell, such as he is.

"Okay, fine," Brit says, directing her attention back to Al. "So where do we find them? Richemerion. Where is the Warden located?"

Almeister blinks and lifts his gaze from the pebble, finally seeming to register the conversation fully. He gestures vaguely toward the horizon. "To reach Richemerion, one must pass through the . . . Sanctuary Threshold."

I mouth it to Brit. *Sanctuary Threshold?* She raises her eyebrows and shakes her head.

"Right, Sanctuary Threshold," I say. ". . . What's that?"

Almeister rubs his temple, as if dredging up old knowledge takes an amount of physical effort. "It is the first gate. A boundary woven from Mezmer itself. It does not open for just anyone; one must first be acknowledged."

"Acknowledged by who, homie?" Perg seems equally anxious to get this train moving.

Almeister frowns, searching for a name he can't seem to remember. Then, it comes to him. "By the Keepers of the Threshold."

He stops talking again, giving just the barest of answers to the last questions asked. Dude would be excellent on a witness stand.

Brit makes a small, circular motion with her hand. "And the Keepers of the Threshold are . . . ?"

Almeister's frown deepens, the lines on his face becoming ruminative valleys. "Beings of unfaltering devotion, set to guard the path to Richemerion. They are even more ancient than Richemerion themself. Inescapable. Only by proving ourselves in their eyes may we be permitted to journey further."

I groan and ask, even though I really don't want to hear the answer, "Prove ourselves how?"

Almeister nods as though this is an excellent question. "The Keepers require that all who approach Richemerion's domain for the first time must pass a trial."

"What kind of trial?"

"One that demonstrates the essential virtue of protection: Vigilance."

"Okay. And so, if we pass that—"

"And then endurance."

Oh, he wasn't done.

"Oh, yeah, alright. Great, well, that doesn't sound too—"

"And, obviously, sacrifice."

There's a pause while we wait to see if there's anything more. When he doesn't keep speaking, Brit claps her hands together and says, "Okay, super, then let's get moving. At some point DONG is going to come—"

"And, lastly, trust."

"Are you fucking kidding me?!"

"I am not. And before one may stand before Richemerion, they must be recognized finally by not only the Keepers but also the essences of all those who have come before."

"And what exactly does that mean?" I ask.

"After the final trial, we shall be judged by the Echoes of the Convocation, who will assess our journey. And if they are unsatisfied . . . well."

"Well what?" I ask.

Almeister lifts a single finger. "*We* will become echoes ourselves."

"So lemme get this straight, fool. We have to complete four challenges designed to test our sincerity or whatever, and if we don't score high enough in the eyes of some chumps who came before us, we get dusted?"

"In so many words."

Perg sucks at his snail teeth, and his moustache bounces in what I would describe as a luxurious anger. There's a beat before I turn to Seph.

"Do you have any other ideas?"

She shakes her head sheepishly and nibbles at her lip. Which flippin' kills me.

"Okay! Fine! It's not so bad. All we have to do is pass less than a handful of trials and then have it acknowledged by four all-powerful, eternal Keepers and a spectral jury of the dead that we're worthy to be in Richemerion's presence by having proved we embody the concept of protection. Complicated? Maybe. A little. But we're used to that. And will it be challenging? Probably, but again, we've—"

"And then—" Almeister interrupts.

"Oh, Jesus Christ."

"—there is the Final Ascension."

"The Final . . . Which is what?"

Almeister folds his hands together. "The final step one must take to stand before Richemerion is to endure the Measure of Burden."

Jameson, who has been listening silently up until this point, toking away, ashes on the ground, asks, "And dat be what, exactly? How de burden gon' be measured, nah?"

Almeister frowns slightly, as if recalling something deeply unpleasant. "The weight of every choice you have made. Every life affected by your actions. The physical manifestation of all that you carry, placed upon your shoulders. One must ascend to Richemerion's sanctum while bearing it."

"So, basically, if you feel guilty about anything you've ever done in your whole life, you're gonna get pancaked before you make it to the top, fool?" Perg's moustache twitches again.

Almeister nods approvingly. "Exactly."

The snail looks at me like this is going to be uniquely problematic and says, "Good luck, homie," before scooching away, swearing to himself in Spanish.

I turn back to Almeister. "Are you *absolutely* sure this is the only way to reach Richemerion? There aren't any other options?"

I always wrote about various scenarios in Riftbreaker. There was never just one way to skin a grimalk.

"No, there is another way."

"Excellent. What—"

"But it is far more perilous."

"For fuck's sake!"

Brit wanders off to join Perg while Seph shoots me a look of worry. I shake my head. "They're fine."

A Notification appears.

You have been offered a Quest!
"Your Mentor, [Almeister T. Wizard] has been CORRUPTED(!) by Disciples of the Ninth Guardian! A possible remedy may be found by requesting audience with [Richemerion, the Warden of Protection]. To hold audience, you must first pass a series of trials! Fun!"
Do you wish to accept this Quest?
[Yes] [No]

I sigh, press [Yes], and then, clapping my hands together, I exclaim, "Alright, great! Decision made. We're doing this. Uh, Perg? Nightwind? Wanna join the rest of the class?"

I wave them back over and they shamble, petulantly, to reassemble. Rubbing my hands together, I'm about to ask if anyone needs to use the bathroom before we head out—fully embracing my teacher-on-a-field-trip energy—when Waslan exhales sharply through his nose, drawing my attention to the now docile Ronine, and as I take in his size and power and force, I have a realization . . .

We're not all gonna fit.

CHAPTER SEVEN

The Porsche Panamera is probably the most spacious luxury sports car on the market, but it's still way too small for me, three magicians, and a small menagerie of exotic beasts. Notably Waslan. Sheila's roomy, but not "can comfortably seat a family of six and a seven-foot half lion, half rat" roomy.

If I'm driving and Brit's in the passenger seat, Perg can go small and sit on the console. Seph, her dad, and Jameson can take up the rear, but Waslan . . . I just can't figure out a way to get him inside as well. And, obviously, even if I could cram him in, he and Almeister have beef, and an additional internal beef is something we simply can't afford. We're gonna have unknown battles to fight; if there are known ones that can be avoided, we have to avoid them.

I stand off to the side of the group with the lion-rat amalgamation designed to bring me down by raising up my deeply buried traumatic memories, stroking its mane, no longer freaked out by the prospect.

"Eiiiinzgeeeeaaar," he purrs.

"Was," I say, "can I call you Was? I guess I can; I made up the name in the first place. Was . . . um . . ." I look into his beady, rat eyes, which are still beady and ratlike but I now also see a kindness in them. An understanding. "Was . . . I don't think you can come with us where we're going next."

"Eiiiinzgeeeeaaar?"

"Yeah, I know." (I don't actually know; I'm just being placating.) "But it's better if you stay here. You can guard Bell's View, really guard it, and keep anyone from showing up here to ravage the place."

He must understand me because he looks around at the burned down remnants of the town and then back at me as if to say, "*Seriously?*"

"Yeah, no, I get it," I acknowledge. "Ravage it . . . worse. I guess."

His brow furrows inasmuch as it can, and then he lets out a low, soft *Ooooooooo* sound.

He did this back in the Tower too. It sounds like he's saying "Bruuuuuce." I blew it off when I heard it the first time because the idea of him calling out my name seemed absurd, but now . . . Shit, now I dunno.

And, honestly, I don't really care.

I give him one last pat and he nods, gently, like Mufasa or Aslan the original or something. Kind of a benevolent but still powerful gesture that transmits a real, "and so it shall be done" vibe, and then he wanders away, back into the alleys of Bell's View and out of sight.

I feel a pang of sorrow watching him walk off. A sort of empathy I never thought I could summon for anything that's even got a hint of rat about it, much less a gigantic fifty percent.

Seph comes to stand next to me. "Saviour?"

"Yeah?"

"Since you are requesting that the beast remain here, does that mean . . . ?"

She pauses. Nibbles at her bottom lip. Which, again, *kills me*. Ugh. Pretty and sad. It's my goddamn Kryptonite.

"Does that mean what?"

"Does that mean that I am welcome to attend you this time instead?"

Oof. It's amazing how quickly a lump can form in your throat. I clear it out before answering, "Yes, yes, of course. Of course you are. I mean . . . he's *your* father. This was *your* idea. And, I mean . . . you're part of my Heart Guard now! I can't let you . . . ! Yes. Is what I'm saying. You silly goose." I give her a gentle shove. She giggles and shoves me back like it's the first time she's ever done such a thing.

Thump-THUMP.

My Heart feels like it's gonna rip clean outta my mesh suit.

"Okay!" I declare. "Time to go!"

She's got me so all up in my feels that I gotta get us outta here before I go into cardiac arrest for a second time today. I really can't decide what the proper thing to do with her is. Like, should I tell her the truth about who I am? Who we are? Or should I just invest in the Carpathianization of myself and feel free to get down to freak town with this cutie patootie who's clearly warm for my form?

The choice should probably be simpler. Stop being a ninny, lean into my natural Carpathian mojo, have sexy fun times with the sexy fun-time girl who thinks I'm hot jam, save the world, and go on about my business.

But . . .

Especially with all this "Brucillian" noise all up in the narrative mix, I dunno. I feel like if I go doling out details like "my name is Bruce, and I fell here from the sky," it might cause some additional consternation. And with my existing consternation, which now includes an angry Goliath of a Catarincian called Mael who's pissed at me and prepared to do who knows what to get even?

(Can't say for sure that's what's on the docket, but if I were writing all this, that's what I'd plot, so it doesn't feel far-fetched.)

I feel like I should leave any apple carts that haven't yet been tipped standing in the upright and secure position. i.e. I'm too deep into the lie to start telling the truth now.

Seph smiles and heads to gather Almeister, stroking my arm as she goes, while Brit strides over, map in hand, a little smirk on her lips.

"How are you and your fantasy girl doing?"

"Please . . . don't."

"Sorry, I was just . . . Sorry." She holds up one of the maps and shows it to me. "Alright," she says, "I think I've kind of figured out, approximately, which way we need to head."

"How?"

"Cross-referenced the ridge line with a passage I remembered from book six about 'a gate unseen, where only the worthy may tread.' Sounds like the Sanctuary Threshold to me."

"That's . . . incredible deduction."

"I do what I can."

"It's also incredibly speculative."

"I do what I can." She takes a breath, then asks, "Your Heart okay?"

"Still pumping."

She nods, also strokes my arm, and makes her way to Sheila.

I have no idea if this trying to find Richemerion business is half smart or half stupid, but it's six of one, half a dozen of the other, I reckon. Which is a doubly tautological thought, but whatever. Word-copping myself isn't going to help.

Shit. I wish we had Mael with us. I mean, from an occupancy standpoint, he would still pose a problem, but from a navigating-difficult-trials POV, there's probably no one better. He's an amalgamation of all the greatest, overpowered badasses ever imagined. He's got strength, speed, intellect, and resolve. He is the very essence of protection itself.

But. We don't have him. And I don't know if we'll ever have him again, so, no value in pondering the improbable. (Doesn't mean I won't. Just that there's no point in doing it.)

"Me Saviour?" Jameson wanders over, spliff hanging out of his mouth, still favoring slightly the wound he took from the Templar's blade but, on balance, not too worse for wear.

"What's up?"

He sticks out his monkey paw and offers me a toke.

Ninety-nine times out of a hundred, I'd be more than happy to get smoked out with him, but today . . . I dunno. I'm feeling like I need to keep my focus a little more, uh . . .

Man, it smells good. I wonder if Mezmer weed is different than what I'm used to on Earth. I knew a guy once who grew something he called Magick Stick, but . . .

. . . Wait. What was I thinking?

Oh! I need to stay focused. That's it.

"Thanks, Jame," I tell him, waving off the blunt, "but not now. Maybe later."

"Alright, me gen'ral, but just 'member, de best 'ting help repair up a broken heart gon' be de' herb. Me keep one aside for ye, now."

He blows a puff of smoke in my direction and walks off.

I consider his wisdom. It's not wrong. Willie Nelson once said, "The biggest killer on the planet is stress, and I still think the best medicine is and always has been cannabis."

Nice thoughts from two great philosophers, Willie and Jameson, but it does cause me to wonder . . . just how many goddamn forests of shit would Mael have to burn for him to decide he wants to be part of my Heart Guard once more?

The drive we're on has been long enough that the initial excitement of setting off has settled into a low hum of road-worn silence. The landscape has changed from the scorched remains of Bell's View into something wilder, rougher, the terrain shifting from cracked stone to patches of scrubland to wide, flat stretches of salt-like earth glowing faintly under the waning light of the twin suns.

Sheila's suspension has held up admirably, but even she wasn't built for a journey like this one. The Panamera is fast, sleek, and luxurious, but cramming a group of battle-bruised fugitives and one increasingly catatonic wizard into a four-door sports car isn't exactly ideal.

I'm driving. Brittany's in the passenger seat, her knee propped against the door, flipping absently through maps that may or may not tell us half of what we need to know.

Perg is perched on the console between us, about the size of a house cat now, his shell glinting faintly in the fading light. He occasionally makes little grumbling noises, shifting his weight as though trying to get comfortable. Given that he's essentially just a big, muscular foot inside a mobile fortress, I don't have the heart to tell him comfort isn't really in the cards.

In the back seat, Persephone has positioned herself next to Almeister, one hand resting lightly on his arm as though she's worried he might just slip away if she's not holding him here. He's staring out the window, unblinking, his face unreadable. He doesn't look like he's thinking about anything in particular. That's the part that unsettles me most. The Almeister I knew—the one I *wrote, anyway*—was always thinking, always calculating, always about three steps ahead of everyone else. This Almeister is just . . . drifting.

Jameson's wedged in on the other side, trying to make himself as small as possible. He's been vibing in his own world for most of the trip, but the sudden, restless movement of his tail against the seat lets me know he's growing fidgety.

"Me Saviour?"

"Yeah, J?"

"Mi need go make tinkle, me brethren."

Goddammit. I *knew* I should've asked.

I exhale through my nose. "Can you hold it?"

"Mi tink. But mi bladder not be as young as it once was."

"We're basically there," Brittany says, eyes still on the map. "Just a little further."

Jameson mutters something under his breath that sounds vaguely like "bumboclaat directions," but then settles back in without further protest. I hope he doesn't go on the leather. I know from my time with Crystal that monkey pee on leather seats never comes out.

My old supervisor's desk chair knows it too.

I tighten my grip on the wheel, eyes flicking to the rearview. Persephone is still watching Almeister, her brow knit with quiet worry.

"Almeister," I say, trying to inject a note of casual conversation into the thick silence. "How we feeling, buddy?"

Nothing. Not even a blink.

"Hey, Al?" I press, forcing a little more levity into my tone. "You wanna tell us what we're looking for? I assume Richemerion didn't just slap a sign on the door saying: This Way to Richemerion's Place!"

For a long, agonizing moment, there's no response. Then, just as I'm about to turn to Brit and confirm that, yes, maybe our wizard *is* completely fried, Almeister speaks.

"It is close."

His voice is distant. Dull. Like he's answering a question someone asked him years ago and it's only just now reaching his brain.

"How close?" Brit asks.

Almeister's fingers twitch against his knee. His lips part slightly, like he wants to say more, but then he just shakes his head, turning his gaze back out the window.

That's reassuring.

"Oh, wait." Brit perks up.

"What? What do you see?"

"There."

She points, and up ahead, I see . . .

Are you kidding me?

There is a big sign reading "Sanctuary Threshold Ahead. This Way to Richemerion's Place."

"¿*En serio*?" Perg says. "They just put it out there like that for anyone to stumble across?"

"No," Almeister murmurs from the back seat.

"What do you mean 'no,' *abuelo*?"

Before an answer can be offered, Jameson makes a little whimpering noise. "Me bladder be struggling, me boss."

Goddammit. "Alright, fine," I say to the macaque, "but be quick and be careful. We brought down the Tower, but there could still be some DONG anywhere." Perg starts giggling and begins to say something, I presume, about Jameson's need to pee, but I cut that shit off with a quickness. "Don't. Just . . . don't."

He looks as penitent as a moderately embiggened snail can look and zips it.

Jameson crawls over Seph and Almeister and opens the door.

"Back in a right jiff, Saviour mine."

I watch Jameson disappear into the scrubland, tail flicking, muttering to himself in what I assume is a mix of irritation and bladder distress. The moment the door clicks shut behind him, the car settles into an uneasy quiet again.

Almeister's eyes don't leave the window, but his fingers curl slightly, like he's gripping something invisible. His mouth works soundlessly for a moment before he exhales a slow, breathy, "The Keepers . . ."

"The Keepers of the Threshold?" I ask, repeating what he told us earlier for no reason other than I'm antsy and, I think, a little hungry. Normally, after collapsing a tower, the gang would all go to Denny's or something.

"Yes," he replies, voice hollow.

"What about them?"

"They are preparing."

"They are?"

"They are."

"You can feel that?"

"I can."

"Cool. 'Kay. Um. Preparing to . . . what? Exactly?"

"To judge. To judge us all."

Brit's fingers tap against the map. "Can I . . . ? Just for clarification, what are we being judged on, exactly? Is this a 'look within your soul' thing, or are we talking a 'prove your worth in a fight' type of deal? Because if it's that second one, we need to have a strategy before we—"

"Worthy," Almeister interrupts. His voice is paper thin, like it's unraveling from his own throat. "Only the worthy will be able to pass on to meet with the Warden."

Persephone's grip on her father's arm tightens. "And what is it, Father, that makes someone worthy in their eyes?"

Almeister's breath catches. For the first time since he went all catatonic, something in his face changes. Just a flicker, a tremor in his expression. A hesitation.

"That is what the trials are designed to reveal. It allows them to look within," he finally says. "Beyond words, beyond actions. The Keepers do not judge what we claim to be. Based on the trials, it allows them to evaluate what we truly are."

Brit straightens and mutters something like, "Cool. Add that to the list of cryptic bullshit we have to navigate," before folding the map angrily and shoving it in her cloak.

"Al, can you elaborate at all? Would be great to know more about how this is going to go before we stumble into it," I plead.

Almeister leans forward, his voice low. "The Trial of Vigilance will show whether we see clearly, or if we deceive ourselves. The Trial of Endurance will expose what we are willing to suffer for, and what will break us. The Trial of Sacrifice will demand that we give up something precious; something we may not even realize we are holding on to. And the Trial of Trust . . ." He pauses, his expression grim. "The Trial of Trust will lay bare who we truly believe in, and who believes in us."

"That seems like . . . a lot," I note.

"They actually trimmed it down since I first sought the Warden. You no longer have to endure a forty-eight-hour silent reflection period, a barefoot pilgrimage across hot coals, or have to milk an extremely uncooperative goat."

There is a lengthy silence before Persephone lets out a quiet sound. Something between a hum and a murmur of thought.

"Seph?"

"Hm?"

"What is it?"

"I'm just . . . If we are to be 'evaluated,' truly, then we must be ready to confront truths about ourselves we might otherwise wish"—her eyes meet mine in the rearview mirror—"remained hidden."

I don't know if she's implying something about her or about me, but in either case, it causes my hands to tighten on the wheel.

"Jameson feels like he's taking a long time, huh? Where's he gotten off to?" I roll down the window and shout into the air, "J? Where are you? You doing okay out there?"

No sooner has the sentence left my lips than there is a *THUD* on the hood of the car.

"AH!" we all bark some version of the sound. I don't think anyone could blame us. It's been a day.

I spin to see Jameson standing there. Just standing. Legs apart, feet planted, tail curled, hands at his sides. His eyes are open but unfocused, like he's looking *through* us instead of *at* us.

"Jame?" I call to him. "What are you—?"

Before I can finish, his mouth opens, and a voice that is absent of a charming and occasionally hard to decipher patois proclaims, **"You approach the Threshold."**

The air around us changes, grows heavy, charged, like a storm pressing down just before the first crack of lightning.

"Um, what is happening?" Brit asks.

"I have no . . . Al? Hey, Al? Is this normal?"

He doesn't respond, so Seph gives it a try. "Father? Father, is this part of the trial?"

Almeister exhales and nods slowly. "Yes," he whispers. "It has begun."

Jameson tilts his head. **"You approach the Threshold."**

It's weird hearing that voice come out of him. Kind of like hearing Brit's voice come out of Carol the Tentasaurian back at the Tower.

"Uh, yeeeees?" I hiss out, unsure if I really want to go through with this now. It suddenly occurs to me that having to pass a series of trials to engage with the Warden of Protection seems wildly counterintuitive. If I had written something like this, Brit or my editor would have surely made a notation in the margins like, *"Why does he have to overcome a bunch of obstacles just to meet with the one who gave him the Heart to begin with?"*

To which I would have pushed back with, *"Because greatness is earned, not given,"* or some equally wilted aphorism.

But, here we are! So, as ever, life is stranger than fiction.

Jameson's eyes are radiating a light as he stares at me. Or, no, not at me, *through* me.

"So . . . can we come ahead now? Or . . . ?"

There is another filled beat where Jameson doesn't blink, doesn't move, until finally, after what feels like a much longer time than I believe a monkey peering into your soul without speaking should be, he finally says, **"Step forward! And . . . be known!"**

And just like that, now my bladder feels like it's gonna spring a leak too. As the light around us shifts, the road, the scrubland, the twin suns, everything bends and warps, twisting like reality itself is being peeled back. The Threshold opens . . .

. . . and we are pulled inside.

CHAPTER EIGHT

Crucible of Tomorrows, Riftbreaker Book Two, Chapter Ten

The wind moved through the clearing in a low, steady murmur. Carpathian watched the fire as it crackled and spit, eyes steady, posture composed. The flames threw shadows across Almeister's face, deepening the lines around his eyes, but his gaze was calm.

For a while, neither of them spoke. The silence was not uncomfortable, more a reprieve after the long day's battle. Carpathian flexed his fingers absently, feeling the ache in his knuckles and the faint tremor of fatigue that lingered in his bones. The scent of ash and iron hung thick in the air, mingling with the crisp bite of the oncoming night.

"They were waiting for us," he said at last, voice low but steady. Not a question.

Almeister's eyes flicked to him, dark and reflective in the firelight. "Yes," he replied simply.

They sat in silence for a time more. At last, Carpathian spoke again.

"May I ask a question?"

"You just did."

Carpathian rolled his eyes. Barely. In truth, small jibes such as that amused the young Saviour. It let him know his mentor felt comfortable enough to make them.

"You have never explained," Carpathian said, "why."

"Why what?" the old wizard replied, although it was clear from his tone that he already knew the answer.

"Why the Warden—why Richemerion—chose to grant me this." His eyes flicked down, fingers resting lightly over the skin of his chest, where beneath, the unrelenting pulse of the Mechanical Heart thrummed with precise rhythm. "Or why they did so in this manner."

Almeister's expression softened just a fraction. "Richemerion is not easy to explain, nor are their choices," he said. "And what they gave you was not a gift."

Carpathian's eyes remained on the fire, unblinking. His hand rested still against his breast, the pulse beneath bone and flesh foreign in its consistency. Never fast, never slow. Just unceasing.

"Then, why did they choose me?" Carpathian asked.

Almeister's gaze drifted, as if seeing beyond the firelight into a darkness Carpathian could not reach. "Richemerion is the Warden of Protection," he said. "But protection is not a shield. It is a choice. It is the weight of knowing what must be done and doing it, regardless of the cost."

Carpathian's fingers rested lightly over the faint outline of the Heart inside his body. "Then it was never about my survival."

Almeister's eyes darkened. "In a manner of speaking. Survival is incidental. It was about what you would sacrifice to protect others. What you would endure. It is about the survival of something far greater than yourself."

The firelight flickered, carving deeper lines into the old man's face. Carpathian's expression remained even. "But I did not ask for this," he said.

"No," Almeister replied. "You did not."

Carpathian's gaze did not waver. "Then why?"

Almeister remained patient. It was not a new question. It was one he had answered at least half a dozen times before. But, as long as Carpathian felt the need to ask, Almeister would answer. Just as Carpathian's oath was to Meridia itself, Almeister's oath was to Carpathian.

"Because Richemerion does not choose those who seek power," Almeister explained. "They choose those who have never asked for it but will bear it nonetheless. The Warden of Protection does not guard those who need nothing. They guard those who would carry the weight of a responsibility they did not ask for. Those willing to, as they say, answer the call."

The fire snapped, sending a spray of sparks spiraling upward. Carpathian's fingers moved absently, tracing the line of his collarbone, the pulse of the Heart beneath yet unchanging.

"Then it is not power," he said. "It is a burden."

Almeister inclined his head, a slow gesture. "It is both. Protection always is."

Carpathian's eyes remained on the fire. "And what is the cost?" he asked.

"To endure," Almeister replied. "Without reprieve. Without end. To guard others even when they do not ask to be guarded."

The fire snapped again, and Carpathian's eyes drifted closed, just briefly, the weight of the pulse beneath his chest a dull ache, steady and hollow.

For a moment longer, neither spoke. Then, with the same regulated precision, Carpathian inclined his head.

"Then I will bear it," he said.

Almeister's hand settled lightly on his shoulder. "You are not alone."

Carpathian's eyes remained on the fire. "I know."

And for a time, there was only the firelight and the quiet, steady beating of the Heart.

ACT TWO

WHAT DOESN'T KILL YOU (STILL KINDA KILLS YOU)

CHAPTER NINE

I don't scream as we plummet into the darkness. I *do* say, "OH, *COME ON*," which is basically the same thing, I suppose.

We fall.

For about two seconds.

Not all that dramatic, actually. Maybe twenty feet tops.

But the landing? Ugh. Falling twenty feet inside a Panamera still packs a wallop.

"Sheila!" My instinct is to protect her—she was not designed for this much off-roading.

The car groans (not literally, she actually hasn't said anything in a while, but the metal makes a sound), settling at an awkward angle on what feels like soft, uneven ground. A pulse runs through the air, deep and reverberating, like the echo of a massive bell. The world around us shifts again, settling into something new. The landscape isn't just dark; it's disjointed, warping in and out of focus, like pieces of it are refusing to hold shape.

Dust swirls around us, thick and shimmering, catching in the dim glow still radiating from Jameson's eyes. He hasn't shifted from the hood, still standing there, unmoving, staring down at us with an eerie, weightless stillness. Then, as if some unseen force tugs at his strings, his head tilts, and his mouth moves.

"The Trial of Vigilance will begin."

"What exactly has happened to him?" I ask.

Almeister exhales. "The Keepers do not appear as we might expect. Their presence is . . . overwhelming. To interact with them directly would be like trying to hold a conversation with a storm. They require a conduit, a voice through which they may be understood."

Brit squints. "And they chose *him*?"

Jameson's glowing eyes flick toward her. "A vessel must be neutral, unburdened by intent. The monkey is . . . Well, he's sufficient."

"How long will he stay this way?" I query.

"They will release him when our task is complete."

Jameson (or, I guess, the Keepers wearing a Jameson costume) remains still, the glow in his eyes steady. No restless tail flicking, no muttered commentary. Just waiting. Watching.

It's very odd to see him not chilled out and blazing. Kind of like one of those monkeys in a movie about a killer virus who go from cute to disturbingly intense in a moment.

I shift uncomfortably in my seat. "And what is our task? Our first one? Exactly? What does 'vigilance' mean?"

"Vigilance is not a test of strength or willpower. It is a test of perception. The Keepers will not ask you to endure suffering or prove your resolve or anything as common as that. They will ask if you are capable of *seeing* the world as it truly is."

"What the hell does that mean?" Brit asks, her old ally—agitation—sliding in.

Almeister gestures at the terrain before us. "We are being observed, but we do not yet know by whom or by what. Our task is not to *fight*, not to *run*, but to *recognize*. There will be distractions, misdirection, things that seem urgent but are not. The *truth* is here, but only if we are vigilant enough to find it."

Perg's moustache twitches. "And what happens if we don't, fool?"

Jameson, apparently also granted superhearing, responds. **"Then you will not move forward."**

A pause. Looks all around. Then . . .

"Yeah, okay." I step out of the car, scanning the terrain. No obvious signs of movement. No path, no markers, no clear objective. Just the subtle, nagging sensation of us *being seen*.

The wind shifts. A small sound, too faint to place, drifts through the air. Not threatening. Not urgent. Just . . . present.

Whatever we're supposed to find isn't hiding.

It's here. Now. Waiting for us to notice it.

Brit gets out and steps up next to me like Phillip Seymour Hoffman approaching Bill Paxton in the original *Twister* to ask if he was feeling something in the air. After a beat, she asks, "Thoughts?"

I look to Jameson, but he's just staring at me all *Children of the Corn* style, still fully possessed by the Keepers. I don't recognize him. Not so much because of the possession but because he's not puffing away on a fatty. It's like seeing Slash without a top hat and sunglasses.

I turn in place, scanning the terrain again, but nothing has changed. No movement, no obvious marker, just that low thrum of *presence* pressing against the edges of my awareness. The more I focus on it, the more it feels like something is breathing in tandem with us, just beyond reach.

Perg comes scooching up, uneasy. "Feels like we're being played with, *vato*. Like something's waiting for us to slip up."

Persephone joins, holding Almeister by the arm. Watching them shuffle along, the thought occurs to me that we're putting a lot of faith in the word of a guy who's been corrupted by dirty Mezmer. Who's to say that he's not leading us into a trap?

"You really need to start thinking of these things before you set off on Quests, Bruce."

I ignore my other half because . . . Whatever. He's not wrong, but I don't need that shit now. If Brain Bruce is so canny, he should've thought of it earlier himself. Those who live in Bruce's brain shouldn't be so quick to judge. As the saying goes.

Almeister clears his throat. "The Keepers do not play games. If you are feeling pressure, it is because they want you to acknowledge it. The question will be . . . why?"

A flicker, just for an instant, at the corner of my vision. Movement? I snap my head toward it, but there's nothing. Just shifting dust and jagged rock.

Then Brit mutters, "Look at that."

"What?"

She points at the ground, where a small stone is rolling as if being pushed along. But then it stops, suddenly, like it's hit something that isn't there. The ground hums in a way that presses against the air, like a held breath finally being released. The space where the stone stopped ripples, a distortion just barely visible. A shallow groove etches itself into the dirt, starting as nothing then deepening as if carved by an invisible hand. The dust around it shifts, pulled inward like a tide reversing course.

Then, the impression sharpens. It's no longer just a groove.

It's a footprint.

Old, half faded, now settling back into place as though it had been erased and is only now being allowed to exist again. Then . . . another footprint. And another. And another.

The prints continue to press into the dirt, forming a clear trail ahead. Brit exchanges a look with me. "Guess we follow them?"

"I guess. Al? We follow these, yeah?"

Almeister turns his head to me, smiles, and says, "Of course."

Hmmm. I really don't care for his smirky affirmation, but . . .

I take a step anyway. Because I am reckless.

The trail stretches ahead, winding through the shifting terrain. The prints appear in clusters, spaced apart like someone walked this path with purpose. The further we go, the more solid they seem, pressed deeper into the earth as if reinforcing their own existence.

We move cautiously at first, then with more confidence, boots crunching against the dry ground. The path leads us between jagged rock formations, their edges blurred as if the world itself hasn't fully decided they should exist. The air is charged with something unseen, but nothing moves now except us.

Perg stops scuttling forward. I stop and look back.

"What's wrong?"

"This feels too easy, homes."

I mean, I don't disagree. But the footprints keep forming, one after another, a beckoning depression of pressed earth guiding us forward. Maybe, just maybe, something can be easy for once.

"I hear you, but—"

However, before I can finish articulating the thought, the ground drops out beneath us.

No warning crack, no shifting of stone, just instant nothingness. Where solid ground was just seconds ago, there is suddenly nothing and we're falling.

Brit curses, arms flailing for balance. Seph gasps, grabbing for Almeister, whose nightgown is once again all up in the air, exposing his elderly nethers. Perg lets out a half prayer, half swear in Spanish.

I try to twist in the midst of my free fall, to see where we're headed, but it's chaos. Brit's cloak flares wildly, Perg tumbles shell-first, Seph's fingers slip from Almeister's sleeve as we all plummet. After not as long as it could be but longer than I would like, I hit something.

Not rock. Not soil.

Something soft.

Like a cushion of air, dense and unmoving. It doesn't break my fall—it stops it, like I never had momentum at all.

And then—

The world snaps like a reel of film jammed in reverse, and the falling is gone. The wind is gone. The rush of panic still lingers in my chest, but I realize . . .

We're standing.

On solid ground.

Right next to the car.

Exactly where we started from. Jameson is still perched on the hood, glowing eyes fixed on us, completely unchanged. He blinks, slow and deliberate.

"You were not vigilant. You will try again."

"Not vigilant? We saw invisible footprints come to life and followed them! Al, you said we had to follow them, right?!"

"I did," the old guy wheezes, catching his breath from our fall that wasn't really a fall. "But those were clearly not the right ones."

"What?!"

Jameson's mouth opens, and the creepy Keeper voice clarifies, **"The Trial of Vigilance is not about following. It is about seeing."**

He doesn't move, doesn't blink, just stares with those glowing eyes that aren't quite his. The words stretch long between us, the implication taking its time to sink in.

By which I mean . . . it doesn't sink in. At all.

"What are you saying?" Brit asks. "We did see. We saw the footprints, we followed them. What exactly did we not see?"

No answer.

Almeister gives his robe a slow shake, dusting off the nonexistent residue of the fall that wasn't a fall. He doesn't look rattled. If anything, he looks like he expected this.

Which is annoying.

Alright, think this through, Bruce. Puzzles are your favorite part of most of the games you've played.

"You mean like Portal*?"*

"Yes! Like Portal*! There's always a solution, even if the rules of physics are actively conspiring against you."*

That's true. It is, actually, what made *Portal* so much fun. Or infuriating. Or both. Honestly, it depended on how many times I accidentally launched myself into toxic goo and how condescending GLaDOS was feeling that day.

I stare at the ground and think it through. The footprints are still there, resetting, reforming in the dirt, some more solid than others.

I narrow my eyes. "Hold on."

Stepping forward, I crouch near the closest footprint, pressing my fingers into its edge. The dirt is firm, compacted. I move to another print beside it, one that formed in front of us. When I press my fingers against its edge, the soil crumbles slightly, like a sandcastle before the tide pulls it back to sea.

I frown. "These aren't the same."

Seph steps closer. "How so?"

I press my palm flat against the deeper one. "This one was always here."

"Always here?"

"Yeah. It's solid. The weight settled into the dirt long before we got here." Then I shift to the other. "This one is recent. Like it was . . . placed in front of us."

Brit catches on, her focus sharpening. "So you're saying—"

"We're not supposed to follow all of them," I declare. "Some were already here. Some were put here like bait."

I glance at Jameson. His expression hasn't changed, but something about his posture makes me feel like he's waiting.

I look back at the prints. I know the difference now. The ones that sink deeper, that never changed—those are real. The ones that reset, that appeared in front of us—those are the trap.

I exhale. "It's not a path. It's a test to see if we remember."

"Remember?"

"Yeah, like Hüsker Dü."

"What is Hüsker Dü?" Seph asks.

"Um . . . the name of a wonderful group of very fine musicians whose music serenaded us on many an adventure, but also, and more relevant to this situation, a type of game."

"It literally means 'Do you remember,' in, um, ancient . . . Danish . . . ark . . . ian," Brit adds.

"I do not know this language."

"You don't need to. It's not common," I hasten to say.

Brit lets out a slow breath, stepping beside me. "Alright. So, we do this again. Properly."

I nod and look carefully at the floor beneath us. Not just at where the prints are but how they settle. Which ones belong. Which ones never left.

I press my boot into the first one. One of the real ones. The ground holds. I take another step. Another. The false prints shift slightly, as if trying to lure us toward them, but I ignore them. They're meant to be distractions.

The others follow my path. We keep moving, step by step, tracing only the ones that were always here. Then the ground firms beneath us, settling into place, but we don't move right away. The false prints are gone, erased like they were never there. The real ones remain, pressed deep, solid. The only path forward.

I take a slow breath and scan the space ahead. Nothing has changed, and yet, everything has. The pressure of unseen eyes hasn't lifted. If anything, it feels stronger now, like something is still waiting for us to act.

But, this time, we don't rush.

I test each footprint before shifting my weight, feeling for the difference between what's firm and what crumbles. Brit walks behind me, her focus sharp, tracking the pattern. Seph moves carefully, her eyes flicking to the prints then to the space around us, as if sensing something beyond what we can see. Almeister follows without a word, hands clasped behind his back, his expression unreadable. Perg mutters under his breath, half to himself, half to the universe.

The path winds. The landscape stretches ahead. The prints remain steady, appearing in a rhythm we now recognize. Five steps. A pause. Three more. A slight turn to the left. Another pause. Something about the pattern feels familiar now. Not just in the way it moves but in the way it forces us to move with it. We step when the ground tells us to step. We stop when the prints stop.

The more I pay attention, the more I realize it isn't guiding us toward something—it's guiding us away from something else. I glance to the side. The false prints are still trying to lead us astray. They reappear when we pause, as if waiting to tempt us. Each time, they fade when we move forward correctly.

This isn't just about seeing what's real. It's about trusting that what's real won't change.

The further we walk, the more it solidifies. The prints no longer feel like clues. They feel like certainties. Like this path was always going to bring us exactly here, step by step, moment by moment.

Then . . . the footprints stop.

"Do you think that's it?" Brit asks.

"I'm not sure."

There's nothing in front of us. No grand exit or clear indicator that we have come to a fork in the road or anything like it. I wonder if—

"THIS CONCLUDES THE TRIAL OF VIGILANCE!"

Oh, shit!

Jameson is, somehow, now sitting on my shoulder and *screaming into my ear.*

"How'd you get there?"

He doesn't answer, hopping off my shoulder to stand firm in front of us and say . . .

"The Trial of Endurance will now commence!"

CHAPTER TEN

Wait, that's it? That was the whole Trial of Vigilance?"

"Yes. That is why I said it was concluded."

"But—"

"The Trial of Vigilance is about more than discovering which path to take. It is about learning to understand that it was always there. That is why the false prints shift, appearing ahead, tempting one to follow. The real ones never move. They wait to be recognized. You remained vigilant, saw what was there to be seen, and now, the path is gone. Because you no longer need it."

I can feel what he's talking about. Pressing into my feet, the ground beneath us feels more sturdy, as if the uncertainty we walked through has finally anchored itself some kind of way.

"Okay, so—"

"The Trial of Endurance will now commence!"

"Yeah, no, I know, you said that. What—"

"The Trial of Endurance will test not only what you can withstand but what you believe you must."

"What does that—?"

"The Trial of Vigilance was about seeing." (He's gotten very interrupt-y.) **"The Trial of Endurance is about *bearing*."**

"About bearing . . . what? Exactly?"

"Weight."

"Riiiiight. Do you mean physically or—?"

"I mean both!"

There is no crack of thunder, but it's the kind of thing that, were I writing it, I might suggest contained a distant sound of one, just to add dramatic tension. Instead, the words just disappear into the air, and Jameson waits for us to, I dunno, be awed, I guess.

I nod a couple of times.

"Cool. So, nonphysically, what are we—?"

"The Trial of Endurance is about that which we carry with us and refuse to set down."

Hearing that kind of makes me wish we just had to lug a boulder up a hill instead.

"Okay, but—"

"The trial begins!"

He claps his monkey paws, and the world detonates.

One second, we're standing on stable ground, still catching our breath from the first trial. The next, the entire landscape shreds itself apart like someone ripped a tablecloth out from under reality and sent everything tumbling into the void.

I don't know how we land, or if we even land. The transition is instant—no slow fade, no disorienting shift—just the immediate, gut-punch realization that we are running for our lives.

And this? This is not some measured test of perception. This is Arnold Schwarzenegger, *Running Man*, full-tilt mayhem.

"Uh," Brit shouts over the absolute carnage unfolding around us, "does this seem like kind of a dramatic escalation?"

"Little bit!" I shout back.

It really does. Whereas the Trial of Vigilance was a pretty chill, "let's see if you can spot the subtle differences" kind of a deal, this is a hellscape in motion. A shifting, snarling gauntlet of death traps that wants us, well, dead, I guess.

A massive pendulum blade the size of a bus swings down from nowhere, slicing the space we occupied a heartbeat ago. The wind howls with the force of its passage, sending shards of rock flying like shrapnel. Brit yells—she's already ahead, moving fast, her cloak snapping behind her as she vaults over a crumbling ledge.

I barely have time to process that before the floor beneath me collapses.

I jump, hit unstable ground, and immediately have to dodge left as a rolling boulder the size of a small house barrels toward me. Perg shouts something in Spanish, his voice a mix of outrage and terror, but I don't catch it because I am actively trying not to die.

I think. It sure feels like death is chasing us, but . . .

"Al?!" I yell.

"Yes?" his thin voice responds, barely audible in the maelstrom.

"If we get tagged, we don't actually die, right? We just have to start over? Like last time?"

"It depends," he coughs.

"On what?"

"On how the Keepers decide to interpret the failure."

Well, that's supremely vague. Having my fate determined by the interpretive vicissitudes of a group of faceless arbiters speaking through the appropriated husk of my monkey companion is not the kind of ironclad set of rules I feel like a game like this should be played by.

"Father, look out!"

I whip my head around just in time to see Seph jerking Almeister out of the path of a swinging bladed pendulum the size of a carriage wheel as the terrain warps violently beneath them. One second, they're on a solid incline; the next, the whole thing is tilting, shifting into a vertical drop. Seph, once more, reacts with lightning speed, grappling Almeister with one hand and throwing herself toward a ledge with the other.

I don't have time to check if they make it because I am suddenly airborne.

A gust of wind slams into me from the side, ripping me off course like a rag doll. I twist in midair, flailing for balance, but the environment doesn't care if

I stabilize—it just keeps trying to kill me. Below me, the ground fractures into moving platforms, each one drifting at different speeds, some flipping unexpectedly, others simply evaporating into mist the second they're touched. I hit one—and immediately jump off as it begins to crumble.

I land hard, rolling onto my feet, only to duck as another blade scythes out of the rock wall.

Brit is ahead, still moving—she kicks off a platform, grabs the edge of a floating slab, swings up, and lands running. The way she moves is effortless, controlled—like she's been doing this her whole life.

I, on the other hand, am less smooth.

I land on a rolling stone, trip slightly, correct myself, and leap onto a more stable surface, only for the gravity beneath me to reverse. I slam into the ceiling.

It knocks the wind out of me—hard. Like getting gut punched by an endurance trial concocted by gatekeepers meant to test your resolve in seeking a Warden of Protection.

Or, no, it's not *like* that. That is what it is. I'm having a hard time organizing my thoughts given the ass-whooping I'm taking.

I gasp, trying to pull in air, but the second I adjust, gravity flips again, slamming me right back down onto the shifting platform below. I land awkwardly, momentum rolling me onto my shoulder before I wrench myself upright, stumbling for balance. Up ahead, Perg clings to the edge of a rock formation, muttering something like, "*Chinga tu madre*, Keepers, *esto no es* endurance, *esto es puro pinche abuso!*" his shell scraping against the stone as he tries to pull himself up.

(Good news is I think my ability to understand Spanish is getting better.)

Brit is a blur of motion, flipping between surfaces with a precision that makes my chaotic flailing feel especially inelegant. The terrain isn't just trying to kill us: it's trying to keep us off-balance. No pattern, no warning. Just relentless movement. And I think I know why . . .

I reach for my Mezmer, purely on instinct, but the second I do, a column of jagged stone erupts from the ground. It knocks my feet out from under me, sending me sprawling onto a narrow ledge that immediately begins to break apart.

No Mezmer. I can't focus, can't even hold on to it for more than a second before the course punishes me for trying.

"Anyone else having trouble using Mezmer?" I shout, scrambling back to my feet.

"Yeah!" Brit yells back, still running.

"The second you try, the course gets worse!"

Brit vaults over a gap, barely catching the landing. For the first time, she stumbles. Just a fraction of a second, but enough to confirm what I already know.

"No shit," she grits out, hauling herself forward. "I noticed!"

This trial isn't about strength or strategy. It's not about using every trick at our disposal. It's about what happens when there are no tricks, no shortcuts, no power to fall back on.

It's about how much you can take before you break.

I throw myself onto another platform just as the one behind me disintegrates. The wind slams into me midair, twisting my descent. I manage to catch an outcrop at the last second, fingertips straining against the crumbling surface.

"Carpathian!" Seph calls out.

"I'm okay!"

I'm not okay, but it doesn't do anyone any good to hear that shit.

I'm tempted to just let go, let myself drop and see if the Keepers judge me worthy to try again. But then I realize . . . I already did that.

That's how I wound up here—in Meridia—in the first place.

This test is kind of a microversion of what's happening to me, writ large.

What are you able to endure? What do you refuse to set down? What are you willing to shoulder and keep going?

Shit.

So, I continue dangling from the ledge, fingers clawed into loose, crumbling earth, legs kicking against nothing. A sudden wind rips past, trying to pry me loose, and my arms scream in protest. Then . . . a noise cuts through it all.

"Does everyone hear that?" I call out.

"Yeah!" Brit yells back. "What is that?"

I'm not sure. It's not wind, not crumbling rock. It's . . . a roar. Something alive. I look up. And I see them.

. . . Thingamajigs.

That's really all I can think of to describe them. They're not the same, but they're all similar in that they ain't looking like nothing I've seen before.

The first lurches forward, long limbed and unnaturally stretched, like a greyhound flayed of all pretense of skin. Sinew and tendon coil like tension cables, twisting beneath a translucent membrane. Its arms are too long, its spine too sharp, and where a head should be, there is only a gaping maw lined with too many teeth.

The second one moves like something that forgot it was supposed to be dead, jerked, stitched, and stapled together with too many joints, too many wrong angles, like an anatomical drawing where the artist got bored halfway through and just started adding extra parts. Its eyes are wet, black, gleaming, too round. Like marbles stuffed into sockets that don't quite fit.

The third is the smallest but fastest, a spindly thing that skitters on all fours like a cockroach crossed with a greyhound. Its mouth doesn't open the right way; it peels back from the center, wide and yawning. Something inside it is clicking.

And then . . . more. Various shapes, sizes, and degrees of "ahhhh!" to them. They emerge from the shifting dark, one moving like a hunting cat but with too many elbows; another crawling low to the ground, leaving wet tracks where it passes. Another walks upright, human shaped but with no actual body to speak of, just a collection of what seems to be . . . cactuses? Yeah, it's a cactus monster.

Oh, for the love of—

"Carpathian!" Persephone shouts again.

I appreciate so much that she's worried about me, but I'm also kind of embarrassed that she has to worry about me *so* much.

I grit my teeth, fingers cramping as the ledge crumbles a little more beneath my grip. The Thingamajigs shift, their too-many limbs flexing, their clicking mouths working at the empty space between us, as if tasting the air. They're . . . waiting.

For what, I don't know. For me to fall? For us to move? For the gauntlet itself to decide we've been pushed far enough and either let us go or make us start again or . . . something worse?

Or maybe they're just waiting for the most dramatic moment to pounce. Which seems to be . . .

Now.

The smallest one moves first, that skittering-cockroach thing with the inside-out mouth. It moves in short bursts, too fast to track, zigzagging like it's waiting for an opening. Then, a second one joins, then a third, and before I can even process the escalation, the entire pack is in motion. A blur of too-long limbs and snapping jaws, of wet, clawed feet scraping against unstable platforms, of tendon and teeth and the undeniable sense that I am about to be very, very outnumbered.

"Shit, shit, shit," I mutter, trying to find some leverage to pull myself up, but the second I move, one of them leaps and—

Suddenly, everything shifts.

Not the gauntlet this time. Or at least, not of its own accord. But because the rest of my crew has snapped into action to assist me.

A slab of stone hurtles through the air like a discus. The lunging Thingamajig is clipped midair, spiraling into the abyss with a sound that makes my stomach tighten, something between a scream and a laugh, like it's delighted to be obliterated.

I crane my neck to see Brit's hands moving in that circular motion, *Summoner of Something* crackling in the air. The rest of the Thingamajig pack falters, sensing something they don't understand. The way they twitch, heads tilting at odd angles, makes my skin crawl.

Then, in a single breath, Brit whispers to them, "Run."

And *they do*. The fastest ones move first, not to attack but to *obey*, their bodies snapping into coordinated action, muscles tensing as they sprint away into the gauntlet itself, rushing headlong into their own demise, diving into swinging pendulums, collapsing ledges, walls that shift and grind like the jaws of some enormous machine.

Beast Mastery. She can control beasts of creation as well.

Well, that's gonna come in handy, you gotta imagine.

A bladed platform tilts and drops, taking down dozens upon dozens more. A wind tunnel activates, sending another straight into the path of a rolling boulder, where it's flattened with a wet *crunch*. The rest scramble, confused, instinct warring with whatever invisible force Brit has pressed into their minds.

But . . . the biggest of the bunch resists, a hulking, multijointed horror that moves like an oil slick trying to shape itself into something vaguely humanoid. It fights against Brit's pull, claws gouging into the ground, twisting in protest.

And that's when Perg hits it like a battering ram.

One second, he's midsize, travel Perg, muttering in Spanish and looking extremely unhappy with our situation. The next?

BAM.

Dude *embiggens* midsprint, shell expanding to the size of a freight truck. The sound of his impact is seismic, a deep *WHUMP* that rattles my ribs as he slams into the resisting creature like a wrecking ball. It screeches, a sound that barely lasts before it's *launched* into a swinging pendulum and gets split in half like a piñata filled with bad decisions.

Perg skids to a stop, retracts slightly, then grunts. "That's right, *pendejo*. I'm the last thing you ever see. Suck on it, bitch."

Unfortunately, the gauntlet itself remains unaffected by this little show of force. It isn't letting up, the ground still shifting, the obstacles still relentless. The last remaining creatures aren't moving anymore, but the world itself *is*. Wind slams into me again, forcing me to very nearly go flying off the edge of this ledge, my fingernails gripping with all the bony endurance they can muster. I grit my teeth. I need to focus. We need to *end* this.

Seeing the success Perg and Brit are having, I try to tap into my Mezmer as well, but it still *won't hold*. Every time I attempt to touch it, the gauntlet reacts, throwing another wrench in, keeping me off-balance.

Unless . . .

I grind my teeth harder, groaning with a resoluteness that I'm not even sure I possess but might be able to will into being, pushing past the burning in my muscles, and reach not just for my Mezmer . . . but for theirs.

Synchron.

The second it clicks, I can feel it. Like I've been plugged into a current, into something vast and *real*. I thought I had to be physically connected to the wielder of Mezmer for it to work, but it would seem that I can be connected to them in other ways as well. Emotionally. Spiritually. Metaphysically.

Brit's Summoner of Something. Perg's sheer, unbreakable strength. Seph's—Seph's—

Hey. Where'd Seph go?

Looking around for her, I now see that she didn't actually go anywhere.

She's gone *everywhere*.

I blink, trying to track them, but my brain *won't* process it. One version of her is vaulting over a ledge, another is flanking Brit, while another is standing right next to me, eyes locked onto mine.

"Hi," I say to her. Or it. Or . . . both.

"Hi," she says back with a smile. And then . . . I synchronize with *all* of them.

Brit thrusts her hands forward, and the very terrain itself moves as if *obeying* her. The gauntlet tries to shift against us, but it's *too late*. She's in control now.

Perg moves next, throwing himself forward at full speed, his shell slamming into the platforms, snapping the moving pieces into place, forcing a path through the chaos.

And Seph . . . Seph and her copies become *one force*, multiplying their reach, their movements precise and inevitable. Where one falters, another takes over. Where one stumbles, another lifts them forward.

And me? I hold *all of it*. Every surge of power, every perfect connection between them. And, together, we *demolish* the course.

Pendulums snap from their chains. Boulders shatter midroll. The gravity shifts *once*, as if in protest, then *locks back into place because we decided it would.*

The gauntlet isn't a test anymore. It's *our* arena. And we just friggin' *won.*

Then . . . silence. The world stops shifting. The obstacles fade. The wind dies.

And standing there, right where I *know* he wasn't a second ago, is Jameson. Still glowing. Still not *really* Jameson.

I pull myself up over the ledge as the multiple Persephones once more become one and she goes to her father's side. Al's eyes are wide, hair windswept and unkempt, looking all kinds of wild man of the wilderness. She holds him up and smiles at me. Perg shrinks back down to a more manageable physique, and Brit comes wandering over, dusting her hands off on her cloak and saying, "Too easy."

I tilt my head at her to imply, *"Let's not get all hubristic now, shall we?"* and she kind of sticks her tongue out and rolls her eyes.

Jameson stares at us. Finally, I hazard the question . . . "Is that it? Did we pass?"

Several long beats pass before he opens his mouth and, for the first time, his Keeper-infested voice sounds . . . uncertain. **"This . . ."** He hesitates. **"This has never happened before."**

CHAPTER ELEVEN

"What do you mean it's never happened before? What's never happened before?"

I'm anxious because Jameson does not say that we passed. Instead, the Keepers inside him seem to be deliberating in eerie silence, their unseen presence pressing heavy against the air, as if waiting for something we haven't yet done.

Finally, he speaks.

"The Trial of Endurance is not merely about survival. It is about bearing weight. About suffering. You did not break."

"So what? We were *too* competent?" Brit asks.

Jameson's mouth twitches, his head tilting slightly. Again, deeply unsettling.

"No."

"'No' we weren't too competent? Or 'no' something else? You need to be specific, *ese*."

"The next trial must now be adjusted," Jameson's Keeper voice rumbles.

"Oh," Almeister murmurs.

"Oh?" I repeat. "Oh, what? Like, 'oh, good'? Or 'oh, no'?"

"Oh," he says, redundantly and unhelpfully.

"The Trial of Sacrifice has been adjusted," Jameson speaks. **"Your endurance exceeded expectation, rendering the original parameters insufficient."**

"Oh," Almeister says again.

"Okay, Al, I really need—"

Before I can finish asking for what I really need, the landscape blinks out of existence entirely. One second, we're standing in the aftermath of our victory, sweat soaked and battle worn. The next, a void. But, unlike the previous circumstance, it doesn't warp, doesn't crumble, doesn't suddenly become a giant gauntlet of things that want to kill us. It just . . . sits there. Heavy. Expectant.

Which, frankly, is kind of worse?

I hate when an empty void is expecting something from me.

In the center of the nothingness, a table appears.

Simple, unassuming, and ominous in a way only furniture can be when it's conjured by ancient forces set to test your soul. On the table are three identical boxes; not cool, mystical glowing boxes or anything, just plain, unadorned red boxes that look like they might be made out of stiff cardboard or really thin plastic.

Perg squints at them, rubbing against his own shell like he's trying to ward off a headache. "You know this is some trickster shit, *hombre*. Ain't no real test that starts with picking a *box*. This is like that carnival dude who says he'll guess your weight but then just insults your mom instead."

I continue to be impressed with the highly specific way Perg references things in life that he's never had firsthand experience of. It shows a real attention to things that he's witnessed. I applaud his dialed-in observational skills.

Jameson—still possessed, still glowing, still standing there like an extremely judgmental Christmas decoration—intones, **"The Trial of Sacrifice begins now."**

Brit gestures, hesitantly, to the boxes. "What, precisely, are we to be sacrificing?"

Jameson moves to the first box.

"One contains an object you hold dear. Something you have sworn to protect."

Then the middle.

"One contains a piece of yourself. Something you cannot regain."

And the third.

"One contains a future you will never see."

The silence that follows is as thick as partisan news commentary.

Perg glares. "So, just to be clear, we have to sacrifice one of these things?"

"Yes."

"Blind," Brit adds.

"Yes."

"And, this is a literal sacrifice?" Persephone inquires. "Once we have sacrificed it, it will be gone forever?"

"Correct. And . . ."

"And?"

"And one must choose for all."

A long beat before I say, "Come again?"

"You bested the Trial of Endurance as one, so you must now choose as one what shall be sacrificed. First, select your delegate."

Looks all around before Brit says, "Yeah, no, that's horseshit."

"Incorrect," Jameson replies, the Keeper voice as neutral as ever. **"They are boxes."**

"No," Brit cuts back. "I wasn't saying—I . . . Argh!" She balls her fists.

"Don't hit him," I caution. "It's not Jameson's fault."

"I don't want to hit *him*; I wanna knock the Keeper out of him. Why the hell is all of this necessary to see the Warden of Protection? Isn't he supposed to be protecting *us*?"

I point at her because, "I had the same thought!"

"The Warden protects themself first. As all wise protectors must," Jameson reasons.

"Ah," Brit breathes. "The selfish, bureaucratic approach to protection. Super."

Almeister clears his throat, robe sleeves twitching nervously. "The Warden's duty is to preserve the balance. To do so, they must ensure that those who seek them are worthy."

Brit makes a face. "Worthy of what? Giving up their shit?"

"Of being able to bear the cost of what they ask," Almeister corrects, voice strained but steady, like he's having trouble focusing or remembering but is digging in.

"Screw that, homes," Perg growls. "I'm not playing 'Guess What's in the Box' with ancient spooky monkey gods who can't even make a straightforward trial. Feels like a trick. And I ain't nobody's fool, fool."

Perg's got a point. The first two trials were annoying, but this one feels like a setup. Like one of those carnival games that look easy but are rigged to make you feel like an idiot. Or one of those claw machines where the claw is so weak it couldn't lift a potato chip.

What it really feels like is that we were too good at the first two trials and so, now, we're being asked to give something away so we have to work harder as we move ahead. Which follows the premise of a lot of stuff in Riftbreaker: that one only progresses and strengthens themselves via suffering. But . . . I dunno. Just feels like we've already given up enough.

"The Trial of Sacrifice is not a trick," Jameson states. **"It is a test of willingness."**

"Willingness to what? To give up things which are important to us?" Brit asks.

"Correct."

"And what if we don't want to give up anything?" she challenges.

"Then you may turn back. Without what you seek."

I scratch my head, glaring at the boxes. "Okay, so just to recap: To see the Warden of Protection we have to basically play Russian roulette with our futures, our souls, or our favorite objects?"

"Correct. The Warden of Protection cannot protect those who cannot first protect themselves."

"What the hell kind of backward-ass logic is that?" Brit exclaims.

"If you cannot choose what to let go, you will, eventually, be destroyed by what you refuse to release."

I blink, because . . . "That's . . . That actually kind of makes sense?"

"Do not agree with him!" Brit snaps. "It only encourages them." She pinches the bridge of her nose. "So, either one of us picks a box or we all turn back empty-handed."

"Correct. Choose."

The three boxes sit there, plain and unassuming, in the middle of the empty void, as if they've always been there, just waiting.

I look at Brit. Brit looks at Perg. Perg glares at all three boxes like he's considering headbutting them, then declares, "Forget this, fool. Why can't we just open them all up, see what's inside, and then decide?"

He moves forward to, I guess, bulldog the boxes, and is . . . instantly gone. Just *poof.*

Brit yelps, Seph jerks forward, and I spin, but there's nothing there.

"Where'd he go? What happened to him?!"

Then Perg reappears violently, gasping like he just got dunked in ice water.

"Oh, shit!" he rasps. "*¡Por eso dicen que nunca confíes en un maldito mono!*"

Brit rushes to him. "What happened?! Where did you go?!"

Perg shudders. "I didn't go *anywhere*; I just stopped, like, existing. Like I was never here at all. I didn't like that. It was not cool."

Brit groans. "Okay. Okay. Fine. Who wants to do it?"

Everyone looks at me. Because duh.

I roll my shoulders, stretch my neck out, and take a slow step forward. "Yeah, okay."

The boxes sit there, unassuming but intimidating at once. Like . . . I dunno. Like a graveyard at night or something.

Shit.

What if one of these is, like, I don't know, the memory of how to breathe? Or, or the ability to taste food? I *like* tasting food. I'd go so far as to say I love it. I don't wanna give that up.

Seph steps up next to me, pressing her shoulder against mine. Her expression is thoughtful. "Perhaps, the point is that we all possess something within us that is worth relinquishing our hold on? Perhaps, if we see it as an opportunity rather than a test, the choice will be easier."

I nod and stare at the boxes, my hand hovering, fingers twitching slightly. It's stupid. They're just plain boxes, the kind that you'd find in a gift shop if the gift shop also happened to be a cosmic torture chamber for the soul.

Seph's shoulder remains pressed lightly against mine, a reminder that I'm not alone in this. But that only makes it harder. It's one thing to pick a box and deal with whatever comes out. It's another to pick for everyone and risk losing something that doesn't just hurt me.

"Carpathian," she says softly. "We're with you."

I swallow, jaw clenched so tight it hurts. I can feel Perg's eyes on me, the tension radiating off him in waves. Brit shifts impatiently, arms crossed, eyes narrowed at the boxes like she can intimidate them into explaining themselves. Almeister stands a little behind, the sleeves of his robe still twitching, the only sign that he's not as calm as he's appearing to be.

The void around us presses close with the oppressive stillness of something watching, waiting to see what we do.

I take a breath and try to steady my hands. This isn't the gauntlet; it's not swinging blades and collapsing platforms and monsters who want to eat us alive. It's quiet. Simple. But somehow, it feels heavier. Dare I say . . . worse.

I wipe my palm against my mesh, which does nothing but make the sweat on my hand feel kind of tacky. I pull back. Close my eyes.

A future I'll never see. A piece of me I can't regain. An object I hold dear.

I open my eyes back up, staring at them again. The middle one, especially, seems to be watching. Which doesn't make sense because it's a box, but I swear it's watching.

Seph's hand now slips into mine, her grip warm and firm. I glance at her, surprised, and she offers a faint smile, eyes soft. "Whichever one you choose," she says quietly, "we'll all endure it together."

Her palm in mine is warm. Too warm. Like it's drawing all the heat left in the void. My Heart beats in my grip—*thump-thump*—and, for a second, I forget about the boxes, about the trial, everything. It feels like a promise, something I should pull away from but can't. I swallow hard, squeeze her hand back, and hope she doesn't notice how my hand is shaking.

The squeeze helps. Not much, but enough to let me breathe. Enough to get my fingers to stop shaking like leaves in a storm.

I curl the fingers of my free hand into a fist, release, reach out again.

And freeze.

Because what if it's the wrong one? What if I choose a future I'll never see, and it's something we need to survive? What if it's a piece of me I can't get back and it's something vital? What if it's something Seph or Brit or Perg needs more than I do, and I just—

"Jesus, Bruce! Either pick one or get the hell out of the way and let someone else do it."

"Hey, hey, Bruce. Don't be a dick."

"Sorry. Just . . . the trials are making me cranky. But seriously, pull your mesh up."

I grit my teeth, swallow hard. This is what the test is about. It's not about the boxes. It's not what's inside. It's whether we can choose to lose something to move forward. It's about cutting away, about what we're willing to set down.

I breathe in, slow and deep, then exhale through my nose.

This is just like every other impossible choice I've had to make. Just like all the times I had to move forward without knowing if I'd even survive, just like every time I had to decide who to trust, what to sacrifice, what to leave behind to get to where we need to be.

I flex my fingers one last time and reach for the middle box. The one that contains pieces of self that cannot be regained.

My Heart is slamming against my ribs, each beat like a sledgehammer, but I press my palm against the lid. The cardboard is smooth, cool, and for a second, I hesitate.

But Seph's hand tightens on mine, so I grit my teeth, curl my fingers around the lid, and open the box to find . . .

Nothing.

Literally. Nothing.

No great revelation. No flash of insight. No mystical severing of something intimate and unyieldingly precious. Just . . . empty space.

I blink. "Uh . . ."

Jameson's expression doesn't change. **"The trial is complete."**

Brit steps up, looks around me. "Wait. That's it?"

"Yes."

"Are you telling me this was a test of whether we'd be willing to give something up but we didn't actually lose anything?!"

"Yes."

Perg curses. "*¡Ay, dios mío!* I told you it was a trick, bro!"

I glance at the empty box.

I don't know what I was expecting. Something to hit. Something to change. I know it was all a very stupid ruse, but still, it feels like maybe *something* should have changed, right? Or am I just disappointed that I don't have a magic Delete function for an aspect of myself that might be gnarly or bad in some way? I dunno. I just feel . . . the same.

Which is, perhaps, the point.

And then, the world shifts yet once more, and the void evaporates. The table is gone. The boxes are gone.

Brit spins on Jameson. "I just have to say . . . that was the stupidest, most stressful, least satisfying trial of all time."

"Then why are you so upset?"

She starts to answer, but then cuts herself off. Presumably, because there is no answer. Because the sacrifice was in the doing, not in the result of the doing. She sacrificed her need to control the outcome, I sacrificed my fear of disappointment, Perg sacrificed his apparent propensity for violence and, to a greater or lesser degree, his ego, and Persephone sacrificed . . . Well, nothing really today, but she's already sacrificed a lot.

(I'm not sure what Almeister sacrificed, if anything, but he once said that he's held audience with Richemerion many times, so I'm not sure it's on him to have to deal with it again today.)

Jameson assumes his authoritative stance before us once more, his glowing eyes pulsing all spookily. As opposed to the normal bloodshot pulsation they normally have.

"The Trial of Trust will now begin."

And the world shifts again.

CHAPTER TWELVE

This is the last one, right?" Brit asks as the void gives way to a soft, sudden dusk all around.

"I think so. Al, this is the last one? Before we have to get judged on how we did by the . . ."

"The Echoes of the Convocation."

"Right. By them. Then we get to take that final trek up Mount Burden to see Richemerion?"

"Yes," Almeister mumbles.

"Okay, wonderful. Then—"

"Unless . . ."

Are you flippin' kidding me right now?!

"Unless?! Unless what?!"

"What season is it?"

Season? What season *is it? How the hell should I know what—?*

"It is the season of the Rising Sands, Father."

"Yeah. What she said. Season of the Rising Sands."

I look to Brit, who puts up her hand in a way that manages to convey, *"Yes, it's a thing; you wrote about it at some point. I'll remind you later, don't worry about it,"* all at once.

"Ah," Almeister reflects. "Then the Warden should be there. They normally take two weeks off during the season of Boundless Wonder, but that's not for another few Lunar Cycles."

The dusk stretches around us, vast and unbroken, the air cool with a bitter edge. There's no path forward, no visible door or gate, just the smooth, flat stone extending to the edge of a chasm that swallows the horizon.

"So, what is the Trial of Trust?" I ask Almeister, but it is Keeper Jameson who answers.

"The Trial of Trust is the last of the four trials."

"Right, yeah, no, I know that. But what *is* it?"

"It is the final trial before you will be judged by we, the Keepers, and the Echoes of those who have—"

"I feel like maybe I'm not asking the right question. *What* is the Trial of Trust? Like, what constitutes the trial? What is it composed of?"

"What do we have to do, fool?"

"Yeah, what Perg said."

Jameson's body (I have to remind myself that it is not Jameson, merely his shell) takes a deep, hollow breath and says, **"In order to move forward toward judgment, you must prove that your faith in one another exceeds your faith in yourself."**

I glance at the others. Because . . . "Didn't we just do that?" I ask, carefully. "Like, isn't that what this has *all* been about? Haven't we been doing that this whole time? You said that we accomplished the Trial of Endurance in a way that no one has ever done so before."

Jameson's head tilts a fraction, the glow in his eyes flaring faintly.

"That is true. But this one is actually called 'the Trial of Trust,' and it's been named that for a long time, so . . . we're not going to go changing it now just for you."

I can feel my jaw tightening. Seph looks at me, brow furrowed, but I manage to pull my shit together long enough to give her a nod of reassurance.

"To protect is to trust," Jameson intones. **"To trust is to release control. In this trial, you will confront the limits of what you see, what you know, and what you believe. To move forward, you must choose to step beyond the boundaries of your own perception."**

Brit leans into me and whispers, "If he says one more thing that sounds like a slogan for a life coach, I'm gonna fuckin' lose it."

The dusk hangs heavy and unbroken, the air cool and metallic. No path forward, just a narrow span of stone stretching to the edge of a chasm so wide that the other side is swallowed in shadows. Jameson stands at the edge of a plateau, eyes glowing, shoulders squared with that unnatural stillness that's becoming more and more unsettling the longer it drags on.

"One of you must lead," he intones. **"The others will follow."**

"Lead where, exactly?" I ask, careful to keep my own tone even.

"To where you must go."

"I *swear* to fuck," Brit whispers.

I press my palm down in the *keep it together* move.

"There is no single path," Jameson goes on. **"Each step taken creates the next. Where you walk, the path will form. But only one of you may see it clearly. The rest must follow."**

"How do we know which one of us will see it clearly?"

"That is the essence of the trial. Pick the one you trust the most."

I narrow my eyes at him because suddenly, I'm wondering . . .

"How often do you have a group like ours seek audience with the Warden? As opposed to just one pilgrim or whatever at a time?"

He takes a long beat in which I get the feeling that all the Keepers gathered inside his macaque brain are having a debate about how much to reveal. Then . . .

"Not very. You're the first in a long while."

"So . . . are you just kind of making up rules as you go along?"

Another long beat.

"We prefer to call it being in a flow state."

. . .

That one isn't so much a dolly zoom as it is just kind of a "Yeah, I probably deserve it" kind of moment. More of a sad trombone.

"Okay," I sigh, turning to the quartet with me. "I guess I'll—"

"I think you should let Father lead," Seph interrupts.

"What?"

"What?"

"What?"

"What?"

I'm not sure which one of us says "What" first, but Almeister is definitely the one to say it last. He blinks rapidly, eyes flitting from Seph to the chasm and back, bewildered. "Me?" he manages, voice small and uneven. "I—I don't think that's . . . No, no, I don't think I should . . ."

His hands fumble at his sleeves, fingers curling and uncurling like he's searching for something to hold on to. His eyes dart to the shadows, wide and uncertain, like a man who's wandered into a room and forgotten why he came.

"You should," Seph says softly, her voice warm but firm. "You are the only one who has journeyed the path before."

He breathes out, shaky and thin, a tremor running through his shoulders. "But I—I don't . . . I don't remember . . ." His brow furrows, fingers twitching at the fabric of his gown as he glances back at the dark horizon, eyes searching, unfocused. "It's all . . . so foggy."

His voice wavers, not with fear, but with something closer to embarrassment. Like he's aware he's supposed to know the way forward but can't quite seem to recall the path.

"You don't have to remember everything," Persephone assures him, squeezing his hand. "Just take it one step at a time. We'll be right here."

He stares at her, eyes glassy and uncertain, mouth opening and closing without sound. "I—I don't think . . ." His gaze flits to me, then to Perg, then to the chasm, and back to Seph, movements jerky, disoriented. "Maybe . . . Maybe one of you should—"

Seph glances at me like she's waiting for me to contradict her. It's a quiet, unspoken question; the kind that doesn't need words to be understood. Her hand tightens slightly on Almeister's arm, but her gaze stays steady on me, trust clear and raw in the way her brow softens, the faint lift of her chin.

The weight of it catches me off guard. For a moment, I can't breathe, can't think past the realization that she's looking to me to make this decision, to give the final word.

I see the look in her eyes. I know it. Not because I know *her* so well but because it's a look that I'm familiar with. It's something brittle, something that has nothing to do with the trial or the fear of failure. Or the fear of success. It's not about strategy or logic or even survival.

It's about wanting to believe in her dad, to hold on to a part of him that still feels real and solid, even if everything else is starting to slip.

I get it.

My chest tightens, a dull ache settling. Exhaling slowly, I force a nod. The motion is small, but enough. Her shoulders ease slightly, and some of the tension drains from her jaw. But her eyes stay locked on Almeister, unblinking, like if she lets go for even a second, he might disappear altogether.

"Almeister?" I call, drawing his eyes to mine. "You've gotten us this far," I say, careful to keep my tone steady. "We trust you."

"I—I don't . . ." His voice is small, almost fragile. "I don't remember the way."

He flinches. For a moment, the silence stretches. I can see the conflict there, hope and fear warring behind his eyes, the instinct to shrink away, to let someone else bear the weight.

Yet again . . . I know the feeling.

Then, the strangest thing comes tumbling out of my mouth before I can pull the words back.

"You've been leading me since the beginning," I say. "Long before any of this."

His breath catches, eyes widening, something raw and unguarded bleeding through the cracks. A soft, wavering laugh escapes him, hoarse and brittle. "Ah," he breathes, almost a gasp. "Well. That's . . . That's kind of you to say, but—"

"I wouldn't say it if it wasn't true," I cut in, firmer this time. "We trust you. I trust you."

For a moment, he just stares, lips parted, eyes bright with a shine that looks dangerously close to tears. The silence hangs, heavy and unsteady, and for a moment, I wonder if he'll turn away. If this is a weight he won't be able to carry.

But then, he breathes in, slow and shuddering, and his fingers ease their grip on his sleeves. The tremor in his hands dulls to a faint quiver, his shoulders straightening by degrees. His eyes flicker to Seph, to Perg, then back to me, and the breath that leaves him is soft and fractured but steadier than before.

"Well," he murmurs, voice raw but almost amused. "I suppose there's nothing for it, then."

He swallows, throat bobbing, eyes still flitting nervously between us. His fingers twitch at his sleeves, uncertain, but Seph's hand on his arm steadies him, if only slightly.

"We're with you," Seph says, her voice gentle but unyielding. "Every step."

He breathes out, shaky and shallow, and nods. His foot moves forward, slow and hesitant, and . . .

Nothing happens.

Which is to say nothing *bad* happens, like, whatever bad could happen if this didn't work, doesn't. Which is a triple negative, but I'm just so stoked that things are not falling apart on the heels of this corrupted old wizard that I'm not gonna police my syntax right now.

Almeister glances down, startled, like he can't quite believe he's still standing. The path stretches ahead, and his eyes go wide with wonder and fear intertwined. He looks back at us, nodding with raised eyebrows. We give him a collective thumbs-up.

"Well done, Father," Seph soothes. "Keep moving now."

He swallows hard, turning his gaze ahead, and takes another step, quicker this time, like he's trying to get it over with before his courage runs out. The way forward holds. He blinks, startled, then glances back at us yet again, eyes wide and glistening with uncertainty.

"Still here," I reassure him, forcing my own voice steady. "You're doing great."

He nods still again, jerky and unsure, and steps forward, movements awkward but growing a little less so with each step. His breathing is shallow and uneven, each exhale a shaky stutter in the cool air. The path forms ahead of him, one tentative step at a time, dark stone stretching into shadows. We follow a pace behind, every footfall deliberate, the silence pressing in close. Brit mutters curses under her breath with every footfall, Perg's moustache twitches with suspicion, and Seph's hand stays steady on Almeister's arm, guiding him forward inch by inch.

The stone trembles faintly beneath our feet, not enough to threaten but enough to remind us how uncertain the path is. Almeister flinches at each tremor, head snapping around at shadows that aren't there, eyes wide and uncertain.

"I—I can't—" he stammers, voice raw with confusion. "I don't think . . . Are you sure—"

"You're doing fine," Seph says, voice calm and steady. "We're right behind you."

Almeister manages a nod. Another step. Another. The path curves, twisting left, then right, each shift tight and precarious. The darkness presses close, cold and suffocating, swallowing the edges of vision.

Then he stops yet again.

His foot hesitates, body turning slightly, eyes darting around to the shadows. There is a low humming coming from somewhere, distant but growing more oppressive by the moment. Al's fingers twitch, his tremors worsening. His voice wavers, barely a whisper. "I . . . I don't think this is right," he stammers, thin and high. "I can't see—I can't remember—I don't . . ."

His gaze stays fixed on the shadows beyond, eyes dark and hollow. His shoulders tremble, a shudder that runs down his spine, and for a breathless moment, he sways.

"I—I think we've made a mistake," he breathes, voice tiny and fractured, so unlike the voice I was expecting to hear when we rescued him. "This isn't . . . This isn't the way—"

"It's the only way," I cut in, sharper than intended. "There's nowhere else to go."

But his eyes dart back, wild and unseeing.

"No," he chokes. "No, I—I can't—This isn't—"

Sharply, the stone trembles beneath us, a low, shivering pulse. Cracks web out from Almeister's feet, dark veins splitting through the path. I feel the shudder in my own bones, a sickening vibration that runs up my calves. He draws back a step, breath catching, eyes darting, unfocused and glassy.

"I can't," he chokes, voice strangled. "I can't do this. I don't . . . I can't remember—I don't know—"

The ground shifts, a sudden violent galumph, and the cracking intensifies, seams widening with a groan of stone. I lurch sideways, Heart slamming against my ribs, hands flying to steady myself. Brit curses, one arm flung out to keep balance, and Perg's eyes flash wide with panic.

"Just . . . move!" I snap, voice raw. "Keep going!"

But he doesn't. Almeister's foot draws back another inch, a breathless stumble, and his eyes go wide, mouth parting in a wordless gasp. "I'm sorry," he breathes out, and then . . .

He turns back.

"No!" Seph lunges, fingers outstretched, but it's too late. His foot slips, the stone beneath him tumbling into nothingness, and for one breathless, agonizing heartbeat, the world seems to stop. Almeister's eyes meet mine, wide and startled and human and here and real, and then . . . he falls into the cavernous maw that has presented itself.

Seph's scream splits the silence. Perg lunges (although to what end, I'm not sure, as dude has no arms, but the thought is nice) but before he can do . . . anything, the dark swallows Almeister whole, and the vacuum of silence closes in, deafening and absolute.

My breath hitches, chest seizing. Brit's eyes are wide, white rimmed, hand half raised as if to grab a phantom. Seph drops to her knees, a sound that might be a sob tearing from her throat, hands shaking violently.

"Father!" she wails, long and urgent, the pain-racked scream making my eyes wet.

I kneel beside her, trying to ignore the fact that this means we are all also now about to be sucked down into whatever pit of something-or-another Almeister has been dragged to as the collapse continues. I want to hold her. Comfort her. Tell her everything is going to be all right.

Y'know, lie to her.

More.

But before I can, Almeister's voice echoes up from the dark, small and bewildered and faintly sheepish.

"Oh, right! It's this way! I remember now!"

Seph's breath catches midsob, and we look down. Almeister is there, standing in what looks like the gauntlet's basement, waving up at us.

"I completely forgot. Had we gone forward further, we would have been engulfed by a wall of flame. Which is, by my recollection, very unpleasant."

I look ahead, grab a nearby bit of crumbled earth, toss it ahead, and yep, sure enough . . . *Whoosh*. Fire emerges from out of nowhere and incinerates it.

I suck at my teeth.

"Good work, Al!" I shout down.

Almeister gives a little shrug. "Thank you?"

I glance at the others, feeling the need to say something profound, and come up with, "Trust. Amirite?"

And then, without another word, I jump in after the once and (I hope) future mentor.

CHAPTER THIRTEEN

We land hard, our boots (and snail bottoms) scraping over uneven stone. My knees nearly give out from the drop, but I catch myself, hands pressed to the cold floor. Almeister's standing there, hands folded with the kind of modesty that suggests nearly leading us into a wall of fire was a minor faux pas.

Seph races over and hugs her father. "Father, are you alright?"

"Yes, yes, fine. It's . . . Some things are starting to come back to me."

There is the tiniest hint of assuredness in his voice. I don't have anything real to compare it to, but the idea of the wise old mentor that I always had in my head sounds like it is becoming present a bit. Like, the very act of endeavoring to seek Richemerion is doing something to resurrect the spirit of Almeister to its previous place of agency.

"You have passed the final trial," Jameson intones, his voice reverberating through the chamber. **"YOU WILL NOW BE JUDGED."**

At the saying of those words, the light snaps out of his eyes abruptly like a candle being snuffed. He sways, knees buckling, and then collapses hard. There's a breathless second where no one moves. Then . . .

"Jameson!" I lunge forward, tripping over myself. Brit and Seph are already there, sliding to their knees beside him, breaths coming fast.

I reach and begin feeling for a pulse immediately. It's there, but it's faint.

He needs *healing.* Do I have anything? I grit my teeth, running through my mental Mezmeric Spell book.

Control? No? CloakRender? Pass. Marrowmancy? That's healing for me, not for anyone else. Not unless I want to suck the literal life out of him and replace my own failing cartilage, which would be very metal but also incredibly counterproductive. Toxin Dart? Yeah, no. Mezmeric Microblather? The most useless ability ever in a situation like this unless Jameson needs to be psychically text spammed into the afterlife. I can't think of anything any of the rest has at the moment that would qualify as healing or mending or even gently rejuvenating.

I groan, rubbing a hand down my face. "Why the hell are none of us healers?"

Seph's jaw tightens. "We should have thought of this *before.* We should have with us a healer. A dedicated healer."

I nod. "I'll add it to my list of regrets. Right now . . ."

I stop, look at Jameson's lips.

Oh. *Oh.* There's definitely something I can try. But it ain't Mezmer.

Now's not the time to get squiggly, Bruce! Keep it together, goddammit!

"Stand back," I instruct.

"What shall you do?" Persephone asks.

"I'm going to help him," I declare, then place my lips to his macaque mouth.

"Oh!" Seph gasps. "The Saviour is going to breathe life force back into him!"

Technically, she's not wrong. I did do one summer as a junior lifeguard trainee when I was in middle school, so while the way she phrases it is sort of a grand description of what's about to go down, it's not completely untrue.

I pinch his nose and blow a breath into his open weed hole.

The faint taste of Mary Jane and ash hits my tongue.

I pull back, coughing, swiping at my mouth with the back of my hand. It only makes it worse, the taste clinging. My tongue feels numb and hot at the same time.

"Carpathian! What's wrong?"

"Nothing," I hack. "All—It—I just . . ." I take a deep, cleansing breath and go back for another round.

Breathe . . .

Pulling back, I look at the little dude.

He isn't stirring, his chest remaining still. I pinch his nose once more, lean back down, and force another breath in, trying not to think about THC spores or the fact that my head is starting to feel strangely light.

His chest rises under my hands, then suddenly, he convulses, coughing violently. I rear back just as he shoots upright, hacking hard enough to rattle his ribs. Thin wisps of smoke curl from his nose and mouth. "Lawd Jesus, mi dead an' gone or mi jus' wish mi was?"

"Jame! You're back!"

"Mi never leave, ya nah. Dem bumboclaat Keeper jus' tek mi body fi a joyride."

He drags in a rattling breath, eyes fluttering half shut, and lets out a low, exhausted groan. He retrieves his seemingly eternal Magick Stick with shaky fingers, snaps two fingers on his free hand, sparking a flame, and inhales deep, smoke curling slow and lazy.

I fall back onto my heels, wiping my mouth with my sleeve, tongue still stinging like I just inhaled a bit of bonfire at a Phish concert, pressing my fingertips to my temple, trying to will my head to clear.

It doesn't.

But it's okay. This is fine. Everything is fine.

"You good, fool?" Perg asks.

"Yeah," I tell him. "Yeah, I'm—"

"I meant that fool, fool. He's the one who was possessed by freaky Keepers. What was it like, homes?"

"Like sharin' mi skull wit' a buncha spirits at a town hall meetin'. All talk, no blessin'. It work, though? We gon' bout to meet de Warden now?"

"Yeah," I tell him. "Yeah, I think so."

"Al?"

"Yes . . . Carpathian?"

He doesn't say the name questioningly like he's addressing my asking after him. He says it like he's still not completely convinced that's who I am.

He would not be alone in that misgiving.

"What happens now?"

Instead of getting an answer from the wizard, it comes from the world itself. The floor rumbles beneath us, low and rolling, and walls unfold, pillars sliding out, the ground reforming into what can only be described as a brutalist courtroom.

Voices ripple out from the newly formed chamber of evaluation, deep and resonant, like sound carried through water. Words blend and overlap, coming from everywhere and nowhere at once in a resonant chorus of sound.

"THE ECHOES OF THE CONVOCATION ARE WE," the voices declare, layered and vast. "THE RESIDUAL SPIRITS OF THE ANCIENTS WHO FIRST LAID CLAIM TO THIS SOVEREIGN PLACE."

The words roll through the chamber, weighted and deliberate.

"YOU HAVE PASSED THE FOUR TRIALS," the voices continue. "YOU SHALL NOW BE JUDGED."

Brit leans in and whispers to me, "Do you think it's like a spiritual judgment? Or just a performance one? Or—"

"IT IS A DETERMINATION OF YOUR WORTHINESS TO MEET THE WARDEN OF PROTECTION BASED ON A COLLECTION OF FACTORS." A pause. Then, "BUT, GIVEN THE FACT THAT THERE IS A GROUP OF YOU AND IT IS DIFFICULT TO PARSE WHO DID WHAT, EXACTLY, WE WILL JUST BE JUDGING YOU ON IF YOU PASS OR FAIL."

"As opposed to what?" I feel the need to ask.

"OUR TYPICAL GRADING SYSTEM OF TILDE TO OCTOTHORPE."

"You said tilde to octothorpe?"

"YES. WITH SUBGRADES IN CATEGORIES INCLUDING VALOR, PLUCKINESS, AND OVERALL PIZZAZZ."

There's a long pause before they continue with . . .

"PASS." It comes out like rolling thunder, and we all let out a sigh of relief.

"WE COMMEND YOU FOR YOUR RESOLVE IN THE TRIALS. YOU MAY NOW—WAIT!" the Echoes boom, voices dropping with what sounds a lot like disbelief. "IS THAT . . . IS THAT CARPATHIAN?"

The silence that follows is so absolute it might as well be carved in marble.

"Uh, yeah?"

"CARPATHIAN EINZGEAR?"

"Um . . . yeah, that's me."

I can feel the Echoes recoil somehow, throwing up their spectral hands in what can only be described as frustration.

"CARPATHIAN, WHAT ARE YOU DOING?!"

"I don't—"

"WHY DIDN'T YOU JUST TELL US *YOU* WERE HERE?"

"I'm sorry?"

"YOU OBVIOUSLY GET FREE PASSAGE."

"I get free—"

"RICHEMERION GAVE YOU THE HEART SO YOU WOULDN'T HAVE TO JUMP THROUGH ALL THESE HOOPS, YOU SILLY GOOSE!"

". . . Seriously?"

"THERE'S A SAVIOUR BACK ENTRANCE AND EVERYTHING."

I close my eyes, jaw tight. Brittany erupts.

"Are you fucking kidding me?!"

"NO," the Echoes intone, sounding confused, like they've never heard a rhetorical question before. "WHY DIDN'T ANYONE TELL YOU THIS?"

I clear my throat and say, as patiently as possible, "Almeister has been . . . corrupted."

"I'm getting better, I feel like." He waves his hand.

"Yeah, but he probably didn't remember when we started. See, that's the whole reason we're here now. It's to see if Richemerion can—"

"AH! AH! GOT IT! OKAY, SAY NO MORE! WELL, TERRIFIC. SO, GO ON THEN."

I blow out a breath, opting to choose gratitude over frustration. "Okay. Thanks. I—"

"GO ON, THEN, TO THE FINAL STEP: THE MEASURE OF BURDEN."

I snap my gaze up, *now* choosing to embrace the frustration. "WHAT?! You're saying I could have skipped the trials, but I still have to endure the Measure of Burden?"

"CORRECT."

"Why?!"

There's a long pause.

"BECAUSE."

"That's not an answer."

"UM . . . TRADITION."

I get the distinct impression that they're just making things up as they go along because no one wants to take accountability for screwing up the fact that they didn't recognize the World Saviour in their midst.

"Okay," I acquiesce. "So what exactly is the Measure of Burden? Another trial? A final boss fight? What?"

"IT IS NOTHING SO PEDESTRIAN."

The air waffles around us, and a pair of grand metal doors emerge. Massive, dark, unyielding. They rise higher than I can see, disappearing into . . . Well, I dunno. As noted, I can't see.

"YOU MUST TAKE THE MEASURE OF YOURSELF," the Echoes intone. "WITHOUT TURNING AWAY."

"What does that mean? Take the measure of myself?"

"YOU KNOW THE EXPRESSION, 'TAKE THE MEASURE OF A MAN'?"

"Sure."

"LIKE THAT. BUT FOR YOURSELF."

The doors stand before us, black and immense. No one moves. No one seems sure of what to do next.

Brit leans in, voice low. "So . . . are we supposed to just, like, meditate or . . . ?"

"YES!" the Echoes boom.

"Jesus!" she jumps.

"SORRY. WE THOUGHT YOU COULDN'T HEAR US. YES," they say again, quieter. "TAKE A PRIVATE MOMENT. TAKE STOCK. WEAR THE CAPE OF YOUR BURDEN, AND THE DOORS WILL OPEN."

God.

Meridia is just one heavy-handed metaphor after another, I swear.

CHAPTER FOURTEEN

There's a long pause. We look at each other; I assume because no one wants to be the first to close their eyes.

I put my hands up like a patient schoolteacher.

"Okay, everyone, let's just do what the disembodied voices say and take a moment to just reflect on all of our life choices, and then go forward to talk to the mystical Warden of Protection, who will do whatever they do to make sure that Almeister here"—he waves—"can reenter the Heart Guard uncorrupted by the dark, malignant forces that have conspired to keep him from serving in his role as ambassador for the forces of good. Everybody okay with that?"

A general shrug of *yeah, sure, I guess.*

I smile, indicate with a gesture that I'll go first, and then close my eyes and . . . reflect.

I try to focus, I really do, but my brain is apparently a bit of a dick. Instead of serene reflection, I get a rapid-fire highlight reel of every bad decision I've ever made. No fade-ins or gentle transitions, just smash cuts of mistakes, regrets, and the occasional slow-motion humiliation for artistic flair that might've been funny if they weren't about me.

There's me, at thirteen, being pantsed by Brandon Ahrenholz in front of my seventh-grade class.

It wasn't the pantsing that bothered me, really; I've always had nice calves and never been afraid to show them. It's more that Brandon and I were bros. Or at least, I *thought* we were bros. That may have been the moment when I became the fundamentally skeptical version of myself that I have remained ever since. I had already been through kind of a lot by the age of eleven, but that feels like it was another tipping point.

A visual shift, and I am standing in front of a counter waiting to order a turkey sub. A cute woman with sandy-blonde hair cut into a trendy bob is giving me a placating smile.

This is me getting rejected by that Carlissa girl who used to frequent the same sandwich shop that I did. It was the one down the street from the bus depot. It was always awkward seeing her after that, which is why I started bringing my own lunch.

A few more embarrassments and follies bubble in. I gotta say, this is a touch more self-flagellating than I typically experience recollections, and I have to wonder . . . why now?

Oh. I have an instant realization. *This isn't my brain deciding it hates me. This is the direct influence of whatever delinquent woo-woo forces control this apparent "Measure of Burden."*

I guess it's comforting to know that at least it's an external process and not me suddenly deciding to pull the rip cord on pity and negative self-esteem. Which feels like progress.

Now that I see what's going on, I think it's a lot like the images that ran through my mind in my office back in St. Louis the night I told Brittany that I had killed off Carpathian. Though, that one had been au naturel. However, as I remember it, the image itself blossoms in my mind: Her, standing in front of me, holding the manuscript in her hands, and that look in her eyes . . . The one where she already knows I've let her down with my apparent betrayal.

I tap my teeth together, suck in a breath, and try to breathe slow, even inhales and exhales, but it feels like my lungs are full of ice water. The air is cold and thin, and my pulse thuds too hard at the back of my skull, having migrated from its usual mechanized thumping in my chest to other parts of my body.

Thump-thump. Thump-thump.

I count breaths—*one, two, three*—trying to drown out the rising tide of anxiety clawing at my . . . everywhere.

And, despite my efforts at maintaining a measured engagement with myself, there she is . . .

Mollie.

Eyes wet and confused, voice tight and raw with hurt.

I wince, shoulders curling in, like I can somehow physically dodge it. Gritting my teeth, I try to focus on literally anything else. The doors. The floor. The distant sound of Perg breathing through his weird snail nostrils. But the second I try to shift gears, the weight slams into me.

Not a metaphorical weight. A real, actual weight, like someone dropped a boulder on my shoulders while whispering, *"You thought you could run, bitch?"* A crushing, sinking pressure spreads across my back, down my spine, settling into my ribs like said massive rock is trying to press me into the ground. My breath catches, and my legs bend slightly under the force of it.

My knees buckle. I grunt, muscles tensing to keep me upright. *Oooooooooh. So that's how this works. Measure of BURDEN. Got it.*

I adjust myself. I straighten my spine. I shake it off.

It's fine. I can handle this.

"Sure you can, Bruce!"

"Thanks for the encouragement, Bruce."

"I'm here for you, Bruce."

Somewhere nearby, Brit makes a soft, strained exhale. It's not a gasp, not a grunt, just a quiet sound of discomfort. I can't see her, and I sure as hell don't dare open my eyes, but I know her well enough to picture her. Yet, that sound makes me very suspicious she's resisting harder than she'll ever admit.

Perg curses. Almeister groans. Jameson hisses. Seph is silent. Which is . . . not comforting.

The pressure increases.

Fine.

If this is how it works, I'll push back. I've carried worse; this is child's play. Not even—infant's play. Hell, maybe embryo's play. I've survived worse. It doesn't matter if this is some silly ancient test; it's just another thing trying to make me feel small, trying to break me down.

I refuse to let it.

A low groan of metal makes my eyes snap open. For a second, I think we've done it. The doors shift an inch, just a fraction—

WHAM!

—before slamming shut with enough force to rattle my molars.

"YOU MUST NOT INTERRUPT THE MEASURING," the Echoes chide, voices resonant and deeply scolding. "NO PEEKING!"

I glance at Persephone, the avatar for Mollie now come to life. She has her head cocked, eyes closed, but her face is pointed at me in a way that suggests she can see inside my thoughts. I know that's *probably* not the case? But then again, she is a . . . Well, I honestly don't know what her proper designation is. Sorcerer? Like Teleri? There are some elements there, but I know she isn't explicitly a wizard, considering she doesn't use any tools and she was admonished about using Rituals, but . . .

It doesn't matter. She's *strong*, a wizard's daughter. And, as of yet, I don't have a clear portrait of her capacity. Before we brought down the Tower, I should have thought to inventory her as the newest member of my Heart Guard, but in my defense, there was kind of a lot going on. Sue me for not thinking of it.

"Got it, got it," I mutter in response to the Echoes. "No peeky. Noted."

Brit cracks one eye open, glances at me with a *get it together* look of encouragement (or like she's considering homicide) and closes it again with a sigh that somehow sounds like a low-key threat. I blow out a breath, press my fingertips to my temple, and shut my eyes again, forcing my thoughts still.

It lasts about three seconds.

The memories keep coming. People I've let down, words I can't take back, moments I should've handled better. No grand betrayals, just a thousand small failures, each one heavy in a different way. It's not guilt that sticks but the simple, brutal acceptance that it was my choice, every time.

The doors groan again, inch open a fraction. *This is stupid,* I think, or maybe I mutter it out loud; it's hard to tell. My eyes crack open instinctively, seeing light spill through from the emerging passageway before . . .

The doors slam shut once more.

Shit.

"Bruce?"

"Yeah, Bruce?"

"What's going on?"

"I dunno. Do you still believe in me?"

". . ."

"Bruce?"

"Yeah, I'm still here, Bruce."

"You still believe in me, right?"

". . . Sure do, tiger!"

I hate it when I lie to myself. Shit.

The problem isn't the guilt. I've dealt with guilt before; it's kind of my thing. The problem is stopping long enough to actually look at it, to hold the worst parts up to the light and not flinch away.

My hands start to tremble, fingertips going cold and numb. The truth stirs, unfiltered and raw, and it takes a breathless moment to choke it down. The weight presses harder, deep and insistent, approaching a level I'd be tempted to label unbearable, until it's not about the trials or the doors or the damn Warden but the simple admission I've been trying to sidestep since this whole nightmare started.

It's my fault.

"What is, Bruce?"

I don't answer Other Bruce right away. I'm still considering what I've just said because I didn't even realize *that* fully, really, and wholly until I said it in my own brain. I mean, yeah, I could try to pass off some of the blame. I could say I didn't know what would happen. I could say I was tricked, or that some force beyond me led things here.

But at the end of the day . . . ?

"All of it." I finally relent. *"Whether or not I was used by this world or manipulated or anything, it's all my fault. I'm the reason we're here. I'm the reason people are dead. I'm the reason . . . It's me."*

Something like understanding unlocks within me, and there's a click in my chest. The Heart? Maybe. I'm not sure. Whatever it is, it's like a knot of tension unravels and the weight inside me shifts, sudden and sharp, and for a terrifying moment, I think it might crush me. But then it steadies, cold but bearable, and the silence settles lighter than before. But it doesn't go away.

It rests.

Not easier. Just acknowledged.

"That's an interesting reaction, Bruce."

". . . Is it?"

There's no response.

And then I hear the doors groaning, slower and more deliberately this time, a low creak that rumbles through the Meridian floor. I don't open my eyes, don't dare even twitch, until the shuddering stops and I can feel light spilling cold and bright across my eyelids.

"Good job, Bruce. I never doubted you!"

"Thanks, Bruce. Feels like a breakthrough, huh?"

"Don't get all overconfident, Bruce. I think all you really did was get a couple of big-ass metal doors to open up, but it's a start. It's enough for now."

When I finally open my eyes to look, the doors are, in fact, open, wide and waiting. Light spills out from them, warm and oddly inviting.

Brit is standing perfectly still, arms crossed, her expression unreadable. She doesn't speak, doesn't meet my gaze right away. Seph looks . . . steady. Not untouched, but like she's already made peace with whatever she saw. Almeister looks older, as if whatever he had to reckon with took more out of him than he was expecting. Perg is in his shell. I don't know if he's doing okay. I'm not going to ask.

No one says anything. Because who would want to admit to whatever mortifying shame they'd just experienced? It was deeply personal. However, someone needs to say *something*.

I clear my throat. "Well. That sucked."

Brit lets out a long, slow breath, pressing her fingers to her temple. "Yeah."

"Not, like, Cavern of Sorrows bad, but—"

"Carpathian?" Brit asks. "Shut up, please."

I nod and turn to the air, looking up a little because I have decided that, for some reason, that's where the Echoes reside. I'm still annoyed despite everything. "Alright. We did your big self-reflection thing. The doors are open. We good now?"

"YOU MAY NOW PROCEED TO HOLD AUDIENCE WITH RICHEMERION, THE WARDEN OF PROTECTION," the Echoes declare.

Congratulations!
Quest: "Your Mentor, [Almeister T. Wizard] has been CORRUPTED(!) by Disciples of the Ninth Guardian! A possible remedy may be found by requesting audience with [Richemerion, the Warden of Protection]. To hold audience, you must first pass a series of trials! Fun!"
[COMPLETE]

No one moves for a long second, like we're collectively waiting for something else to go wrong. But, finally, I take the lead and step forward, feeling the beat of my Heart get stronger, like it knows it's going home. I feel . . . anxious? Yeah, but also excited.

You are right to feel that way, Saviour! And heads up . . . The Warden is, well, the Warden Particular. Just thought you should know.

"Particular"? The hell does that mean?

. . . You'll see.
{COURTESY MESSAGE #31}

Great. I now no longer feel the "excited" part.

CHAPTER FIFTEEN

The path we're walking curves gently downward, the incline so gradual and smooth that it feels intentional, like a welcome invitation rather than just a descent to a place. The walls on either side are carved from dark stone, polished to a subtle gleam, inlaid with faint patterns that catch the light when I turn my head just right. Not runes or symbols or anything as Lara Croft-y as all that, just lines and arcs and spirals that flow naturally, like vines or river currents.

Lanterns hang at intervals, suspended from iron hooks shaped like lotus petals, their light warm and golden. (Which, admittedly, is kind of Lara Croft-y.) The air is cooler here, crisp and clean, carrying the scent of sandalwood and something lighter, like jasmine or green tea. Our footsteps are muffled by woven mats that stretch beneath us, patterns of jade winding through the fabric with an artistry that feels ancient and also freshly made.

There's a quiet here. Not the heavy, breath-holding silence of a tomb but the calm stillness of a garden at dawn, when the world is waking slowly. The kind of quiet that makes it hard to remember why you would ever have been nervous to come here in the first place.

The corridor widens gradually, the ceiling arching higher into shadow. Pillars rise at even intervals, slender and smooth, each one wrapped in silk banners—deep blue and dark yellow—embroidered with scenes that seem to shift with the lantern light.

I catch glimpses as we pass; warriors in lacquered armor, blades at rest; a phoenix rising with wings outstretched; a robed figure standing at the edge of a tranquil lake, head bowed in meditation.

Perg whistles low as he scooches along, eyes drifting from one banner to the next. "Yo, this place is swank," he mutters. "Like one of them fancy spa joints rich folks go to when they're exhausted from, like, yacht shopping or whatever."

"It is beautiful," Seph murmurs, fingers brushing one of the banners with something like reverence. "I have never seen anything quite like it."

Almeister moves beside her with a kind of calm I haven't seen in him since we rescued him. No twitch of fingers. No uncertainty. His head is high, shoulders relaxed, eyes drifting over the banners and the statues with an air that's almost nostalgic.

"Father?" Seph whispers.

"It is as it has ever been," he says, voice low, reverent.

Given what all has changed for him, I can appreciate how he might feel a sense of relief that this place, this place that is supposed to be the genesis of protection, appears to remain protected itself.

"It's . . ." I hesitate, glancing around, a warmth spreading through my chest that I can't explain. ". . . Perfect."

The word slips out unguarded, quieter than I meant, and for a second, I feel almost embarrassed. But it's true. There's something about this place that feels like stepping into a memory I can't quite place, familiar and distant at once.

We move slowly, eyes darting from one shadow to the next, but the longer we walk, the less I feel the urge to glance over my shoulder. It's like the walls themselves are breathing calmness into me, steady and serene, radiating a warmth that seeps into my bones.

The path takes another curve, opening out into a broader passage lined with statues: figures in long robes, heads bowed, hands clasped before them. The original Wardens, maybe. The faces are smooth and calm, eyes closed, mouths relaxed, radiating a kind of tranquility that makes my own shoulders ease down a notch without me realizing.

Perg snorts. "Fool, this place feels like one of those Thai bathhouses I've heard about," he mutters. "Bet they got, like, towels folded into little animal shapes somewhere."

He's right. The air is warm, fragrant; sandalwood and cedar, touched with something sweeter, like lotus or magnolia.

A faint hint of lilac.

The corridor widens again, spilling out into a vast hall with a polished floor that gleams like dark water. No tiles or seams, just one smooth expanse of stone stretching out beneath our feet.

More lanterns hang above, their light warm and steady. There are no doors here, no visible exits, just shadowed alcoves set into the walls, their depths softened by the lantern glow.

Brit shifts beside me, eyes narrowed but shoulders a little looser than before. "Okay," she mutters. "This is . . . kind of nice."

"Yeah," I breathe. "I think it's supposed to be."

Seph takes a slow step forward, eyes wide and bright. "This place . . . it feels like . . ." She hesitates, searching for the word. "Like sanctuary."

The word sits on the air as the light shifts, catching on the silk banners that sway gently in a breeze I can't feel, and I now hear . . . music. I can't make out what it is, but it sounds vaguely familiar. Low and steady, a slow thrumming that comes from the walls themselves, resonating through the stone.

"Well," I murmur, and this time, the words come out quieter, almost reverent. "I guess we follow the music."

The music leads us down a narrow passageway. It's hard to describe what it's like. The music. It's sort of vaguely, I guess, Far Eastern sounding? Like, I can sort of hear what sounds like a guzheng? A Chinese zither? But there's something beneath it, a kind of pulsing rhythm that I just know I've encountered in the past, but I just can't place it. It's not really comparable to anything, not derivative, but its draw is undeniable.

We reach a small, arched doorway that wouldn't look out of place in a traditional Japanese or Chinese home. Like the kind you'd see in a Kyoto teahouse or an old courtyard residence in Beijing. The frame is dark wood, deep and rich, polished to a low sheen that reflects the lantern light in warm tones. A narrow strip of gold is inlaid along the inner edge, so fine it's almost invisible unless you're right up close.

The doors are sliding panels made from a material that looks like paper, translucent with a faint texture, like shoji screens, the kind that divide rooms in a traditional ryokan. A pattern runs across them. Cranes in flight, wings stretched wide, inked with faint strokes of black and gold. It's like something out of a woodblock print.

It's like we've walked out of *A Song of Fire and Ice* and into *Ashes of Love*.

The music gets louder.

I feel like—

"Richemerion is through here, Father?" Seph's voice is hopeful. Anxious.

Almeister nods. "Yes." He reaches out to slide the door open, then pauses with his hand hovering just above the handle. For a moment, he doesn't move, fingers twitching. His eyes are distant, glassy, like he's seeing something beyond the door. Then he blinks, breathes in slow, and whatever he's seeing falls away. "Before we enter, you should know something about the Warden."

"What?" I ask.

"The Warden is . . . particular."

That's the same thing the Heart told me. *What the hell does that mean?*

"I dunno, Bruce."

"Sorry, Bruce, I wasn't asking you."

"Good, because I don't know. You know what you should do?"

"Ask Almeister instead?"

"What I would do."

"Good call, Bruce."

"Thanks, Bruce."

"What does that mean?" I ask, upon advice from me. "*Particular*?"

"The Warden values sincerity," Almeister says. "Speak plainly, answer truthfully. The Warden will know if you don't."

"Okay."

"And do not interrupt. Even if the Warden appears conversational."

"Conversational?" Brit asks.

"Yes. The Warden has a tendency to . . . wander. In thought. Do not let it distract you."

"So, just let them talk, even if it sounds like they're not making sense?"

"Precisely." Almeister nods. "Do you think you can you do that?"

Brittany looks at me. "I can manage it. I have practice."

I make a "not right now, please" face, and she backs off.

I nod slowly, making sure I have the rules. "So, don't lie, don't interrupt, and if they start talking about the meaning of life or how to properly fold pocket squares or whatever, we should just roll with it."

"Yes," Almeister replies. "And, lastly, if they ask questions that seem strange, answer them. Even if they feel irrelevant to you."

It's now my turn to glance at Brit.

"Fine," she grits out. "Again . . . I have practice."

"Should we bow or something, fool?" Perg asks.

"That will not be necessary."

"Should we tell 'dem how handsome dey be? Put on the butter spread nice and thick?" Jameson asks.

"No," Almeister responds. "Richemerion is just particular, not a narcissist. They seek to protect the Meridian Plane, not to rule it."

Perg lets out a breath. "Fyah day, nah. Jus' checkin'."

Almeister stares at Jameson for a moment. It's nice to have the macaque back, smoking and joking.

"However . . ." the wizard says, looking at the blunt.

"Wha gwan? Ya need me put it out?"

There is a hint of worry in the question, like he's afraid he's going to be required to do something that violates his moral code.

"No," Almeister replies. "Just the opposite."

Huh. Odd thing to say. But—

"Let us enter now," Almeister says, sliding the screen door open. The moment he does, the music stops. Which is mildly irritating because I feel like I was just about to ID it.

Something, something, something . . . Something . . . Something, something . . .

Fragments of lyrics detached from melody bounce around before disappearing.

Warm light greets us along with the scent of tea leaves and jasmine. A low table waits in the center of the room set with a tea service, delicate porcelain cups painted with koi and bamboo. Steam curls from a cast-iron teapot as trays of bright orange slices dipped in dark chocolate and sugar-dusted pastries sit nearby.

Perg hesitates at the doorway, eyes darting between us and the table. "Is this for us, homes?"

"If it is offered," Almeister says, "it would be impolite to refuse."

Perg moves faster than any snail in history has ever moved and begins *housing* snacks. Can't blame him; I don't remember the last time we ate and, now that I know he's been suffering through eggshells and crap he hates for forever and a day, I'm not going to begrudge him a well-earned chow down.

Of all the surreality I've encountered here, there's a particular kind of surrealism to this moment specifically. Because I've met people in this world whom I knew about, or thought I did; characters whose arcs I'd planned out, whose endings I'd written in the margins with tidy notes. And they've all been at least close(ish) to what I imagined. If you squint. Different enough to make me second-guess everything, but still following the general lines I laid out.

And then, there are the ones I never planned for at all. The out-of-nowhere, what-the-hell-are-you-doing-here characters who didn't even exist in the drafts. Figures like Jameson, who, if I'm being honest, I probably would've cut from the final manuscript for being too implausible. But there he is, blunt in hand, chatting like it's a Sunday barbecue.

Or . . . Tavrella. Who . . .

Not now. I can't. Not now.

But . . . Richemerion is a third category altogether.

A Warden. A legend. A character whose existence I knew about, whose influence I scattered in whispers and half-remembered tales across the books, but who never got a scene, never got a face, never even got a line of dialogue. Just like the Ninth Guardian, always present in the lore but faceless and abstract. A title. A placeholder in a prophecy I felt in my gut but couldn't make sense of.

Silhouettes on the horizon, always out of focus. Names to fill out the world's lore. Plot devices with voices like clear bells and hearts like monks'. As much a mystery to myself as to my readers. More legend than person.

So, yeah, this is uniquely surreal.

I try to build an image in my head of whom we're about to meet. The tea, the wood panels, the cranes and gold inlay all point to something traditional, serene, a kind of spiritual minimalism.

In my mind, Richemerion is a figure who glides instead of walking, who never raises their voice because they never need to. I'm picturing long robes, hands hidden inside wide sleeves. Eyes that glint with ageless wisdom but don't quite meet yours. The kind of person who speaks in parables and never gives a straight answer. A Zen master straight out of Central Casting.

Incense wafting off them, maybe? *Yeah. Definitely incense.*

But I've been wrong about pretty much everything else so far, so I'm not sure why I think I'll be right about this. The MO on everything thus far has been subversion. So maybe what I should be preparing for instead is the opposite of what I anticipate.

Looking around at the soft, warm light seeping through the paper panels—spilling in puddles across the floor—and the overstuffed cushions and tea that smells like it was brewed with actual sunlight, a projected energy of coziness overwhelms

It's the kind of place you'd come to get your fortune read by a well-meaning but probably scamming old woman with too many cats and a shitload of gauzy scarves everywhere.

Which is maybe why I'm so skeptical.

It's not that I distrust cozy places. It's just that I've built enough of them in fiction to know how quickly they can turn. Like a mirror with just a crack at the edge. Just enough to keep you watching for the spiderweb to spread.

My eyes drift to a side door, half hidden by a panel painted with lotus flowers and water reeds.

The music stopped when we came in, but now, it resumes again. That same twanging zither and, now that we're in here, I can tell it's a faint thump, almost a . . . bassline? It's muffled by the walls, but it's definitely there. It doesn't fit the vibe. Too steady, too modern, too . . . familiar.

I glance at Brit, "You hear that?" She nods. "Does it sound—"

"Familiar?" I nod. "Mm-hm."

Perg pauses midsnack, antennae twitching. He looks over as well. "Is that—?"

But before he can ask, the door from which the music emanates slides open with a soft shush.

And a wall of smoke rolls out. And I mean a WALL.

Jameson's eyes go wide, like he's seeing the face of a god, and he whispers, "Mi gen'ral . . ."

I cough, waving a hand in front of my face, eyes watering. The scent hits first, strong and skunky with a faint hint of something herbal, and the sound gets clearer. It's not "temple music." It's not even close. It's—

"Yo," a voice calls through the smoke. "Y'all get shit started without me?"

The smoke thins, and Richemerion steps forward, backlit by warm light and thumping beats.

They wear a sleek black bomber jacket adorned with subtle gold embroidery along the cuffs and collar. Underneath, a crisp white tee peeks out, paired with tailored dark jeans that taper neatly into high-top sneakers. A simple gold chain rests against their chest, catching the ambient light.

Their hair is neatly braided beneath a black skull cap that fits snug, embroidered with an intricate symbol in gold thread, something abstract, like interlocking circles, but stylized.

"Richemerion," Almeister greets, inclining his head.

Richemerion takes a long drag, blows out a cloud of smoke that drifts lazily toward the ceiling, and grins. The Warden reaches their hand back, as does Almeister, and then . . .

. . . they dap each other off, then Richemerion pulls the wizard in for a hug.

"Meister, what's good, my boi? Yo, they gotchu looking beat up from the feet up."

"It has been a challenging time," Almeister replies, leaning into the hug.

"Well, it's all good now, baby. Richie Rich gonna smooth shit out nice. I gotchu. Gon' protect ya neck, ya heard?"

. . .

Richemerion. The fabled Warden of Protection. The one who gifted Carpathian, me, my Mechanical Heart . . .

. . . Is RZA.

The RZA.

From the Wu-Tang Clan.

Or, at least, a doppelgänger approximation.

Well.

Huh.

Okay.

As I suspected: Not what I expected.

Which is, of course . . .

Exactly what I should've expected.

CHAPTER SIXTEEN

Richemerion steps back from Almeister, giving him a long, slow once-over, like he's assessing the state of an old, beloved record someone left in the sun too long. The grin fades into something more contemplative. A head tilt. A slow, knowing nod.

"Damn, son," Richemerion exhales, hands sliding into the pockets of their jacket. "You the last cat I expected to come walkin' through my door, lookin' all types of busted. Ain't gon' front, Meister, this shit? This shit hurts me, yo."

Almeister offers the faintest shadow of a smile, but it barely meets his eyes. "It is good to see you as well, old friend."

Richemerion breathes in deep, rolling their shoulders. The casual ease of their stance—one hip cocked, chin slightly lifted—should be at odds with the weight of the moment, but it isn't. The presence they carry isn't just that of a Warden but of someone who's been bearing something larger than themselves for a long time.

"And this right here, this here is Carpathian Einzgear. Carpathian himself, word? The one who 'answers the call,' as they say?"

Richemerion bobs their head at me a few times. It doesn't sound like they're asking a real question as much as . . . I'm not sure. Evaluating, I suppose.

I would normally expect Almeister to step forward and present me, but as he's currently still in a bit of a state and, as he seems to have as of yet fully accepted that I am whatever I say I am (if not, then why would I say I am?), Persephone takes up the role of presenter instead.

"Yes, Warden. This is Carpathian, our Saviour and your charge."

Again, Richemerion eyes me, blowing out smoke (To be clear, the Warden is not currently smoking; smoke just billows out when they open their mouth.) and says, ". . . Bet."

Thump-thump. Thump-thump.

I'm noticing that the Heart beats differently here. I assume it has something to do with some kind of Mezmeric resonance or something? This being the cradle of the Heart's invention. There is an intense pull on the energy, kind of the way a puppy tugs at its leash when it knows it's getting close to home.

"Yes, Warden," Seph goes on. "He was felled, as you may know, but he is now reconstitute."

"Facts," Richemerion replies.

"And in so having recarbonified, he led the charge upon the Tower to rescue Father."

"Word, word."

"But, as you may sense, Father has been . . . The Super Vizier, the Templars, and all of DONG seem to have interfered with Father's Mezmer. With his very life force. And we have sought you that you might be equipped to assist in restoring his wellness."

"No doubt."

There is a long pause as Richemerion continues staring at us. Or, more accurately, at me.

"So . . . can you?" Seph asks. "Will you? Help us?"

Richemerion squints their eyes at me tightly and, finally, rubbing their palms together, says, "Say less; I got you. Come through, fam." They turn on their heel and we start to follow, but then, they turn back sharply, and we all stumble into one another. "Y'all gotta keep it real Zen in here, ya feel me? No perpetratin' on my spiritual geomancy. This place is a *harmonized* space, ya heard? Step in with the wrong frequency, you throw off the whole groove. And trust? You ain't wanna know what happens when the groove gets thrown."

Brit asks, "What does that mean? Exactly?"

Richemerion narrows their eyes at her. "Means don't be disrespectful, shawty. Know what I'm sayin'?"

Brit's mouth tightens into a fine line.

Perg snorts and mutters under his breath, "Fool clocked you fast."

Brit glares.

Seph watches Richemerion with an expression like she's trying to figure out the shape of the space they occupy.

Jameson, who has clearly already decided that Richemerion is a deity in mortal form, bobs his head, murmuring, "Harmonized space, mi big boss, mi understand, mi overstand . . ."

"Respect," Richemerion finishes, turning and leading the way toward a new set of doors, tall and curved, shaped like a gateway into another world. And when they slide open . . .

The courtyard is quite breathtaking.

Smooth cobblestone paths wind through carefully cultivated gardens split by small, flowing streams that trickle over artfully placed stones. Cherry blossom trees stretch their ancient, knotted limbs overhead, their petals drifting lazily through the air, carried by a breeze that feels intentional, like the world itself is exhaling in perfect rhythm.

A stone bridge, low and simple, arches over one of the streams. Beyond it, a circular training ground of polished stone, etched with golden sigils that pulse faintly in the late-afternoon light. And beyond that, at the far end of the courtyard, a raised platform with a single, low wooden bench, where a crane sits, motionless.

It watches us.

Its long, elegant neck is tucked slightly, but its dark eyes glint with something more than simple animal instinct.

It *knows* something. Maybe. Or maybe it's just a crane.

Either way, I don't like that.

I narrow my eyes at it. It narrows its eyes back.

Great. Now I'm beefin' with a bird. Fantastic.

"Yo, Pathe," Richemerion calls, startling me out of my silent battle of wills with the crane.

I turn back. "Yeah?"

"How's the Heart, B?"

"The Heart?"

"Yeah, son. How's it holding up? It stayin' on the beat?"

"Uh . . . Yeah. Why?"

They cock their head. Suck their teeth. "Just curious."

Richemerion turns their attention to Almeister once again, eyes narrowed, head tilted just enough to suggest they're reading something beneath the surface. Their fingers hover an inch above Almeister's chest, moving slowly, precisely, like a DJ spinning vinyl, searching for the right track. They don't speak for a long time, just watching the faint rise and fall of Almeister's breathing. Then, finally: "Damn, son. They really got you good."

"It was unpleasant," Almeister comments.

Seph shifts forward, hands clasped tight in front of her. "Can you help him?"

Richemerion's eyes flick to her, then to me. A long, slow blink. "I got something for him."

They turn back to Almeister, fingers twitching in small, deliberate circles. No light, no flash of Mezmer, just a ripple in the air, subtle and controlled. The Heart picks up on it immediately, a steady *thump* that feels like a bassline on a jungle track.

The fog in Almeister's eyes recedes, just for a moment. His gaze clears, locks on me, sharp, aware, almost desperate. Then, just as quickly, it's gone. His shoulders slump. His eyes glaze over.

Richemerion clicks their tongue, rolling a shoulder like they're working out a kink. "Ain't gon' lie, this might take a minute."

Seph's voice is tight, raw with hope. "But you can do it?"

"Imma try," Richemerion says, already moving. "But Imma need y'all to be up out of my business while I'm doing it."

"What? Why?" I ask.

"Because, son, when I'm in the lab, I like to keep my processes close, know what I'm sayin'? I'm 'bout making sure the sushi is prepared right, but I ain't out here performin' for y'all. This ain't Sarya's Sushi Showcase, fam."

(I would have assumed he'd make a Benihana reference, but they probably don't have those here.)

The Heart stutters, a faint double thump that makes my breath catch. I shift my weight, suddenly aware of my hands hanging loose at my sides.

"You sure that joint's a'ight, yo?" They point at their chest, indicating their own heart. "Ain't been giving you no troubles at all?"

"I mean . . ."

"You know what? When's the last time any of y'all was up in a Well?"

"A Pulse Well?"

"Nah, Terence Trent D'Arby, a wishing well. Yes, son, a Pulse Well."

"Um, not since we brought down the Tower."

"Respect. A'ight, look here, y'all go get y'all selves validated and verified while I do my voodoo that I do on my man, Meister, and then we'll huddle up and chop up what's what. I'm assuming y'all got big plans to lace once everybody's all Heart Guarded up again?"

"Yeah. I guess."

"Figure y'all gonna wanna rescue up the rest of the Guard, get into some Ninth Guardian squabbles, all that?"

"Um . . . yeah?"

"Why you look surprised, yo? I'm the Warden of Protection up in this piece. You think I don't know *everything* that goes on 'round here?"

They lean into that *everything* real hard, looking at me with an extremely pointed stare. I feel like I'm about to be called to the principal's office after having been caught cheating on a French exam. (Which is a thing that did, in fact, happen. And was not *trés bon*. I'd go so far as to say it was a *merde* experience.) My Heart's beating speeds up, and my mouth gets a little dry.

Which is stupid, I know. I'm the friggin' World Saviour, and I just brought down the damn Tower of Zuria, broke every bone in my body, stitched myself back together, and have now led the Party to attend the Warden, but still . . . Historic trauma presents in unexpected ways. As every moment on Meridia seems to reinforce.

"So, y'all get y'alls Well game on while I get into it with my old boy over here," Richemerion adds.

Seph looks nervously at her father, who nods, reassuring. "All will be fine, my dear. Allow me and the Warden to chop it up, and I shall return to you."

Seph's shoulders sag with relief. "Yes. Thank you," she says to Richemerion.

"I got you, boo. Y'all go on. Temple of the Body's down the path. Stay on the pavers, follow the glow. Don't go wanderin' off; ain't no insurance for lost spirits up in here."

Richemerion leads Almeister away, throwing one last look over their shoulder at me. And it's this look, this one right here, that feels like it's straight out of a movie, the all-knowing, all-seeing, I-know-what-you-did-last-summer look that causes the knot in my chest to radiate out and stiffen my whole physical self.

The thing about Meridia is that it keeps throwing me these goddamn curveballs. Not just the "oh, that's not how I wrote it" kind, but the "did I ever really know anything at all?" kind. I've been blindsided enough times now that I should be used to it, but every new encounter still feels like tripping on a stair I could've sworn wasn't there a second ago.

Initially, I think I thought that the worst part of being in this place was the danger, the constant hum of threat under everything. But honestly, the worst part is how sometimes it's not dangerous at all. How sometimes, it's like it is right now. Safe. Warm, even. And how those are the moments that throw me most off-balance. Like I'm always waiting for the other shoe to drop, only to find out that the other shoe is a slipper, and this is actually a pretty nice carpet.

But now, there's Richemerion in their skull cap and track jacket talking like the universe's most enlightened hype man. Which is not only not what I pictured—it's something that I don't think I ever would have pictured. And they're staring at me like they know a truth that no one else sees.

Or almost no one. Because that's becoming a pattern. Those who look the least like they "belong" here, or at least, are the least expected by me, are the ones who seem to have the clearest line of sight. The ones who speak in riddles with punch lines that somehow cut right to the bone.

It's like when you pass a homeless guy screaming on a street corner and you brace yourself for the usual rant about the end of the world or how pigeons are actually government spies, but then he pauses, points right at you, and says something like, "You ain't foolin' nobody, man." And you keep walking because obviously he's out of his mind, but for the next five blocks, all you can think is *how the hell does he know?* He *sees* me.

That's what Richemerion feels like.

The more out of sync someone here is with my expectations, the more I start to wonder if maybe they're the only ones seeing things clearly. Like maybe those who can see through the cracks are the ones who've already made peace with the idea that there are cracks to begin with. And maybe *I'm* the one who's out of focus.

It's starting to hit me that Meridia isn't a place where I get to decide what's real and what isn't. That bridge between me and Carpathian isn't a line I can trace or a wall I can knock down. It's more like a mirror in a dark room. Most of the time, it's just shadows on glass, but sometimes . . . Sometimes, you catch a glimpse of your own face.

I think I figured out what it is, specifically, about what feels different with the Heart here. It's pulsing slow and steady, but it's less mechanized. More organic. Like it's breathing in sync with the rhythm of the place, glad to be home. Which makes me wonder if I'm supposed to feel that way, too. If the reason I can't settle, can't stop the constant crawl of nerves under my skin, is because I know deep down that this isn't home. It's just a place that wears the mask well enough to make me hesitate.

Or maybe that's exactly what I'm supposed to think. Maybe this is all part of the setup, and I'm still falling for it because I want to believe there's a version of this world that isn't just a string of battles and betrayals and hard-won victories that never stick. Maybe I'm simply looking for a place where I can stop fighting for five damn minutes and remember what it felt like to be someone who wasn't responsible for saving anything.

Or maybe that's the real trick. Maybe that's the thing the Heart's trying to teach me. That I don't get to go back to being just Bruce. That I'll never get to go back, no matter what happens here. That I'm stuck halfway across the bridge and the only way out is forward. That the only way to learn how to live with it is to keep moving.

"Carpathian?"

Seph's voice pulls me back from inside my thoughts.

"Yeah? Sorry, yeah?"

"Shall we visit the temple now? The Pulse Well?"

I let out a breath, straighten my shoulders. "Yeah. Let's see what the Well has to tell us."

Because if the only way out is forward, then I need to keep walking.

CHAPTER SEVENTEEN

Keeping with a now recurring theme, the inside of this Temple of the Body looks nothing like the exterior. It resembles a Snap Fitness I worked out at once or twice until this really mean lady trainer started snickering at my form when I was doing lunges. *Like, okay, maybe you wanna give me some tips rather than be an asshole? Coulda gotten a new client, but opted for an air of superiority instead. I mean, do better, lady. Mind your own business.*

The floors are that same rubberized material, with faint scuff marks where weights have been dropped one too many times. Overhead lights glow with a steady, even brightness. No flicker, no buzzing, just clean illumination that makes everything feel sharper. There's a rack of towels near the entrance, neatly folded, and a row of ellipticals and treadmills lined up along one wall, screens dark and waiting.

A water cooler stands in the corner, complete with a stack of plastic cups. The air smells faintly of disinfectant, like someone wiped down every surface in a fit of overachieving cleanliness. Mirrors run along one side of the room, catching reflections in the kind of brutal honesty that makes you second-guess everything about your posture and the state of your hair.

Speaking of which, I catch my own reflection in the mirror across the room: tired eyes, hair longer than I remember curling just past my ears. The beard's starting to fill in too, not just scruff anymore but a real beard, the kind that takes a couple weeks of deliberate neglect to grow. It's uneven, a little wild, but there's no denying the shape of it. For a second, it throws me, because it's not Bruce staring back. Not exactly.

I look like I've been stuck in the wilderness for a month, sure, but more than that, I look . . . heroic? Almost? Not in the clean, square-jawed way I'd pictured Carpathian, but rougher. Like a knight on the twelfth day of a campaign, armor streaked with mud and eyes that haven't seen a good night's sleep since spring. A face that might fit better on some stained glass window in the Sanctum of Saints.

And that's the part that gets me. The way it all feels like it's been heading in this direction without me noticing. Like my reflection's been keeping secrets, only letting them out now that I've got nowhere else to look. The hair, the beard, the weight in my eyes . . . It's all too close to how I'd pictured him. Windswept hair, a jaw set in righteous determination, eyes that seemed to hold every burden at once.

For a second, I wonder if this is the real trick. Not the Mezmer, not the temples, but this. The slow transformation, subtle and almost incidental, until one day I look in the mirror and don't recognize the person staring back. Maybe that's the whole point of this hootenanny.

To make me become the story I wrote without me realizing it.

There's a kind of genius in it, I realize. Making something so profoundly unremarkable that it loops back around to remarkable again. Like a magician who spends an hour talking about card theory just to distract you from the fact that he's been making your watch disappear and reappear the whole time. It's the sort of trick that doesn't get a standing ovation, just a slow nod from the one guy in the audience who actually understood what happened.

And that's the point, isn't it? Of doing anything challenging. To, eventually, make it all look easy. Effortless, even. To work so hard at wrapping everything up in a mundane package that only someone really paying attention would ever see the seams. Like a painting so realistic you think it's a photograph, but the artist has hidden a thousand tiny imperfections that only come into focus when you are inches from the canvas.

The illusion is the magic.

But the real magic is what the illusion lets you ignore.

If you're looking for the show, you're already missing it. If you're waiting for the curtains to pull back and reveal the gears turning underneath, you're going to be standing here a long damn time. The real tricks are the ones that don't ask for your attention, the ones you only catch when you stop trying to catch anything at all.

It's funny. Not in any kind of funny way at all, but in a way that sparks curiosity. I can *feel* Mezmer here. Maybe I could have felt it in the other temples we've been in too, or maybe I'm just getting attuned, but it's palpable here. Obviously, not because the place looks extraordinary or mythical or mysterious, but precisely because it doesn't.

The Mezmer isn't in the walls or the air. It's woven into the ordinary. The way the light catches on the edges of the mirrors, the exact temperature of the room, the soft hum of what I think might be ventilation but can't quite pin down. It's all too smooth, too aligned. Like Richemerion, in designing it all, went to great lengths to make sure everything felt as unmagical as possible.

Maybe *that's* the trick at work. Maybe *that's* what's actually special. The way Meridia keeps hiding the truth behind things that look safe, familiar, even boring. The way every time I think I've got a handle on the rules, it shifts the ground just enough to make me question if I ever understood them at all.

Like Mezmer pretending not to be Mezmer at all is the real magic on display.

Or maybe I'm just tired. It's hard to tell the difference sometimes.

"Alright, well, does someone else wanna jump in and see where their Stats stand?" I put to the group.

"I'll go," Brit volunteers.

She breezes over to the tanning-booth-looking Pulse Well in the corner and lets herself inside. I can tell she is "feeling it," as they say, and—after all of our near-death cavalcade—is eager to know how pumped up her pumped-up kicks are.

The Well lights up immediately, identifying her by name and throwing her intel on the glass.

[Teleri Nightwind]
[Heart Guard Member]

>Mezmer Type:
Three-Type

>Foundation:
Vanguard

>Resonance Tier:
Etherflint

>Affinities:
Convocationist: [High]
Function (Warmarked): [High]
Stellari: [High]

>Statistics:
Mental: Etherflint Level 9
Physical: Etherflint Level 8
Aura: Etherflint Level 5
Animus: Etherflint Level 6

>Armament(s):
Summoner's Cape

>Abilities:
Map Maker [Advanced]
Beast Mastery [Advanced]

>Spell(s):
Summoner of Something [Convocationist] - [Advanced]
Randolf's Radiant Ray [Stellari] - [Novice]
Wall of WOW! [Convocationist] - [Beginner]

Heavens to Babadook. I had surmised that after what we endured in the "Great Tower Breakout" (as I have just decided to start referring to it) and our trek to visit with Richemerion, that everyone would be juiced up, but I didn't expect Brit's stat line to leap up between three and four levels in every category. Not to mention she's now an Advanced Beast Master—which tracks somewhat; she was able to talk to me through the voice of a dragon earlier—and has a brand-new Spell to boot: Wall of WOW! I don't even know what that does, but it's a Convocationist Spell, so it's something she can call up when needed.

Probably a wall. That's probably got a pretty good *WOW!* factor. If the name is accurate.

With luck, we won't be interrupted in the way we were when we visited the Pulse Well in Garr Haven and can try out all our new strengths here in the temple before moving on.

"Bruce? Did you really just think that?"

"Yeah. Why?"

"Do you know nothing about how jinxes work, you lunatic?!"

I push the self-criticizing voice in my head to the rear as Brit exits, looking pretty pleased.

"Feel good?"

"Fuck yeah," she exclaims. "I could tell that I had some hot shit cooking up inside me, but it's nice to know exactly *how* hard I can push this action." She swirls her hands, and Randolf's Radiant Ray begins forming.

"Steady," I caution.

"Sorry," she says, stopping the motion and letting the ray die down before it blooms and, whatever, melts Perg's shell or something.

Speaking of . . .

"*Ese?*" Perg shoots me a look. "Sorry, sorry. You're up."

He scooches inside and, once more, the Pulse Well tells the tale.

[Pergamon Slow Bottom]
[Heart Guard Member]
>Mezmer Type:
One-Type
>Foundation:
Hexkeeper
>Resonance Tier:
Etherflint
>Affinity:
Mutamorph

>Statistics:
Mental: Etherflint Level 9
Physical: Etherflint Level 5
Aura: Etherflint Level 6
Animus: Etherflint Level 8

Damn. Just like Brit, Perg has jumped up appreciably more than I could have anticipated. He and Brit are both on the precipice of graduating to Ironspark in their mental Stats. The intellectually inclined part of my ego gets some kind of odd satisfaction out of knowing that my cohort appears to be amplifying their cerebral strength faster than their physical or even metaphysical strengths. Although, as the old saying goes, "clever can get you killed," so I don't want to get too sassy about it.

"Jameson?" I ask. He ignores me, too focused on keeping the cherry lit on his joint which *finally* seems like it's dying out a little bit. "J? Jame? Jameson? Yo, J.R.R. Toking?"

That gets his attention. "Ye know me full name?" he asks, bloodshot eyes wide with surprise.

". . . What?"

"Me name. Jameson Righteous Ragamuffin Toking. Me never tell you dat. How ye know?"

I start to say something, but honestly, the stakes are too high to get side-tracked by the absurdity of the whole thing. Even for someone as easily Sidesy McSidetracky as I am.

"It doesn't . . . Just . . . Would you like to step into the Pulse Well so we can verify your details?"

"No," he responds.

"No?"

"No. Me no truck wit dem Pulse Well juju."

"It's not juju. It's . . . Everybody uses the Pulse Well to validate their statuses. Otherwise, you won't be able to know what your strengths and weaknesses are and how to use them."

"Me don't need no validation. Me grant me self me own knowledge. You know dem say. Ignorance be bliss."

He smiles and nods to himself. I mean, I can't argue that he's the most blissed out of the bunch of us. He took a sword to the gut and is looking just fine, so I can't argue with him.

"Okay, then. Seph?"

She hesitates. "You first?" she requests.

"Um . . . yeah, sure, okay."

She smiles, daintily, as I step in.

The Well fires up (so to speak, not actually, thankfully), and I get the first look at my new and improved lowdown following "The Great Tower Breakout." (It really does sound so cool.)

[Carpathian Einzgear, aka "World Saviour"]

>Mezmer Type:
All-Type

>Foundation:
Synchron

>Resonance Tier:
Etherflint

>Highest Affinities:
Elemist (Stoneheart): **[Experienced]**
Mutamorph: **[Above Average]**
Technomancy: **[Average]**

>Statistics:
Mental: ***Etherflint Level 10***
Physical: ***Ironspark Level 2***
Aura: ***Etherflint Level 8***
Animus: ***Etherflint Level 10***

>Armament(s):
Mechanical Heart
[Elder Tier] ***Blade of the Starfallen***

>Inventory:
[Medium Tier] ***Stoneheart Gloves***
[Elder Tier] ***Blade of the Starfallen***
[1] New Slot Available!

>Abilities:
Scaredy Cat
Sharpshooter

>Spell(s):
Control **[Chronoshift]**
CloakRender I **[Aetherpulse]**
Marrowmancy **[Mutamorph]**
Toxin Dart **[Mutamorph]**
Mezmeric Microblather **[Technomancy]**

Ho-lee Katzenjammer Kids.

While my Resonance Tier does remain at Etherflint, it won't be there much longer, because my Mental, Aura, *and* Animus Stats have jumped up like a House of Pain song.

Mental and Animus at Etherflint Level Ten? *Ten*? That means the next time I get a boost, both of those will be at Ironspark. Mother Mandy. I'm passing through the "first filter" far faster than Carpathian ever did. Honestly? The pace at which I'm leveling up my game is a little worrying. Because . . . if the nature of things operates as I understand and have been further led to believe, then the strength at which I'm operating owes to the fact that I'm gonna need to be ready to handle some heavy shit sooner rather than later.

The doors slide open, and I step out. Brit nods.

"We're starting to be on some Avengers shit, huh?"

"I was thinking Super Friends, but sure."

Brit and I have had a long-standing DC vs Marvel disagreement. I tend to favor the aspirational qualities I feel like are represented in the DC canon, whereas Brit responds to the satirical/political commentary aspects of the Marvelverse. We're both very on brand.

"Who are the avenging super friends?" Persephone asks.

"Uh, nothing, just . . . Let's get you in there," I change the subject, gracelessly.

Once more, though, she hedges, shuffling her feet. Hesitating.

"Hey, seriously, what's wrong?" I ask, stepping close to her. "Everything okay?"

"Yes. I just . . ."

"Do you not want to see what your Abilities look like? I'll bet they're alright."

Maybe she's embarrassed? She was just stuck in Bell's View for forever and a day, waiting on me to return, doing who knows what. There was no way for her to build up her capacity the way one does in real-world interactions.

But . . . That's . . . She shouldn't . . . I mean, I've seen her in action. She can replicate herself; she can put up spheres of protection. Hell, she even crafted vision versions of *me* back in the Tower when I popped Almeister out of his cage. Maybe she's not as feisty as the rest of us, but she's surely got some impressive things going on for herself.

And, honestly, I just really wanna know what they are.

"It's alright," I say again, nodding gently. My hand brushes her arm, and she smiles and nods. Stepping over to the tube, she takes a breath, walks inside, the doors close, and then . . .

. . . the weirdest thing happens.

It's like in the movies when the nerdy girl lets her hair down and removes her glasses, and the audience has the tragically misogynistic shared realization that she'd been hot the whole time.

Whatever is happening as Seph is in the Pulse Well is like the Mezmeric version of *She's All That*, except where Seph was already gorgeous before, the incarnate form of beauty I am currently beholding is hard to look at directly.

Her red hair cascades down her back like liquid fire, skin catching the refracted light inside the Well in a way that makes it difficult to take in. It's like trying to stare at the sun. I damn near have to avert my eyes.

She offers me a smile from inside the tube that makes my heart do jumping jacks, and I'm pretty sure I let out a slight whimper.

"You good?" Brit asks.

"Yeah, just . . . Are you seeing—?"

She cuts me off. "Yeah, no, I see it. It's . . . quite something."

"What do you think is going on?"

"Dunno." Brit shrugs. "Maybe it's just verifying that she's a fuckin' smoke show."

Brit and I stare, both of our mouths slightly agape. Sorcery, indeed.

Just then, Seph's current standings light up on the glass, and the awe I feel is now for an entirely different set of reasons.

[Persephone Vizardsdottir]
[Heart Guard Member]

>Mezmer Type:
Four-Type

>Foundation:
Pulsariel

>Resonance Tier:
Ironspark

>Affinities:
Dreamweave: **[Perfect]**
Elemist (Pyreheart): **[High]**
Nexabind: **[High]**
Mutamorph: **[Above Average]**

>Statistics:
Mental: *Ironspark Level 7*
Physical: *Ironspark Level 3*
Aura: *Ironspark Level 9*
Animus: *Ironspark Level 7*

>Abilities:
Thaumaturgic Amalgamation III
Ritual Forge
Rotary Bicursal Virtuosity IV
Double Your Pleasure
Alchemical Proficiency IX

>Spell(s):
Instantaneous Doppel III **[Dreamweave]**
[Steelshard] ***DoppelShift*** **[Dreamweave/Nexabind]**
Somnium Kennel **[Dreamweave]**
Ignition Chain **[Elemist (Pyreheart)]**
Chrysalis **[Nexabind]**
Flamestriker **[Elemist (Pyreheart)]**
Pierce the Veil **[Nexabind]**
Imbue **[Mutamorph]**
Remedial Reversion **[Mutamorph]**
Rift Anchor **[Nexabind]**

I, who am never at a loss for words—indeed, some might say I could afford to lose more words more often—am founded dumb.

"Do you see that?" I ask Brittany.

She nods, feebly.

"Do you know what all that is?"

She nods in near catatonia a second time.

"That's . . ." I trail off.

"It is," she mumbles.

I don't even understand all of it. I'm sure Brit does, which probably means she's more overwhelmed than I am. But even what I do grasp . . .

Thaumaturgic Amalgamation? That's the ability to know how to forge spells together and create new ones, which, I guess, she did back in the Tower, but at a level of three?!

Ignition Chain? That's something I only remember one other person in all of Riftbreaker having. Cinderath, the Flame Scalder, was a bad-guy-girl in . . . one of the books (can't remember which) who had it. It's pretty much a whip-cracking Spell but that uses a chain of fire as the whip and it explodes on contact. It's as badass as badass can ass badly, and Seph has it.

I have no idea what Rotary Bicursal Virtuosity is. And the fact that she's got the level four version of a thing I don't even know about . . . ?

"Yo, this *chica*'s a beast, fool!"

Perg, as usual, is not wrong.

The doors to the Well open, and Seph steps out, crossing to me timidly.

"So . . ." she says, shrugging her shoulders.

"How . . . How . . . How?" I ask, like a stuttering dummy.

"While you were away, I had lots of time to just . . . practice. On myself."

Brit's eyebrows go up, and she starts to say something cheeky—I can just feel it—but I shake my head at her tightly to ward off her inappropriate sassafras.

"I see," I breathe out. "Well. All that hard work clearly paid off." I take a second to gather my thoughts. "I'm really glad you're with us."

"As am I." She smiles.

Swallowing hard, I try to put my attention back onto business. "Very good. So, let's see how Richemerion is doing with your father and—"

"No need to find the Warden, yo. The Warden finds you."

I look over to see Richemerion strolling in, icier than a debt collector's handshake. Jameson perks up at the appearance of his spirit Warden. He offers Richemerion a puff of his blunt, but the Warden waves him off and, once again, blows out smoke that must just live in their lungs. If ancient mystics even have lungs; I dunno what's going on in there.

"So . . ." Seph starts, running over with hope, "how is he? Is he restored?"

"Yes and no."

Her face drops. "What does that mean?"

They don't answer outright, instead putting their hand on her shoulder. "It's gonna be alright. I just need a second with the Pathe maker over here."

"Me?" I point at myself, redundantly. Richemerion nods "What do you need to—?"

"Just need to chin-wag with you, my boi." They rub their palms together. "Got a couple small . . . let's say . . . details . . . we need to conversate about."

CHAPTER EIGHTEEN

The space Richemerion has led us to looks like someone blended a Kyoto teahouse with a recording studio designed for royalty. It's minimalist but warm, with dark wood walls split by shoji screens that glow softly from behind. The floor is polished bamboo, smooth and seamless, reflecting the light just enough to catch faint silhouettes.

High-end speakers are built discreetly into the walls, matte black with subtle gold accents, and they look like they could blow a hole clean through reality if someone ever turned them up to full blast. A mixing console sits along one side of the room, its knobs and sliders gleaming under recessed lighting, paired with a pair of turntables that look both ancient and brand new at once.

There's a low table in the center with a few floor cushions arranged around it, each one stitched with intricate patterns in black and gold. A pair of headphones rests on the console, the kind with oversized ear cups and gold-plated connectors that suggest a level of sound quality that borders on religious experience.

"You do a lot of, um, beat making?" I ask, trying to make small talk.

"I call it 'creating harmonic convergence,' but words is words, know what I'm sayin'?"

"Yeah," I sigh. "I do."

"I know that's right."

Opposite the console, a glass wall stretches from floor to ceiling, so clear I almost miss it at first. It has a faint iridescence, catching the light in a way that suggests it's not just glass but something reinforced, something that could take a hit and not so much as shiver.

Through it, I can see into an adjoining chamber that looks almost like a spa. Soft, ambient lighting, walls lined with bamboo, a mist rolling lazily along the floor. Almeister is reclined on a stone platform in the center, eyes half lidded, surrounded by a haze that's either steam or something Mezmeric in nature. His breathing is slow, methodical.

Invisible . . . attendants? I guess? move around him, hands made of light or energy or something in between weaving in slow, deliberate motions. They smooth over his chest and arms, each pass causing a faint ripple in the air, like heat off asphalt. Almeister's fingers twitch now and then, but he doesn't resist.

Richemerion throws themself into a low-backed armchair with the kind of ease that suggests the chair was built specifically for them. Which they confirm by saying, "My boy Lank Freud Wrong designed this joint, custom."

One leg draped over the armrest, fingers laced behind their head, watching me with an expression that lands somewhere between amused and analytical, they sigh. The smoke that follows them seems to have thinned, lingering just enough to blur the edges of things, to make the corners of the room seem a little less defined than they should be.

For a moment, I just wait there, taking in the scene. The silence isn't heavy, but it's full. Like . . . Well, like the quiet between tracks on a record. There is the faint trickle of water from a small fountain set into the far wall, its surface broken by smooth stones arranged with acute precision. Even the air smells curated: cedar, citrus, a hint of ozone that makes my skin prickle.

"So," Richemerion drawls, breaking the silence without really breaking it. "Your man's at the end of the process. Few more cycles and he should be back to runnin' right."

I drag my eyes away from Almeister, trying to ignore the way the light plays over him, too bright and too soft all at once. "And by 'runnin' right,' you mean . . . ?"

Richemerion grins, flashing white teeth, but it doesn't reach the eyes. "Mean he'll be able to hold a conversation without starin' through you like you a bad memory. Mind might need a minute to recalibrate, but he'll be straight. Eventually." The Warden flicks a bit of invisible lint from his jacket sleeve, casual, almost bored. "Thing is, though, he said some real interestin' shit while we was workin' on him."

That brings me up short. "Oh, yeah?"

"Word."

"Uh-huh. Uh . . . interesting like how?"

"Interestin' like you and me need to have a sit-down," Richemerion replies, tipping their chin toward an armchair that matches the one they're in. "Mans had a lot to say."

"About what?"

"About you, lil' bruh."

That drags my attention back to Almeister, to the faint furrow in his brow, the way his fingers flex and relax against the sheets in a slow, rhythmic pattern. I can feel the Heart in my chest pick up its pace; not fast, but deeper somehow, each beat reverberating down to the flippin' marrow. I hesitate, half a step from the chair, glancing back through the glass at Almeister.

"Look, man, he's fine. Or, he will be. Ain't nothin' to do now but let the process finish marinating. Get comfortable, boi."

I drop into the armchair, which turns out to be way softer than it looks. I try to keep my back straight, to ignore the way my shoulders immediately start to uncoil, a knot of tension unraveling without my permission. Richemerion chuckles low, almost to themself, like they can see the whole mental fight play out in real time.

"You know," they start, lacing their fingers behind their head again, "for a cat who's supposed to be the World Saviour, you stay lookin' like somebody's about to call on you in class and you didn't do the homework."

I can feel my face blanch, the color draining right out of it. *Is the Warden . . . in my brain?*

"I ain't in your brain. But I can feel your thoughts," they tell me.

"How?"

They tap their chest and then point in the direction of mine. They lean further back in the chair, almost sinking into the floor itself. Their eyes are half lidded but sharp underneath. There's a pause that hangs just long enough to make me think they're waiting for something; maybe for me to speak, maybe just for the hell of it. When they finally do talk, it's slow and measured, like they're telling a story that they've thought about a thousand times but never really told out loud before.

"You know," the Warden starts, offhand, "back when the first Saviour got pulled, back when the First Guardian came into being . . . You know about all that, right?"

"Enough-ish," I tell Richemerion. I don't actually know nearly enough-ish, to be honest, but at this very moment, I am appreciably more interested in what's about to be said regarding this Saviour and the First Guardian. I don't want to get sidetracked with a history lesson. Eventually, but not now.

"Yeah, well, wasn't no Heart involved," they go on. "Just a lotta blind faith, sharpened bronze, and gods with too much time on their hands. Know what I'm sayin'? Whole thing was raw as hell; heroes lurchin' from one bloodbath to the next, hopin' the gods might smile their way. The first Saviour? Mans was out there buildin' a legend one body at a time, seein' what stuck and what broke under pressure."

Looks like I am getting a bit of a history lesson, after all. Oh well. Those who don't learn from the past are destined to repeat it, I suppose.

"So, what happened?"

"I mean, for a while, shit worked," Richemerion continues. "First Saviour did their thing, took down the First Guardian, bought the world a little more time. But peace don't last. Ain't meant to. Eventually, some new evil starts crawlin' out the dark, some new Guardian gets to feelin' themselves a little too much, and the world starts beggin' for a hero again. Then another Saviour gets pulled. And another. Each time a little messier, a little harder to put back together.

"So, you know, each Saviour needed somethin' different to keep 'em in the game. Second one was all blood and thunder, so they got the Bloodbound Gauntlets. Kept 'em swingin' even when they was half dead. Third Saviour needed clarity, so I made the Silver Eyes. Let 'em see through lies, through illusions. Fourth needed lungs that wouldn't burn out, and so on and so forth. Eighth needed a mind that could hold the whole damn world without splittin' at the seams."

"But . . . I needed . . . a Heart?"

They lean forward, elbows on knees, eyes gleaming dark and warm. "Yeah, fam. You needed a Heart. Well, not exactly. You just needed . . . an upgrade. You needed a heart that didn't *bleed*."

Something about it hurts my feelings, which is, I suppose, the point.

I blink. "You mean . . . metaphorically?"

"Everything's a metaphor, bruh. But also nah, I mean literally. Heart that couldn't break, couldn't bleed. Shit keeps pumpin', makes you hard to kill, my boi!" They breathe in, breathe out. "But then . . . you did die, didn't you?"

"Oh, uh . . ."

"See, 'cuz to the metaphor point? Yours wasn't supposed to be able to get twisted up by grief or guilt or any of that heavy shit that turns Saviours into martyrs. You was gonna be the kind of Saviour that wasn't just out here swingin' for glory. You needed to survive. And to survive, you needed a heart that wasn't afraid to get dirty. A Heart that didn't flinch."

"Oh. Well—"

"See, that's what don't sit right," the Warden murmurs, almost to themselves. "What's in you wasn't supposed to break. It wasn't supposed to bleed. None of that. But it did. And you died, word?"

"Um, word . . . But I came back? So . . ."

The words hang for a second, heavy and pointed. I try not to fidget in my seat, but it's like sitting on a live wire.

"Yeah, that's the part," they sigh, shaking their head. "Like, don't get me wrong, I'm glad you're back. But how you back? Either I messed up—which, nah—or there's somethin' else in play. Somethin' I wasn't told about. And, see, yo, more than that, how come the System let it slide? YOU'RE supposed to be the World Saviour, right? Carpathian Einzgear? But Almeister"—they jerk a thumb toward the glass wall, where Almeister's fingers twitch in the mist—"man's been droppin' some real interestin' rumors about Brucillian."

I can feel the blood drain out of my face. "Brucillian," I repeat, voice coming out a little more strangled than I intend.

"Mm-hmm. Now, I ain't the type to buy into tall tales and bedtime stories," Richemerion continues. "I mean, if some false prophet was gonna flip the whole game on its head, you'd think a Warden might get the memo, yeah? But Almeister's been real chatty while he's been detoxin'. And the shit he's sayin' ain't just some 'oh no, the end is nigh' type deal. Nah, this is specifics. Like he's got the script before the shit's even been written, you feel me?"

"Richemerion, I—"

"Look, fam, don't get it twisted. I ain't tryin' to blow up your spot. I'm just letting you know that whoever you are, whether you really are you, Carpathian, and you got caught slippin' and came back, or whether you're . . . not, I don't give two bounty mantras in a flim-flam slop, you know what I'm saying?"

"Like, possibly not at all, but—?"

"I'm sayin' the thing about myths, y'see, is they need continuity. Ain't enough to have heroes and villains. Gotta have the spaces between. The breathin' room. The parts that don't make it into the songs or the books, where the hero's just tryna remember which way is north and the villain's wonderin' if this is really worth the price of admission.

"See, fam, *you* are the one strapped with the Heart. *You* are the one who's set to do what needs to be done. And *you* are the one who needs to decide that that's not bullshit. If nothing else, ain't nobody want to hear a mothafucka questioning their place in the world for I don't know however many Lunar Cycles. You dig what I'm sayin'?"

"Yeah . . . Yeah, I . . . dig."

"So, you know, if I was you, I would just come correct, decide that you're HIM. Feel me? And trust that as long as you stay a real one, ain't nobody gonna trip. You can't be having someone's back unless you *up-front* with them first. Ya heard?"

I let my gaze drift through the glass wall to Almeister lying slack on the platform, fingers twitching now and then like he's mid-dream. Maybe he is. Maybe whatever Mezmer is being woven around him is pulling memories to the surface, sifting through them like someone sorting a junk drawer for anything useful.

I should be relieved to see him like this, to know that he might actually come back to us. Instead, all I feel is this tightness in my chest, a slow, turning guilt that coils around my spine and doesn't let up. But it's not about Almeister, not really.

It's about Seph.

About the look in her eyes every time she asks me a question and I have to figure out how much truth I can get away with telling.

She deserves better. Deserves the absolute truth, all of it. I've been telling myself I'm doing it for her, for everyone, that there's no point in ripping the rug out from under anybody until I'm sure there's actually a trapdoor for us to escape to underneath. But the longer this whole thing goes on, the more it feels like I'm just stalling. Like maybe I'm not actually trying to protect anyone else from the truth; maybe I'm just trying to protect myself from what happens when everyone finds out.

Almeister's fingers curl, tighten. I lean forward instinctively, like I could maybe catch some fragment of the visions or memories or whatever the hell's playing out in his head. Richemerion's eyes flick from me to Almeister, one eyebrow lifting just enough to look amused.

"Um," I say, trying to sound casual and not like someone whose Heart rate has decided to run wind sprints. "Can I ask a question?"

"Technically, you just did."

Jesus. Life imitates art imitates whatever the hell this is.

"I was just going to ask how you two know each other in the first place. You and Almeister."

"Oh, me and the Meister go way back, fam. We was in a group once."

I blink. "A . . . Like . . . Like a *musical* group?"

"Hells yeah." They grin, eyes half lidded but glinting. "We was called 'Soulforge Syndicate.' Shit was live as fuck, yo. I was on the decks, Meister on vocals. Had a whole, like, dank-ass vibe, too. Dark, ethereal, lotta echo, reverb. Problem was . . . mans couldn't hold a key to save his life. Sounded like a banshee with asthma tryin' to recite a hymn. Ended up partin' ways, creatively speakin'. I got into, y'know, protectin' reality from collapse and shit, and he got into what he got into." They gesture lazily at Almeister, fingers trailing smoke that doesn't burn.

I can't tell if they're serious or if I've just wandered into some *Twilight Zone* version of *Behind the Music*.

"Seriously?" I ask, squinting.

"Nah, bruh! Not seriously. You playin'? I'm a Warden, fam. My shit is ancient. Been here since the time before time began. Meister's maybe, like, a couple hundred? Tops? Nah, yo. I just met him back in the day and me and the *maestro* fucks with each other. That's all."

"Oh. Right." I glance back through the glass at Almeister's slack features, at the invisible hands weaving light and energy over him in smooth, deliberate arcs. Complicated doesn't even begin to cover it. "Is he . . . Is he gonna be okay?"

"Yeah, bruh, he'll be a'ight. Next thing after we wrap him in there is to get him plugged back into your Heart Guard. Can't be running all over the universe unguarded. Might get CTE and shit. More, I mean."

The Warden stands. I join.

"Warden—"

"You can just call me Richemerion. Or Rich Homie Mary. Or the Protectifier. Or Sluice the Framework Pony. Or Warden is also fine, I guess."

"Yeah. Warden . . . I—" Before I can finish the thought—a thought I'm not even sure I have fully formed yet—Richemerion takes me by the shoulders and looks me in the eye.

"You know the biggest misconception about reality?"

"That you can fold a fitted sheet successfully by yourself?"

"Okay, the second biggest misconception." I shake my head. "Is that your fate is actually predetermined."

"It's not?" They shake *their* head. "That's so . . . I used to think that way, but now—"

"It's like this: The fortunate one will say 'fate is kind.' The unfortunate one will say 'fate is cruel.' It's neither. It's fate. Shit ain't personal."

I consider this. The look on my face must show how hard it hits because Richemerion goes on to say . . . "I be droppin' BARS, son! Believe." Then they add, "You can change your fate, if you really want. You *can* flip the script. Just because the record is spinning don't mean the groove is set. There's always a B side, you feel me?"

I nod, slowly. "I do. But . . . how?"

"I got you. Follow me."

They start to exit. I follow. They stop, turn back, and add . . .

"Oh, also? We gotta get you some new vines, bruh. This mesh suit? It ain't cute like that, B."

I look down and notice that the suit is showing signs of wear and tear. It's starting to kind of sag, not as formfitting as it once was. Kind of a poopy pamper vibe. It's a little cringe.

"Oh," I note. "I hadn't realized."

"It's all good. But Warden of Protection means I also gotta protect my rep. Can't have you out here Saviouring all around town looking like a Drakonar's dinner, know what I mean?"

"I just don't have any other gear to change into."

"That's a'ight, my boi . . ." They smile a deep, broad, knowing smile. "I do."

CHAPTER NINETEEN

Jesus Christ," Brit says. "That's a fuckin' upgrade."

She ain't lying.

I'm not a fashion maven. I don't typically geek out over fits; at least not my own. I will spend hours laboring over a precise outfit for, say, a character in a D&D campaign, however. So, on the basis of that, I'm pretty friggin' turnt about what Richemerion has slid me into.

It's got that old-world, knight-in-shadowlands aesthetic, but laced with a street-born energy that causes the asphalt to crack when you walk.

A long, deep-black topcoat, heavy enough to feel like armor but cut for movement. Broad shoulders, tapered just right, its hem dusting the back of my heels when I walk. The sleeves are fitted, cuffed with gold-threaded embroidery, and the interior is lined with hidden pockets deep enough to stash essentials without weighing me down; there's one at chest level just big enough for something secret. Which should make Brittany very happy, as she'll no longer have to haul my crap around, *and* it frees up storage slots for things that actually need storing someplace more discreet. Speaking of which . . .

Underneath the coat, I'm wearing a tunic in deep charcoal, lightweight but structured, layered with a sleeveless, close-cut vest. The fabric moves like . . . I dunno. Like . . . liquid shadow. (Yeah, that's good.) But it's reinforced at key points: shoulders, ribs, spine. Built so that I can take hits and keep going even before reaching my naturally enforced physical self.

The waist is cinched with a sash of deep crimson, thick and textured, tied asymmetrically with trailing ends that shift in the air. And woven into it, a sheath sits against my hip, almost hidden. It will allow the Blade of the Starfallen to finally have a proper repository for chilling out when it's not being waved around, carving shit up. Again, Brit is gonna be *stoked*.

The pants are cut like classic combat trousers but tailored to fit, with even more deep-set pockets along the thighs. They sit easy but firm, tucked into boots that are built for silence and speed. Heavy enough to ground me; light enough to let me ghost through a battlefield if I have to. Thick soles, steel-toed, laced up but folded slightly at the top for that effortless edge.

Shit is cash.

"Damn, fool. Now we're talking. That's on some hero shit, huh?" Perg compliments.

"Yow, mi Saviour. Yuh done step be lookin' like prophecy an' problem at di same time. History, but also fresh rain pon de cobblestone."

"Thanks, Jame," I respond.

Persephone draws close, shy and coquettish. "It does look very nice, Carpathian. You look more like . . . yourself."

Richemerion drops their head and eyeballs me with a tired look, gazing up kind of through their eyebrows. I have to say, all this pressure I feel to tell people or, specifically, Seph the truth about what's going on is having the opposite effect of that which is intended. I won't deny that I have a bit of a contrarian streak, and being pushed to do things is one of the triggers that brings it out. But that's also childish, so . . . But whatever. I just need everyone off my back for a second.

I adjust the coat, sliding a hand into one of the hidden pockets, feeling the weight settle around me, and ask a question to change the subject. "Where did this even come from?"

Richemerion says, "Wardens keep the archives, my guy. Ain't just books and myths; we keep the *drip*, too." They flick their wrist like they just conjured magic, then slap my shoulder. "But enough about how GQ down you lookin'. We gotta get mans into the *Pulse Well* and get you off onto your next adventure. Which is where, by the way? Whatch'all gon' get up to next?"

"Um, well, we're still missing Party members, so we're thinking we'd go find them."

"Say word, son," Richemerion volunteers. "I fucks with that plan." That's encouraging. If the Warden of Protection is corroborating an idea, it must be the right one. "So, bet. Who you 'bout to seek out?"

"Zerastian," I tell them. "Our precog."

"I feel that."

"She's also our Technomancer. She can hack basic systems and handle breakdowns of things like vehicles and so forth."

"Buckabuck," Richemerion mumbles.

"I mean, we also need to get Xanaraxa back at some point, but . . . Zerastian first?"

Richemerion pauses, then says, "Are y'all looking for me to approve the shit or something?"

"Oh, maybe?" I realize. "You're the Warden of Protection. I figure you know strategy."

Richemerion once more rubs their palms together like they're scheming up something. "Well," they say, "Xanaraxa is a down mothafucka. Warrior poet with mad skillz and the third-eye wisdom."

"Yeah," I acknowledge. "She's also sort of Car—sort of my, um, moral compass? Like, Xanaraxa, beyond being a really good fighter, always, well, kept me grounded. I suppose."

Brit nods as if to say, *Yeah, you got it.*

"Facts, facts. But . . . as you note, Zerastian got that precognitive shit." The Warden paces slightly, head nodding. "Mm-hmm. Mm-hmm." Then . . . "Yeah, you should scoop up Zerastian."

"You think Zerastian should be the priority?"

"I mean . . . that's what I just said, ain't it?"

"Because you think we'll need her precognitive and Technomantic skills more?"

"Nah, because—and correct me if I'm wrong—you lost Zerastian in the Mokeisan Desert."

"Yeah, how did you—?"

"I know you're not about to ask *how* I know what happened to the members of your Party. I'm the Warden of mothafuckin' *Protection*, B."

Yeah, okay.

"So, you should go get Zerastian because then you can fuck with the Mid-Meridian Plane."

There's a long pause before I ask, "The what?"

"The Mid-Meridian Plane, son. For real, you need to take a hearing upgrade?"

The pause is because . . . I have no idea what that is. I never wrote about something called "The Mid-Meridian Plane." I never even *imagined* something called a "Mid-Meridian Plane."

"And what, exactly, is the Mid-Meridian Plane?" I dare to query.

Richemerion pulls their head back, studies me, and says, "It's a spot in the Mokeisan Desert."

"And how do we get to this 'Mid-Meridian Plane'?" Brit asks.

"By going to the Mokeisan Desert."

Her fists clench. She absolutely hates tautological answers.

I put up my hand to calm her.

"But," I ask again, "what *is* the Mid-Meridian Plane? We've never heard of it before."

"It's where you go if what you want to do is flip the script."

To be fair to Brit, I feel my fists balling now too. I grit my teeth. "I'm sorry, I'm not—"

Richemerion sighs. "Bruh, do you trust the System?"

"Trust the System?"

"For real, B. You need to see a hearing specialist; you be asking way too many repetition-based questions. Yes. Do you trust the System?"

"Um . . . sure. Of course I do."

"Well, you shouldn't."

"Excuse me?!"

"I mean, it's not your fault. I know that's what everybody's been telling you to do. Because, obviously, that's the way things have always been done. But when a System gets corrupted, it's no longer worthy of that trust. Trust has to be earned, ya heard?"

"I . . ."

I don't know what to say because what's being told to me right now is kind of melting my brain. It's upending my entire worldview. Or, at least, the worldview that I held for Meridia.

Everything I wrote was predicated on the notion of trusting the System. But . . .

"Did you choose to write Riftbreaker or did Riftbreaker choose you?"

Yet again, Brit's question enters my thoughts. The answer seems to be getting clearer and clearer. I'm now embracing the very probable reality that perhaps I'm not as imaginative as I thought I was. I think, maybe, I was just . . . available.

It's a real unique kind of a bummer to discover that what you thought was your creative genius was really just you being the transcriber of someone else's majestic reality. Although, I guess the other way of looking at it is that of all the schmoes in the universe who could've gotten tapped to tell the tale and get nice houses and fancy cars as a result, I was the one who got picked. Maybe it's a compliment; not entirely sure. But the one thing I'm starting to get wise to is that Carpathian Einzgear dying was never part of the narrative this world intended.

That was the one thing that was all my decision.

Nice work, Bruce.

"You talking to me, Bruce?"

"No, I was . . . Maybe? I dunno. Just . . . I'll check back in later."

"You got it, Bruce."

I exhale, adjusting the fit of the coat, the weight of it settling on my shoulders like something more than fabric. Like responsibility. Like a work shift I wasn't ready to punch into but here I am, uniform and all.

"Okay," I say. "But, so, if the System's corrupt, then . . . what about this?" I point at my chest, indicating the Heart. The looks on the faces of my Party people scrunch up just like I feel my own doing.

"What about it?"

"It's . . . It's the enlivened embodiment of the System inside *my* body. What do I . . . ?"

I trail off because the notion that I might have a betrayer in my breast is, well, not the best. (I shouldn't rhyme at a time like this but, I think, subconsciously, I probably want Richemerion to feel that I have fire bars. I can be an accidental code switcher if I'm not careful.)

Richemerion gives me a long, slow blink, like I asked whether fire was hot or if the sun was bright. Then, they shake their head.

"See, that's why I gave *you* the Heart and not some other scrub," they say, tapping their own chest for emphasis. "The System? Yeah, it got fingers in everything, true. It moves like a wraith through time and space, nudgin' pieces where it wants, settin' the stage for what it thinks oughta happen. But the Heart? The Heart don't play by those rules. It's the exception."

"How?"

Richemerion exhales through their nose, like explaining this is some kind of effort (even though I know they love dropping game). "'Cuz I built it that way, B. I ain't just hand you some factory-model conduit for the System's will. I made sure it had fail-safes, redundancies, countermeasures. You got discernment built into your bones, fam. The Heart don't tell you what to do—it lets you *see*. Past the bullshit, past the illusions, past the strings the System tries to pull. You ain't *bound* to the System the way others are. You got the one thing it can't override."

"What's that?"

"Autonomy, my boi. Free will, feel me? No leashes, no whispers in the dark tellin' you to move left when you should be movin' right. That's why you different. That's probably why the System let you die, but now, it ain't got a clue what to do with you now that you came back."

The words settle into my brain, heavy but fitting in ways I hadn't fully grasped before. The Heart *is* the System's creation, but it's also its outlier. Not a cog in the machine but a key. One that can unlock, override . . . maybe even rewrite.

Thump-thump.

I look down at my chest, not like I can see the damn thing, but just feeling it there, steady, constant. Then it occurs to me . . .

"Okay, but then, why should I trust . . . you?"

All heads turn from me back to Richemerion. It's like they're watching a tennis match.

The Warden doesn't flinch. They just roll their shoulders, cracking their neck.

". . . You shouldn't."

Not gonna lie. That catches me off guard. "I—What?"

"I mean, you *should*. I gave you a Heart and then fruit and snacks and shit."

"You have any more, by the way, fool?"

Richemerion snaps their fingers, and a whole new spread appears for Perg to tear into.

"But that's what I'm sayin'. I *earned* that trust. I have proved that you can trust me by my *actions*, ya heard? You shouldn't trust me *just* because I say some nice words and give you a fresh fit. See, that's the System's whole trick, bruh. It gets people to trust titles. Structures. Legacy. Puts the right robes on somebody, slaps a crest on their chest, and boom, you're supposed to believe they know what's best.

"But I ain't been asking for your trust, playboi. I been asking you to *watch*. Watch what I do. Watch where I stand when the real choices come down. Then *decide* if I *deserve* your trust. That's what you need to be doing with everyone you meet. Hell, fam, that's what everyone needs to do with everyone they meet."

I stare at them for a long second, the weight of that answer settling in.

Brit leans into me, whispering, "Gotta be honest. That was kinda bars."

I push her away. "Alright. So, what are you suggesting, then? That . . . what?"

"I'm just sayin' it's going to take more than the bougie but admittedly necessary cleanse I offered to Almeister to get the corruption out of the System itself. I can deprogram an individual, but to un-brainwash the whole machine . . . ? Shit. That's why you're gonna need a fresh blueprint. And that's why you need to get to the Mid-Meridian Plane. Also, to pick up your girl Zerastian, but the other upside to being there is that you will be able to reframe some shit."

I squint as if that will somehow grant me insight that I don't have. It won't. And it doesn't.

"Okaaaaay, fine. So, how do we access this Mid-Meridian Plane, then?"

"You know the serpent? Actually, serpent*s*. There's more than one."

I avoid Perg's stare. "Yeah, yeah, I know them."

"You gotta do battle."

"I figured that much, but are you saying . . . ? Are you saying that the serpents . . . ?"

"I'm saying that the serpents are the gatekeepers for the Mid-Meridian Plane, yes."

Un. Real. *Jesus.* Not only did I not know that this Mid-Meridian Plane existed, I didn't know the Giant Serpent of the Mokeisan is its flippin' gatekeeper. I thought the serpent was just a cool boss to battle. I had no clue it served a purpose greater than just being a baddie in a set piece.

Meridia is like a Russian nesting doll of traumatic obstacles.

"So, to access the plane, we have to defeat the serpents?"

"No, to access the plane you have to defeat *a* serpent. Once *all* the serpents are defeated, access to the plane will be shut down."

"Of course it will."

"What's that, my G?"

"Nothing. This is all very challenging; you know that, right?"

"I mean, obviously, fam. But that's what's up. As the Warden of Protection, I need you to understand something, see: Protection ain't about buildin' walls. It ain't about throwin' up shields and hopin' nothin' gets through. That's just defense. Protection is about knowin' what's worth riskin' yourself for. It's about steppin' up *before* the threat even lands, about holdin' the line even when you know the line is razor thin."

I frown to myself. Because I *think* I get it? But—

"You can lock a door, post up guards, wrap yourself in armor thick as an ironclad oath, but if what's inside ain't solid? If the foundation is already cracked? Then all that defense is just buyin' time."

"Oooooookay. So—"

"Real protection? That's makin' sure what you're guardin' is worth the fight in the first place."

"Right, no, I get that, but—"

"So ask yourself, playboi: When you strip it all back, when you peel off the titles, the System, the expectations . . . what are you really protectin'? And, who's protectin' you?"

I stare at them to make sure they're finished. After a moment, when it seems that no more is forthcoming, I start. "Fine, so then—"

"You gotta—"

"I got it! Okay! I got it! Thank you! That's . . . extremely helpful. Now, may we get Almeister into the Pulse Well now and reconnect him to the Heart Guard, please?"

"Ain't no thing but a chicken wing, baby."

Richemerion heads out to retrieve Almeister while Seph cozies up to me.

"The Warden is very wise, are they not?"

I look at her big, earnest, hopeful eyes and with only a passing amount of guilt about the number of lies I feel like I'm heaping on her, say, "Pfft. The wisest."

You have been offered a Quest!
"Heart Guard Member [Zerastian Teronia] is currently in holding on the [Mid-Meridian Plane]. Seek [Zerastian] on the [Mid-Meridian Plane] by defeating a [Giant Serpent of the Mokeisan]."
Do you wish to accept this Quest?
[Yes] [No]

Blowing out my lips (quietly, so that everyone doesn't know how kind of ambivalent I'm feeling about it all), I reach out and press [Yes].

Tremendous!
Quest: "Seek [Zerastian] on the [Mid-Meridian Plane] . . ."
[ACCEPTED]

Welp. I'm in it now. And I hope that getting Almeister reconnected to the Heart Guard is successful, because, frankly, I'm also still holding out some kind of hope that if he can once again become the Almeister I knew (well, not *knew*, exactly, but expected and planned to know), then I'll get just that much additional amount of steer when it comes to plotting next steps.

So to speak.

I look at the wizard floating in the Well, his arms drifting slightly at his sides, fingers moving like he's feeling the texture of the space itself. His eyes are half lidded, but not in exhaustion, more like a man listening to a song he once knew, trying to hum along before the melody returns to him fully or something.

I turn to Richemerion. "How much of him do we actually *have* back?" I ask, keeping my voice low, like speaking too loudly might break the spell. "Like, *back* back? How much of the old Almeister is with us now."

Richemerion tilts their head, considering. "I mean . . . we *definitely* got more wizard than we got weirdo, so that's a big W. But, like . . . what percentage of mans is precorruption versus still maybe a little scrambled? Hard to say exactly. The whole process of reintegrating him won't be completely complete until he's Guarded up. After that, I'd say try to keep him from being exposed to any kind of Dark Mezmer for, like, I dunno, a full Lunar Rotation. He'll need time to set."

I love that we're talking about the guy like he's a soufflé that might collapse if someone slams a door too hard.

Almeister, who has been listening but not interrupting, clears his throat lightly. "If I might be so bold as to contribute to an analysis of my own existential state"—he lifts a hand, flexing his fingers like he's trying to recall a forgotten spell—"I feel quite whole. And if there are lingering fractures, I daresay they are likely to only add character."

Persephone claps her hands and tugs on my new coat. "That sounds like him. Like Father has always spoken. Father?"

"Yes, Daughter?"

"You feel better?"

"At the least, I no longer feel like an old kettle that someone's been using to brew nightmares, so I'd say it's an improvement."

"Okay," I breathe. "So, Al, first let's take a look at your Stats and all that good stuff, see how you're situated, and then we'll get you reconnected to the Heart Guard, yeah?" By which I mean, check to see if there's any residual funk baked into his cake, but I don't say that, obviously.

He eyes me, still a little unsure seeming. I'm hoping that once he's reconnected to the Heart Guard, we can put this whole "Brucillian" thing away. For now. I know I'm going to have to deal with it at some point (by which I mean figure out exactly where the whole Brucillian runner got started and who started it), but for now, I just want to keep moving forward, knock out this next Quest, and see what this whole "flip the script" ambiguity that Richemerion is being all cagey about is all about.

Y'know . . .

Progressing.

Almeister's personal details are now projected for us all to see.

[Almeister T. Wizard]

>Mezmer Type:
Two-Type

>Foundation:
Wizard

>Resonance Tier:
Steelshard [Recovering – Current: Ironspark]

>Affinities:
***Stellari:* [High]**
***Splicecraft:* [High]**

>Statistics:
Mental: *Steelshard Level 2 [Recovering]*
Physical: *Steelshard Level 3 [Recovering]*
Aura: *Steelshard Level 1 [Recovering]*
Animus: *Manasteel Level 1 [Recovering]*

>Abilities:
Gravitas VIII

Shaking Off the Dust
Seen Too Much XXI
The Long Pause II
Old Hands III
Final Kindness III
Crook Spine, Steel Back I

>Spell(s):
***Starflare II* [Stellari]**
***Void Busk* [Stellari]**
***Whisper Magnetar III* [Stellari]**
***Threadtouch I* [Splicecraft]**
***Borrowed Pulse IV* [Splicecraft]**
***Binding Bind V* [Splicecraft]**
***Concordance Veil* [Splicecraft]**
***Symbiotic Latch* [Splicecraft]**
***Orbitwalker* [Stellari]**
***Luminary Brand* [Stellari]**
***Eventide Crown* [Stellari]**
***Singularity Merge IX* [Splicecraft]**

Heart Guard Member [Almeister T. Wizard] is requesting [Full Reintegration] into your Heart Guard. Do you wish to allow this reintegration?
[Yes] [No]

Hell. Yes.

I reach out, press [Yes], and breathe a sigh of relief. Thank Richemerion. It worked! It appears to have actually worked. Finally, *finally*, something seems to be going right.

"Bruce!"

"What?"

"Did you seriously not listen earlier when I said don't jinx yourself?"

"Oh, stop being so superstitious, Bruce. That's not how jinxes—"

Before I can think out the remainder to myself, the Pulse Well *shudders*. It begins glowing in a different way than it normally glows, and then the glow intensifies, flooding the chamber with a sudden burst of too-bright light.

"My eyestalks!" Perg shouts.

I also avert my eyes to avoid having my corneas fried by a Mezmeric blast, and that's when . . .

The whispers begin.

A layered chorus of voices, thin, distant, and *many*.

"What the hell is that?"

"I dunno, Bruce. Does that sound like Mandarin to you?"

"Nightwind?" I call for Brit.

"Yeah?" she asks, squinting to avoid the light.

"You hear that?"

"What? The whispers?"

"Yeah. You know what language that is? What they're saying?"

"No. I've never heard it before."

"It's the vestiges," Richemerion says.

"Vestiges of what?" I ask.

"The residual echoes of the corruption workin' their way outta his core self. Like smoke leavin' old wood, know what I'm sayin'?"

"I do, mi Warden," Jameson notes.

The whispers swell, rising and falling in strange, wavering patterns, as if whatever's unraveling inside him is protesting its departure. Then . . . they *escalate.* Physically. Like old ghosts, they swirl in the air, vibrating throughout the Well, and for a split second, I feel something reaching. Not physically, exactly, but . . . reaching all the same.

And Almeister's eyes *snap open.*

His pupils are *huge*, irises glinting with something sharp and ancient. He inhales sharply, mouth slightly open, like something is crawling into—or out of—his throat.

"Is this normal?" I ask Richemerion.

"Compared to what, my boi? Ain't no normal. All corruption is a perturbation, and perturbation be perturbin' in their own way."

"Al?" I call out. "How we doing?"

Almeister's mouth *moves*, but it's not his voice that comes out. The sound is jagged, distorted. Like two voices layered atop one another; one his, the other something else. **"The vessel is reclaimed, but the remnants remain. The roots of old rot do not release without protest. Witness. Grieve. Forget."**

And then—

Clap.

The sound cracks through the chamber, sharp and immediate.

But it's not a thunderclap or anything like that. It's Almeister's own hands. He's clapped them together with force, a sudden snap that sends a pulse of controlled magic through the air.

And while the Well *still* shudders, the whispers . . .

Cut out. They just cease. Stop. The end.

The glow dims. The air settles. And the presence, the *vestiges*, retract. Or go away. Or do whatever vestiges do when their vestigial manifestations are no more.

"That was intense, fool."

It was.

Almeister exhales slowly, rolling his shoulders as though shaking off something heavy. His eyes flick toward me, clearer now. Normal. Entirely his.

"Carpathian!" he calls out. "When did you get here?"

ACT THREE

A DISH BEST SERVED COLD (BLOODED)

CHAPTER TWENTY

Richemerion is being good enough to escort us back to Sheila so that we don't have to run a reverse trial gauntlet. They walk us out with that same effortless, almost lazy gait, the kind that says, "I have all the time in the world, and none of it is wasted."

Almeister moves with quiet assurance now, his presence steadier. The frantic edge is gone, replaced by a deliberate ease, like one who has found the shore after drifting at sea for too long. There's a clarity in his gaze, a sense of someone who may remember everything but is no longer ruled by it. The experience lingers in him, not as a burden but as a mark of what he's endured and overcome.

And that shit is a relief, I won't lie. Between being in the presence of Richemerion and a now fully reintegrated Almeister, for the first time . . . I feel like being in control isn't just a Spell: it's a state of being that I can embrace.

But then . . . I see that crane. The one who was watching before. And I don't like it. It seems like it's up to something.

I ask Richemerion, "Hey, what's the deal with the crane?"

"Which crane?"

"That crane. The one staring at us."

Richemerion looks at the bird. The crane seems to nod. Richemerion nods back.

"That's Percival," he tells me.

"Who is Percival?"

"They are."

"No, I know that, I mean—"

"I know what you mean, fam. They just be protectin'."

"Protecting what? I thought you're the Protector."

"Even Protectors need protection, know what I'm sayin'?"

"Oh, sure," I lie. Because . . . who cares? We're almost at Sheila.

Upon arriving, the car appears to have been given a detail job by some unknown (but appreciated) cleaning team, and Richemerion claps their hands together. "A'ight, this where we part ways, troop. But lemme pull your coat for a minute, Carpathian?"

They wag their finger, drawing me to the side. I gesture to the others *I'll be right back* as the Warden of Protection leads me away.

"Yes?" I ask, noticing the crane, still craned over being all cranelike.

"Look here, yo. I know you got shit to do. People to see, battles to win, choices to make, and whatnot. But, more than anything, you got *you* to figure out, know what I'm sayin'?"

I don't answer because I assume that's rhetorical. They go on . . .

"I ain't sayin' you lost, word? But you ain't exactly found neither. And that's the real battle. So don't be out here fightin' the whole world 'til you get that straight first, ya feel me?"

That hangs in the air for a long moment before I realize it isn't rhetorical.

"Yeah, I—"

"Ya ain't gotta answer, fam. Don't know about it; be about it. Ya heard?" I nod. Then . . . "Nah, bruh, shit ain't rhetorical, tell me you heard. You've got that hearing problem."

"Oh, yes, I heard."

"Bet."

Richemerion gives me a gentle tap on my chest, right where the Heart lives, and we head back over to the car. They nod at the others, then they look at Almeister one last time.

"Glad to see you, maestro. Don't be a stranger."

"You as well, Warden."

Richemerion licks their lips, nods at the lot of us, and says, "Hold steady, troop. Y'all gonna be a'ight. But, you know, if you need the Rich Mary, holla, and the Rich Mary shall appear . . . Unless it's the season of Boundless Wonder, then I might be chillin' and it'll take me a minute, but I still got you."

They tilt their head back, inhale deep like they're tasting the air, and then grin. "A'ight, then. Time to ghost."

They slap their palms together once, and the space around them ripples like heat off summer pavement. The crane, Percival, lets out a low, throaty warble and spreads its wings. Just as it does, a gust of wind kicks up from nowhere, sweeping dust and loose leaves into a tight spiral. It sounds like the turning of ancient pages or the shuffle of footsteps too distant to place.

Then, Richemerion steps backward . . . and vanishes.

Not fades, not blinks, not even a dramatic *poof.* Just *gone.* Like they were never there at all.

Percival lingers for a moment more, regarding us with what I perceive as a look of smug satisfaction. Then, with a slow and deliberate motion, they lift off, banking hard into the sky until they're nothing but a dark shape against the horizon.

We just stand there for a second.

". . . Okay, honestly, that was pretty fuckin' sick," Brit finally says.

Jameson grins like he just witnessed a legend in the making. "Mi nah lie; if coolness had a Warden, mi tink mi just meet dem."

"Properly enigmatic," Almeister muses, adjusting his cuffs. "Theatric, yet efficient. So very Rich Mary."

Persephone nods with satisfaction. "A true Warden's exit. Always present, even when unseen."

And Perg rounds out the commentary with, "How come the crane got a big, dramatic exit too, fool? Like, was that shit coordinated, or . . . ?"

I exhale. "Let's just load up. We got squabbles to attend to, fam. Uh, sorry. We have battles to . . . It . . . They . . . It's a very addictive pattern of speech to slip into."

"This is one dusty-ass desert, fool," Perg says, coughing hard as we make our way toward the town of Elderkeep, the horizon glimmering in the late afternoon suns like a mirage. "You're sure this is the place we're supposed to be headed?"

Brit's maps very clearly indicated that Elderkeep is the epicenter of the Mokeisan Desert, the last known location of Zerastian, and the location where we are to seek the Gauntlet of Sorenthali.

Even though he didn't get his own hands on it until book seven, the Gauntlet of Sorenthali was actually the first artifact I ever dreamed of. It was, to a greater or lesser degree, kind of the inspiration for everything that came next: the Blade of the Starfallen, the Obsidian Shield of Baelus, the Cerulean Tunic . . . It's possible none of it would exist without the Gauntlet. I was going to have Carpathian find it first, in book one, but then the Blade of the Starfallen popped into my mind, and I couldn't shake it. I kept wanting to introduce the Gauntlet sooner, but, as we know, stories will take themselves where they want to go sometimes.

Canonically speaking: Forged in the lost city of Sorenthali, the Gauntlet was created by early Mezmeric scholars as a stabilizing force designed to harness and refine the chaotic flow of Mezmer into pure, unerring intent. Unlike crude amplifiers of power, the Gauntlet does not simply magnify Mezmer, it translates will **into reality**, allowing its wielder to manipulate Mezmer without the risk of instability or corruption. It's hidden beneath Elderkeep itself, in a place called Origin Pass.

Like the Gauntlet, Origin Pass was also one of the first places I thought of—or had placed into my brain—when Meridia started growing there. Which is why it's called Origin Pass. It was kind of loosely based on this tunnel I had to navigate to get to my locker at work. It was this gray, municipal shaft of sadness that I kind of have to be grateful for because it triggered my ruminations about a world far removed from my reality.

Careful what you wish for.

In any case, the Gauntlet landed there and was sealed away after the Great Collapse. (Or maybe it was the other way around? Maybe Origin Pass collapsed because the Gauntlet needed to be sealed? I can't remember exactly.)

But I *do* know that, in my mind, the Gauntlet wasn't just hidden for safety. It was locked away to share space with something that came into being before even Mezmer itself.

A thing called "the Gnarl."

Not a tangible being of any kind but an artifact of twisting pressure and stone that was riven and never healed straight. A force that couldn't be destroyed, only tricked into slumber. Until, of course, someone dared come for the Gauntlet.

(To be clear: That never actually made it into the book because I was on a deadline and decided to skip it, but that's the backstory. It's fine. Nobody necessarily needs to know all that shit, but it's probably good that I know about it, given our current predicament.)

Regardless, I did become slightly worried when I asked Sheila to direct us to where we are now and she paused for a long moment before saying, "It's your choice."

I have rolled all the windows down to avoid everyone getting high as hell from Jameson's smoke, but now that we're into the Mokeisan, the wind whipping the sand and dust into the car is worse. We're likely not even gonna get giggly. Just Mezmer-lung.

"Well, it is a desert," Brit chokes out.

"Yeah," Perg gasps, "but this is like a desert you find inside another desert. Desert 2.0."

Glancing in the rearview, I see Jameson, unbothered, smoking, and Persephone covering her mouth to avoid getting high and/or suffocated. Almeister is looking at me, smiling. He nods in an affirmation that he is back to form and with us once more. I nod in return, grateful to have an actual guide in our company. I finally feel like, perhaps, our journey will have greater focus. Direction. Intention. He made sure Carpathian was centered in the books; I'm relieved to know that he will now be able to do the same for us.

We zip past a knotty, gnarled sign nailed to a crooked post that marks the town's entrance. The faded lettering reads "Elderkeep," barely legible through layers of peeling paint and accumulated grime. The sign creaks in the hot breeze, a haunting reminder of a place that time forgot. It has much more of a "gunfight at the O.K. Corral" energy than I was expecting.

The Mokeisan Desert has a certain rugged beauty to it, not unlike the Mojave—which is how I imagined, or at least described it in the books—but Perg is right. It's more than that. Or less.

The ground is cracked and parched, ridges of desiccation spiderwebbing across the landscape. Scraggly, lifeless plants dot the terrain, branches reaching out like skeletal hands clawing at the air, while the suns beat down relentlessly.

Instinctively, I worry that I need to find some Banana Boat SPF 1500 sunscreen. I have always had an evolutionary disadvantage when it comes to the sunrays. I fry easily. Or, I did, when I was still a clearly less complicated version of myself. Just Bruce. Now that I have gained a few notches in the ol' Resonance Tier, I may be more burn resistant. If I can bounce back after getting lit up with a spellsword like I did at Jeomandi's, I suppose I'm at less of a risk of overtanning than I used to be.

Jameson takes a long drag from his seemingly never-dying doobie. He exhales slowly, the smoke curling upward before dissipating. "Dis place be mad lookin' like de end of de world, mon."

Persephone leans forward and whispers, "I can feel the remnants of some type of ancient Mezmer here, but—"

She is interrupted by Almeister shouting something unintelligible as he begins spasming, his body jerking back, forth, and side to side like a Ludacris song.

"Father!"

"Al?!"

"What's happening to him?" Brit shouts.

"Is it ants?" Perg—now grown to approximately the size of a French Bulldog—calls out. "Does he got ants in his . . . robe? Desert ants are the worst!"

Persephone and Jameson grab hold of the old codger in an attempt to settle him down.

"Wha gwan, mi big wizard?! Ya bout gon' crazy again nah!"

"Father. Father, what is it? What's taken you over?"

His eyes, wild and cloudy, dart back around, panic pouring out of him.

Then, out of nowhere, he LEAPS forward into the front seat and grabs me about the neck like Homer Simpson choking out Bart back in the days when we all still thought choking children was funny. (Privately, I still find it pretty hilarious. I'm just not gonna say it out loud.)

"Father!"

I try to wrench his hands away, but he is showing a far greater amount of strength than seems reasonable for an old man in his postresurrectioned state.

"Get. Him. Off. Get. Him. Off," I work out between breaths.

Everyone else is now tugging at his hands and arms, but to no avail. It's some straight up Linda Blair in *The Exorcist* type shit. But now, I can make out the words he's garbling.

He's saying, "False Prophet! Fake Saviour!"

Which is not something anyone wants to be called, but certainly not me.

"Father! Stop! Father! Please!"

I can feel my eyes bugging out of my head, and I wish Toxin Darts had modulation. As in, I wish they weren't fatal. If I could just hit him with one as a knockout drop, that would be helpful.

Before I have to make a decision about what to do or not do to pry his Crypt Keeper's mitts off my esophagus, Persephone lets out a cry of "CANDLION-OGRUMNIAC!" or something like that. I'm piecing it out in my head phonetically.

Almeister's grip loosens, his eyes roll back in his head, and he falls back, drained of hostility juice.

I feel at my neck the way people do when they've been choked by old wizards. Or probably anybody.

"What did you say?" I cough.

"A passivity Ritual. An old family recipe, as it were, that Father used to use on me when I was a child and did not wish to go to sleep. Normally, it is reserved for use on unruly children, but . . ."

Her shoulders sag. She's realizing something similar to what Carpathian realized in book nine: The child has become the parent.

"Thank you," I say, clearing my throat. Then . . . "What the hell just happened?! I thought he was fixed! I THOUGHT HE WAS FIXED!"

"I-I . . . don't know," Seph stammers, looking at her dad with renewed anxiety.

"What were you starting to say?" I ask. "About feeling some kind of ancient Mezmer when we came across the border?"

"It was . . . old. But not just in the sense of age. More like . . . like a residue. Not alive but not gone either. Lingering. Stuck to the place."

Probably should have seen that coming. The place is called friggin' Elderkeep.

Jameson blows out some smoke. "Ya mean it be like when ya leave a kettle pon de stove too long an' even after ya take it off, de metal still hot?"

Seph nods. "Precisely. Like heat that loiters long after the fire has gone out."

Brit drums her fingers against the door. "Shit."

"What is it?" I ask.

"Richemerion did say, clearly, that we'd need to keep him from being exposed to Dark Mezmer for a full Lunar Rotation."

"Shit."

"Exactly. But . . ."

"But what?"

"I dunno, just . . . I get that it's leftover energy, residual Mezmer, but it still shouldn't cause him to flip that much."

"You know that for sure?" I ask.

"No, not for sure, but extending the hot-pot analogy: If I touch still heated metal, I pull my hand back. I don't, y'know, go off choking motherfuckers."

There's a long beat. Brit turns around to look at Seph, whom I see in the rearview mirror cocking her head and frowning.

"What is it?" Brit asks.

"I'm sorry, I've just yet to become fully acclimated to your recarbonified speech patterns." Her eyes flit back to her father's slack form. "Perhaps it reacted to something within him. If it was a residue, then perhaps it has clung to something yet fully purged from his essence. Some reality he has yet to let go of."

"You think so?" I ask.

"I don't know. I'm just freeballing."

Another beat.

"Say again?"

"Free spitting? I'm trying to adopt some of your reconstitutional idioms."

"Oh, uh, spitballing, I think you mean."

"Yes. That."

She puts on a strained smile that doesn't reach her eyes. She's trying so hard to connect with us. Me. It thumps my Heart.

"You're suggesting that whatever Mezmer is here has disentombed some buried . . . ?" Brit trails off.

"Yes?" Seph half answers, half asks. "Yes. If the Mezmer here has clung to something unresolved within him, something Father might not want to admit to even himself . . ."

She meets my eyes in the mirror with what I would call—for the first time—suspicion.

A terrible feeling crawls up my spine.

I've talked about it before, but . . .

I've always liked the idea of allies turning out to be enemies. It's one of my oldest tricks. Lull the reader into a sense of security and then rip the rug out. Give the heroes someone to trust and then make that trust a weapon. I did it in book seven, when one of Clan Catarinci's lieutenants, a guy called Shambonio, tried to run Carpathian over with a Soul Tractor.

A betrayal that comes from inside . . . Those always hit the hardest. That's the rule. Always someone who seemed above suspicion, too central to fall. Always someone the hero trusted completely.

I worried that Seph was that kind of figure when we first connected with her in Bell's View. I even kind of had some suspicions about Richemerion when we were heading there to meet. I suppose the Ninth Guardian could, somehow, be using Almeister as such a figure.

But . . .

And this is the part that really burns . . .

Maybe . . .

It's actually . . .

Me.

Maybe that's who *I* am to the others.

False Prophet. Fake Saviour.

Maybe *I'm* the villain.

"Should we turn back?" Brit asks.

"What?"

"Get him away from whatever this is that's causing him to have a relapse."

"That's maybe not a bad idea."

"As you suggested earlier, we shouldn't be trying to take on battles until we're at full strength. And if we're going to have to—" But that's all she's able to get out before an unholy noise shatters all of our concentrations.

Which isn't quite accurate, because "noise" doesn't fully capture the scope of what this is. It's more like . . . like all of the atoms in the universe colliding at the same time and ripping apart the heavens above and the earth below.

"Is that—?" Brit yells.

"I think so!" I shout back.

Sheila starts rumbling like she's thrown a gasket. The car shakes like we're in a Vitamix turned to level four, but quickly escalating.

And that's when I see it through the windshield. It's barely possible to make it out through the tempestuous wall of swirling brown that has been kicked up, but as it hurtles closer, it gets easier to see, emerging from within the maelstrom like a brutal magic trick.

It's . . .

It's . . .

Yep. There it is.

It's the giant fangs of a giant serpent, mouth open wide, motoring hard in our direction.

CHAPTER TWENTY-ONE

Fuuuuuuuuuuuuuuuck ME!" I hear Brit shout as the unhinged jaw of the snake opens wider still. But . . . when I look over at Brittany, I see that while her eyes are wide, her mouth is still closed.

It wasn't her who just shouted.

. . . It was Persephone.

Huh.

Well, while it seems very, very bad that she's reacting that way from the perspective of assessing how much danger we're in, given that it's not her normal reaction to stuff, on the positive side, she really is starting to pick up some idioms.

"*That* is the Giant Serpent of the Mokeisan?!" she wails.

"Technically, it's *a* Giant Serpent of the Mokeisan!" I respond, half shouting, half groaning. "But yes!"

"It's huge!"

"Yeah, well, 'giant' isn't intended to be ironic!"

However, it *is* an underreporting, because my literary depiction of the Giant Serpent of the Mokeisan Desert was—like I'm finding so many of my depictions to have been—woefully inadequate.

In the text, the length of the thing was said "to stretch well over three hundred feet." Which is true, but in this case, "well over" means, like, more than three times that. It's close to a thousand feet long, easy. The coils of the body appear as thick as a fortress wall, and the scales shimmer with a molten sheen, reflecting the blistering desert suns in hues of fiery gold and obsidian black, which kind of causes it to blend seamlessly with the storm and the dunes all around.

In other words: It's big, tough, and hard to see. We may be in even more trouble than I prepared myself for.

"We don't have the Gauntlet yet, fool!" Perg hollers in my ear.

I don't even bother to respond because I'm not sure what he wants me to do about it.

This whole situation reminds me somehow of that scene with Azteral the Punisher. The one when Carpathian was bludgeoned and seemed doomed, and he asked for Richemerion to save him. Richemerion granted him the inaugural Temple of the Body and kept him alive long enough to fight another day. That's how I feel now. Like I'm cornered and need help and . . .

I wonder if . . . now that we've met, and we're besties and all . . . ?

Richemerion? Uh, my G? I don't know if you can hear me, but if you can . . . I mean, you said to trust what you do, not what you say, so . . . if, y'know, if you can find the time, it would go a long way toward building that trust if you could, I dunno, provide some assistance here?

Please?

Your Quest has been [MODIFIED]!

Oh shit! Oh, shit! Ask and ye shall receive! Ye, of moderate but deeply skeptical faith!

Current Quest:
"Heart Guard Member [Zerastian Teronia] is currently in holding on the [Mid-Meridian Plane]. Seek [Zerastian] on the [Mid-Meridian Plane] by **DEFEATING a [Giant Serpent of the Mokeisan]."**

Has been [MODIFIED] to:
"Heart Guard Member [Zerastian Teronia] is currently in holding on the [Mid-Meridian Plane.] Seek [Zerastian] on the [Mid-Meridian Plane] by ***BINDING* a [Giant Serpent of the Mokeisan]."**

Wait. The "modification" isn't granting me the Gauntlet or firing down lightning bolts on the serpent or some shit but just changing it so that I now have to wrestle it into submission rather than just defeat it?

Yes. That is exactly right!

How is that better?!

You are being, if we may say, quite bossy for someone asking for help.
Do you wish to accept this [MODIFIED] Quest?
[Yes] [No]

Man, come on! This isn't—

"TURN! TURN! TURN!" Perg's screaming loud enough to shatter glass, his eyes bulging from his shell.

"I AM TURNING!" I haul the wheel hard to the left, and Sheila lurches, tires skidding over sand that's more liquid than solid now. The rear end fishtails, and I see the serpent's jaws clamp shut right where we'd been a heartbeat ago. Its teeth, each one the size of a grown man (a big, grown man, defensive lineman size), slam together with a crunch that vibrates through my bones.

"The Quest has been modified!"

"What?" Brit asks.

"The Quest! It's been modified!"

"I heard you! What do you *mean*?"

"We no longer have to defeat the serpent!"

"What do we have to do?!"

"We have to *bind* it!"

"Huh?!"

"What I said!"

"*Bind* it?"

"Yes!"

"Is that going to be harder or easier?"

"How the hell do I know?!"

The Notification hasn't yet disappeared because I've yet to accept or decline it.

Your Quest has been [MODIFIED]!
"Heart Guard Member [Zerastian Teronia] is currently in holding on the [Mid-Meridian Plane. Seek [Zerastian] on the [Mid-Meridian Plane] by *****BINDING*** a [Giant Serpent of the Mokeisan]."**
Do you wish to accept this [MODIFIED] Quest?
[Yes] [No]

Son of a Bisquick batter! Obviously, I mean *obviously*, I have to say "yes," but as much as I wasn't sure how we would defeat it, I have even less of an idea how we bind it. In the last book, it took an enormously OP Carpathian and some equally pumped-up Pergamon and Teleri to bring down the one they bested. But the group of us is supposed to make this one tap out?

This does not feel like a fair fight!

Regardless, I press [Yes] and get a follow-up Notification.

Excellent!
[MODIFIED] Quest: "Seek [Zerastian] on the [Mid-Meridian Plane] by binding a [Giant Serpent of the Mokeisan]."
[ACCEPTED]

Quest Requirements:
You may not forfeit any Party member prior to seeking.

Oh, for funky butt's sake!

There are innumerable things I don't like about that requirement, but most of all is the fact that I'm starting to learn that when I get certain Notifications and requirements and so forth, it seems to be a type of foreshadowing. Which is something I do in my writing all the time. Which, of course, means that it's something that happens on Meridia all the time, and that's likely where I developed the wont to do it, but—

"Bruce! Jesus! How many times do we have to have the jinx conversation?!"

"Shut up, Bruce! I need to focus! I don't have time for a debate!"

"Well . . . to be fair, all of your thoughts are happening in the blink of an eye. It's not like you're writing them all out in a book. You have as much time as you want."

"Yeah . . . I guess you're right. Okay, well, in that case, look . . . I still don't know if I believe the whole 'jinxing myself' thing is really— "

"Look out!" Persephone calls, causing me to realize that I am just kind of zoning out here, still staring at the Notification.

"Goddammit, Bruce! I told you I didn't have time for a debate!"

I spin the wheel again just as the serpent turns back on me and unhinges its jaws so wide it could swallow an orca whole, bellowing forth a roar that lets me know we all must have Mezmer-protected hearing or something that's keeping us from being deafened because it sounds like every fire engine and police car in New York City has set off their sirens at once.

The desert is a nightmare of howling winds and the wail of a serpent so massive it feels like the sound alone should be crushing us. I still have the window down to let out the weed smoke, and now, sand and serpent breath blast me in the face as suddenly—almost impossibly suddenly—the serpent is attacking from the side. And also, once more from behind. And . . . unless my eyes deceive me (which they very well might, let's be real), from the other side as well. I squint around at the ascending chaos, trying to pinpoint exactly how that's possible. It feels like it's coming at us from all places at once.

And that's when I realize . . .

Duh.

It is.

"It's all of them!"

"What?" I barely hear Seph's voice call out.

"It's . . ." Realizing that there's no way my voice will carry over the tempest of noise, and remembering that I still have a Microblather Spell, I send the message to the whole Party.

"There's not just one serpent. There's a whole brood. No time to get into the details, just accept and adapt, please. Thanks. Love, Carpathian."

I try to be calm and don't put exclamation points at the ends of the sentences because I don't want anyone to panic. Which is probably stupid. But it made sense to me while I was composing them.

All four of the original giant serpent's giant serpent kin have us quartered and are ready to strike. I have a blinding sandstorm in my eyes, and I can't hear shit other than the overwhelming wail of the megasnakes singing out like an orchestra of doom, but in a sucky, gonna-end-my-life way rather than a cool, Wagnerian way.

For some reason, I decide to start screaming too. Like King Lear thundering back at the thundering storm thundering upon him. I don't manage anything as poetic as "Blow winds and crack your cheeks!" What I say just comes out as, "Gooblebohoodeedonow!" But it seems to do something, because, in an instant . . .

ZZZZZZZZZZWWWWWAAAAAHHHHHMMMMM.

Thump-thump. Thump-thump.

Control! My old friend! How I've missed you!

Mere feet from competing to see which of the four remaining members of the Giant Serpent Clan gets to swallow us like we were desert Jonah, the Spell lights up, and their huge, fangy faces freeze in place. I can feel that I (and by extension, Sheila) is just *that* much swifter now. I can sense Control is stepping up. We're not locked into their rhythm, explicitly. We can move slightly closer to my standard, normal, Bruce-moving-through-the-world pace.

It's pretty wild, this feeling of being able to move myself a little swifter than the frozen world around me. When Control levels up some more, I bet I'll be able to do all kinds of funny things when everyone else is frozen. Practical jokes like yanking the pants down on some bad guy or cracking an egg over their head or something. Such a thing would be an absolutely offensive waste of this kind of power, but it's kind of a nice distraction to my current level of existential threat to think about. It's gonna take a lot more than an egg crack to get out of this shit.

Control has also steadied the whirling sandstorm so that I can make out the details of the family of serpents. Unfortunately, it makes them more frightening rather than less. They're worse than anything I wrote.

Scales like black-glass mosaic, edges catching what little suns light pierces the storm, reflect fractured slashes of crimson and gold. Their eyes are pits of igneous brass, slitted pupils narrowing with a cold, intelligent malice that doesn't belong in a creature that size. Each one is a living warship, massive coils sliding over dunes with a low, ominous rumble that I can feel reverberating in my rib cage.

Which, I gotta be honest, is a pretty good bit of descriptive prose that creates a pang of regret that I'm only just thinking it to myself and not writing it down. Oh, well.

I lock eyes with Persephone in the back seat. I nod to her, reassuring, letting her know that everything is going to be all right. She nods back.

Wait.

She nods back?

She nods back. Just like me. In real time. Everyone else in the car is moving in slow motion, having been stilled to a greater or lesser degree by Control. But Seph doesn't appear affected by it in the same way. I'm not sure if it owes to her now being a part of the Heart Guard and her (as I now know she has) super pumped-up Mezmer levels that allows her to somehow piggyback off of my innate Abilities? Like, maybe because of her status and the fact that I synced with her before, now we share something in a similar way that Sheila and I do?

Whatever the reason, she is moving at full speed. At full speed . . . when she . . .

. . . opens the rear door and leaps out of the car . . .

"Protect Father!" she shouts.

"Seph!" I reach back for her, but she's gone, out of the barely-there-but-better-than-nothing safety of the Panamera and into the Thunderdome of serpent and sand.

Thump-thump. Thump . . . Thump.

SHWOOOOOOOOOOOOOOMMMMMMMMPPP.

As things go full speed again, two things happen at almost the exact same time.

I jerk hard on the wheel, and the serpents, so dead set on annihilation that they seem to have forgotten reason, all crash into one another.

And,

Persephone vaults toward them with a grace that shouldn't be possible on shifting sand, her garments snapping around her. Her hands flare with raw, unfiltered power, bright enough to burn spots into my vision.

With fluid precision, she pulls her arms into a tight circle, Mezmer flaring at her fingertips. She does a quarter spin, a move that—now that I know she has the Pulsariel Foundation—makes a lot of sense. Pulsariels are the equivalent of magical capoeiristas who can use their *sick dance moves* to control their powers. She's about to do history's most violent Tarantella on the group I am now choosing to identify as the Four Serpents of the Apocalypse.

A shimmer of light bursts from her hands, curling into a transparent dome around the serpents' collective heads. For a heartbeat, the beasts stop thrashing, their eight glowing eyes narrowing as one, as if searching for something unseen. Seph's managing a Mezmer-generated rope-a-dope. But the reprieve is short-lived. The shimmering sphere cracks under the sheer weight of the serpents' assembled wills, like glass under a boulder. The dome shatters, fragments of Mezmer spiraling away in glowing shards, sending Persephone tumbling off with them.

"Seph!"

And then . . .

Well. And then . . . as if this wasn't adequately blech-y enough, something *really* unfortunate happens.

The serpents, all four of them, begin, um, eating each other.

Which, on the one hand, could seem like a positive. Like, they're having an intrafamily squabble over which of them got the rest into this predicament where they find themselves being hammered on by a bunch of lesser-powered entities. And if that were the cause of their, uh, cannibalism, it would be fine. Let 'em turn on each other and take the group out that way.

But that's not what this appears to be.

What this appears to be is . . . they're consolidating themselves into one larger than large, mightier than mighty, bigger than the biggest big that ever bigged super snake.

Which is not something anybody wants. Except, probably, them.

I see one's head slide into the mouth of the second. The second into the third. And the third into the fourth. And now . . .

Now, the thing is easily a mile, a mile long, and we . . .

We are miles from home without a plan.

. . . Which is a huge flippin' drag. I'll be super honest.

CHAPTER TWENTY-TWO

"Ay, ay, ay, fool! What the fuck just happened?!" Brittany yells. (Or, no, that was Perg. Got confused for a second. I'm very freaked out right now at the four-serpents-in-one combo.)

"They're doing some kind of Voltron thing!"

"Did you know that could happen?!" Brit shouts. (This time, it *is* her. She's also hitting my arm while she yells at me.)

"Yeah, I just thought it would be funny not to mention it to anyone. NO, I didn't know!"

"So, now we have to bind all four at once?!"

"It would seem!"

The car jolts as the serpent's now small-town-size tail slams into the ground, kicking up a tidal wave of sand that all but buries us in seconds. The windshield is a wall of swirling brown, and the only thing I can hear is the roar of the storm and the overlapping bellows of a mile-long super snake.

"I can't see shit!" I shout, trying to shake enough sand off the windshield to get a glimpse of anything.

"Go! Just go!" Brit yells back.

"Go where?!"

"Look out! It's surrounding us, fool!" Perg yells. Sure enough, the serpent's entire body is now starting to encircle the vehicle. "It's going to try and squeeze us to death like a boa squeezewhelk!"

"The fuck's a squeezewhelk?!" Brit shouts.

"It's like a constrictor slug kind of a thing! Like a boa constrictor! But a slug!"

"Did you just make that up?" I ask him.

"Maybe? I can't tell what's real and what's not anymore!"

The serpent's tail coils inward, walls of muscle and scale slithering into place around us, closing in like a vise.

"It's boxing us in!" Brit's voice is tight, her eyes fixed on the encroaching scales of crushification.

"We're surrounded, fool!" Perg wails.

"No shit!" I let him know.

I can't see Persephone. I don't know what's happened to her. All I can see is the massive wall of serpent closing in on all sides like a living moat.

Then a thought occurs to me . . . "Ray!"

"What?" Brit asks.

"Randolf's Radiant! Triple R! You wanted to see what you could do with it since it's been pumped up to Novice? Now is the time to find out!"

She doesn't linger long in the devilish look that sneaks onto her face, but it appears adequately impish enough to let me know that she's just been waiting for this moment. She starts working her hands in a ball, in the Tai Chi manner that precedes the expulsion of the Ray from her fingertips, and then . . .

"Wait!" I shout.

"What do you mean, wait?!"

"I don't know what will happen if you unleash it inside the car. We have to get out."

"Get out, fool? You really think that's the move?"

"I think we don't have a lot of good options, *ese*!"

"Yo! Easy on the *ese* shit!"

"Sorry, sorry. But yes, I think we have to—It's gonna crush us! We gotta move!"

Brit doesn't wait. She throws the passenger door open and leaps out, still forming the Ray with her hands. Perg mumbles something that sounds like "This some funky bullshit," but then he stumbles out of Sheila as well. I spin my head around to see a still-unconscious Almeister and unusually nonplussed Jameson chilling in the back seat.

"You got him?" I ask the monkey.

"Gwan, mi big Saviour. Don't gon' be no harm to find him."

He takes a puff of the joint, sticks out his hand, and offers me a hit; for just a moment, I consider that it might be the courage that I require, but then, realizing that since I ain't never got none of that Meridian chronic all up in me yet, I don't want to choose this moment to experiment. I wave him off, throw open the driver's side door, and leap out just in time to see Brittany let loose with a full blast of her newly amplified Ray game.

And, I'll tell ya, the difference between Beginner and Novice is no small potatoes.

The blast isn't just light—it's a column of sun's fire, raw and unfiltered, roaring forth from Brit's outstretched hands with a heat that singes the air and a brightness that momentarily turns the whole world white. A searing beam that slams into the serpent's coiling mass with the force of a meteor strike.

The serpent's scales light up in a cascade of hues, crimson and gold flaring with every point of contact. The air cracks with the sound of shattering crystal as Triple R carves a path across the humongous serpent's side, scales blistering, a shock wave rippling out that sends dunes collapsing in on themselves.

It rears back with a roar that rattles the plane, peeling away from the car in an instinctual recoil, exposed flesh hissing where the Triple R's heat has peeled back its natural armor and left raw, reddened patches of mortal vulnerability.

"Holy shit, yo!" Perg yelps, antennae quivering with what I hope is excitement and not imminent defecation.

Looking around, I can't find Persephone, which worries me more than almost everything else, if I'm being fantastically honest with myself.

"Where are you going?" Brit calls as I take advantage of the injured beast and leap into the air, somehow skying far higher than I thought I could, antigravitationally landing on top of its injured body and preparing to jump off to the other side.

"Just keep it busy!" I shout back in my most Carpathian-y way. I feel like I even hear a hint of an accent, just like I heard Brittany using in Garr Haven.

Just as I set myself to leap down . . . it decides to rise up, throwing me to the ground and lifting itself into the air, Slitherus Prime's mighty shadow now passing over my head, blotting out any hint of the suns light still trying to make its way through the melee. An omen of disaster if I've ever seen one.

"Damn it! Perg, try and flank it!" I bark as I hit the ground in a roll and bounce to my feet.

"How do you expect me to flank it?! I'm a snail, not a ninja, *cabrón*!"

"Get big! Go Mothra to its Godzilla!"

"Mothra lost!"

"You know what I mean!"

Perg curses in Spanish, but then embiggens the ever-loving shell out of himself and grows to almost-but-not-quite half the size of the serpent. It feels like we are attempting to fight off the Mississippi River with our bare hands—if the Mississippi River had both teeth and a personal vendetta, and could also raise itself into the sky and whip around violently and was, y'know, a snake.

BOOM!

The serpent's vast body comes crashing down, causing the whole desert to jump in response. It is, quite literally, a small earthquake. One that causes a fissure in the Meridia that I can see. And out of that fissure . . . energy. Some kind of tangible energy that I *can't* quite see, but I can feel. It's not exactly Mezmer, but it is Mezmer adjacent.

Oh, snap. That must be it. The Mid-Meridian Plane. The place Zerastian is being held.

I have half a mind to just jump into the newly formed fjord and see if I can escape the serpent's wrath that way, but the Quest clearly stated that I need to bind the creature while not forfeiting a member of my soul patrol. (Which is what I almost thought of naming the Heart Guard back in the day, because they are bound to Carpathian "Heart and Soul," but there are already tons of usages of soul patrol in twentieth-century pop culture and I didn't wanna risk a lawsuit. Also, I worried that there might be implications of cultural appropriation, so I thought it best to steer clear. Momma ain't raise no fool.)

Also, there's no goddamn way I'm going anywhere without Mollie again. Uh . . . Persephone. Seph. Not without her. Just . . .

No.

And out of the blue . . . a Notification from the Heart.

Hello, Saviour! Just checking in. Things appear, from here, to be awfully perilous. And, while—as previously discussed—the preference would be that you come to learn to make these decisions on your own, you can only do that if you are still alive. So, with

that in mind, one would be remiss not to remind you that . . . YOU HAVE THE BLADE OF THE STARFALLEN AVAILABLE TO YOU. Perhaps that could be helpful? {COURTESY MESSAGE #32}

Well, don't I just feel like a big old dip dop?

Shit! Yes! The Blade! I go to reach for it in my new fancy hip holster, but . . . ! It's not there.

Crap! Where is it?

Aw, damn, I now recall that I shrunk it down and gave it to Brit for safekeeping, but then forgot to get it back when I got the new gear. (So many moving parts.)

I look to see if I can find where she might be in all the tumult. She's now blasting more Radiant Ray, which, despite her improved dexterity with it, might as well be called Flickering Flybys for all the good they're doing now that the serpent knows they're coming and is able to dodge, showing an impressive nimbleness given its bulk. But, whatever, the blasts at least allow me to identify where she is.

"Yo! Nightwind!" I shout in her direction.

"What?" her strained voice returns.

"Blade!"

"What?!"

"The Blade of the Starfallen! I need it!"

"Jesus fuck, man! Why didn't you take it back when you got fucking pockets?!"

"I didn't think about it!" I start to go into an apology, but then, remembering that we are enduring an existential threat that would make Frank Herbert blush, I stop myself. "Whatever! Just let me get the friggin' Blade! Please!"

We make our way to join one another far closer to the head of the long, slithering Satan than I would like. Thankfully, Perg is distracting it by backing that giant snail ass up into its snake temple and causing it to snap at him instead of chomping down on us. I'm also trying not to look back at the impossible length of the thing, thinking that it's like the horizontal version of standing on the edge of a skyscraper. Don't look to see how far the fall is and you might not throw up.

"Here!" Brit shouts, reaching into her garb and withdrawing the miniature Blade of the Starfallen. I somehow manage to grab it from her palm and avoid dropping it into the churning sea of sand (which would just be *too* too), and make it full size just in time to hear a voice yell . . .

"Look out!"

And at that Valkyrie-like warning, I turn to see Seph, rising into the sky like a phoenix.

"Where were you?!" I call to her elevating form.

"I took a tumble! But, again, I need to say . . . Look out!"

She points and I turn my head to see the serpent swatting big Perg away, sending him flailing off with an "*Ayiiiiiiiiiii*," before turning back to take me and Brit into its screaming mouth. I'm hoping it just gulps us up rather than skewer us with its gigantic fangs. I'd kind of like to die in one piece for some reason. I guess, just in case we aren't completely disintegrated by its stomach acid, and someone can dig us out for an open-casket funeral. I think that would be classier and give everyone a sense of closure.

But, before either fate can befall we three . . .

. . . a dozen glowing figures explode into existence between us and maceration.

Persephone (Persephone*s*? Persephoneses? Persephoni?) Whatever. A pluralization of Persephone appears in a flash of brilliance, confusing the snake and causing it to turn its attention to the swarm of sorcerers instead of me and Brit.

"Holy shit," I whisper, watching in awe the power she's able to wield. It's like staring into the heart of a star, beautiful and terrifying in equal measure. A reminder that there's a reason the gods keep fire and wrath to themselves.

The Persephones move as one, their forms flickering between singularity and multiplicity, like echoes of light bending through time. Each of them lifts a hand, fingers carving symbols into the air, and from the trails of their movements, golden lassos form, ropes of pure luminescence woven from energy itself. The light crackles, bright as molten dawn, humming with the force of something both ancient and impossibly new.

The serpent recoils, its massive body twisting through the sand, its scales flashing against the glow of the lassos as they arc through the air. One Persephone snaps her wrist, and a loop tightens around the beast's throat, another circling its coiled body, sinking into the storm-hued hide. The serpent thrashes, the impact of its struggle sending waves of sand cascading into the sky, but the lassos hold.

"She's binding it!" Brit shouts.

She sure is. She's become like a whole phalanx of sexy, Mezmeric rodeo clowns.

The Persephones pull in unison. The air trembles, and the golden binds constrict, locking the super snake into place as the Persephone copies berate the serpent with a synchronized dance of devastation.

But here's the thing: see, about a mile-long animal with an intensely malleable vertebrae, as previously established, can whip that articulated spine around so that it's attacking you from all sides at once.

Turning my head, I see the tail end thrashing laterally in my direction. Ironically, it's not aiming for me and Brit, per se. It's just that an unintended side effect of it focusing its full attention on the kick line of Persephones (Persephonalia?) that's currently bothering it is that its tail is spraying wild and, at the moment, zipping in our direction.

Thump-thump. Thump-thump.

Oh, shit. My Heart is filled again to the point where I can use Control. Sweet.

But before I get the chance to set it off . . .

WOW!

That's what I hear.

It's weird. It quite literally sounds like someone shouting the word "Wow," but in actuality, what it appears to be is the sound of the serpent's tail smacking against some kind of invisible barrier and bounding back in the opposite direction.

My eyes go wide when I see Brit with her arms spread out to the sides of her body like Charlton Heston as Moses parting the Red Sea in *The Ten Commandments.*

"What are you doing?"

"The new Spell I got!"

Oooooh. Her new Spell, "Wall of WOW!" Huh. A bit literal, but clearly effective.

The Spell seems to have allowed her to do exactly what it promises: Throw up a protective wall that, in this case, has shielded us from being tail whipped into the next dimension.

Now that I know to look for it—the Wall—I can see it's not entirely translucent; there's a faint shimmer around the edges. Being able to spot the perimeter, it looks like it's only a few feet wide and a few feet high, just enough to insulate us. I have to imagine that as she builds up its strength, it will be able to encompass larger and larger areas, but for now . . .

Wow.

Glad it's here.

"How long can you hold it?!" I ask.

"I dunno!"

"Can you move with it? Can it work like Perg's shell but invisible?"

"I don't fuckin' know! I just found out I have the shit, dude!"

The answer to the question about the Wall of WOW!'s durability is answered in short order as the serpent's tail slaps back in our direction once again and, effectively, shatters it. I know it is shattered because instead of "WOW!" the sound it makes this time is a "WHOA!" as the barrier dissipates entirely.

The serpent's tail, slapping through the protection, comes dangerously close to lacerating us both. In fact, it would have chopped us down were it not for the fact that I, in a reflexive response, wrist snap the Blade of the Starfallen just as the tail is about to bowl us over and chop off the very end of the thing.

It slices straight through the glistening, near unsliceable hide of the monster, severing it deeply enough that the flame from the Blade blazes through the dense remainder of the flesh that I can't possibly carve with my regular, human-size wingspan, and sends sparks of sky shower raining down upon the whole of the bisected fragment, burning it all away instantly and intermingling it into the existing cloud of sand like golden stardust.

The bellowing scream the partially bound snake emits is higher pitched and replicates the sound of ten million balloons being squeaked by ten million annoying children at a birthday party for the world's most assholish kids.

The noise causes me and Brit to lose hold of whatever modicum of control we were holding on to (which wasn't much, I gotta tell ya) and fall to the desert floor, writhing in pain.

More problematically, it induces the same effect on all the Persephonasia dancing in the air. They poof out of being, and the real Persephone, the foundation, also falls hard to the ground, smacking into the desert floor, clenching her ears, causing her to lose her magical hold on the sausage-wrapped serpent. The bindings remain, but her control of the lassos do not.

"Seph!" I start to race for where she has landed. Her body has fallen about halfway down the length of the snake's bound, tubular shell, and it feels like every step I take toward her she gets pulled farther away by the swirling sands.

The thrashing, keening serpent who is now tied with magical light and also missing a portion of its torso (which means, technically, a portion of *four* torsos—which is probably adding insult to injury), convulses and bellows, spiraling up into the sky, trying to shed itself of its restraints, readying itself to descend upon all of us and deliver what I have to presume is going to be its finishing move. Probably called "The Sandstorm Slam Down" or something.

And that's when I hear . . .

VROOM!

I look over my shoulder to see Sheila barreling toward us.

Oh, shit! Has she been fully autonomous this whole time and I didn't know? I am so bad about reading user manuals.

But no, she's not. She's not driving over on her own. I can't see the driver's head, but I can see the bright, beaming cherry of the tip of a blunt peeking up from just behind the steering wheel.

Sheila screeches to a stop beside us and the snake, the window rolls down, and Jameson yells out, "Get in, ya Saviour and family! Me not gon' let de bumboclaat serpent get dem dirty mouth round me masta ace numba one star who brought ole Jameson back from de dead now!"

And people accuse me of using ten words when two will do.

"You heard the little simian! Let's go!"

I lunge for the car, Brit following close behind, and we load our carcasses into Sheila.

"Let me drive," I say, shoving Jameson aside.

"Jameson got it, nah!"

"Bro, your feet barely reach the accelerator, and your head is hardly high enough to see over the steering wheel!" I mean it literally. Less literally, his head is plenty high.

He acquiesces and jumps into the back. I plop the Blade next to the seat, take hold of the steering wheel, and . . .

And have a decision to make.

Seph is in front of us. I can see her up ahead just barely, unconscious on the hard desert floor. Perg is on the other side of the serpent's body, still large, still dealing with the effects of having been smacked in the chops.

They're in two, diametrically opposite positions from one another.

Which one do I attempt to rescue first?

Goddammit. Options. So many options. Always, always, always so many options.

It's always, "Pick this Skill, pick that one. Use this Spell, use the other one."

Save Seph. No, save Perg.

Of all the obstacles that trip me up in my life, this one may be the most persistent.

How do I simply . . . choose?

There was a time, not so very long ago, when a moment like this would have resulted in me having to have a whole, big-ass conversation with myself (either figuratively or literally) about how to decide what to do. Weighing my history with Perg against my feelings about Seph, what she's been through, and what she represents. But for reasons I also decide not to wonder about just now, I don't place the thoughts onto the scales at all and, instead, slam down on the accelerator as we take off toward . . .

"What about Perg?" Brit shouts.

"I'll circle back for him," I say, quieter and more focused than is my usual manner in a situation like this one as Sheila zips toward Seph through the Sturm und Drang like she's being directed by George Miller.

"Come on, come on," I mutter to myself, pushing Sheila as hard as I can, knuckles turning white against the wheel. The speedometer is maxed out. I'm working as hard as I can to keep her from skidding out or coming apart at the seams. And that's when I realize . . .

. . . we're not going to make it.

I'm not going to get to her in time. I'm not going to be able to scoop her up and keep her from perishing in this brutal, unforgiving wasteland. She waited for me. For Carpathian. She waited and waited and waited, and the second he came back—*I* came for her—and took her away from her self-relegation, she's going to die.

And so is Perg. Perg, who told me how cool it was that he got to come along and go on this adventure with me. He's not going to make it either.

Both of them. My oldest friend and my newest friend. They're both going to die.

SHIT!

I lean forward in my seat as if that will somehow make us get there quicker. It won't. All it will do is allow me to see, in more vivid detail, the moment when both Persephone and Perg are eviscerated by the living mountain of fury bearing down on the land.

The chasm—the open rift in the earth—is also expanding, energy of some kind now seeping up to pour over the plains.

And, as if I needed a goddamn reminder, on the stupid PCM screen I see . . .

It looks as though you could use a reminder!
As a Quest Requirement, *you may not forfeit any Party member prior to seeking.*
{COURTESY MESSAGE #33}

"I KNOW!" I shout, punching the screen with my fist.

Which, in turn, causes the screen to light up.

***Chaos Chain**
***Fog of Decimation**

***Sonic Torment**
***Oscillating Vortex**
***Lightning Rider Strike**

I stare at it for about half a second.

"Which one?" Brit asks. "What do we choose?!"

Always a choice to make. Always a decision. With consequences. Always.

Write another dozen books.

Kill Carpathian and see just what happens.

Choices.

I reach my fingertip out—the jostling mayhem of the car causing it to quiver—and I let it hover over the choices just long enough . . .

I'm tired of having to choose.

. . . to decide to hell with it and, flattening my palm . . .

. . . choose them all.

CHAPTER TWENTY-THREE

The moment my hand slams onto the screen, all five icons light up at once, a menacing glow pulsing through Sheila's dashboard, the steering wheel, and into my fingertips, and I'm not sure exactly, but I think I feel it in my coccyx. The car suddenly jerks, the engine emitting a *roar* so deep it feels like it's coming from the earth below us itself. The desert vibrates with a resonance so violent that for a fleeting, horrified moment, I think the serpent's body has started tunneling directly below. But no. This is something else.

Chaos Chain. Fog of Decimation. Sonic Torment. Oscillating Vortex. Lightning Rider Strike. All of them activate at once, and Brit asks, politely . . .

"WHAT THE HELL DID YOU JUST DO?!"

"I made a choice!" I tell her.

Boy did I ever. I can barely hold the wheel steady as Sheila . . . lifts off the ground.

Literally. Lifts. Off. The. Ground.

"BRI—NIGHTWIND!" I shout, gripping the steering wheel so tight it's now a blue-knuckled panic. "DID YOU KNOW SHEILA COULD FLY?!"

"Sure I did!"

"Really?"

"NO! OF COURSE I DIDN'T KNOW SHE COULD FLY!" she screams back, holding on to the dashboard for dear life. "I don't think she's supposed to! This is NOT NORMAL!"

Normal compared to what, McAfee? I want to ask.

The serpent, seeing us rising into the air, hesitates midstrike, its massive body coiling up, glowing eyes narrowing as if it's suddenly *aware* that something even more insane is about to happen.

It ain't wrong.

CHAOS CHAIN!

It hits like a thunderclap. The air around the serpent flashes white hot, and something like molten lightning snakes out from Sheila's undercarriage, lashing itself around the serpent's body. It's not unlike the Flamestriker Spell Persephone apparently has. Only, y'know, being shot out of the ass of a hundred-and-twenty-thousand-dollar, three-hundred-forty-eight-horsepower, two-point-nine-liter V6. That's now also charged with Saviour Mezmer.

The serpent roars in agony, flailing wildly as the chains tighten and sear its scales, carving molten scars into its otherwise invulnerable hide.

FOG OF DECIMATION!

Sheila starts pouring out a thick, dark smoke that doesn't rise. It sinks. It oozes down the serpent's coils like a living liquid, dissolving sand and stone into nothingness wherever it touches. The serpent screams again, its glowing eyes wide with terror as its body writhes and thrashes, trying to escape the creeping fog that now seems *alive.*

SONIC TORMENT!

A wave of pure sonorous energy explodes out of the car in a deafening *BOOM* that shatters the air. Somehow, inside the car, it's not unendurable. But outside . . . Serpy's massive head snaps back like it's been punched by God, its own roar drowned out by a noise so loud I can feel my bones vibrating.

OSCILLATING VORTEX!

The last time I used it, it sucked away all the Templars chasing us out of Garr Haven. Which was super weird. This time . . . This time is somehow even weirder. If that's possible.

The sandstorm around us changes direction. It doesn't *stop*—it just reverses, swirling up into a massive funnel cloud that glows with an eerie, electric-blue light. The serpent, still bound by the Chaos Chains and writhing in the Fog of Decimation, is now being dragged *upward* into the vortex, its enormous body flailing helplessly as it's sucked into the center of the storm.

I have the nervous impulse to make yet another *Wizard of Oz* joke, but I'm frankly too terrified to speak anymore, so, to what I'm sure is everyone's great relief, I stay dumb.

LIGHTNING RIDER STRIKE!

Oh boy.

From the heart of the vortex-ing vortex of a tornado, a single bolt of lightning tears downward, striking the snake square in the center of its massive four-body problem.

The serpent convulses violently, its body locking in a twisted coil as energy floods through it, arcs of wild Mezmer lashing out in every direction. The storm howls louder, the wind shrieking like a living thing. Sand and debris explode further into the air, creating a cyclone of pure, unrelenting chaos.

Seph's chains hold it, kind of, restricting its ability to move about in a focused way, but they aren't stopping the serpent from thrashing. Which is, like, maybe worse? Because the more it fights, the more the Mezmer seems to feed on itself, escalating, compounding.

It's not subduing—it's escalating.

And then . . . Sheila starts plummeting toward the ground.

"AHHHHHHHHHH!" is the collected sound from within the car from me, Brit, and even Jameson. The first time I've seen anything break-a-his stride. Slow-a-him down.

You gotta figure that's bad.

"Shit!"

The sound of me swearing is probably indistinguishable from the rest of the shouting, but my "shit" is about something distinctly separate from the fall itself . . .

It's that we're about to fall onto Seph, who is still prostrate below us on the desert floor.

Sunuvabitch!

I pull back on the steering wheel like a pilot attempting to pull a plane out of a nosedive. Except Sheila's not a plane, and the wheel doesn't really pull back. The best I can hope for is that I rip the whole steering column out and maybe we slide to the side or something and miss crushing her under the weight of the whip.

And then . . . Perg shows up.

Big, giant Perg. He comes zipping his double-speed, giant snail body over to where Seph is and puts himself in between her and us, zooming down on top of her. The sight makes my heart feel full. My, I guess, metaphorical one. My actual, mechanical one also appears full again, at least according to the last icon I glanced, but . . . Whatever! It makes me happy seeing teammates looking out for each other! It's nice! That's all I'm saying.

However . . . him being there, running a body block for Seph, means that we're gonna bounce hard off his enlarged shell and, I have to imagine, either go pinging off into who knows where or smash against his backside. Neither scenario feels all that tasty.

But fortunately—or not fortunately at all, bordering on tragically unfortunately, depending on how you look at it—something happens that obviates the concern.

I can feel a sudden *shift* in the air around us. And before you can say, "What is that down there? Is that a portal?" there's a sound like the ripping of fabric, amplified a thousandfold. The fissure that had begun expanding when the serpent smacked it into being now expands. The whole world seems to warp as the sands twist and reality itself begins to collapse inward as a hole in the Meridia under Persephone and Perg opens up, dragging them into the unknown.

In response, instead of pulling back on the wheel, I find myself leaning forward, pressing my foot onto the accelerator, willing Sheila to move faster toward the hole that just swallowed up the pretty redheaded sorcerer who only just got a chance to venture out into the world, and the awesome snail homie who's done nothing but have my six ever since he became sapient before the great cavern closes itself up . . . as it looks like it is starting to.

"Hey . . ." Brit says, tugging at my elbow.

I ignore her, focused on plummeting us down into the dark after the two *amigos*. (Technically, one *amigo* and one *amiga*, but I think the plural is masculine. I'll ask Perg, if we make it.)

"Hey . . ." Brit calls again, now pointing at the closing desert lid.

"I see it," I say, probably too quietly to be heard.

"Me big Saviour?" Jameson questions.

"I am," I say again, too softly to be heard. "I am the goddamn big Saviour," I repeat, really trying to hype myself up. It's kind of working? I'm at least more determined than afraid. Which is not nothing.

And before another word can be spoken by any of us, we nosedive into the hole just as the desert closes above us and we are torpedoed down, down, down, into . . .

I'm not sure what.

[MODIFIED] Quest: "Seek [Zerastian] on the [Mid-Meridian Plane] by binding a [Giant Serpent of the Mokeisan]." [COMPLETE]

Seeing the words projected onto Sheila's windshield, I'm unsure if I'm alive or dead.

"Are we alive?" Brit's voice chimes in, letting me know that, since she's also asking, we must be, at least, alive adjacent.

"Looks like we made it. We're on the Mid-Meridian Plane."

I yank up my Heart Guard Evaluation to make sure that Seph and Perg are also still . . . Well . . . Still.

Heart Guard Evaluation
Heart Guard Member [Teleri Nightwind]. Status: Present
Heart Guard Member [Almeister T. Wizard]. Status: Present
Heart Guard Member [Pergamon Slow Bottom]. Status: Available
Heart Guard Member [Persephone Vizardsdottir]. Status: Available
Heart Guard Member [Tavrella Redacted]. Status: Deleted
(Do you wish to permanently delete member? [Yes] [No])
Heart Guard Member [Xanaraxa Caputrukahs]. Status: Missing
Heart Guard Member [Zerastian Teronia]. Status: Available

Thank god. Not only are we, it seems, alive, but Perg and Seph are too. I presumed that had to be the case, since the requirement of the modified Quest was that before we could seek Zerastian, we had to bind the serpent without forfeiting any of my Party members. (I don't know if I could have given up Jameson, as he's not actually in the Party, but I wouldn't do that to the little guy. In my mind, he's a steady.)

Beyond which, if they weren't still alive, I assume the eval would tell me they're "Deleted," like Tavrella. Which is a shitty way to say it, but I have to remember that the System doesn't technically *care* about things like feelings and all that. It is the pure essence of nihilism. It just "does" what it is prescribed to do by whatever force created it. (Theoretically, me, but . . . remains to be seen.)

In any case, Perg and Seph are not "Deleted." So, I'm breathing a little easier. However . . . their statuses have gone from "Present" to "Available." (Zerastian's has also gone from "Missing" to "Available," which is . . . encouraging, I suppose.) So, by the properties of simple inference, while they're not here with us, they're somewhere seekable.

(Mael's name is no longer there at all, which clearly was going to be the case once I removed him, per request, but it still bites to see. Or not see.)

But. Focusing on the positive: We're in the right place to reunite with Zerastian, and Perg and Seph are around here somewhere. Killer. The only question is how we track them, but I know, based on empirical evidence, that as members of my Heart Guard, I can use the Heart like a homing beacon to—

Note: Whilst on the [Mid-Meridian Plane], Mezmer is ATTENUATED. Functionality will be LIMITED. And, as a result, this feature of your instrumentation will now enter into SLEEP MODE for the duration of your stay.

Wait, what?!

I said: Whilst on the [Mid-Meridian Plane], Mezmer is ATTENUATED. Functionality will be LIMITED. And, as a result, this feature of your instrumentation will now enter—

"I heard what you said! What do you mean you're entering *SLEEP MODE*?!"

"Who are you talking to?" Brit asks.

"The Heart! It says it's going into 'sleep mode'!"

"What?"

"What it say, nah?" Jameson chimes in.

Almeister snores.

"But how will we find Zerastian?!" I shout. "How do we find Seph and Perg?! How—?"

All excellent questions! With luck, you can find someone who has some answers. Because it ain't gonna be me for a minute! Good luck! {COURTESY MESSAGE #34}

Thump-thump. Thump-thuuuuuump. Thuuuuuuump-thum . . . p.

And with that, I can feel the Mezmer part of the heart go dark.

I slam at my chest with my hand.

"What are you doing?" Brit asks.

"It just went offline!"

"What do you mean it went 'offline'?"

"*Offline* means that it's no longer connected to—"

"I know what *offline* means, dummy! I'm asking what you mean by it!"

"Just what it said! It went to sleep!"

Almeister again snores in an ill-timed mockery of the situation.

"Shit," Brit huffs.

"Yeah . . . Shit." I don't expect anyone to be as concerned as me, but a little more anxiety would be nice.

"Does that mean . . . ya gwan die, mi big Saviour?"

Oh, crap. I didn't even think about that.

"I don't . . . I don't . . . think so?" I take a few breaths to make sure I still can. "No. I don't think so. I think it just means that it won't work as, like, a guide here. Or as a tool. It says that Mezmer is attenuated on the Mid-Meridian Plane."

"And what the fuck does *that* mean?"

"*Attenuated* means—"

"Are you serious?" She balls her fists. "I know what the fuck *attenuated* means! I mean what does Mezmer being attenuated mean?"

Rather than wait for an answer, she tries forming a ball of Triple R. And rather than anything radiant or raylike, she just gets a small puff of energy. A burst that then dies out. She then tries throwing up a Wall of WOW! but all that happens is a sound like a failure to win on *The Price Is Right*. "Waa-waa-waa."

"So, exactly what the fuck it sounds like," she says.

I pick up the Blade to see for myself.

"The hell are you doing?"

"Checking to see if the Blade works."

"In the car?!"

I hear her point, but it doesn't matter because as I touch it, tiny sparks of energy crackle, but nothing anywhere near the kind of thing I've been able to do on Meridia. Not completely devoid of Mezmer like what happened in the upper floors of the Tower, but definitely diminished.

"Yeah. We're operating on low power mode."

We sit for a second in the quiet, looking around.

I have to be honest, what I see outside the car doesn't look like what I would have anticipated a liminal space in between realities to look like. In fact, it looks . . . beautiful.

Like, the sky above is a clear blue with puffy white clouds. The area all around where we've landed is a vast, verdant meadow with wildflowers, and a bright yellow sun is shining down on it all. It looks like it goes on forever.

It also looks like this recurring dream that I have had for a long time.

In the dream, I'm in a field where I used to play baseball as a kid, but the grass is too green, too perfect. Like someone turned up the saturation on the memory.

It's the same field from back home; the one behind my old elementary school where the dirt was packed too hard and the bases were just scraps of white painted onto it. But in the dream, the dirt is soft, the bases gleam, and the outfield stretches forever, no chain-link fence, no neighboring houses, just an endless expanse of golden meadow blending into a sky so blue it kind of makes my eyes water.

There's always a warm breeze rustling through the grass, carrying the scent of cut clover and leather and something older. Something I can't place. The air is thick with late summer, the way it used to be when we'd play until the streetlights flickered on, when I'd sprint around the bases with my whole chest, arms pumping, believing for half a second that I could outrun the throw.

Which, of course, I couldn't. Not in real life. Which is why my high school coach suggested I join the chess team instead. But that's why dreams are the best.

In the dream, there's never anyone else there. No outfielders calling for a catch, no coach shouting from the dugout for me to slide, no heckling from other jerky kids waiting their turns. Just me, and the wind, and the sun sitting heavy in the sky like it's watching me be my best, most idealized self.

And always, past the infield, past where the outfield wall should be but isn't, there's a shape. Something just beyond sight. I'm not sure what it is because every time I've tried to approach it to find out, something happens that stops me. Like, I trip and land on my face and everybody laughs. Or a hole in the field will open up and swallow me.

I never get close enough to see what's there.

I never reach it before I wake up.

It has ever remained a mystery.

Actually, it's, to a greater or lesser degree, how I imagined the concept of Meridia. The original Meridia. Meridia before the Ninth Guardian took over. The green Eden that was violated by the Guardian and DONG. I never wrote a flashback or anything into Riftbreaker; I just had characters describe it a couple of times to other characters. But this is what I based it on in my head. Memories of the days back before . . .

Anyway.

All that is what this Mid-Meridian Plane joint looks like.

"Check the maps," I request of Brit. "Do they show anything?"

She pulls out the sheaf of papers that have been steadily updating themselves since she verified her Advanced Map Maker Skill and what they show is . . .

"Nothing."

"What do you mean, nothing?" I ask.

"I mean nothing. Not only do they not show anything new or useful, they show literally nothing. At all. Look." She lets me look at the parchments, and that is, indeed, all they are. Blank parchments. Any kind of anything indicating place—either where we are or where we've been—is completely absent.

"That's weird."

"Ya think?" she asks, fanning through the sheets.

"Even when we were at the Cavern of Sorrows and the Tower, they still showed the outline of the places, even though they had no details about the interior."

"Yeah, no shit, I was there," she says, getting more agitated by the second.

"Well—"

"What's that?" she asks.

"What's what?"

"There. Over there."

I look through the windshield to see what she's talking about, and that's when I spy it, arcing in the sky near us.

Holy shit.

A rainbow.

Sort of.

It's more of a kind of, I guess, *broken* rainbow. Or an incomplete rainbow, only comprising the ROY G. B part of ROY G. BIV. Just the red, orange, yellow, green, and blue. It pulses faintly, intensifying and then settling back, almost like the heartbeat of my currently dormant chest companion.

And it's out of order. The yellow is first, followed by the red, then the green, then orange, and blue. I don't know how you'd create a pneumonic from that. YRGOB. I guess maybe if you spoke Romanian or some—

"Look over there, big boss. What dat 'bout now?"

Jameson draws my attention to . . . something . . . that . . .

"You're kidding," I say.

"Me no kid. 'Dis no kiddin' matter, mi gen'ral."

"What. The. Fucketing fuck?" Brittany sees it at the same time.

Standing in the middle of this place—this so-called "Mid-Meridian Plane"—is a police call box. A *British* police call box. A big, British police call box. In other words . . .

"A fucking TARDIS?" Brit says.

"Looks like."

"Why is there a TARDIS here?"

"I don't know."

"What be a TARDIS?" Jameson asks.

I don't even attempt to answer, turning my attention instead to trying to rouse Almeister once more. Richemerion said he'd be able to guide us once we got here, so, I'm hoping he can tell us why there's a prop from *Doctor Who* just sitting here.

"Almeister? Al? Hey, Al?"

I shake him, but he doesn't become alert; just snores once loudly and then goes back to his heavily breathed sleep. Goddammit.

"Talk to you for a sec?" I ask Brit. She nods and opens the door to get out. Turning to Jameson, I say, "We'll be right back. Watch him for a minute?"

"It's what ole' Jameson do, mon." Jameson leans back, puffing away. I roll the windows down to mitigate just how high he and Al can get then hop out and round the front of the car to meet up with Brit.

"I don't understand what this is," I whisper quietly. Extra quietly. *A Quiet Place* quietly.

Because I also just noticed that there seems to be no sound here. Virtually none at all. Maybe not minus twenty-plus decibels like that anechoic chamber I visited at the Orfield Lab in Minneapolis, which I did just to see how long I'd make it before I freaked out (Answer: longer than I thought. Almost an hour. They said most people start to flip way sooner when they hear their bones grinding and blood flowing, but I just dug into the meditation and started to question whether or not I really exist, and the minutes just flew by!), but it's still pretty silent.

"Yeah, me neither," Brit whispers back. "Let's just . . . I dunno. Decide what's next. You have any intel at all? From . . . ?" She points at my chest.

"A little. I'm pretty sure that Seph, Perg, and Zerastian are around somewhere. We just have to find them."

"Without maps."

"Without maps."

She looks around, clicks her tongue, says, "Quiet."

I nod.

We look together once more at the TARDIS. We're both huge *Doctor Who* enthusiasts. Brittany even used to run a *Doctor Who* fan page before a bunch of *Doctor Who* bros found out she was a woman and started getting all skeevy about it and she shut it down. Something she said to me once that I've also definitely found to be true: "Cultures may be diverse, customs may be varied, languages may separate us, but one unifying constant remains no matter where in the universe you find yourself: People will be dicks. Especially toward those who aren't like them."

That's stuck with me ever since I first heard it. Maybe it's why Brit and I have always gotten along despite our superficially apparent differences. Despite appearances, underneath it all, in the ways that actually really matter, we're almost exactly alike.

And, in this moment, that means that we both know what happens next.

Without another word exchanged between us, we both march toward the TARDIS.

Placing hands on it, feeling all around, it seems solid. As in, it's really here and not just some figment of our imaginations. (Insofar as anything is real and not a figment of our imaginations.)

"Maybe it's some kind of art installation?" Brit offers.

"Maybe . . ." I say slowly, continuing to explore its shape.

Then, I feel something. Some kind of sensation. An energy. Maybe . . . a presence. I look around.

"What are you looking for?"

"Not sure. Something . . ."

I get this odd feeling, this weird tingle I used to get at the base of my neck when I was writing and I'd have a sudden idea for a plot point or some kind of direction to take the story, or a new character would pop into my—

"Hello," a voice comes from behind. A plummy, British voice that sounds a lot like the voice I hear when the Heart speaks to me.

Brit and I turn as one, both of us in attack stance (however limited it may be) to see . . .

A guy. Sort of. For the most part, he looks like a normal, human-seeming guy, except for the four tiny horns sprouting symmetrically from his forehead. He's barefoot, wearing loose trousers that have seen better days, an equally loose-fitting poet blouse, and has a scarf draped around his neck.

Something about him causes a fresh itch to sprout inside the front of my own forehead.

"Fuck are you?" Brit asks, defensively. Obviously.

He puts his hands up in a gesture of "no threat here" and says . . .

"My name. Is Sumnut. Babu Sumnut." He bows deeply at the waist. "How do you do?"

ACT FOUR

STUCK IN THE MIDDLE WITH YOU.
(AND YOU, AND YOU,
AND YOU, AND . . . YOU.)

CHAPTER TWENTY-FOUR

Turns out the TARDIS is not actually a TARDIS, but is something Babu Sumnut (or just Sumnut, as he has offered) is calling a CHRONOS, which stands for "Chronological Heuristic Reconnaissance Object for Navigating Other Spacetimes." So, in other words . . . it's a TARDIS.

And—exactly like the TARDIS on *Doctor Who*—inside, it is unexpectedly much larger and more spacious than the shape of the exterior would imply. (I guess it's not that unexpected, given that it's clearly just a rip-off from the TV show and whoever is in charge of shit on the Mid-Meridian Plane is as big a believer in the concept of "homage" as I am, but . . .)

The interior of the CHRONOS is a big, shiny space with all kinds of floating consoles and holographic interfaces around the joint. We have plopped Almeister in a tufted club chair in the corner next to a side table upon which is stacked a haphazard pile of books with titles like *The Art of Ignoring Temporal Distortions*, *Soup Recipes for Multidimensional Entities,* and *The World's Okayest Sherpa*, and Jameson, Brit, and I stand by the tea station as Sumnut pours from a samovar and gives us the lowdown on where we have managed to find ourselves.

"So, you have found the Mid-Meridian Plane, eh?"

"Yeah," I tell him. "I mean, we were kind of looking for it. We just didn't know what, exactly, we were looking for."

"I see. Then you must be interested in a revision?"

"A revision?"

"Yes."

"I'm not sure what that means? What, precisely, is the Mid-Meridian Plane? Please?"

Sumnut turns a cup in his hands thoughtfully before passing it to Jameson, who sniffs it suspiciously then sips and raises a thumb in approval before pounding back the whole thing. "The Mid-Meridian Plane is, well, it is whatever you wish it to be."

"Whatever I wish it to be?"

"Whatever anyone wishes it to be. You see, the Mid-Meridian Plane does not *exist* on its own in any way that is explicable. Everything within the MMP is either something brought in from another reality or a construct of the traveler's own subconscious, shaped by latent intention rather than conscious desire."

I'm attempting to work out what he's saying, but it's not hitting. "Try again?"

He sighs. "The Mid-Meridian Plane does not create. Nor was it created. It is individual; bespoke, if you like. It *reflects*. Everything here—every structure, every environment, every moment—is either something brought in from another reality or something *you*—or someone else—has unintentionally shaped from the raw material of your own subconscious. And, moreover, it allows you to refine those raw materials however you like."

Sumnut lets that sit for a second, watching my face like he's waiting for something to click.

I rub my temple, trying to put it together in a way that makes sense outside of my own brain. "So . . . lemme try to . . . It's not a real place."

"No."

"Not in the way we think of places."

"That's right."

"It's not even a dream, really?"

"Not as such."

"It's . . . a projection."

"Precisely."

Jameson makes a low noise, rolling his empty teacup between his hands. "So, ye sayin' we hallucinatin'? Like we been smokin' dem Wizard Tears?"

I have no idea what, exactly, "Wizard Tears" is a euphemism for, but I can't get into it now.

"No," I respond, heading Sumnut off and thinking it through as I go. "It's not imagined, per se. It's just . . . It only exists because we think it does. It's like—and tell me if I'm wrong?" Sumnut nods. "It's like that thing where you assume something's going to go badly, and then it *does* go badly, but you can't tell if it was actually going to happen that way or if you just, like, *willed* it into existence? Is that what we're talking about?"

I feel like getting an explanation would be much easier if we had common frames of reference like, I don't know, the entire backlog of psychological horror films where a character's perception dictates their reality. Or like *The Matrix*, or *Inception*, or *The Others*, or that one episode of *The Twilight Zone* where the guy thinks he's in a normal town, but it turns out he's actually a doll in some kid's toy box.

But, of course, Sumnut doesn't have those references because he is, himself, his own frame of reference. A derivative and yet totally unique sort of identity.

He lifts a finger in response to my continued postulation. "Very much like what you say, but on a far larger scale. The Mid-Meridian Plane responds to *will*, not desire. It does not give you what you want; it gives you what you *will into being*, even if you don't realize you are willing it. The Mid-Meridian Plane is, at its most basic, the place from where journeys are conceived of before they are commenced."

"Journeys are conceived of before they are commenced."

"Yes. To use a vehicular comparison: You would not set off on an adventure without some type of road map, would you?"

I start to say, *Of course not*, but then I take a pause. Because that's not true at all. In a nonliteral sense, that's how I've started just about every story I've ever written. In an absolutely literal sense, I've also done it a thousand times. Just gotten in the car and started driving. Or been on a hike and wandered off the trail despite the signs stating very clearly, "DO NOT WANDER OFF TRAIL."

Call it a curious nature or call it a lack of an ability to focus (or call it both, because that's what it is), but it's how I've tended to operate my whole life. It's why my life before I started writing was so hard for me to take. Not because it was a bad job, being a bus driver. Bus drivers are a crucial part of society. They take people on their journeys. They get them where they're going. They help people in a tangible, essential way.

But bus drivers also have routes, paths, rules that they follow day in and day out. They know what's coming up next. And, honestly, it made me feel like I was stuck in a time loop where every day bled into the next, and sunrises and sunsets started to feel indistinguishable from one another. Which was, to name its impact on me, a real friggin' drag.

So, being honest with all that about myself, I answer, "Doesn't matter what I would do. Say more, please?"

"The Mid-Meridian Plane is gestational," he continues.

Brit repeats this time. "Gestational?"

"Yes. It means the process of carrying or developing something, especially in the womb. That is, I believe, the precise definition."

"Yeah, no, I know what 'gestational' means. Jesus Christ, bro, why does everyone think I need a goddamn vocabulary lesson every time they open their mouths? I mean, *what do you mean by it*? What's being gestated? Us?"

"No. Not 'you.' Your . . . stories."

My pulse quickens—which is strange, given that I technically have no heartbeat at the moment, but conventional biological function is not high on my list of curiosities at the moment.

"What do you mean, 'our stories'?"

"The Mid-Meridian Plane is where narratives can be written or rewritten, depending on the storyteller's needs. But rather than taking place in a necessarily terminal environment where there might be dire consequences, here, one can explore possibilities. Alternate realities. Concurrent timelines and, sometimes with the help of others, sometimes on their own, fashion a version of events that may or may not resonate once they are once again back in their own dimension."

A writers' room. He's talking about a writers' room. Or group. Or workshop. Or whatever. He's basically just described what is (although I don't use them, famously) an outline.

I think he's suggesting that this is a realm where you can try out the notion of who you are or maybe even who you want to be without risk of, I suppose, being publicly flayed in the process. But . . . there is one thing about it that confuses me. (Actually, many things about it confuse me, but I'm going to try and focus on one thing at a time.)

"Right," I let out slowly. "But . . . let me try and . . . Let's say we were in the middle of a journey already. Like we already had road maps and stuff"—Brit grabs and holds up her sheafs of now blank parchment—"then, the fact that we've arrived here gives us the opportunity to, uh, reroute ourselves somehow?"

"Yes. That's right. The Mid-Meridian Plane also provides the opportunity for a revision, if you like."

Hm. When I thought before that I wished I could figure out a way to throw out this draft of our lives out and start over with a virtual page-one rewrite, I was kind of joking, assuming such a thing would be impossible. But here, in this realm . . .

"You mean . . . flip the script?" I ask.

He considers the phrase. "Flip . . . the script. I like that. Yes. Because nothing here is shaped by anything as pedestrian as time or geography, but rather by aspects much more meaningful . . ." He pauses, blowing at his tea and taking a sip. I wait for him to finish. He takes another sip. I wait again. He takes another—

"Can you please tell us what is 'more meaningful'?!" I finally blurt out.

He swallows and says, "Yes. Memory. Regret. And, as I said before, intent."

Sumnut strikes me as one of those gurus who manage to convince people that what they're saying is just dripping with profundity when, in fact, all they're doing is saying random words in an orderly syntax that vaguely approximates sense. I mean, I know I have done that too from time to time, but the stakes here demand a little more clarity, I feel like.

"Can you expound on that at all? In a way that's more, I dunno, comprehensible? 'Intent.' Intent toward what?"

"The Mid-Meridian Plane does not function as a passive realm. It is not an echo of a world already shaped, nor is it a realm of simple indulgence. It is a crucible; a place where the raw elements of who you are or who you might be can be tested, refined, and reconsidered."

I open my mouth to ask another question, but he's already pressing forward.

"Every journey is built on decisions. But not all decisions are made consciously. Some paths we walk simply because they are beneath our feet when we begin. Others we choose without knowing why. Here, you are given the opportunity to step outside the momentum of your own life. To ask, with full clarity, why it is you move in the direction you do. And if that direction still serves you."

"Babu—"

"Eh, eh, eh. Sumnut, please. Babu is my father."

"Er, fine. Sumnut, can you just—"

"Let me ask you a question," he cuts me off. "Do you know what you are seeking?"

"What? Yeah," Brit answers. "Of course. We're seeking our friends."

"Are you?"

The way he asks it makes me consider that I thought that's what we were on about, but now, I'm not sure. I hate it when people do that.

"Yes," she answers decisively. "We got separated when we landed here, and we need to find them before we, whatever, keep going."

He nods to himself for a moment, then looks directly at me. "What did it look like? Outside?"

"Huh?"

"Before you joined me here in the CHRONOS, what was outside?"

"I . . . This feels like a trick question."

"I assure you, it is not. What did it look like?"

"It looked like . . . It looked like a place I remember even though I've never seen it before."

"Well said." He smiles.

"So, like, how is that possible?" Brit asks.

Sumnut sighs deep into his chest. "The Mid-Meridian Plane has no origin; not in the way one understands origination. It was not built, not carved, not spoken into being by a god with a grand vision. It was not discovered by some ancient traveler who planted a flag and named it. It simply . . . *was.* Or rather, it *became,* when the first lost thing needed a place to land."

"What lost thing are we talking about?" I ask.

"Like how mi sometime lose mi fyah and mi no find a way to light mi stick?" Jameson asks.

"I don't know what that means, but no." Sumnut turns his cup in his hands, watching the liquid ripple as if stirred by something unseen. "You see, in the beginning, before there were worlds and systems and rules, there were stories. Not written, not spoken, just *held* in the minds of those who would one day tell them. And where did those untold stories live before they found a tongue to shape them? Where did the ideas go before they had form?" He looks at me then, eyes knowing.

"I . . . Here?"

"And places like it. Yes."

Holy shit. I think this guy is telling me the origin story of the place where origin stories find their origin.

Well, that's original.

"Nice one, Bruce."

"Thanks, Bruce. It just came to me."

Holy hell. I thought Origin Pass was the first place I ever made up, the seed from which the rest of Meridia grew. But the more Sumnut talks, the more it hits me: The Mid-Meridian Plane came before even that. Before narrative. Before invention. It's not the birthplace of the world; it's the place that whispered the idea of a world into existence to begin with.

This shit is like if Sanderson filled three whiteboards with ideas, showed them to David Mitchell, and they handed the notes to a pack of ADHD squirrels and said, "Go write!"

Sumnut continues. "We are in the threshold between what is and what could be. The place where half-shaped thoughts and unrealized possibilities gather, waiting to be chosen. Some say it was the first world, the cradle of creation. Others say it is the echo of every world that has ever been, overlapping at the edges, blurred and blending. But those are just ways of explaining something that does not want explaining."

"Who . . . discovered it?" Brit asks. "Like, who were the first to, I dunno, find it?"

Sumnut sets his cup down. “The first people to walk the plane were not conquerors, not explorers, not scientists, as you might expect. Because you cannot seek the plane. The plane must call to you.”

Shit. This is why we had to fight the serpent. Because we had to put ourselves in the same position Zerastian was in to be drawn to where Zerastian was drawn. Sneaky Peterson.

My fingers twitch. A slow, creeping certainty is settling into my bones. “And once you’re here?”

Sumnut leans forward, steepling his fingers. “Ah, well. That is the real question, isn’t it? Once you are here, you must ask yourself: Are you looking for a way forward? Or a way back?”

“Bro . . .” Brittany is starting to lose patience. Which is not ideal. “I’m reaching a serious inflection point with motherfucker’s Yoda-fying us. Not your fault; you’re just doing you, I get that, but I’m gonna need some remedial education real quick. Are you saying—?”

“He’s saying that it’s up to us.”

“What is?”

“All of what happens next. It’s all up to us.”

“Precisely.” Sumnut smiles again. Sips tea.

“Dude—” she starts.

“Just . . .” I put up my hand. She chills for a second, huffing and puffing. “I think what he’s saying is that we might—*might*—have a chance to, for lack of a better phrase, rewrite the story.”

“Which story?”

“Ours. Or . . . the one we find ourselves in. We’re in a tabula rasa version of Meridia. The one that existed before . . . Before. We might be able to . . . revise it. Play it out here in a testing ground and then—and correct me if I’m wrong,” I offer to Sumnut, who nods, “carry it back to Meridia proper somehow and draft events in a new way. A better way.”

I look to the little man with the horns. “Yeah, that’s it. You’ve got it. Your longings, your questions, your unfinished thoughts, the pieces of you that have not yet become whole. You may indulge any of them. Or not. Up to you. But . . .”

Of course there’s a *but*.

“But what?” I ask.

“But, if you do choose not to address what it is you wish to revise, the Mid-Meridian Plane will choose for you.”

He says it so casually that it takes me a second to process what he actually means.

Brit, of course, has no patience for the slow burn. “I’m sorry. What do you mean, ‘it decides for us’? The fuck?”

Sumnut shrugs. “Time does not pass here in the traditional way, but it *does* move. And if you do not shape your path with intention, the plane will do so on your behalf. It will enter into something we call . . .”

No. No. No. He can't—He doesn't mean—No. Don't say it, don't say it, don't say it—

". . . flow state."

Son of a—

CHAPTER TWENTY-FIVE

Brit looks like her whole body is about to implode.

"So, let me get this straight," I say, rubbing my face, trying to remain calm. "If we don't make a clear decision on what we're doing here, what we're revising, what we're changing, the plane is just gonna dredge up some unresolved baggage and force us into *that* story?"

Sumnut nods, pleased, like I just solved an elementary riddle. "Yes."

"Yeah, okay, no, see? That's bullshit," Brit declares. "That's a fucking *ambush*."

"It is no more an ambush than a tide is an ambush," Sumnut says. "You knew you were stepping into the ocean; you simply did not consider the current."

He turns around, and I manage to grab Brit's arm and spin her away before she manages to clock the dude on the back of the head with the samovar. He turns back around just as I wheel her away.

"Sorry." He beams. "Did you say something?"

"No, just . . . Can you give us a second?" I ask.

"I can give you a hundred and eleven seconds," he replies, stepping away, allowing us to kibitz amongst ourselves.

"This is funky bullshit!" Brit whisper-shouts.

"I know, I know."

"We're in some sort of in-between place where we get to, whatever, flesh out the details of our own personal histories and come to grips with ourselves; only, if we don't, we get robbed of the chance to even try? Or something?"

"What it sounds like."

Jameson points his long finger at me and then at Brit. "That what I tink too."

She takes a breath. "Fuckin' . . . Mid-Meridian . . . Suck my . . . Cock smoking . . . Okay, fine. So? What do you want to do?"

"I mean . . . If I'm reading this right, and I think I am, we might have the chance to replay all the things that have happened—losing Zerastian, losing Xanaraxa, Mael . . . Tavrella, all of it—and figure out how to keep it from having happened in the first place. Since it's a liminal space and time doesn't exist, per se, we could keep trying drafts of outcomes until we find the one that suits and then bring it back topside with us."

Brit looks at a snoozing Almeister and chews on the inside of her cheek.

"But if that's possible for us, then that means it's possible for everyone else, too."

"Yeah?"

"I mean . . . presumably, that's what Zerastian's been doing here. Rewriting her story."

"Right . . ."

"And, since we don't know where Persephone and Perg are, who knows what kind of version of their stories they might be reworking or whatever the hell."

"What are you saying?"

"I'm saying that, for a change, we should make a plan. And that plan should involve our, y'know, group. Or Party. Or . . . I'm saying that rather than making a wholesale decision now about what's going to happen next without consulting with *the other people it might affect*, we should find them first, get their input on what to do, and then go from there."

She shrugs. Which is her nice way of trying to indicate that she's not mad anymore, just looking to avoid the same haphazard, willy-nilly approach that wound us up where we are in the first place.

"Even if it means we don't get the chance to redraft things the way we want?" I ask.

"I mean . . . Yeah." She says it like it's the most obvious answer in the world.

". . . Okay." I look at the macaque, and in the spirit of collaboration, ask, "Jameson? Thoughts?"

"Mi do whatever the group say. I go any way. Mi not picky."

I take a deep breath in . . .

"Alright. Hey, Sumnut?"

"Oh, has it been a hundred and eleven seconds already?"

. . . and exhale it out, long and slow.

"If we don't want to 'revise' anything right now—"

"Why would you not want to revise anything? Is there nothing in your existence which you would wish to explore what might have happened had things been different?"

"I mean, yeah. Like, maybe almost everything. But we have other concerns we need to address first. Honestly, right now, we just want to find the missing members of our Party."

"Even if it means you miss your chance and the plane chooses for you?"

". . . Yeah."

"Oh. Well. Very noble."

"Is it?"

"Unless you want to kill them or it's just to extort money or something, I would say so."

"Okay. So, operating within the framework of how things play out here, are there any suggestions you can offer as to how we go about finding them?"

"Of course. It is not hard."

"Oh, good. Great. So, how do we do it?"

"Very simple. You must know them," Sumnut says.

"Know them?" Brit repeats. "What do you mean, 'know them'? Of course we know them."

"No, I mean *know* them. Truly. Not just their names, their faces. Not just their place in your Party. You must know *who* they are. What they mean to you.

What they are becoming. The more clarity you bring to that which you seek, the more the plane will give you in return."

I rub the back of my neck, the ache of exhaustion creeping in.

"Okay!" (That was a little more emphatic than I meant it to be. I dial it back.) "Okay . . . Okay. Good. Great. So, then, let's start with what we are clear about. Zerastian, Perg, and Seph are somewhere on the plane, but you're suggesting that they're in places that—"

"There are no 'places' per se."

"*Fine*! Different . . . meow meow meows—"

"How do you know the official term?"

". . . Are you kidding me right now?"

"No. That is what they are called. There are as many meow meow meows in the Mid-Meridian Plane as there are boo-hoos in the Subplane."

"The Subplane?"

"That's right."

"What's the Subplane?"

"That's where those who can't take purchase on the Mid-Meridian Plane may discover themselves being relegated to. It's not like everyone gets a chance to rewrite themselves. Only those deserving of revision."

Oh, for fu—Purgatory.

That's what he's describing.

That's technically where we are.

We're in purgatory. A transitional state where souls undergo a kind of purification to atone for sins before entering heaven. Not eternal punishment but not eternal rest either. An in-between where your story gets to be rewritten. More or less.

Holy Sister Mary Margaret, I think I'm gonna have an aneurysm.

"Okay, fine. So our friends are in different meow meow meows than we are because their desires—"

"Or intentions."

"OR INTENTIONS . . . Can I finish a sentence, please?! Their *intentions* are different from ours?"

"Yes. As they were not with you when you made your arrival, they occupy a different meow meow meow that you must align with, intentionally, if you wish to seek them. The meow meow meow will typically be a fertile ground for allowing their intention to flourish."

"You mean, like, a genre?"

"What is a 'genre'? Silly-sounding word."

"Why?!" Brittany very nearly whines out of nowhere. "Why can't anything be simple?!"

"Because nothing is," Sumnut says without any judgment at all. Matter of fact.

"So we have to surmise what their intentional desires are and then focus our intentions similarly, and we'll track them down?" I ask. For something resembling clarity.

"Yes. Which should be easy, as they are members of your Party, correct?"

"I thought you just said nothing was easy," Brit accuses the guy.

"No, I said nothing is *simple*. A subtle but distinct difference."

While Brit wanders in circles to cool down so that she doesn't break anything irreplaceable in the CHRONOS (which is probably everything), I mull this over. In theory, he's right. As members of my Party, my Heart Guard, I should be able to align my intentions with theirs. But the thing is, I don't really *know* them. I thought I did. I wrote about them. But it turns out that nobody really knows anybody. Not that well.

But I'm gonna have to figure them out ASA-flipping-P if we're going to keep moving forward. Because I will never again abandon a thing I started without completing it to the best of my ability. And I sure as hell ain't gonna leave nobody behind.

"Alright, two more questions," I say.

"Ask as many as you like; it is the reason I am here, as whatever Mezmeric consults you are used to conversing with are likely attenuated."

"That's my first question. Why is Mezmer attenuated here?"

"The same reason Mezmer fades when one is too far outside the reach of Meridia's pull. It is a function of Meridia's terrestrial infrastructure. The fact that it functions here at all is a wonder."

"So, you don't actually know either."

"Not 'actually,' no. Just the way it's always been. Probably to do with it being a safe place for exploration or something."

"Super cool. Second, how do we, um, travel to wherever the others are? Actually. Once we've, y'know, figured out how to get on their intentional wavelength or whatever? Do we use this? The CHRONOS?"

"You may use *A* CHRONOS. This one happens to be *MY* CHRONOS. It is how *I* get around to other meow meow meows. It is specific to what my intentional reality looks like."

I look around at the clear TARDIS homage, and I just have to ask . . .

"Soooooo . . . you're a big *Doctor Who* fan?"

"Dr. Who?"

"Yeah."

"No, Dr. Who?"

"That's what I'm saying."

"But, no, Dr. Who?"

"What?"

"Who is Dr. Who?"

"Yes. Obviously, Who is Dr. Who."

"But—"

"Oh for the love of Richemerion, stop," Brit interjects. "He obviously doesn't know who you're talking about."

"Yes," Sumnut says. "*Who* are—?"

"Stop!" she declares again, more . . . emphatically. "Who gives a shit?"

"He does?" I point at Sumnut.

"QUIT IT!" She shakes her fists at both of us like she wants to say, *Why, I oughta* . . . "So, if this is your thing, Sumnut, how will *we* get to where we need to go?"

He scratches at one of the horns on his head and says, "I don't actually know. My job is just to help people understand the purpose and potential available here and leave them to their devices. Tracking is above my pay grade."

So, he's HR. He onboards, welcomes new hires, does orientation, and then peaces out never to be seen again. Man, bureaucratic bullshit is inescapable no matter where you are. I look at the stack of books and see, once again, the title *The World's Okayest Sherpa*, and it carries a whole new meaning for me.

He shrugs. "You just have to be clear enough about what you're looking for, and the plane will give it to you. Usually."

"Usually?"

"Don't worry about it."

"That's a very worrying thing to say."

"Then don't think about it. I noticed that you arrived here in a vehicle?"

". . . Yeah. Her name's Sheila."

"It is a very beautiful carriage."

"Thanks. I'll tell her you said so."

"In theory . . ."

"Yeah? In theory, what?"

"In theory, she could be used as a CHRONOS of her own if she is a dedicated vessel? Is she? Are you the Titleholder?"

"Yeah."

"Then, as she operates as an extension of your own Mezmeric reservoir, your intentions will be aligned. Even as your other Mezmeric functions are attenuated."

"Seriously . . . ?"

He smiles, and a sparkle lights his eye. "Just because things are never simple doesn't mean they can't sometimes be convenient."

"You're welcome to leave him here until he awakens," Sumnut says, referring to the curled-up Almeister in the back seat.

"I appreciate it, but . . ." I trail off, not wanting to risk offending the four-horned rando who just showed up and started telling us stuff that we have no way of verifying. Brittany, however, has no such reservations.

"But we don't know you and can't be sure you aren't totally full of shit and are luring us into some kind of gnarly trap."

He smiles placidly and says, "I think that's probably wise. Alright, then I'll leave you to it. I have to go provide a tutorial to another recent group arrival anyway. Another quartet, actually. Four young people." He starts off, and watching him go, I see something. Something that causes my blood to chill and my spine to seize up . . .

An owl.

There's an owl sitting on the branch of one of the trees in the field near the CHRONOS. And I'm overcome with a realization that causes the rest of my body to shake. I couldn't contextualize it back in the Tower. It gnawed at the back of my brain, but I couldn't fully unearth the latent memory. But here . . . now . . .

"Hey!" I call out as Sumnut is walking away.

"Yes?"

"This other quartet. Do you know their names?"

"They are on my list, yes."

"They're not called . . . Ycul, Retep, Nasus, and Dnumde, are they?"

He bends his head, eyes narrowed. "Yes. How do you know?"

". . . Lucky guess."

He huffs a laugh and then meanders back over to his TARDIS-y looking CHRONOS, goes inside, and after a moment, the thing starts to vibrate, shimmer, and disappears.

"The fuck did you know that?" Brit asks.

"Yeah, how you know dem name?" Jameson follows.

Rolling it over in my head, I don't answer directly, instead noting, "I think the Ninth Guardian knows we're here."

"What? How?" Brit asks.

"I don't know how, but I feel certain they do. We need to find Seph, Perg, and Zero-ass—"

"That what you gonna call Zerastian to her face?"

"Haven't decided yet. But we need to find them and get back to Meridia proper. Richemerion and Sumnut are spot-on about one thing: We need to start changing the narrative."

"Which narrative?"

"The one the Ninth Guardian is controlling."

"I don't under—"

"I'll explain it later. I promise. For now . . ."

I put Sheila into drive, press down on the accelerator, and head off into I have no idea where—to do I have no idea what—in an attempt to find Perg, Seph, and Zerastian before the Ninth Guardian does.

CHAPTER TWENTY-SIX

We've been driving for a good long while now, passing an ever-changing terrain as we go. Or, I guess, allowing ever-changing meow meow meows to pass us.

My thoughts race along with the transient landscape. What I see—and am trying to ignore—is a panorama of images from times in my life I can recollect: Family vacations with Mom before she died. Holidays and birthdays. Other random locations from other random memories.

Meridia before Meridia had its reality shattered into a killion little pieces.

I'm sorely tempted to take a little detour and indulge in building the story anew. But then, I think . . .

That's exactly what one would expect me to do.

The owl . . . The owl in the tree . . .

I stop the car. Turn it off.

"What are you doing?" Brit asks.

Ignoring the question, I turn around and shake the wizard's leg, seeing again if I can get him to wake up. "Al? Al? Rise and shine, please? We're having a grand adventure, and you're missing it."

Nothing. He rolls over and sucks his thumb.

"Bruce, uh, Carp? What's going on?"

"I have a theory."

"What kind of theory?"

"I don't wanna say too much about it yet. I don't have a way to prove it."

"Yeah, that's the definition of a theory."

"Touché."

"Just . . . What is it? A theory about what?"

I look at Jameson, who appears to be listening with a look of detached interest.

"Okay, so, the Mid-Meridian Plane, due to its Mezmer attenuation, can't be touched by the Ninth Guardian the way Meridia proper can, right? Since the way the Guardian wields power is by controlling the flow of Mezmer, here they'd be without that advantage."

"Alright."

"So, presumably, because the Ninth Guardian can't reach the plane without either exposing themself or, alternately, sacrificing one of their minions to come here, they can't hold direct sway over it. If the nature of the Mid-Meridian Plane is purgatorial, which it seems to be, that means that anyone who enters the plane can't be, quote-unquote, 'all bad.'"

"Say again?"

"I'm suggesting that one may be flawed, corrupted, but as Sumnut said, in order to get a shot at manipulating your history, your story, you have to at least be worthy of redemption. And presuming that's true, it would discount anyone who has signed onto the Guardian's agenda. Pure evil, so to speak, would be kicked straight out of here and onto the Subplane."

"Okay."

"So, in order to monkey around—"

"You need me do something, me gen'ral?"

"No, sorry, figure of speech. In order to *mess* around on the Mid-Meridian Plane—to, in some way, disrupt the incubator of narrative propulsion by the individuals here and co-opt it for their own needs the same way they have on Meridia—the Guardian would need to send an *inadvertent* emissary. Someone who is not completely in service to the Guardian but who has been, oh, I dunno . . . corrupted by them . . . to scout it out, as it were. To traverse the plane, find its weak spots, its entry points, the ways in which it can be manipulated . . ."

Almeister's soft snoring continues from the back seat.

"Oh, shit," Brit breathes.

"Yep. They've got a homing beacon."

Jameson lets out a low whistle, rolling the window down like he suddenly needs more air. "So wha' yuh sayin' is . . . dis whole time, de Guardian been lookin' fe one way in, but dem cah breach it unless dem send in a scout. A scout who cyan exist in both realms. Who cyan get corrupted, but nat be fully lost. Who cyan set de groundwork fe dem plans, even if dem nuh even know dem doin' it."

"I mean, that is *literally* what I just said. So, yeah."

"Son. Of. A. Bitch," Brit says. "So they've been working on a backdoor."

"Not just a backdoor," I murmur. "A *blueprint.*" I glance back at Almeister, still snoozing in his corner of the back seat, blissfully unaware of the existential crisis he's about to wake up to. "He's the test case. They're using him to see how far corruption can spread without fully losing someone to the void. How much of a person they can twist before they snap. And more than that, how much of the Mid-Meridian Plane they can manipulate before it fights back."

Brit exhales through her nose. "Why would they do something like that?"

"Because then they can rewrite the rules," I say grimly. "Permanently. They turn the Mid-Meridian Plane into just another piece of their empire. Another place to control. And once they do that? There's no safe haven left. No place beyond their reach. No way to change things without them seeing it coming first."

Brit blows out a deep breath. "But he was de-corrupted."

"Not completely. That's why he flipped out when the ancient Mezmer got into him in the desert."

"Yeah, but . . . I mean, we also reconnected him. To the Heart Guard."

"I know. Which is what worries me."

"What do you mean?"

"Babu Sumnut."

"What about him?"

"Babu is another word for 'mister.' Sumnut is an anagram. And it's not even a very clever one. It's just 'Tumnus' spelled backward."

Her face drops. "Mr. Tumnus." I nod. "That's why you asked if the four he was going to welcome in were called Ycul, Retep, Nasus, and Dnumde."

"Edmund, Susan, Peter, and Lucy. Yup. Same thing I do sometimes. 'Xanaraxa Caputrukahs?"

". . . Tupac Shakur."

I nod. "Homage."

(The first time I told her I was doing that, she rolled her eyes. Not because she thought it was stupid, I don't think, but because she was mad at herself for not catching it. I was surprised how many people didn't. I always thought it was pretty obvious. Anyway . . .)

Edmund, Susan, Peter, Lucy, Tumnus. All characters from *The Chronicles of Narnia.*

I suppose it could just be a coincidence, but . . . it's not. I know it's not.

Because of the owl.

The owl iconography at the Tower.

An owl sitting in the tree on the Mid-Meridian Plane, a place that otherwise looks to me like the idealized versions of a life I long for in various ways . . .

I've never told Brit the owl story, but now isn't the time. Fortunately, one of the things I like the most about Brittany is her ability to grasp a concept without a ton of explanation. Not that I don't always offer a ton of explanation. I do. It's why she's so frequently annoyed with my speechifying. She's already five steps ahead and has to wait for me to get all the words out of my system. I don't even want to think about how frustrated she would have been back before I discovered Adderall. So, she gets what I'm suggesting without me having to pour everything out. Maybe at some point I'll tell her all of the details about . . .

But not now. Not with Jameson sitting in the back seat and not . . . Just not now.

Her breathing speeds up. "Jesus fuck. How—?"

"Perfect storm. We didn't give Al's de-corruption time to reset, *and* we reconnected him to the Heart Guard. So now, the Ninth Guardian doesn't just have a Manchurian candidate on the Mid-Meridian Plane—they have one who can link to me. To us. And they're giving us hints, I think. Reminders."

"What do you mean, reminders?"

"The Ninth Guardian is letting us know that even though they may not be *here,* they're still here. That even if they can't technically touch us right now, they can still see us. Or feel us. Or more accurately, I suppose they're letting me know all that."

"Why?"

"It's fun for them? It's a game? They're just really, really mean? All of the above?"

"But how's it even possible? For them to know those things about you?"

"I'm not sure. But when I said we need to start changing the narrative?"

"Yeah?"

"I don't just mean it the way Sumnut talked about it. Not just here in the lab but in our actual reality. With every step we take moving forward."

"What are you suggesting?"

"I'm suggesting that we *think* we're operating of our own free will, but are we? We brought down the Tower. Great. But . . . that is what Carp—What I was *supposed* to do. That was, eventually, what I would have done had I not, y'know, died." Her eyes narrow, and she pieces together what I'm pitching. "I think it's possible the Ninth Guardian knows what we're going to do before we do it."

She lets it wash over her for a second before saying, ". . . Fuck."

"Yeah."

"We think we're making choices, but we're just following the trail of crumbs they already set down. Like, they knew we would reconnect Almeister and bring him with us to the Mid-Meridian Plane."

"Yeah."

"Fuck."

"Yeah."

"So, what do we do?"

"I'm not sure yet. But it certainly reinforces Richemerion's point about questioning how much we should trust the System."

We sit in silence for a second. I feel like this is where a *thump-thump, thump-thump* would normally happen.

"We really need to find our precog," I sigh, placing my hands on the steering wheel meditatively and closing my eyes.

"What are you doing now?"

"Not entirely sure. But driving aimlessly isn't getting us anywhere. I'm going to try focusing my intention."

"On what?"

"Zerastian, I guess? I'm going to see if I can, whatever, 'identify' her in my mind."

I close my eyes again and strive to imagine Zerastian. Which is not easy, since I've never actually met her. I think about what I do know about her, how she and Carpathian came to meet. How she became part of his Heart Guard. I'm so bad about recalling details that . . . But this is important.

So.

I dig as deeply as I can into my hidden box of recollection and attempt to recall what I wrote back when I thought this was all just a story I was telling . . .

Ages of Alumos, Riftbreaker Book Four, Chapter Thirteen

Einzgear the Saviour squinted at the rusting metallic hulk sitting before him in the "Abandoned Vehicles for Hire" facility in the small mountain town of Colandeen where he, Almeister, Teleri, and Pergamon had fled to after suffering an unfortunate setback in their attempt to unseat the mayor of Dorieximore. It had become clear that they needed a vessel of some kind—of any kind—if they were to continue to fight "road wars," which were becoming increasingly more frequent in the struggle for supremacy.

"What do you think of this vehicle?" Almeister asked.

"This," Carpathian declared, "is not a vehicle. It is an insult on wheels. We'd be better off in my old conveyance vessel. At least it was serviced with some regularity."

Next to him, Nightwind crossed her arms, equally unimpressed. In the time since he had met her, he had learned that while she was a faithful ally, she did not suffer fools nor truck with the wasting of time. She had become as committed to the journey they were on as the Saviour himself. However, Carpathian also knew her to be pragmatic to the core.

"It is a wretched device," she acknowledged, "but considering our limited resources to acquire such a thing, I suppose we're lucky it has wheels at all."

"If I may," Pergamon's rugged voice chimed in, "my concern's that the wheels are square. That seems a cause for concern, does it not?"

Carpathian looked over again to his aged mentor for some sort of guidance in the matter. The old wizard shrugged. "What did you expect? A Mezmer-ready battle chariot?"

"Ideally," Carpathian said flatly.

The four of them stared for another moment at the . . . thing in front of them when a woman came into view. She stepped out of the shadows of the garage, her chunky boots crunching on loose scrap metal, and strode toward the quartet.

She wore garb composed of leather and some sort of metallic fabric. Her bare forearms were covered in intricate tattoos that glowed faintly in the afternoons suns. Her crimson hair was tied back in a sleek braid, and her eyes had an otherworldly sheen, like twin mirrors reflecting secrets she was unlikely ever to share.

As she drew closer, Carpathian could read the glowing name badge on her top.

It read: Zerastian.

"Hello," this "Zerastian" said, her voice calm and somehow knowing. Her accent was strange; clipped and efficient. "You're looking for a vehicle to hire?"

Teleri raised an eyebrow. "We're looking for something that can actually move. This thing looks like it would give up halfway down a hill."

"If it made it that far," Pergamon added.

Zerastian did not seem offended. If anything, she looked amused. "I'm sure you would. So would everyone. But transports like you're talking about are in short supply. If you want something fancier, you'll have to deal with the official agencies who are in possession of such things. But anyone who comes here isn't really in a position to go through more . . . municipal channels, usually. So, this is what we've got." Her smile widened and her eyes narrowed as she looked at Carpathian. "I know you," she said.

Everyone stiffened as Carpathian's hand went to the hilt of his treasured Blade of the Starfallen. "I don't believe so," he responded warily.

"Don't be worried." Her smile widened, and she leaned her head forward. "I've been waiting for you," she said with an air of relief, like someone who had been waiting to utter those words for a long time.

Again, there were looks all around before Almeister finally asked, "What do you mean you've been waiting for us, my child?"

Rather than answer directly, she said, "I know this heap of junk looks like scrap, but it's the exact transport you'll need to handle the kind of terrain you're going to be heading into."

"How do you know what terrain we're heading into?" Carpathian queried.

"The same way I know how we're going to get out of it." She grinned. "Or, at least, the way I believe we will with enough of a statistical probability that I can get rid of this now." She pulled off her name badge, let it drop to the ground, and started back toward the garage. "Give me just a moment to gather a couple of personal items and we can go."

Carpathian shook his head. "Wait, what? What do you mean, we? What are you talking about? Who are you?"

"She's a precog," said Almeister, awareness dawning over him.

"A precog?" Nightwind asked. "She can see the future?"

Zerastian responded, "Sometimes. More accurately, I can see future possibilities. I usually get some kind of likelihood percentage along with whatever the vision is. The percentage I saw that I would meet you all and join in your efforts to combat the Ninth Guardian was close to ninety-five percent, so I felt good about it. In any case, I actually just decided I don't need anything, really. We can just go." She started for the car. Reaching the decrepit machine, she opened the door while Carpathian simply stared at her.

"Truly," she said, "we should leave before they arrive."

"Before who arrives?" Carpathian asked with worry.

"The Disciples of the Ninth Guardian. They know you're here. Or they will soon. I don't have as accurate a picture of the timeline, but I'm fairly confident about the outcome if we don't go soon."

"Why do you want to come with us?" Pergamon asked the young precog.

"Because . . ." She paused to think. "Because I saw it. But more than that, I felt it. When I see it and feel it at the same time, it tends to be right. Sometimes, I have to parse, but when it's as strong as what I have in this situation, I don't question it. There are a few possible outcomes for you all, but as far as I've been able to project, none of them happen without me there. So, y'know, I'm excited to find out what's going to happen as well!"

She beamed at them, and Carpathian drew the others into an impromptu huddle.

"Almeister?" he asked, leaving the specifics of the question open.

"I can sense no malice from her. And it would not hurt to have a precog with us."

"You don't worry that she's a spy or something of the like?" Nightwind, ever cautious, asked.

They turned to stare at her, and Zerastian waved her tiny hand.

"Perhaps. But I don't think so," Almeister confessed. "However, it is ultimately the Saviour's decision. Carpathian? What say you?"

Carpathian ran his tongue across his teeth and then broke company, striding over to the small, self-proclaimed precog.

"What else do you offer? Besides this supposed precognitive Ability of yours?"

Once again, she did not appear offended. She simply smiled and said, "I knew you would ask that." Einzgear rolled his eyes. "I have a kind of Mezmer that not everyone does."

"What kind is that?" Carpathian queried, interest piqued.

"Technomancy," she replied. "Which can come in handy in certain sticky situations. Like, oh, I don't know, when you need to bypass security to infiltrate the office of the mayor of Dorieximore." Carpathian raised his eyebrows. She shrugged. "Just for example."

"You know—" Carpathian started, but before he could finish, she became giddy and added, "Or when you need to get an old hunk of junk up and running to combat standards!"

She pulled a small device from her belt, a gleaming orb covered in etched runes and delicate wiring. Placing it against the vehicle's hull, she began muttering under her breath as her tattoos pulsed slightly. The sound of grinding metal filled the air, and after a moment, the vehicle's engine roared to life, a low, guttural sound that echoed throughout the yard.

Carpathian watched with wonder as faint lines of blue light coursed through the frame and the square wheels shifted, smoothing themselves into much more useful circular shapes.

"See?" Zerastian said with a satisfied grin. "Handy."

Carpathian took a moment to regard this curious young woman and this unexpected turn of events, lifting his chin in a skeptical assaying of the moment. Then, he looked at the members of his burgeoning Heart Guard and said, "Let's go," calling them over with a wave of his hand.

The other three made their way to the newly imbued vehicle as Carpathian took the driver's seat. Teleri climbed into the passenger's seat next to him, holding Pergamon in her lap, with Almeister settling into the rear and Zerastian hopping in next to the wizard.

Carpathian assessed what was now a quintet, and for the hundredth time in the last couple of Lunar Cycles, wondered over how it was that life could change so quickly.

"That's not how they met."

I stare at Brit in half confusion and half superconfusion.

"What? What are you talking about?"

"I mean, it is approximately how they . . . uh, *we* met Zerastian." She glances in the back seat at a snoozing Almeister and a distracted-by-a-piece-of-lint Jameson and whispers, "But that's not the way the interaction with her went. That was an early draft."

"Huh?"

"That was an early draft before I went in and made a bunch of suggestions to try and tie some stuff together and clean it up. It was overwritten as shit. You seriously don't remember at all?"

I do now. Damn. She's right. *Ages of Alumos* was, famously, the messiest of all the books in the Riftbreaker series. It was the first book Brit was aboard for from start to finish, and I think I wanted to impress her with how clever I was, so I overwrote myself into a corner. Repeatedly. Complicating the simple. Sometimes, rewriting a chapter twenty or twenty-five times.

I know a couple of writers who do that, and it works. My friend Matt, for example, has talked about how he does that until he gets everything just so, and it's been wildly successful for him. But for me, the only thing it seemed to do was get my new assistant-at-the-time really frustrated about how badly I was blowing past deadlines, as she was the one who had to field anxious phone calls from my publisher.

"Damn. Yeah. I remember. Or, I remember that I don't remember. What was it in the end? How did we decide . . . ?"

"It was decided that she needed to be less noble? That not everyone has pure intentions when they join up with what is supposed to be seen as a righteous cause?"

"Oh, right."

"What do you mean, 'oh, right.' Why'd you say it like that?"

"Like what?"

"Like you resent the change."

"I didn't."

"You did."

"I didn't."

"You totally did."

She's right. I totally did.

Because that wasn't what I wanted for Zerastian. It's what, as Brit just said, was decided. I never really wanted Zerastian to be a sassy, wisecracking street hustler. I always wanted her to be more . . . *elevated.* More *otherworldly.*

The first version of Zerastian wasn't just some wayward scoundrel scrabbling for a better deal. She was *above* that. She was untethered by the grime and desperation that the revision shackled her with. She wasn't some scrappy survivor clawing her way through the world's cruelties; she was *of* the world but not *in* it. A presence. A beacon.

Because I like that kind of shit.

But I got persuaded (to put it politely) by other people—Brit, my editor, a couple of early readers drawn from a contest the publisher ran to give Riftbreakerers a chance to vote on the story's direction—into the idea that "*realism*" means "*relatability.*" That Zerastian needed to be *accessible.* That no one would believe in a character who seemed too untouchable, too *formed.*

Basically, I wound up letting the work be crafted by committee.

Because something other people pay a lot more attention to than I do is what I guess one would call "theme." I can usually tell you the story and the plot to a greater or lesser degree, but I don't really go into writing stuff knowing what it's *about*. That's a subtle distinction that people don't normally pick up on, I don't think. What happens in a story versus what the story is actually trying to say.

Hell, I don't know if *I* know what I'm trying to say sometimes. Just that I feel like I need to say *something*. In any case . . .

"So, I don't think I can find her," I tell Brittany.

"Why not?"

"Because, if I can barely even recall what she's all about, there's no way I can align intentions with her. I don't know what she wants."

Brit sighs and mumbles, barely audibly, "You may have come from me, Bruce, but I'll be damned if I can understand you . . ."

"Yeah. Something like that."

"Okay, so, let's see if we can get a twenty on either Perg or Seph," Brit suggests.

"Sure. Alright. Theoretically, I should be able to figure out Perg's intentions. He's my familiar. And he's a pretty simple guy whom I've known for, like, a dozen years."

"Or . . . he's known you."

"What do you mean?"

"I mean, he's known you. He's watched you and paid attention to everything you do but, until recently, you only really considered him when it was time to feed him."

I blink at her a couple of times. I don't know if she's calling me a selfish prick deliberately, or if it's just a statement of fact and I now feel like a selfish prick, but tomato/asshole, I reckon.

"Still, I feel like I know him better than I know Seph. Maybe."

"Mi know her," Jameson's voice interrupts from the rear.

"What?" I turn to face the heavy-lidded macaque as he finally (finally) blows the last of the doobie out of the window and rolls it up.

"Mi hear ya up there talkin' about who know who and someone mi know 'bout is Miss Persephone."

Of course. *Of course*. She brought him back from the dead. She took what was left of him as a bloodstain on the floor of Garr Haven and summoned it back into existence. That's the kind of thing that gives people a real intimate understanding of each other, you gotta figure.

"So, do you think you can find her? Align with where she is on the plane?"

"Maybe. Maybe not. But more important, nah, mi need to ask question, Saviour mine."

"Uh, yeah, sure. What's up?"

"Who be Bruce, mi gen'ral?"

CHAPTER TWENTY-SEVEN

We're out of the car, standing a distance away so as not to be heard by whoever might be listening in. What I thought was the "last" of the spliff appears to have been not even close to the conclusion of the sweet stick-icky Jameson has available, because he's now puffing away aggressively enough to send Smokey the Bear into a paroxysm of anxiety. "Paroxysm of anxiety" also being an apt description of the normally chill monkey's mood at having been told what is, more or less, the whole story.

We've been pretty sloppy about "staying in character." Brit's called me Bruce, I've referred to "Carpathian" in the third person (which only psychotic narcissists do when speaking of themselves, and that's not the look I wanna project for a World Saviour), and we've talked probably a little too freely about the books in general.

Jameson clocking it is now the third or fourth time we've been called out on it, but this time, I felt like there was no point in trying to dodgeball our way around it. There is a simple truth about Jameson that I neglected to pay attention to; something I know very well: High people are the most observant and unceasingly suspicious people you'll ever meet.

When I'm high, I notice stuff all the time that feels small but hits big. Like realizing that the reason I'm so into the pizza I get from this one local place I like in Ellisville called Faraci is because there's just the faintest hint of cardamom baked into the crust. Mind. Blown. Or the night I was doing what I call "writing and lighting" while listening to Sufjan Stevens's "No Shade in the Shadow of the Cross" and heard this faint, rhythmic hum in the background.

I paused the track, backed it up, and listened again. It was an air conditioner running. Not in my house (I have a whisper-quiet HVAC system. I love my whisper-quiet HVAC system. I miss my whisper-quiet HVAC system.), but in the background of the song. It painted this incredibly vivid picture of Sufjan holed up in some small apartment, alone on a sweltering summer day, fiddling with his guitar, trying to chase the perfect melody while the heat bore down on him.

I later learned that the reason it was there was because Sufjan recorded that song on a friggin' iPhone (which is both ballsy and kind of genius), and that all the ambient noises—the hum, the clicks, the barely there creaks of the piano bench—were part of the song because they were part of the moment. That stuck with me. How sometimes the unintentional details are what make art truly resonate. It made me cry. Possibly because I was also high when I learned that tidbit, but also because it's beautiful.

Speaking of people crying when they're high . . .

"So . . . you *not* Carpathian Einzgear, the World Saviour?" Jameson says, eyes glistening, like his whole reality has been shattered.

You and me both, pal.

"No," I tell him with a big sigh. "No. I'm bestselling author and American literary treasure Bruce Silver from St. Louis."

Brit gives me a tense look. As I say, I'm giving him "more or less" the whole story.

He looks around, blinking, trying to make sense.

"No."

"Yeah."

"No, no, no."

"Yeah, man. I'm sorry."

He shakes his head, exhaling another heavy plume of smoke. "Mi not high enough for this."

I don't know if coming clean was the right decision or not, but I figure Jameson is, if nothing else, a good test audience; i.e. if hearing the truth makes him bug out, then I'll know for sure that the, shall we say, less lifted and more invested denizens of the RLU (the Riftbreaker Literary Universe) will not take the news well at all.

And, given the hand-shaking nervousness he is trying to calm by smoking up all the weed in the universe at once, I think I have my answer about how stressful this information is to hear. Watching him stand here, more freaked out over this than any of the other stuff that's happened to him—being Spell-summoned back to life, being run through with a sword and surviving, bringing down the whole goddamn Tower—has me almost more freaked out than I've been about anything that's happened. (*Almost.* Let's not be overly dramatic about it.)

I reach out and, without asking, I grab the spliff from Jameson.

"What are you doing?" Brit asks.

"Clearing my head," I answer, raising the blunt in a half salute and putting it to my lips.

Two things: One, just recalling the Sufjan story made me realize how long it's been since I've gotten high, and possibly, I need some "adventuring and chill" in my life to refocus me. Maybe it'll help dial in my objectives. And two, I'm thinking that if I show Jame that I'm still just a cool dude who he can get smoked out with, it'll make him less fearful. Kind of like saying, "Okay, yes, I'm not exactly who you thought I was, but I'm not a narc, bro."

Or, more honestly, I just wanna see if I can escape from unreality for a second.

So, popping it into my mouth and drawing in a long, rich, full pull of the sweet, sweet—

COUGH. COUGH. COUGH.

Oh, god. Omigod. Wow. *WOW.* Either because it's been a minute since I smoked or because this Meridian diesel just hit different, I was not prepared for the intensity of this shit.

"I'm fine, I'm fine," I gasp between coughs. Even though no one is asking if I'm fine or not.

Jameson grabs the stick back and pops it into his mouth, still eyeing me with skepticism.

"Bruce ya be, then?"

"Yup," I gargle, still working out the remnants of the hyperweed from my lungs.

He directs his questioning to Brit. "And what ye be called, for the true?"

She looks at me pounding on my chest. I try to give her a thumbs-up.

"Brittany," she sighs. "Brittany McAfee."

Jame nods, taking it in. He sucks in more smoke, which now just amazes me. I can seriously barely breathe. Holy monkey weed, that's the heaviest pull I can ever remember taking. These Meridian macaques are built different.

"De snail?"

"His name was 'Gonzo,' but he's requested a formal change, so it is now actually Perg. We didn't fill out paperwork or anything, but it's what he's requesting, so we're honoring it," Brittany affirms.

"Aye. A Perg by any other name . . ."

I don't even bother to ask if Jameson knows he's paraphrasing the Bard or if it's just a coincidence. Doesn't really matter.

I spit, which is gross but necessary, and take in a semicleansing breath before saying, "Yeah. So, that's the story. So far. That's who we are, how we got here, and, well, you know the rest."

He squints at me. "How come ya not tell nobody?"

"I dunno, man. I . . . At first, because I wasn't sure this was all real, and then because, y'know, once you get deep into a lie, it's just easier to keep lying, I guess. Besides, I'm not sure what good it would do."

"Why not?"

"Because if everyone sees me as Carpathian and sees her as Teleri, they feel hopeful. People already had their Saviour taken from them. If, in their minds, he's back, who I am to disabuse them of that belief? Carpathian isn't just a person."

"He's not? What he be?"

"He's an idea," Brit moans. "A symbol for what we can all become if we just believe in ourselves and a bunch of shit like that."

I scowl at her because even though she might be over it, it's still a nice idea.

"Yes," I say. "That's right. So . . . y'know . . . when seen through that prism, who's to say I'm *not* Carpathian? Y'know?"

He puffs and thinks. And thinks and puffs.

"S'pose."

"So . . ." I begin, cautiously. "So, we're cool?"

"Yeah, mon, we cool."

I breathe a little easier.

"And you won't tell anyone?"

"Nah, mon. Jameson keep him mouth closed tight like a virgin's knees."

Specific simile, but okay.

"Thank you."

"But you need tell."

"What? Who?"

"Mi girl. Mi Persephone. She been long waiting for the Einzgear, him to come back to her. She need to know the truth."

God. Is everyone following the same guilt-inducing playbook?

"No, no, no," I say. Emphatically. "No. Why? No. In fact, I would argue that she's the *last* person who needs to know the truth. At least not yet."

"How come, ya say?"

"Because of what I just friggin' said! If anyone needs to believe in Carpathian's presence here, it's her. Given what she's been through? What she's still going through? You really think she needs this news dumped on her? I may not be the Carpathian she wants, but right now, I'm the Carpathian she's got. Can't that be enough?" He considers my plea with uncertainty, so I keep selling. "We don't even know where she is or what she's dealing with at the moment. Can we at least figure out that part and then make a decision about what to do?"

He scratches the back of his head, and it calls to mind when I used to scratch Crystal the capuchin behind the ears. Finally, after a long moment, he says . . .

"Alright, me gen'ral. I see how we go."

He points at both of us like, "tread carefully," and then heads back to the car. Brittany turns to me and asks . . .

"Do you think—?"

"I dunno," I interrupt, continuing the habit she and I have developed of her starting to ask me about things for which I do not have an answer and me just heading it off at the pass before I get too far into my own thoughts, seeking remedies that don't exist for maladies I don't understand.

Following close behind, Brit and I take our places inside Sheila, and as I slam the door shut, it jolts Almeister finally awake with a, "Brucillian?!"

Jameson and I make eye contact in the rearview mirror. He raises his furry eyebrows.

"No, no, ya sleepyhead, you. Brucillian's not here. It's me. Carpathian."

Continuing to work with my theory that the DONG Mezmer that has kept its residual hold on Almeister despite our best efforts has somehow also made him an unwitting tool in the Ninth Guardian's plans is yet another reason I need to keep "the truth" (such as it is) close to my vest. I need to treat Al like he's wearing a wire and anything that gets talked about in his presence is likely also being transmitted somehow to Ninth Guardian HQ. Better safe than sorry.

"Oh, oh," he says, looking around. "Where are we?"

"We're in the Mid-Meridian Plane."

"Mid-Meridian Plane?" He blinks his eyes. Looks around.

"Yeah. Remember? Richemerion told us to come here?"

"Oh . . . Yes." He looks around. "Where are the others?"

"Well, we haven't found Zerastian yet, and we managed to lose Perg and Seph, unfortunately."

"Seph?"

Oh shit. Does he not . . . ?

"Yeah, Persephone. Your daughter? You remember her, right?"

"Of course I do. I just wasn't sure I heard you correctly. My ears haven't popped." He opens his jaw, trying to unclog his canals. "What do you mean, we 'lost' her?"

"I mean, she's somewhere on the plane. And we need to, uh, localize our estimation of . . ."

"We need to dial into her, intentionally," Brit interjects. "Assess where her essence might have drawn her, atmospherically, and collect her up. Jameson thinks he can do it."

"True tale, mi wizard," Jame affirms.

"Oh." Almeister ruminates, not speaking for a moment. I glance at him and notice he's staring down at his lap.

"What's wrong?" I ask. "You need to pee or . . . ?"

"I should have . . ." His lip starts to quiver. "I should have . . ."

"Should have what?"

"I should have been a better father to her!" he exclaims, causing the three of us to jump.

"Whoa. Al . . ."

"I have not been as present in her life as I might have been! After her mother passed . . ."

WAIT, WHAT?! MOTHER?! PERSEPHONE HAD A MOTHER?!

I mean, duh, obviously. Of course she did. The mechanics of reproduction on Meridia are the same as on Earth . . . I suppose . . . Never wrote a birthing scene. BUT . . . I guess I just never even considered the fact that Almeister would've had a wife at some point. Maybe he didn't. Maybe they weren't married. Maybe younger Al was a playboy who got around the block. In which case, he could have who knows how many babies and baby mamas!

"Calm down, Bruce. Don't run riot now. You have bigger Persephones to catch."

"You're right. Thanks Bruce."

"I gotcha, Bruce."

". . . I fear I wasn't dutiful in my fatherly obligations!" Al concludes, breaking down.

Jesus Christ. Are you kidding me?!

Man, oh man, is *this* ever a diversion we don't need. I'm starting to understand better the critics of my past work who took issue with how much granular detail I threw into my writing. I mean, sure, this is a spicy tidbit that might be interesting at some point in the future, but is NOW the time I need to be finding this out?! (Rhetorical. *No,* is the answer.) And then, the realization lands like a brick in my gut.

Almeister could fix it here.

Here, on the Mid-Meridian Plane, where everything is malleable, where you can rewrite yourself, your story, your regrets, your failures . . . If Almeister leans into this guilt, the plane might be inclined to bend itself around him to accommodate.

He could craft a new past, a new truth, a reality where he was there for Persephone in all the ways he wasn't before. And why wouldn't he? If I were him, wouldn't I? If I were given the chance to revise the worst things about myself, wouldn't I take it? Wouldn't anyone?

Isn't that the central journey that I'm on right now? (Again, rhetorical. Obviously, it is.)

But we do not have the time for this.

If Al gets sucked into a personal redemption arc, we will never get him back. And we need to get out of here together.

Right now, I have to get this train back on the tracks and keep us moving forward. Because the *last* thing I need is for Al to attempt to do a revision on his life's story by throwing himself into a narrative reality where he wins a Father of the Year trophy or some shit and we have to drag him out of his own meow meow meow and back to us again.

I reach back and pat him on his old, bony, kind-of-ashy knee.

"Bah, don't worry about it. Nobody's father is perfect!" I clear my throat. "Look, we're gonna figure out where she is, and we're gonna—"

CRACK.

Before I can finish, there is a sound that splits through the air like the universe just popped a joint back into place. It's not thunder. Not an explosion. It's the sound of *something* giving way, like a fault line snapping, like a pane of glass under too much pressure, like . . .

Like maybe a plane that got tired of waiting for us to move it along and decided to just give us a shove instead.

"The fuck was that?"

"I think—"

Another *CRACK*, and the air turns dense. The light bends sideways.

"I don't like this," Brit moans.

"I don't either," I mumble as I watch the world around us tilt. Not physically, not like we're about to slide off some cosmic table, but conceptually, like the idea of where we are just changed its mind midthought. Like a painter, unsatisfied, dragging a brush over what once was, layering something new over something erased.

The landscape dissolves, not into nothing but into possibility, colors bleeding, textures melting into impressions waiting to be filled. I can feel it: the indecision, the impatience.

The plane is editing.

I grip the wheel on instinct; though I can feel it, the car doesn't matter anymore. The whole concept of a car barely holds together in the shifting logic of a world that is actively reconsidering its own structure.

Brit's hand reaches over, and her fingers dig into my sleeve. "This is fucked," she hisses.

No shit. But I don't know what to—

I close my eyes and try—like really, really try—to focus my intention. Not on finding Seph or Perg, but on the one thing I can think to truly try and take another run at.

Zerastian.

I picture her as I originally wrote her: calm, composed, knowing. A force of quiet certainty, someone who had already seen the future and accepted it, waiting for the right moment to step in. A precog who played her cards close to her chest because she already knew the hand. Someone who had already run the calculations, already factored in all the variables, and was simply waiting for the rest of us to catch up.

I want *that* version of her. Not the scrappy hustler, not the survivor clawing her way through the wreckage, not the version everyone argued was more realistic. I want the one who was *waiting for us*. The one who, from the moment we met her, made us feel like we weren't just fumbling forward in the dark, but that maybe, just maybe, we were exactly where we were supposed to be.

"Us?"

"What's that, Bruce?"

"You keep saying 'us.' That Zerastian was waiting for 'us.'"

"I do?"

"Mm-hmm."

"Well . . . Okay. Whatever."

I don't have time for this. I have to change the plane before we wind up getting shuffled off into who knows what.

So, I press into that thought of Zerastian, into that idea of her, and the plane stirs again.

The colors in the sky don't just shift; they *reconsider themselves*. The road beneath us buckles, not like it's breaking but like it's *adjusting*, rolling and settling into something new, something revised.

I open my eyes. And . . .

The junkyard stretches out before me. Not in my head. Not on a page. *Here*. Real.

Not real in the way the junkyards back home are real. It's exactly as I wrote it, or wanted to write it. Not a crumbling expanse of rusted-out wrecks, but a place where the abandoned wasn't necessarily the forgotten. A space where things came to wait, not to rot.

The stacks of metal and machinery aren't random heaps of scrap; they're arranged almost *intentionally*, like the bones of something unfinished waiting to be pieced back together. The rust flickers in and out of time, shifting between decay and restoration as if the junk itself can't decide which version of itself it wants to be.

And then . . .

She steps out.

Boots crunch against loose scrap metal, deliberate and unhurried. The sound carries, crisp and clear in the heavy silence that has settled.

She wears leather and metallic fabric, not terribly practical in the way a scavenger would demand, but practical in the way someone who *chooses* their place in the world decides to present themselves. Her bare forearms are lined with intricate tattoos that pulse faintly. Her crimson hair is sleek and bound, catching just enough of the light to mark her against the scrap and steel around her. Her eyes that reflect more than what they see; twin mirrors holding depths I was only ever able to describe but never truly understand.

And yet, standing here now, I *do* understand.

She isn't hesitant. She isn't uncertain. She isn't improvising her way through a world that doesn't care. She's exactly as I once imagined her.

She stops a short distance from us, and I prepare to hear that efficient, clipped tone I once wrote about.

And that is exactly what I do hear when she speaks.

"Hello . . ."

Kind of.

"Carpathian."

Um . . . actually . . . more like . . .

"I wondered when you might show up here."

. . . Björk.

"This is your new farartæki? She's very nice."

She sounds like Björk.

CHAPTER TWENTY-EIGHT

"Once Upon a Time in Meridia." Part 5

Zerastian held her breath as she tumbled through the void, her body twisting and flailing as the tether dissolved into an unholy snag of snarling energy that seared at her flesh and spirit. The sensation was unlike anything she'd felt before—a combination of falling, drowning, and being torn apart atom by atom, all while being shoved through some type of sadistic kaleidoscope.

Had she been tasked with anticipating what she expected the Mid-Meridian Plane to be like, she didn't know if she would have been able to express in language what she expected, but whatever it was, she felt certain this was probably it.

She might have suggested it would be a black abyss. Some sort of timeless limbo. Something grim but comprehensible. And she would have been right.

At least for her.

And when the chaos finally spat her out, she found herself precisely where she wanted to be. A hazy, empty space filled with black smoke. A place that was neither here nor there, and with an inability to see into what had been called before "realms unknown."

It was an unfamiliar feeling, this sensation of not being able to project the future. But it was one she relished.

As a precog, she had spent her whole life feeling—to a greater or lesser degree—unsurprised. Of course, there were always aberrations, deviations to the expected order of events, but by and large, she could anticipate the outcome of most inevitable situations. At a minimum, she could foretell that which was merely probable and that which was inevitable.

A good example of the inevitable was having met Carpathian Einzgear and his burgeoning Heart Guard in the first place. She had seen the moment that he, along with his sorcerer friend, Teleri, his snail companion, Pergamon, and the old wizard, Almeister, had first wandered into the "Abandoned Vehicles for Hire" facility in the small mountain town of Colandeen where she worked as a leasing agent.

Her parents had questioned her decision to take a job so seemingly beneath her. After having been identified as one of the seldom—the rare—precognitive progeny of the land by the great Endershadow of the Deepvoid, it had always been believed that she would one day assume a role of prominence in the Meridian High Council, the chief advisers to the principal governors of the world.

But it was precisely because of her clairvoyance that she knew what would happen if she did. She would become subject to capriciousness of the Ninth Guardian and be impelled to play a role in their theater of cruelty. She could glimpse what that future would hold for her, and it was bleak. Zerastian Teronia's remarkable gift would have been reduced to nothing more than an instrument to be used for someone else's bidding. And, oriented as she was—emotionally—that was a future she would not abide.

So, she took a "regular" job. An ordinary, everyday role as a vehicular leasing agent, the benefit of such a thing being twofold.

First, it kept her largely hidden. At a minimum, it made her less conspicuous. She was able to go about her day, focusing on developing her talents in relative obscurity and accruing Mezmeric Skills she found interesting, one such Skill being Technomancy. She had always loved tinkering with things, devices. And working around abandoned vehicles all day, preparing them for lease to needy citizens, gave her the chance to indulge in her hobby. Which she knew she would need for the second reason . . .

Her earliest memory of being able to glimpse the future involved a man whose name she did not know but whose face she could see clearly. The specific vision would occasionally change—sometimes he would appear to her dressed in the uniform of a conveyance conductor, sometimes in the garb of an emerging hero; sometimes with a beard, sometimes clean-shaven; sometimes alone, other times with a coterie in tow—but always with a purpose that felt, to her, greater than herself.

So when Carpathian approached her that fated day—as she stood in the garage of the leasing office attempting to engineer a rusted old hunk of metal back into something like working order—she was not surprised. She had been waiting for him her entire life. And when she persuaded him to let her join his cohort and serve as his warning system and his technical adviser of sorts, she felt that her life's mission had finally begun.

Which is what had made his betrayal hurt all the more.

She had wanted to say something. To confront the Saviour. To ask him why he was planning to forfeit all they had struggled for and simply "give up" on the Fields of Rendalia. But she waited, because it hadn't yet happened. Because he did not yet know he would. And because she held out hope that perhaps the future she predicted would not come to pass.

But then . . .

There was the battle with the Giant Serpent of the Mokeisan. A battle in which her Omen Ability, as it was called, seemed to be rendered dumb. At the time, she could not understand why. She could not make sense of all the ways in which her Skills, Talents, and Abilities were being compromised. At least not until the portal that swallowed her up opened its great maw and dragged her down to where she found herself ultimately deposited.

But somehow, some way, she knew that Carpathian had done this to her. Perhaps not intentionally. Perhaps not maliciously. But it was his hubris, his unwillingness to look into his own Heart and admit that he could not be all things to all people that precipitated this great fall. And she knew—not precognitively but in her very core—that she would not be the last who fell because of those qualities within the Saviour that, while admirable, also wielded a costly counterblade.

When she finally landed, she laid there for a long moment, just gasping for breath and blinking at the empty void around her, the sensation of not knowing causing her to breathe just ever so slightly faster.

What is this place? she wondered to herself. In all the permutations and possible realities she had ever witnessed in her mind's eye, a realm like this had never entered her consciousness. Her first instinct was to run a scan, but she quickly realized how little that would help. The readings struggling to make themselves seen to her seemed useless—patterns looping in on themselves. It was data that defied logic. The place wasn't just unfamiliar; it was actively defying categorization.

She could not imagine, or more accurately, will into her imagination the name for this place, but her instincts screamed that she had entered somewhere entirely *other*. A whole new world that didn't operate by the rules she had played by her whole life.

But she had a burning feeling somewhere in the far recesses of her brain that let her know she had, in fact, seen something like this place before. Perhaps in a dream.

Just as she began puzzling together where she might have encountered such a noncorporeal environment, someone spoke to her.

"Welcome," she heard them say, "to the Mid-Meridian Plane."

Spinning, Zerastian attempted to activate the Rebuker, but its opalescent shield failed to flare to life as she expected it to, which only further enhanced the sense of wrongness she felt.

"Do not be frightened," the voice, which sounded an awful lot like it was coming from inside her own head, went on. "I'm not here to harm you."

"Who are you?" Zerastian asked.

"I am your guide. I am to introduce you to the plane and explain how it works."

"Show yourself," Zerastian demanded.

"I cannot," the voice replied.

"Why not?"

"Because you are the architect, and you have not designed a form."

"What?"

The voice began whispering to her, explaining the rules of order on the Mid-Meridian Plane. Defining for her what was possible here. It spoke of intent, of stepping outside one's own life and asking why. Asking if the direction you'd been moving prior to now still served you.

As she listened, she found herself drawing in deeper and deeper inhalations; anxious, short inhalations that caused her to feel as though she was consuming nothing but grave and unfamiliar uncertainty.

But, much to her surprise, it was the uncertainty that caused her to also feel that, for the first time in her life, she could truly and freely . . . breathe.

She let out the anxiety and sucked in another resonant, pacifying chest full of . . .

. . . She didn't know.

She didn't know what to call it or what might happen next or if she might be trapped in this place for all of eternity. She just knew that she was finally free from the anchoring burden of her so-called "gift."

And it caused her to smile.

CHAPTER TWENTY-NINE

Wow," I say, the word tumbling out of my mouth before I can stop it.

Because it's a dumb thing to say. It's too small, too insignificant for what Zerastian has just told me. Too inconsequential. But it's what I've got.

There have only been a handful of times in my life when I've been genuinely at a loss for words.

Finding out that *Riftbreaker: The Graphic Novel* was about to be scuttled because the publisher thought it was going to be "too cerebral for their target demo." That was one. Walking into a surprise birthday party Mollie had arranged and discovering that everyone, literally *everyone,* I had ever met had been invited, including my high school gym teacher whom I hadn't seen in like fifteen years and who greeted me with, "Damn, Silvert, you got old." (As if I needed another reason to hate surprise parties.) That was another. But this? This moment?

This moment of meeting Zerastian for the first time, only to discover that she had been harboring doubts about (and a kind of resentment for) Carpathian for at least a couple books worth of story . . . ? That's taken the usually robust amount of language I toss around right outta my old yapper.

Because I feel like shit. I let others determine what I wanted to say with her. To turn her into what she was. To turn her into a character who came along on the journey because she was compelled to rather than because she wanted to.

Because, not unlike the published version of Zerastian, I didn't want to disappoint anyone. I didn't want to let anyone down. And so, at the end of the day, I wound up with a character I eventually learned to love but who it seems like she never loved herself all that much.

And now that I know she exists . . .

Ugh.

"Yes," she says. "Wow."

I'm having trouble adjusting to her voice. The narrator from the audiobooks chose to go with a more traditional "mystical, British faerie" type of a thing, but this Björk vibe she has going on wears well on her too, honestly. More of an . . . Icelandic faerie, I guess. It's kind of charming.

(Turns out she speaks it too. *"Farartæki" means "vehicle," Brit said.)*

Makes sense, I suppose. There's a reason they shot half of Game of Thrones in Iceland. Place feels like a fantasy realm.

"Um," I go on. "I had no idea you felt that way about, uh, me. And everything."

"How could you?"

There's kind of a wink in it. An "of course you didn't, you're not the precog" thing.

"Why didn't you ever say anything?"

It's a weird question to have to ask. Because, up until very recently, I was under the impression that nobody in Meridia said anything I didn't write for them to say. But, given that I couldn't even recall which version of Zerastian went to print, I'm also starting to consider the possibility that what was happening when I would draft stuff out was just the Meridia-story-funnel blasting realities through my imagination until I landed on the "right" one. (Or that may just be me looking for ways to rid myself of guilt. I suppose it doesn't have to be an either/or proposition.)

Regardless, I genuinely had no idea that Zero-ass (No, actually, I don't like that; may just go with Zerry instead—we'll see if she hates it.) . . . I truly did have no idea that she already knew Carpathian was going to let everyone down before even I did. One of my characters knew what I was going to write before I wrote it. That's some serious H.G. Wells shit.

"Because," she says, all Sugarcubes sounding, "the more someone knows about their future, the more they become trapped by it. The moment you tell a person of their fate, you risk pushing them toward that very outcome."

"But you always told them—us—about events in the past." I look to Brit for backup.

"Yeah," she says. "Like, we never would have been able to fight off that sea Valkeetrian if you hadn't pulled our coattails to it."

"I do not remember tugging on anyone's garments."

"Oh, uh, it's just an expression."

Zerastian tilts her head at us both.

"You do not seem to speak as yourselves any longer."

"Remort," we say at the same time.

Zerastian nods her head thoughtfully. "Warnings about sea monsters are not the same as telling the World Saviour about his own future choices." She looks at me with something like compassion. "You already carry the unbearable weight of being Carpathian Einzgear, the chosen one. You are under constant scrutiny, every decision measured against the impossible standards of the role you were forced into. If I had told you, *'You will fail in Rendalia,'* do you think that would have stopped you from failing? Or would it have just made you hesitate, second-guess every move, and ultimately crumble faster?"

As ever, she's talking about Carpathian, but she's also talking about Bruce.

"Besides," she goes on, "if I had told you, and you still failed . . . The one thing I knew you to always have, even in the worst moments, was belief. Belief that we could win. Belief that our fight wasn't futile. Belief that, somehow, we would make it through. If I'd told you that failure was inevitable, if I'd put that seed in your mind, you might have stopped believing. And if Carpathian Einzgear stopped believing, everyone else in the world would too."

It's a strange thing, being told that your failure was both inevitable and necessary. That withholding the truth from you wasn't just an act of kindness but a calculated decision to preserve something more valuable than victory: Belief.

I'm not sure how to sit with that.

Because the part of me that is Bruce Silver, regular human with an ego and an inflated belief that I have any say over the way the universe functions (or at least the way the universe I believed I created functions), wants to reject it outright. Wants to say, *No, you should have told me. I could have done something different. I could have changed the outcome.*

But the part of me that is Carpathian Einzgear, the one who learned lessons that I don't know if I ever learned myself, knows she's probably right.

Because I *do* hesitate. I *do* overthink. (As is in evidence all the time.) And, maybe, if I'd known Rendalia was doomed, I wouldn't have fought harder to save it. I might have given up before the battle even began. Or worse, I might have tried so desperately to change my fate that I would have made it happen faster.

I swallow hard, throat tight, looking at Zerastian's calm, knowing expression. She's always seen more than others. She's always known. And now, I have to live with the fact that my failure wasn't an accident—it was part of the design. A stepping stone toward something else.

But *what*? Exactly?

"Okay, fair enough," I acquiesce. "So, then, what have you been doing here all this time?"

It occurs to me that I don't really know how much time "all this time" is. I don't know how time works here. If we are able to escape the Mid-Meridian Plane back to Meridia, will it be the future? Will it be like the end of *The Chronicles of Narnia,* where Edmund, Susan, Peter, and Lucy pop back through the wardrobe to find themselves right back to the way they were when they left? Still kids? I hope I get the chance to find out.

"I have been . . ." she says, then stops, trailing off.

"You have been . . . what?"

"Just that. I have been," she replies. "It has been very nice."

She's far more chill than she is in the books. Much less *Zer*astian and more *Zen*astian; the original way I imagined her. Which suggests that, at least to a degree, the promise of revising truths on the Mid-Meridian Plane is kind of working, it seems like. Encouraging.

"So, is your precognitive Ability . . . gone?"

I'm stoked that life is better for her, but part of the hope in retrieving her now was that she'd be able to offer us some direction as we sally forth. She was one of the Heart Guard's most valuable weapons owing to her ability to see around the corner.

"Not exactly 'gone,' but altered."

"Altered."

"Yes. While I am no longer a precog in the traditional sense, my connection to the mechanics of fate still exists. Being here, being able to clear my mind, it is now part of me, just as being the World Saviour is a part of you. But it has adapted into something else."

"Adapted how?"

"On the Mid-Meridian Plane, intent, perception, and cohesion shape existence."

"Yeah, I heard about that."

"So, what that means for me is that I am no longer shackled by the constraints of *seeing* the future. Instead, I have developed an ability that, in many ways, is more powerful."

"More powerful? Than being able to see the future?" She nods. I find myself almost afraid to ask, but when in the Mid-Meridian Plane . . . "What could be—?"

"*Influence over probability itself*," she answers with a polite smile. Then, seeing that I clearly look dumb about it—because I am—she lets out a long sigh. "Here, on the MMP . . ."

God. Of course there's an acronym. Everyone here just loves acronyms.

". . . I don't see things from a distance as I do on Meridia proper. I *am* the distance."

"Say again, now?"

"Ahhh," Jameson interjects, pointing his finger. "Mi understand."

"You do?"

He nods. "She saying she exist beyond perception, waiting, always waiting, for de moment when her presence—her intention, ya might say—register."

"That's right. The monkey seems to understand." Zerastian nods.

I look at him and ask, "Is that because you've been brought back from another plane yourself, or because . . . ?" I indicate "smokey-smokey" with my hand.

He shrugs. "Who can say? Mi no precog, mi just know what mi know. Mi point is, Lady Zerastian here now, she like the writer. The skilled, famous writer who know she can plant dem perfect plot device two, three books earlier so when de ting happen, it gon' *feel* inevitable, but really, she just putting herself in dem exact right intersection of time, perception, and whatcha might call *narrative weight* to go on ahead and step forward. Maybe ya understand better now?"

In the absence of Perg and the Insight Persephone granted him, Jameson seems to have taken over the role of "unlikely oracle." He puffs away and looks at me with a heavy-lidded expression that reminds me of Denzel Washington in *Training Day* and kind of scares the shit out of me.

However, his somewhat pointed and on-the-nose metaphor makes sense. Zerastian's like Goku when he first stepped into the Hyperbolic Time Chamber on Kami's Lookout: eyes blazing with resolve, every movement deliberate, like he could already feel the trepidation of the insane training ahead but still knew he'd come out stronger. It's that kind of quiet, terrifying focus that makes you think, "Oh yeah, this person's about to punch reality's face in into next week."

Or, more simply, she's still wielding an enormous amount of woo-woo even without having her full Mezmer tank topped off. Somehow, being deprived of a natural Mezmeric reservoir has made her almost more potent rather than less.

I'm glad she's here.

And not just because of all that but because, I don't know, I feel an affection for her. She gives me hope. I've never met her before, but I missed her.

The her I always hoped she would be.

I look at Brit and Jameson, then at Almeister. The prior know everything about what's going on, and the latter knows . . . Well, honestly, it seems he knows less and less. But Zerastian . . .

I, frankly, don't know what she knows and doesn't know. I have to assume that her being down here on the MMP when Brit, Perg, and I showed up on Meridia is why she also doesn't know the "truth" about us, insofar as truth exists. But I don't know what will happen to her recognition of circumstances if we drag her back up with us (assuming we figure out how to get back), if the powers that she's achieved on the MMP combined with her Meridian Resonance will cause some kind of cosmic collapse given that, as of right now, she's operating on a whole other level of universe-bending communion with a shot of dormant precognitive Ability on the side . . .

However, given the possibilities that suggests and given that I now believe the Ninth Guardian is also all-seeing and all-knowing, we could use someone with Zerastian's pumped-up skill sets back with us even more than I anticipated.

"Zerry—Oh, may I call you Zerry?"

"I don't . . . think so?"

"Okay, sorry, Zerastian. So, a couple of things . . ." She waits patiently, staring at me. "One, Perg—you remember Perg—"

"Pergamon?"

"Yeah."

"He lets you call him Perg now?"

"Uh, yeah."

"Hm." She thinks for a second, then says, "Then I suppose you may call me Zerry."

Oh, right. Zerastian always had a soft spot for Pergamon. They shared some sort of bond that I never really explained—because I didn't have a good explanation for it—but that always made for fun side banter. I thought it was cute that this tatted-up, Technomantic precog would be besties with a snail.

And, y'know, I guess on something of a more "thematic" level that Brittany would know more about than me . . . Pergamon was slow, deliberate, steady; a creature of process, patience. Zerastian was the opposite. Lightning-fast cognition, her mind constantly leaping ahead, processing futures before they even had a chance to form. So, he didn't just counterbalance her—he anchored her. While everyone else saw her as an oracle, he saw her as a person. He forced her to exist in the now, to stop treating every moment like an inevitable prelude to something else.

Like I said, besties.

"Okay, great. So, Zerry . . ." She nods assent. "One, we have to find Perg. He's here too. So, given your current state as . . . What did you say? Distance itself?"

"I *am* the distance, yes."

"Super. Given that, you can help us get our hands on him? Can you?"

She thinks for a tick. Blinks.

"I think so."

"Okay, excellent. And then, once we have him, the second thing: We need to find Persephone."

Zerastian doesn't react immediately. She doesn't blink, doesn't nod, doesn't even shift her weight. It's a beat too long, that silence, and it makes something in my stomach twist.

"I see," she finally says, but there's something careful about it. Like she's measuring the shape of the name in her mouth before she commits to anything else.

I don't know what I expected. Maybe a flicker of recognition? Maybe some kind of *Oh, Almeister's daughter, of course.* Or *Ah, I've foreseen this moment.* Something definitive. But instead, she just watches me.

"So, like, do you have any thoughts on how we align with her? Intentionally? To find her?"

Zerastian tilts her head slightly, eyes narrowing just enough to make it clear she's thinking *too* much about the question. Not in the way someone stalls for time but in the way someone is trying to find the edges of something that might not actually have them.

"Persephone," she repeats, not like she's unsure of the name but like she's testing it against something. Then, finally, she says, "No. I don't know."

"You *don't* know?"

"No. Sorry. I don't know enough about her."

Goddammit.

It's the way she says it. Not like she *missed* something, not like Persephone just happened to slip under the radar, but more like . . . More like Seph was left out of the story. Not misplaced—deliberately omitted. A blank space. A missing page. A part of the world that existed without ever really *being* in it.

God, I suck.

"But," Zerastian continues, "I believe I can align with Pergamon. Now that I know he's here."

"Okay, yeah, sure. Let's see if we can locate him first, then."

Zerastian closes her eyes. Not like she's concentrating or like she's reaching for some deep cosmic power but like she's listening for something just out of reach. A whisper in the fabric of the plane.

"We will find him by making space for him," she finally speaks.

The air around us feels heavier in a way that makes me feel like I'm stumbling my way through a sentence that I didn't know the end of when I started it. Like the world is waiting for the right words to land.

Zerastian lifts a hand, and the landscape exhales. The edges of the junkyard blur like wet ink, and . . . the distance between where we are and where Perg is intended to be starts collapsing. The world rewritten. Like where we are now was never there at all. And then . . .

A suspiciously familiar vista appears in the salvage yard's place.

Like, *suspiciously* familiar.

Like the set from a TV show that a snail, sitting in an aquarium in my office with nothing better to do would have had a chance to see hundreds of times over . . .

CHAPTER THIRTY

A fortress of gray stone stands with high walls thick and weathered. Crenellations line the battlements, and round towers rise at intervals, some taller than others, capped with slate roofs. A central keep looms, its structure reinforced with heavy buttresses.

A wooden gate, bound with iron, marks the entrance, flanked by squat guard towers. The walls enclose a large courtyard surrounded by stone buildings—armories, stables, and barracks. Smoke drifts from chimneys set into the walls. Wooden walkways and staircases connect different levels. A second, inner wall protects the stronghold's core. In the distance, beyond the stone, the branches of an ancient tree stretch skyward.

Brit moves over so that she can whisper in my ear. "It's Winterfell."

"What?" I whisper back.

"It's *Winterfell*," she says again with slightly more emphasis.

I check to see if Zerry is paying attention, but she appears to still be . . . doing whatever it is that she's doing that's bringing us to this place. Or, us to it. Whatever. "What? No . . ."

"His tank did sit awfully close to the TV a couple of years ago when you were doing your GOT rewatch. Maybe it got baked into his fledgling memory banks. He's impressionable."

"You think that Perg's ideal revisionist history would place him in . . . ?" Before I can finish, a shadow passes over the snow ahead of us.

A dragon-shaped shadow.

You have got to be . . .

The shadow comes around again, this time accompanied by the unmistakable sound of massive wings cutting through the air. Its serpentine form glides into view, pale, shimmering body twisting like a ribbon of light. It's huge, easily as long as a bus, and its wings sparkle with a faint iridescence as they catch the light.

"He is here," Zerastian says, opening up her eyes fully. "Pergamon is nearby."

The dragon lands in front of us in a billowing spray of snow, its enormous bulk settling with an elegance that seems almost impossible for something its size. For a moment, none of us speak, the surreal majesty of the creature silencing even Brit's usual snark. (In a variety of other circumstances, I might expect her to say something like, ". . . Because sure, let's just add 'blinded by swirling snow' to the list of things making this moment more dramatic than it already is," but . . . nothing.)

The leviathan lowers its long, shimmering neck, its massive head tilting slightly as it surveys us with intelligent, glinting eyes.

Then . . . it laughs.

Not a roar. Not a growl. A . . . laugh. More of a titter, actually. Kind of a guttural *hee hee*. It's still deep in its way, coming from the back of the throat, sounding almost like . . . Well, almost like Ray Romano? I mean, not *exactly*? More like if you crossed Ray Romano with Kermit the Frog. But it's odd. Then . . . it speaks.

"Hey. Hi there. Oh, boy, look at you. You look so worried. Hey, no, be not afraid. You shall not be harmed, for here, in Tierras de la Corona? Eh . . . you are friends."

Soooo . . . Kermit Romano, speaking in formal, welcoming, herald jargon. That's what we've got. (Clearly somebody was also paying attention when I went through my *Get Shorty* phase.)

"Okay. Thanks," I say, raising my hand in salutation. "Sorry. Where are we? *Tierras*—?

"Tierras de la Corona," Brit says. "Crownlands. Technically, 'lands of the crown.'"

"That one gets it," the dragon says, nodding to Brit. "I am Don Esteban Alejandro Ricardo de la Luz y Bravura. It's an honor for me to escort you to the throne of our beloved Rey Pergamon Gonzo Sarita Montiel Slow Bottom."

Oh, dear god. I think Perg wrote his own fanfic and has now made it real.

"Rey . . . ?" I repeat.

"Rey Pergamon Gonzo Sarita Montiel Slow Bottom. Of the Santus Luminous Slow Bottoms."

Amazing, I'm not gonna lie. Perg has been given a chance to rewrite his story, and he's clearly going all out.

"Okay," I sigh. "Thanks. Which way is—?"

"But first," Don Esteban, the talking dragon, interrupts, "there's the matter of the duel."

I feel my lips tightening, but I let them go with a *POP.* "The what now?"

"The duel, fair guest," Don Esteban repeats, unhelpfully. "To enter the hallowed territory of the *rey*. Thems the rules, like they say."

I look around at the others. No one seems to know what to say, so they all just stare at me and kind of shrug. I look back at Don Esteban.

"When you say duel . . . ?"

"Duel. Y'know. A duel. Swords. Sabers. Other jabby things. Whatever you want. You get to pick the weapon; it's one of the many ways that the *rey* is a benevolent ruler."

He genuflects, his giant dragon-y wings flapping up snow behind him.

"Right, but . . . why do we have to . . . duel?"

"What do you mean?"

"I mean . . . you just said that we would not be harmed. Now you're telling us we have to duel? Doesn't the fact that we have to duel necessarily imply that harm might be inflicted upon us?"

Don Esteban ponders this for a moment, as if it's the first time anyone has ever asked him such a question.

". . . Only if you lose, I suppose?"

I scratch the top of my head and sigh. "Is there any chance that I could speak with the, uh, *rey*? Before the duel, I mean?"

"Oh, I don't know, that's a most irregular request. I might have to run it up the flagpole. Who should I say is making the request?"

"Br—Carpathian. Carpathian Einzgear." Don Esteban stares at me blankly. "The World Saviour?"

Don Esteban Alejandro Ricardo de la Luz y Bravura, the talking Ray Romano/Kermit the Frog–sounding dragon, narrows his giant gleaming eyes at me, his long iridescent neck tilting like he's trying to puzzle out a particularly complicated crossword clue.

Then . . . "Ohhh, yeah, yeah, yeah," he says, dragging the words out like he's flipping through an internal Rolodex. "Carpathian Einzgear, the World Saviour." He looks skyward. "Nope. Sorry. Not ringing a bell."

"Are you kidding me?"

"No, no, I wouldn't joke about something like that. I mean, I joke a lot. Just not about *that*."

I pinch the bridge of my nose. "Can you just tell Perg that I'm here?"

Don Esteban braces, every scale on his scaly body going rigid. His tone sharpens with a freshly injected sense of menace that reiterates the reality of him being a giant dragon who could probably both burn us alive and/or eat us, given the attenuation to our ability to fight back; presuming he's real enough in his manifestation to do such a thing. I don't know if someone else's imagined reality can craft tangible threats to our lives, but mine kind of has, so I suppose anything is possible.

Regardless, at hearing me refer to his monarch so casually, he growls, "What did you say?"

"Sorry, sorry. I mean . . . Can you please let your *rey*, Pergamon Gonzo Sarita Slow Bottom, know that Carpathian is here?"

"Rey Pergamon Gonzo Sarita *Montiel* Slow Bottom," Don Esteban corrects.

"Yes. Sorry again. Can you please let him know?"

The dragon lets out a long, exaggerated *hmm*, wings fluttering slightly, scattering more sparkling snow into the air. "I don't know. The *rey* is very busy, very important. Lots of matters of state. Big decisions. Things to decree, laws to enact. Like the one that says *no one may enter until they have dueled* . . ."

I turn my head and look at Brit, shrugging my shoulders with the intention of suggesting, *WTF is going on?*

She shakes her head for a second, then whispers, "Agency."

"What? What does that mean?"

"What I said. Agency. Everyone wants to feel like they have agency. So, if one gets to work out one's own ideal narrative drawn from one's experiences, and one's experiences are largely limited to . . . what his have been limited to?" She pauses, then continues carefully, "One might wind up trying out their King Joffrey impression, maybe."

Looking at the other faces around me, they all kind of raise their eyebrows and shrug in confused affirmation. Even Almeister. I feel like I'm in a goddamn Preston Sturges movie.

I turn back around, face Don Esteban, and say, "Yeah, okay. Fine. FINE. Who do I have to duel?"

"I mean, the champion. Obviously."

"Yeah, no, of course. *Obviously*. And who is the champion?"

Esteban inhales deeply and lets it out, causing the snow all around to billow in a mild blizzard. Then, with what I would describe as his most "authorial" voice, says, "The champion! Is the indomitable, the fearsome, the undefeated, the scourge of all cowards, the bane of all weaklings, the sword-swinging executioner of the unworthy!" Don Esteban takes a dramatic pause, then, in a lower, reverent timbre, intones, "Dagger McCloud."

Silence.

I blink. Brit blinks. Everyone collectively processes that name.

"Dagger . . . McCloud?" I finally ask.

Don Esteban nods solemnly, like I should know. "Yes. Dagger McCloud."

"Dagger . . . McCloud."

"As I said."

"That's his name."

"You heard me."

I glance over at Brit, whose mouth is twitching like she's physically restraining a comment. Jameson raises an eyebrow. Zerastian remains unflinching, but I sense a hint of sadness still. Like she thought she had finally gotten out of all this Carpathian drama and now finds herself pulled back in like Pacino in *Godfather Part III*.

Almeister is back to staring into the middle distance like he's seen the unraveling of existence itself, which is a super bummer. Gods, we were so close. And now . . .

I blow out my cheeks. "Where did . . . the *rey* . . . find this . . . champion?"

"The *rey* did not 'find' him!" Don Esteban scoffs. "Dagger McCloud manifested! Called forth from the deepest recesses of the *rey's* noble, kingly mind! His essence, a tapestry woven from the mightiest warriors of lore; his spirit, honed from the most legendary battles! Battles like . . . the Siege of Helm's Deep, the Betrayal at Castle Greyskull, the Undying Slaughter at Shao Kahn's Arena, the Battle of Marineford, the Eclipse of Griffith's Betrayal . . ."

Jesus Christ.

Lord of the Rings, He-Man, Mortal Kombat, One Piece, Berserk . . .

". . . and, of course, Goku vs Frieza. On Namek!"

Sure. Obviously.

Two things leap out at me:

Perg paid a lot more attention to the world around him as seen from his aquarium than I ever would have thought possible. And,

I watch a *LOT* of TV.

Don Esteban continues, now sounding like Ray Romano doing his best impression of Kermit the Frog doing his best impression of Michael Buffer. "He is, uh, the greatest warrior to ever exist within the hallowed walls of the Tierras de la Corona! A champion forged from battle, tempered in the fires of conflict, clad in the mythic steel of—"

"Okay!" I interrupt. "I got it."

Don Esteban puffs out his chest. Or at least, I assume that's what he's doing; it's hard to tell when a dragon's entire torso is already a glistening wall of impenetrable muscle and scales. But then, after a sufficiently long pause meant to build dramatic tension, he steps back and flaps his massive wings.

"Alright! I shall summon him," he declares, all de-nasally. "Prepare yourselves, for you stand upon the precipice of battle with the greatest warrior to ever grace these sacred lands."

He takes off with a gust of wind that rumbles the earth around us.

"Dagger McCloud?" Brit says, as if saying it again will make it sound less stupid.

I scratch my temples. "Yes, that's the name of the champion Perg has selected for the *duel*."

A sentence that quite literally no one in history has ever uttered before now.

Brit exhales. "Sounds like the name of a guy who'd challenge you to a fight at a food court."

And then, as if on cue, a sudden explosion of steam or mist or some other kind of steamy, misty thing manifests from out of nowhere and radiates all around as a dark silhouette begins to take shape inside the foggy ball of ether. And then, he steps forward from within, revealing himself in all his glory.

Dagger McCloud.

Okay . . .

So, imagine if someone at some point in the mid-1990s played every fighting game, watched every Saturday morning action cartoon, saw exactly two bootleg anime VHS tapes, and then, using only those references, tried to create the single coolest person ever.

That's Dagger McCloud.

He's tall. Like, suspiciously tall. As if someone accidentally clicked and dragged his height slider in a video game character creator and forgot to check the proportions. His body is wrapped in a midnight-blue trench coat that billows despite the lack of wind. He wears a belt over the coat for some reason, from which several daggers—too many, frankly, if you ask me—are haphazardly strapped like someone lost control while clicking "Add to Cart" in a weapons catalogue.

His face is obscured by an angular mask that looks like a fusion of Shredder and a Power Rangers villain, and his hair . . . His hair sticks out behind him in spiky, silver anime tufts that defy both gravity and common sense.

Most . . . delightful? Of all?

He is wielding katanas. Dual wielding . . . katanas.

He approaches me in a weighty, deliberate manner, completely unaware that he is, quite possibly, the apex predator of all NPCs. He finally emerges fully from the mist, crosses his arms over his chest, and speaks in a deep, raspy voice that is trying way too hard.

"So . . ." he intones, dragging out the syllable. "You have come."

I sigh. "Uh. Yep. Sure have."

He tilts his head ever so slightly, as if he's assessing me through his extremely impractical mask. "I have been waiting for this moment. A worthy opponent. A rival, perhaps."

He comes across like a guy who has read exactly one volume of *Naruto* and built his entire personality around it.

Jesus lord. I really don't wanna do this. I take one last shot at attempting to do an end run.

"Honestly . . . I do not wish to fight," I say, trying to keep things as diplomatic as possible. "I just want to speak with the *rey*. Really. We go back."

McCloud's eyes flash. "Only the worthy may enter the Minaret of Kings!" He flicks one of his katanas dramatically. "And only through the crucible of combat can worth be proven."

Brit mutters under her breath, "Wow, this dude is just so online."

I start to say something else, but before I can, he cuts me off by instantly teleporting five feet closer. Now standing right in front of my face like a bowed-up drill instructor, he circles his finger in my face then sheathes one of his katanas, dramatically, flicking his coat, also dramatically. "We shall settle this as all great warriors have. With steel. And honor."

"Settle . . . what?"

"No more talking! We fight!"

I once again look around at my cadre.

"You got this." Brittany gives a thumbs-up. "I believe in you."

Something tickles the back of my brain, trying to remember where I've heard that exact expression said that exact way before.

I feel fairly confident it's plagiarized from . . . ?

Eh. It'll come to me.

I turn back to McCloud. "Alright. Fine. But can I at least pick the weapon?"

McCloud gestures magnanimously. "Of course. That is the way of true warriors."

I need to think this through carefully. Yeah, he looks ridiculous, but he also looks like he knows how to wield those katanas with lethal force, and I'm out here free balling it with attenuated Mezmer. Even though he is a derivative figment of Perg's imagination, it remains unclear to me whether or not I can actually suffer a terminal injury on the MMP. No one has bothered to elucidate that point yet, and it now feels too late to ask.

So . . . I think of all the possible options available to me. The Blade, the gloves—which I probably can't even use because they are also Mezmer dependent—my wits. Which at the moment, and much to my great dismay, is probably my most valuable weapon. Scary proposition, but no less true.

Then it comes to me.

Looking McCloud dead in his icy, nearly pastel-blue eyes, I say, "Cool. Then I pick . . . Rock-Paper-Scissors."

For a moment, there is silence. Absolute, baffled silence, and McCloud recoils like I just struck him across the face with a lead pipe.

"Wha—" He shakes his head. "No. That is not how—"

"Nope. Rules are rules," I insist, shrugging my shoulders. "Challenger picks."

Finally, after an enormously filled-ass pause, McCloud exhales sharply through his nose and mutters, ". . . Very well."

He steps away, letting me exit the car, and he lifts his hand, fingers twitching like he's about to perform some arcane magical technique.

I blow into my own fist. Not to prepare; it's just kind of cold out here.

And then . . .

I ready myself for the most goddamn epic game of Rock-Paper-Scissors in history.

CHAPTER THIRTY-ONE

I'm not usually one to brag. In fact, I almost never do. But if there's one thing that I have no problem glazing myself about, it's that I am the goddamn undefeated Rock-Paper-Scissors GRAND CHAMPION of McKinley Classical Leadership Academy grade seven. At the time, I had an almost preternatural ability to guess what my opponent might throw and get out in front.

(Yes, sure, I lost the title the next year to Cristela Montoya, but I had sprained my wrist the previous summer, and I think it affected my game play, so I still count myself as the champ.)

Regardless, Dagger McCloud done gone ahead and stepped himself into a world of humiliation that he ain't even ready for, I tells ya.

I roll my shoulders, lifting my hands and curling my fingers into a loose fist. Dagger watches me closely, his spiked-up hair making him look like an overbleached hedgehog.

"Alright. Let's do this," I growl as I start pounding my left fist into my open right palm. "One, two, three, SHOOT!"

I throw paper, just knowing this joker, with his big ego, is gonna go rock first.

But . . . he doesn't. In fact, he doesn't do anything. He just stares at me.

"What are you doing?" he asks, tilting his head.

"I . . . What? Playing the game," I reply, not breaking eye contact. I'm already running through the mind games. Do I go rock *next*? No, too obvious. Paper again? Bold. A wild card. Scissors, maybe? But is that predictable? I could maybe fake a throw—

"What game?" Dagger interrupts my thoughts, voice ringing with confusion.

"Huh? Rock-Paper-Scissors. What are you—?"

Don Esteban, lingering nearby, lets out a bemused snort. "That is not how you play Rock-Paper-Scissors."

I blink. "What?"

"I don't know what game that is," he continues, shaking his great shimmering head, "but it's not Rock-Paper-Scissors."

My stomach tightens. "What are you talking about? Of course this is how you play Rock-Paper-Scissors."

Dagger lets out a dramatic chuckle and takes a slow step back as something shifts. A low rumble rolls through the ground, shaking the frozen air around us. And then . . .

Three objects materialize in the snow between us.

A jagged, basketball-size rock that looks heavy enough to break bones.

A sheet of paper, but not just any paper; it's the size of one of my Cal King bedsheets, parchment-thick, edges curling with golden embroidery that hums—literally hums—with energy.

And a pair of scissors. Massive, gleaming scissors five feet long, with handles large enough to step through and blades so sharp they could probably cut through solid steel.

I am concerned I have miscalculated terribly.

"Behold," Don Esteban proclaims, his wings flexing, scattering frost into the air. "The tools of battle."

"Um . . ."

Dagger spreads his arms, his coat flaring theatrically. "These are the sacred elements. The foundation of all combat. The balance of nature itself."

Oh, dear.

"It's okay, Bruce. It's fine. You can do this?"

"You really think so? Bruce? . . . Bruce, you still there?"

I think Brain Bruce just passed out.

Okay. Okay, no, it's fine. I can do this. It's just an adjustment. I am still the RPS MASTAH!

"Excellent," I posture. Then . . . "And what, exactly, are the, uh, rules?"

"Simple," Don Esteban says. "When I say, 'go,' you each charge for your weapon. The first one to touch the weapon uses it to battle in that round. The rock smashes, you use the paper in whatever way best counters your foe, and the scissors . . . I mean, they're blades. They cut and stab and everything."

Of course. Of course it's some dramatic, overwrought, anime-tier nonsense. I don't know why I thought . . . *Argh*.

Dagger steps forward. "Best two out of three? What do you say, *challenger*?"

I glance back at the car. Everyone is giving me yet still more encouraging looks. Which, I'll be honest, feel more patronizing than encouraging at the moment.

I sigh. "Yeah. Let's get this over with."

Dagger grins and stands back, assuming a pose like a runner in the starting blocks, ready to dash forward and grab his object of choice. I step back as well, trying to read his eyes like I'm a goalie; anticipate which thing he's going to go for.

Even with the new rules, the rock is still the safe bet. It's big, blunt, and requires no finesse. But that's exactly why Dagger might go for it. Which means maybe I should go for the scissors? No, no, that's ridiculous. I'm not built for giant blade-wielding combat. And the paper . . . What am I supposed to do with the paper? Write him a note asking him not to pummel me to death?

No more time to think. Don Esteban rears up to his full height, wings spread wide, and bellows in Romano-ish exuberance, "GO!"

McCloud launches forward like a bolt of lightning, moving at a speed that should not be possible for someone with that many belts and unnecessarily dramatic accessories.

He does, in fact, go straight for the rock. Because, duh.

Unfortunately, I react half a second too late, stumbling into motion, snow crunching beneath my feet as I make a desperate choice and dive for the paper.

I don't know why. Instinct? Habit? Stupidity? But before I can think better of it, my hands clutch the edges of the massive sheet, the gold embroidery sparking beneath my fingertips like it disapproves of my choice.

C'mon, paper. Don't be a dick. I'm counting on you.

Dagger whirls around, hoisting the massive stone above his head like it weighs nothing. His entire body radiates smugness. He prepares to launch at me like a . . . Well, a giant rock. "Ha! Foolish choice, challenger! The rock—"

Like I've been doing it all my life, I whip the paper forward like a bullwhip, and it *moves* in a way that paper absolutely should not. It extends like a living thing, twisting in the air, folding, wrapping, consuming.

"NO!" Dagger tries to step back, but it's too late. The paper doesn't just cover the rock. It *devours* it.

With a sound like a book slamming shut, the parchment wraps itself around the small boulder, swallowing it whole, the golden embroidery glowing fiercely as it squeezes. And then—*poof*. The rock is just . . . gone.

For a second, neither of us move. Then Dagger makes a strangled sound. "No! How could this be?! That was the rock of smiting! It has never before been smote!"

Don Esteban pauses, eyes wide, before finally making himself announce, "Uh . . . A flawless execution! Point to the challenger!"

Dagger looks at the Sky Dragon like he's been betrayed. The dragon shrugs. I hear a collective, "Hooray!" from behind me. An actual, "hooray," spoken as a word. Which I find weird, but when I turn, I see everyone, even Almeister, cheering me on, and it makes me feel like that invincible eleven-year-old again.

McCloud is *seething*. His face twitches, his hands clench into fists, and I swear I hear the distant rumble of thunder even though the sky is clear. He stares at the parchment, now back in its place, pristine and humming with power once more.

"This means nothing," he growls. "A single victory does not decide the fate of warriors."

"Yeah," I affirm. "I know. That's why it's two out of three."

This displeases the champion.

His gloved hand twitches at his side, fingers flexing like he's picturing wrapping them around my throat. His breathing is controlled, but just barely, and I can see the rippling of tension in his frame. His precious, beloved rock had been consumed in a way that had clearly rocked (*heh*) the very foundation of his understanding of reality.

"Again!" he shouts, his coat flaring as he whips around, stalking back to his starting position. He's rattled. That's good. I can work with that. That's how I took down Daniel Curtis when he cornered me at my locker on the way to biology and challenged me to go best three out of five. I told him okay, but only if we both closed our eyes the whole time and let the gathered crowd tell us who was winning. Shook him straight out of his fresh Vans.

Okay, Bruce. You just have to win one more. Win the next one, and you don't have to deal with this lunatic anymore and can go see the lunatic you're actually here to see.

Don Esteban flaps his wings once, sending another swirl of frost through the air. "And so, we proceed to the second battle! Will the challenger achieve a swift and mighty victory? Or will the champion claim his redemption?! Stay tuned to find out!"

Dagger snaps his head toward me, eyes glowing. "Redemption is unnecessary," he mutters darkly. "Only retribution."

Oh. So he's in *that* kind of headspace. Cool.

"Reconstitute!" Don Esteban shouts, and a new rock materializes alongside the paper and the as yet unused scissors.

I consider my next play while I roll out my shoulders, stretching my arms like I'm getting ready for a two-second drill. Because that's what this is, really. At the end of the day, even with the oversize objects and the high drama, it's just a game. A game I happen to be really, *really* good at.

So . . . should I choose the—?

"GO!" Don Esteban bellows.

Oh shit!

I launch forward, but once again, I'm caught slipping, and Dagger is fast. Or at least faster than I'd expect for someone so weighed down with unnecessary belts and flowing, physics-defying clothing. I feint left toward the scissors (*make him think that's my move*) then pivot hard toward the rock.

Unfortunately, Dagger doesn't fall for it.

Like he *knew* I'd second-guess myself, he shoots past me in a blur and seizes the parchment before I can even process what's happening. I barely even have my hands around the rock when I feel a snap of energy crackling in the air and whip around just in time to see Dagger unfurl the massive sheet of parchment and toss it . . .

. . . at *me.*

Not at the rock in my hand, like I did to him . . . He throws the parchment right at my face, and it engulfs me. Completely. I'm talking total darkness. Not just covering—wrapping, binding.

I thrash, trying to shake it loose, but it has no edges, no gaps to push through. It tightens, constricting, like some ancient scroll that *knows* my sins and wants to punish me for them. Dramatic? Perhaps. But I'm being absorbed by a magic bedsheet, which is foundationally dramatic, so . . . y'know.

I try to call out, but my voice gets swallowed. Panic rises in my chest, a cold weight pressing down as my senses dull. I have a memory of Cristela Montoya throwing scissors when I just *knew* she was gonna throw rock and slicing my sad little paper hand apart. (Part of my memory is her being carried away on the shoulders of the other kids as they shouted "Stella! Stella!" but that's likely just a reminiscent fabrication. Memory is an unreliable narrator.)

In any case, just as I'm sure that the pumpkin is about to be squeezed out of me . . . the paper releases its grip, and I stumble forward, gasping, flailing wildly as I crash onto my hands and knees in the snow.

I look up to see Dagger standing over me, arms crossed, parchment drifting back into place behind him like a cape.

"Pathetic," he sneers.

I cough, shaking off the lingering phantom sensation of being suffocated by *stationery*. "Oh yeah? Well . . . you're . . . *you're* pathetic," I wheeze, pushing myself to my feet.

Dagger cocks his head. "Creative."

Oh, oh hell no. Okay. NOW I'm *pissed*. You can talk all the shit about me you want, making fun of my haircut, my weird obsession with collecting Fabergé eggs, the way I always overexplain movie endings like I wrote them personally, but you will NOT mock my bona fides when it comes to manufacturing a pithy retort!

Don Esteban lets out a laugh. "Well, that was a thrilling reversal, huh?! The champion claims this round! The duel is now *tied*! Boy, oh, boy! So, okay, one final battle remains. The deciding match! Will the challenger prove his mettle and be granted access to have audience with the *rey*? Or will the champion reign *supreme*?!"

I shake out my limbs, taking in deep breaths. The cold air burns my lungs. *Okay. Focus.*

This is it.

One last round.

I cannot—I *will not*—lose to an anime OC made real.

"Oh," Don Esteban says, almost as an afterthought. "I should also mention, the loser of the final battle will be sentenced to . . . Hold on. What's the current decree?" He fishes around in his . . . scales? I guess? And pulls out what looks to be a proclamation. "Let's see. Ah, yes! Eternal entombment in the Obsidian Vault beneath the Minaret, where they shall be left to reflect upon their failure for anywhere between a thousand years and, um, forever."

I stop stretching. "Excuse me?"

Dagger McCloud, still exuding the kind of unique smugness that comes from winning a single round, chuckles. "A fitting fate for the unworthy."

"Wait. No. What? I thought I'd just be denied entry to see—"

"Reconstitute the weapons!" Once again, the battlefield resets. The rock. The parchment. The massive, gleaming scissors. All laid out and ready for dueling.

My blood runs cold. I glance back at my Party people, hoping for some kind of intervention, a plea, an escape clause. But nope. Just the lot of them watching us like this is some kind of high-stakes Olympic event.

I think I'm gonna be sick.

I take another slow breath, shaking out my hands.

Alright, Bruce. Get it together. This is just a game. Just an absolutely insane, physically manifested version of a game you were once a champion at.

Dagger's confidence has returned. He's bouncing in place, loose, relaxed. He points at me, nods, and steps back into position.

My pulse pounds in my ears. This time, there can be no second-guessing. No hesitation. I *have* to win.

"GO!"

Dagger goes straight for the rock.

I bolt, going straight for the scissors.

Grabbing the handles, I see why he hasn't tried to scoop them up before. Their weight is immense, almost too heavy to lift. If I had access to my Mezmer, it would be no problem, but attenuated as I am . . .

"Ha!" He braces his legs, shifting his weight, preparing to throw. "The rock *smashes*—"

Before he can finish, I summon something from inside me. Something deep down. Something not Mezmeric or mystical or cosmic, just a deep, yearning childhood-trauma-born desire to not lose no matter the cost. And . . .

. . . I swing.

And I swing flippin' *hard.*

The massive blades slice through the air, heavy but with a momentum I can *feel.* The weight of the swing carries through me, the force so strong I actually stumble forward slightly as the blades collide—

And cleave the rock *clean in half.*

A deep, splitting *CRACK* shatters the silence, and two neat halves of the rock drop to the snow at Dagger's feet.

And so does the top half of Dagger.

Dagger McCloud's torso doesn't fall so much as it folds. One second, he's standing there, rock still clutched in his hands, mouth frozen in a triumphant grin. The next, his upper half slides off his bottom half like a bad CGI effect in an 90s midbudget, straight-to-video action movie, and the two halves hit the snow with an anticlimactic *plop*. A clean cut. No blood. No gore. Just a neatly bisected anime OC, lying there like someone snapped a plastic action figure in half.

"Oh, shit!" I hear from behind me. I can't really make out which one of them shouted it because, suddenly, there is a bell-like ringing in my ears.

I lower the scissors, which are still vibrating in my hands from the impact. My breath comes in short, sharp bursts, and I realize I'm gripping the handles so tightly my knuckles have gone completely white. My fingers refuse to unclench, like my body hasn't caught up to the fact that it's over. The weight of what just happened presses in.

"Oh . . . Oh god. Oh . . ."

Don Esteban, who had been frozen in place, wings half raised in apparent shock, blinks and stutters like the Munchkins in *The Wizard of Oz* when they see the crushed body of the wicked witch. "You . . . You killed him."

"I know. I . . . I didn't mean to, I just—"

"Huh," he says, completely casually, changing the tone of the moment in a syllable. (Also kind of like what happens in *The Wizard of Oz.*)

"Huh?" I repeat.

"Yeah. I really wasn't expecting that. Gotta be honest. So . . . Okay, great." He clears his throat. "The challenger has emerged victorious! A stunning upset! A momentous triumph! The *rey* will surely be pleased!"

He keeps announcing these things like there's a crowd he's playing to, but . . . Anyway.

"Wait, no, I just killed a guy."

"Eh. He was kind of an asshole."

"What?! But. Okay, but . . ."

"Seriously, don't worry about it."

"Don't worry about it? But he's just lying here and—"

"Oh. Is it bothering you? I can . . . Here."

He claps his talons together, and suddenly, with a sharp gust of wind, the two halves of Dagger's body are . . . gone. Just *gone.* Like they never existed.

I step back. "Where did—?"

"Really, don't sweat it. That's just how things go in Tierras de la Corona."

I start to ask more questions, but deciding it quite literally could not matter less, I turn to the crew yet again. Everyone is goggled. Not literally; they didn't put on goggles. They just look surprised. Whatever.

"You good?" Don Esteban asks. "You seem freaked out."

"No. I'm . . . fine."

"Okay. Then, you wanna see the *rey* now?"

I nod, sort of, I think, catatonically and walk back to where Sheila is still sitting in this new landscape, open the door, and plop down. There is a long moment in which no one speaks. Finally, Brit dares . . .

"Are you—?"

"I don't wanna talk about it."

Don Esteban flares his wings wide, scattering frost and stray snowflakes like he's the star performer in an absurd and flawed yet hypnotically compelling dragon ballet. His voice echoes off the surrounding cliffs *way* too loud. "And so, by the decree of fate and the undeniable might of our victorious challenger, I, Don Esteban Alejandro Ricardo de la Luz y Bravura, shall personally escort you to the sanctum of the *rey*!"

He pauses, as if expecting applause. He clears his throat.

"Ahem. I *said* . . . By the decree of fate and the undeniable might of our victorious challenger, I, Don Esteban Alejandro Ricardo de la Luz y Bravura, shall personally escort you to the sanctum of the *rey*!"

We give him a polite golf clap. He seems grudgingly mollified.

He spins in the air and flaps his wings with somehow even more theatrical intensity, sending a cascade of frost and loose snow swirling into the air.

"Dis a lot of fanfare just to meet back with dem snail."

Jame's not wrong, but this is no longer my story. It's Perg's. And until we can see him, I gotta kinda go where the story takes me. Fortunately, I'm well practiced at that kind of thing.

The icy debris eddies and churns like a frozen tornado before crashing into the rocky mountainside ahead. For a moment, nothing happens. Then, with a deep, groaning rumble, the snow begins to slide and shift, revealing two towering gates carved into the face of the mountain itself.

"Oh, so all the dancing round was functional. Never know how something gon' pay off, eh?"

The gates are monumental, with stylized swirls of gold and silver spiraling outward from the center, forming a pattern that looks both ancient and nouveau modern. Like something you'd see printed on a tote bag at a fancy farmer's market. Additionally, each side of the gate bears an enormous snail shell insignia, their edges inlaid with shimmering gemstones that pulse for no particular reason that I can imagine.

"Okay, friends! You ready to see the *rey* now? He's been expecting you."

I take a long, protracted moment to keep myself from shouting, "*WHAT?*" and instead manage a more civilized . . . "I'm sorry? You say . . . he's been . . . expecting us?"

"Yeah. You're Carpathian Einzgear the Saviour, right?"

". . . Uh-huh."

"Yeah. He said to be on the lookout for you."

I'm doing my best not to LOSE MY SHIT, but it's not easy.

"When I told you, not more than a few minutes ago, who I am and asked you to tell him I was here, you said, and I quote, 'Not ringing a bell.' And when I responded, 'You're joking,' you said—and again, I quote—'I wouldn't joke about something like that.'"

"But I also did admit that I joke a lot, so . . ."

"But you said, 'Not about *that*'!"

"I know. But I also lie a lot."

"Are you fu—!"

"Sorry! I'm sorry! It's just been a minute since we had a really good duel, and I wanted to see what would happen, and . . . and *that* was a great duel! So . . . thanks for that! But, anyway, seriously, you ready to see the *rey*? He has been expecting you. I don't wanna make him wait."

I can feel the veins in my neck pulsing as I grit my teeth and nod my head. And as the great stone gates groan open, revealing a grand, torchlit corridor that stretches for so many kilostrydes I can't see the end, I wave everyone into the car and, once they're all seated, pull Sheila forward with a new appreciation for why readers sometimes develop such strong, negative feelings about a fictional character.

CHAPTER THIRTY-TWO

I CANNOT EMPHASIZE ENOUGH HOW CRUCIAL IT IS THAT THE STAFF REMAIN UNINTERRUPTED DURING MOISTURIZING HOUR. IT IS THE FOUNDATION OF THE KING'S DOMAIN."

Don Esteban is flying ahead of us, shouting back to be heard over the rush of oncoming wind. The long corridor down which we're traveling feels like the grand version of the little tunnels Perg used to carve out in his habitat. He started doing it back when I very first got him. I asked the kid at the aquarium store why he might be digging into the soil like that, but, perhaps unsurprisingly, the seventeen-year-old in the *Mastodon* T-shirt just shrugged and said, "Snail shit?"

Turns out he wasn't wrong. I looked it up online and found out that burrowing is not an uncommon snail behavior. Couldn't ever find out if there's a consensus malacological reason why, but Mid-Meridian Perg seems to have extrapolated out his habit into a full-blown urban development project.

"What the hell do you think 'moisturizing hour' is all about?" Brit asks.

Before I can say, "*I have no idea,*" Don Esteban shouts back, "EVERY AFTERNOON, THE ROYAL STAFF MUST PAUSE ALL DUTIES TO MIST THE *REY*."

"If he can hear us from all the way up there, why does he need to shout?" Brit follows up.

"BECAUSE I HAVE EXCEPTIONAL HEARING AND YOU DO NOT." There's a long pause, and then he asks, "DID YOU HEAR THAT?!"

"Hear what?" I respond.

"I ASKED, AT A LESSER VOLUME, IF YOU COULD HEAR ME. YOU CLEARLY COULD NOT. SO. HAHA! THAT'S WHY I'M SHOUTING!"

Yeah, okay.

"What do you mean 'mist the *rey*? Mist him how?"

"THE MISTING OF THE REY IS WITH A MULTISTEP HYDRATION RITUAL INVOLVING IMPORTED SPRING WATER, CEREMONIAL SEA SPONGES, AND A CHOIR HUMMING A SOOTHING MELODY IN THE BACKGROUND. THE REY SAYS IT CLEARS HIS MIND, ALLOWING HIM TO RULE IN THE MOST MAGNANIMOUS WAY POSSIBLE."

"Are you kidding?" Brit poses, rhetorically.

I don't say it aloud, but, eh, I get it. If my entire existence hinged on being adequately slimy, I'd probably put some safeguards in place too.

I can see a light up ahead. Literal light at the end of the tunnel. There has been precious little conversation since we got into the car, mostly due to the fact that I have not wanted to talk, and, Brit notwithstanding, there is a certain amount of deference granted to the Saviour even if it doesn't always show up as such. When the Saviour says the Saviour doesn't want to talk, allies of the Saviour will dummy up. Usually.

So, I put out to the group, "Everybody hanging in?"

There is a generalized grunt of half-convincing affirmation.

"Zerastian? You okay?"

"I am fine."

There's a beat. A filled, dense moment.

I take a breath, gripping the wheel a little tighter. The words are there, crowding the front of my brain, but finding the right ones, shaping them into something that doesn't feel hollow, is harder than I want it to be.

"I, uh . . ." I start, then immediately regret starting without a full thought prepared. "Look. I just . . . I just wanted to say I'm sorry."

Zerastian turns her head toward me, her expression impassive. "For what?"

"For not knowing," I say. "For not realizing how you felt. For not seeing what was happening with you before. I—" I stop, exhale. "I should have known."

She watches me for a second, then looks forward again. "You could not have known."

"I could have paid more attention."

"Perhaps," she allows, but there's no real weight behind it. Like she's indulging the idea for my sake, but she doesn't actually believe it. "But I did not want you to know."

That stings more than I expect it to.

I glance at her again, trying to read her expression. "Did you—?" The question feels too heavy. I start again. "Do you feel betrayed?"

I consider that not telling Brittany and my readers what I was going to do is not unlike never sharing that same truth with Zerastian.

She tilts her head, considering. "No," she finally answers. "Frustrated, perhaps. But not betrayed. You did not act against me. You simply did not act for me."

That distinction shouldn't make it feel better, but somehow, it does. It's not forgiveness, but it's not condemnation either. It's just . . . fact.

I nod, letting it sit, then shift gears slightly. "So . . . how do you feel about coming back with us? To Meridia? Once we collect Perg and Seph? Persephone?"

She breathes in, slow, steady. "I do not know."

That hits harder than I expect. I don't know what I thought she'd say. That she was eager? That she missed the world she left behind? That she was ready to step back into the fight?

"Do you want me to?" she asks suddenly.

I look at her, not expecting the question. Not expecting the weight of it.

"Yes," I reply, not even hesitating. "Obviously. Of course I do."

"Because you need me?"

That lands like a punch to the gut.

Not *Do you want me there?*

Not *Do you think I should go?*

Not even *Do you believe I belong there?*

Because you need me.

"I mean, yes, but not just because of that."

She looks at me for a moment, then looks ahead. "Then we shall see."

"WE HAVE ARRIVED!"

Sheila's tires crunch over frosted cobblestones as we roll into . . . Well. I'm not sure what it is exactly. Because it's, like, all the things.

A space that looks as if it was designed by someone who got really into *Game of Thrones*, then switched over to take in *Nausicaä of the Valley of the Wind* while playing *Halo*, before pausing to watch a doc on ancient Mesoamerican cities before picking up *Horizon Zero Dawn*, and then falling asleep while watching *Tron: Legacy*, but only held on to the earthy, mystical parts. Not the neon cyberpunk ones.

In other words . . .

It looks like something I would have come up with.

Son of a bitch. I get it. I understand why, or at least how, this is what Perg would have (and obviously has) built for himself.

He's imitating me.

Or, at least, he's imitating the way I work. The way I create. The way I assemble my hodgepodge ideas. He's crafted an homage to the homages I have crafted in homage to the homage crafters who crafted homages to the homages before them.

Jumping Jesus on a pogo stick.

It makes sense. Clearly. Perg's exposure over the years to anything outside of his aquarium is limited to whatever I was exposing him to. So, of course, when he finally got the power to create, he pulled from the only well he ever dipped his ladle into. My well. The bits of pop culture I fed into the air around him, the games I played while he slowly oozed up the glass of his tank, the shows I binge-watched while he burrowed into his little patch of moss.

He absorbed all of it, and now, here I am, standing in what is essentially my *brain* given physical form, only filtered through the logic of a recently sapient snail.

My god. Looking around, I now understand—I mean, *really* understand in a way that I only thought I understood before . . .

. . . why Brittany gets so aggravated with me sometimes.

This shit is mayhem.

The sheer density of ideas crammed into this place is overwhelming. Every inch of it feels like it was built from half-remembered concepts mashed together with the unshakable confidence of someone who has never questioned whether two things *should* go together, only whether or not they *could*. A real Doritos Clam Chowder kind of a vibe. (Which, side note, is a real thing I tried in Tokyo once, and thus I can now also verify that Tokyo emergency rooms run as clockwork smoothly as the rest of the city.)

A towering fortress, equal parts medieval and industrial, looms ahead. The walls are cut from a mix of stone and something that looks suspiciously like a repurposed spaceship hull. Pathways are lined with statues that start off looking like noble warriors but, upon closer inspection, have the subtle proportions of action figures, like the sculptor only had reference material from a limited-edition collector's line.

The courtyard we're pulling into has been carefully arranged into a series of paths and symbols, but something about the design pings the back of my brain. An RPG map, maybe, or a puzzle layout I can't quite place.

Oh! No, I know what it is. It's straight out of *Elden Ring*. Not an exact copy, but the winding stone paths, the strategically placed archways, the sense that every turn is leading you toward something inevitable . . . Yep. That's what I'm rolling all up into.

Banners flapping in the wind bear the insignia of the *rey*. It is a highly stylized snail with an exaggerated but dignified moustache. Embroidered with an unnecessary level of craftsmanship, it's as if the entire royal textile division was tasked with ensuring it had just the right amount of gravitas. And there are roads up ahead that lead deeper into the city wound in a way that suggests there's a peculiar kind of logic at work. I don't know for sure, but given everything else on showcase, I have a sneaking suspicion that if I were to get a bird's-eye view, they'd appear from above as letters spelling out something like, I dunno, "REY RULEZ" or "SNAILS 4EVER," or something.

Everything about this place screams *Bruce's brain on shuffle*, but Perg, in his snail wisdom, has cranked up all the settings even beyond what I might have dared. If I ever entertained a thought about a cool visual or a weird worldbuilding rule, it's *here*, realized in over-the-top, perfectly unnecessary detail.

Guards, or at least something adjacent to guards, are stationed along the walls, standing at attention in full regalia that looks like it was designed for maximum dramatic effect rather than functionality. Their armor glints in the light, heavily embellished with ornate patterns that surely *mean* something, but only in the way that cool logos on fake fantasy currencies mean something.

They see us creeping in and acknowledge us, but there's no tension, no gripping of weapons, no assessing of whether we belong here. *Because I* am an integral piece of the puzzle.

Or it's just because I won a duel. Probably that, actually.

Man. Man, oh man.

Perg didn't just create a world. He built a whole *mythology*.

Don Esteban stops, hovers in the air, and calls, "BEFORE WE PROCEED—"

We all cover our ears because now that the sound from the wind tunnel has ceased, his voice carries like all of the fire engine sirens in Rome going off at once.

"Sorry," he says, realizing and quieting down to a listenable volume. "Before we proceed, there are rules."

He lifts a talon and starts counting them off.

"First, do not interrupt the *rey* when he speaks. He is generous, but his patience is not endless."

Oh, for the love of—

"Second, you will refer to him by his full title: His Luminescence, Architect of the Misted Realm, Sovereign of the Forge, and Keeper of the Glistening Hour, His Royal Royalness, Pergamon Gonzo Sarita Montiel Slow Bottom."

"You really want us to say all that?"

"No."

"No?"

"No. I REQUIRE that you say all that. THIRD! Do not comment on the misting ritual, no matter what happens."

I squint, trying to imagine what that implies. "What could possibly—?"

"NO MATTER *WHAT* HAPPENS!

". . . Okay.

"And last—and I cannot stress this enough—do not under any circumstances attempt to wipe away any excess moisture. This will be taken as a declaration of war."

I sigh, because . . . because I do. "Alright."

Don Esteban looks at me with skepticism. "I mean it."

"I said alright."

"I'm not kidding."

"Neither am I! I won't do anything I'm not supposed to."

"You'd better not. You do not wish to face the wrath of an unnecessarily dry *rey*."

I have to be honest; I am reaching a point where I am questioning the necessity of having Perg along as we continue forth. But then, I remember all of our good times together. Watching him try to climb up the glass of his tank (which I now realize was kind of a prison and holding him in there was fairly messed up), feeding him, uh . . . I mean . . . Honestly . . . that's kind of about it. He's a snail. He only recently got, like, engageable.

Regardless, if I have to humor Perg in this redraft he's doing of his life, so be it. God knows I've been doing my own revision of late.

"I promise. I will adhere to all of the rules of the *rey* and . . . y'know . . . bow and everything."

"No bowing."

"Sorry?"

"He perceives it as mocking."

And with that, Don Esteban adjusts his wings, glances toward another set of massive doors ahead, and takes a breath. "Alright. Let's do this!" he declares before turning and flinging the doors open.

I let out a slow breath and slide Sheila into drive once more, trying to mentally prepare myself for whatever fresh absurdity is waiting on the other side. Because, honestly, after everything I've seen so far, I won't be surprised if . . .

"What's up, homies!"

. . . No. I take it back. I've really got to stop saying that.

CHAPTER THIRTY-THREE

"So, *obviously*, when it came time to establish a governing body, I knew I needed something that both *commanded respect* and *allowed for moisture retention*, and that's when I hit upon the idea of the Misted Seat," Perg is saying as he sits, medium size, on the sprawling throne that is just straight up the Iron Throne; only, the jagged edges that sprout from the back are actually misting tubes, like the kind they have outside restaurants in Palm Springs and other places that tend to be excessively dry and hot.

"You *could* say it's just for individual comfort and a fear of literal desiccation, but I would argue that, if you look deeper, it's a statement about the necessity of learning to control one's own environment if one hopes to experience true growth. You feel me, fool?"

We're seated in what I might describe as a *lounge of conceptual indulgence*. A space designed less for practical gatherings and more for the inevitable *discussions of meaning* that happen in overlong fantasy epics. Everything is deliberately oversize, from the bioluminescent tapestries to the overly tufted chairs sculpted as if to encourage the occupants to lean forward dramatically with steepled fingers.

A group of attendants, small and nimble, are moving soundlessly through the space, adjusting decorative lanterns, subtly replenishing the humidity, and generally maintaining the impossibly curated aesthetic. They never make eye contact, never break stride. It's like someone programmed a setting for *Ideal Background Servant Behavior* and let it run on autopilot.

Perg is draped in a ceremonial robe that appears to be woven out of some kind of perpetually damp silk that shimmers under the mist-heavy air. His shell has been polished to a glossy sheen, and someone has taken the time to carefully etch minuscule decorative patterns into its surface. He munches on a biscuit, getting crumbs all in his stache like it's the first time he's eaten in who knows how long. Or like it's the first time he's eaten something he *likes* in who knows how long, as opposed to the lettuce leaves and eggshells I fed him. He never went hungry on my watch, but he never got to select the menu either, so getting to pick off the menu must be a real hoot for him.

"Oh, I'm sorry, fools. I just realized I didn't offer you anything. Yo! Esteban!"

Don Esteban, who has been hulking in the corner, swoops over.

"Yes, my liege?"

"Can you get the homies something to eat? Drink? I'm trying to be as good a host as Richemerion, fool," he asides to me. "I thought that was classy."

"Of course," Don Esteban replies. "What would you all like?"

"Nothing for me," I say. Given that we're on a narratively reconstructionist plane that barely abides by the laws of physics, I'm not convinced eating wouldn't permanently alter the molecular structure of my digestive tract.

"Me neither," Brit says, presumably exercising the same caution.

Jameson, however . . . "Mi will take di finest fruits, sweet and succulent. Somethin' strong fi di belly. Mi waan real vibes, ye know."

I wave my hand at Almeister. "Al? Al? Would you like anything? Al? You probably haven't eaten in, like, ever?"

Perg leans into me. "Homeboy's still living that corrupted life?"

"Yeah."

"Damn. Yo, Esteban, fool. Get my man some Mender's Biscuits."

"The ones soaked in the Elixir of the Kindly Mind?"

"Yeah. Shit is fire, yo."

"Of course, *Rey*. They're very mild," Esteban says to Almeister. "They help with, uh . . . soothing."

"That sounds good. Thanks." I nod. "So, Perg . . ."

"What's up, homes?"

"Once everyone's fed and we get Persephone, we should talk about—"

"What do you mean 'we,' fool?"

"What do you mean, what do I mean?"

"You can go get homegirl. I'm set."

"Set?"

"Yeah, fool. Look around. I'm locked in."

"No . . . No, this is just supposed to be a liminal space where you can work out—"

"Liminal these nuts, fool. You seen the misting throne? I ain't going nowhere."

Putting aside the "these nuts" of it all, I'm not sure I understand what he's saying.

"Everybody, can you excuse us for a second?" I grab Perg by the shell and draw him down off his throne. Almost immediately, the group of attendants draw weapons of all stripes—knives, samurai swords, photon blasters—and point them in my direction. I lift my hands in surrender.

"It's okay, homies. Fool don't know how shit works yet. I'll break it down for him."

The weapon wielders eye me with suspicion, but they do as their *rey* says and reholster their pew-pews and cutty-slashes. We move our way out of earshot.

"The hell do you mean, you're not going anywhere?" I ask.

"Oh, I'm sorry. I thought you spoke English. Here, I'll try again. *No me voy.* Fool."

"Perg—"

"Of course *you* wanna leave."

"What does that mean?"

"World Saviour? Carpathian Einzgear? Mr. Big Shot?"

"You think I *like* being Carpathian Einzgear?"

"Who wouldn't?"

"Me! I have DONG coming after me! I screwed shit up with Mael! I got a shitload of people killed! And that's just in the last handful of Lunar Rotations!"

"Well then, that's on you, homie. You're the one who made the shit."

"What does *that* mean?"

"I mean, *maybe* if you hadn't been so reckless, things would be different. Look at me. Look around. This is what *I* made, fool. Every single detail. You know how many times in my old life I ever got to make something for myself? *Ninguna.* I lived in a box, bro. Maybe, on a good day, I got to move a rock around or something, but—"

"What happened to 'Thank you, *ese*? My life's turned out pretty cool, homes'?"

"Who said that?"

"You did! In the Cavern of Sorrows! You thanked me for . . . I'm actually not sure what, but you said things were better for you!"

"That was the trauma talking. *This*. This is actually better. Here? I got *everything*. I got power. I got people who listen to me. I got respect. And you want me to go back to being a charming sidekick? Nah. You do you, fool, but I'm staying."

I can't believe this shit. I just stare at him, waiting for him to tell me he's just joking with me like he's done before, but he doesn't. He just stares back. Defiant. Then he says . . .

"Why didn't you make up something new?"

"What do you mean?" I ask.

"I mean, you had the chance to recreate a new reality down here or whatever, right? Make up some new shit? Workshop some ideas for how you see your life going or wanted it to go and whatnot? Didn't you get a guide to explain the rules?"

"Yes, we got a guide. But the three of us"—I point at Brit, Jameson, and myself—"or, four of us, I guess," I add Almeister, who is now fanning mist onto himself like he's in a sauna, "opted not to. In fact, we risked allowing the plane to dictate our futures for us to prioritize finding you and Seph so that we can all try and rewrite our paths together."

"I ain't never ask you to do all that."

I stare at him. Because that is, in almost the exact wording I used, what I told Brittany when she suggested that fans of Riftbreaker would feel betrayed by the choices I made when I killed off Carpathian. She talked about the sacrifices and commitments that they had made to me as the author of the books.

She said, "*The ones who stand in line to get your autograph. The ones who tell you how much what you've written means to them. Those are the ones who are devoted to what you've made. And those are the ones you'll be pulling the rug out from under. You don't feel any responsibility to them to not blow it the hell up?*"

And I said to her . . . "*I never asked anyone to do all that stuff.*" As if that excused me from my responsibility to it.

The snail has come home to roost, as the saying goes.

"You made your own choice, bro. And I . . . I made a *paradiiiiiiise*," he draws the word out, "as you can see."

They say that power corrupts, and absolute power corrupts absolutely, and Perg is showing himself to be the rule that proves the rule.

"Who was your guide?" I ask him. "What was their name?"

Perg opens his mouth to answer, but before he can wag his moustache, someone else answers for him.

"Carpathian Einzgear and company! Hello! You're here!"

I know that voice. That plummy, cheery tone. I turn to see . . .

"It's me! Sumnut!"

"Sumnut? What are you doing here?"

"The same thing I did with you. Did you not notice the CHRONOS?" I look to see the police box nestled in the corner. It was easy to overlook amidst all the other hodgepodgery. "You found your friend's meow meow meow! He's made quite a nice situation for himself, eh?"

"Yeah, it's super. Can you please help me out here?"

"Help you how?"

"Help me explain to Perg that he can't stay here forever?"

"I can do that, yes."

"Thank you."

"But I won't."

"What? Why not?"

"Because . . . it's not altogether true."

"What?"

Sumnut spreads their hands in a very *well, what can you do* sort of way. "It's not altogether true that he can't stay here forever."

I look at Perg, who is grinning like he just won the goddamn lottery. I look back at Sumnut. "Are you kidding?"

"Yes."

"You are?!"

"No, actually. Sorry, I was kidding when I said I was kidding. I'm a bit of a kidder that way."

I'm going to kill someone. And this time, I won't feel bad about it.

"Sumnut—!"

"Well, no, look, 'forever' is a strong word," Sumnut says, rocking on their heels. "But indefinitely? Yes."

I stare at Sumnut. Then I turn back to Perg. He's looking *way* too pleased.

"No. I thought this was just a place to come work shit out and then—"

"Yes, that's true, but leaving this place is an entirely other endeavor."

"What the hell does that mean?"

It suddenly occurs to me that I have failed to ask how one does make their exit when one decides it's time to leave the Mid-Meridian Plane. When one feels that the story they're telling here has run its course.

"You have to understand something," Sumnut starts.

"Oh, do I? Great. What's that?"

"The Mid-Meridian Plane only exists in so far as it exists for *you*, the user."

This is starting to feel like high-level math. *What do you mean there's such a thing as imaginary numbers?! I thought the whole advantage to working with numbers over things like, you know, your imagination is that they're real! Is there nothing in life that's dependable?!*

"What. In. The. Fresh. Funky. Fantasia are you saying?" I ask, trying to keep the exhaustion and frustration out of my voice.

"I am saying that the MMP does not exist *in* between, you see. It *is* the in-between. You cannot exit it. You must compel the MMP to exit you. It is not a space you retreat from; it's a state of being that has to retreat from you. The plane will release you when your story finds resolution, or you abandon it."

I swallow. ". . . Are you kidding?"

He gets an impish look. "I am . . . not." I wait. "No, that's it this time. I am not. Whether that means closing an old chapter, clarifying your purpose, or forging a new path forward, you must decide . . . what you are willing to let go of."

The hairs on my arms stand up, and I don't even know why. Something in his tone.

"What does that mean? 'Let go of'?"

"Exactly what I said. Stories that are crafted on the Mid-Meridian Plane are never actually 'finished.' They are only surrendered."

Again, Brittany's counsel to me back in my old house runs through my mind, "*When you make something, and then you put it out into the universe and ask people to engage with it, you're making an agreement with the audience. A compact. You're saying that you are surrendering the thing you've created to them, and that by them picking it up, it is no longer exclusively yours.*"

If Perg had hands, they'd be extended at his sides when he says, "So what's up now, homes?"

I clear my throat, crack my neck, and feel the weight of it settling in.

Perg is grinning. Sumnut looks entirely pleasant and unaffected. And me? I'm standing here, once again being told that the only way forward is to let something go without knowing what, exactly, that means.

It is, in this case, neither simple nor convenient.

I look at Perg, at his mist-shrouded throne, at the kingdom he's built for himself.

"Yeah," I finally say, the words dry in my mouth. "What's up now?"

CHAPTER THIRTY-FOUR

I have drawn Sumnut over to stand next to a giant dining table that I am *this* close to flipping over (I don't actually think I could flip it, though. It looks pretty heavy.), and am trying to find some angle, some loophole that makes this make sense. But there isn't one. The Mid-Meridian Plane isn't something you *walk out of.* It's something that *lets you go.* And Perg? He hasn't given it a reason to.

I attempt to take a calming breath. "Okay. Let's just . . . Let's break this down, real slow. Perg's story here?"

"Yes?" Sumnut says.

"The whole *Misted Throne, Supreme Moisture Overlord thing? Is* ongoing because he wants it to be?"

Sumnut nods, pleased. "Precisely."

"And if we want him to come back with us, he has to *what*? Decide he's done being the Misting King?"

"More or less," Sumnut agrees. "He has to *let go of it.* He has to stop believing this is the story he wants to live."

"I'm standing right here, fool. You can ask me directly," Perg says, shimmying over and needling his way back into the conversation.

I look at Perg, who is smirking. "And you don't want to do that?"

"Do you need to take this class over again, homes? Why is this hard for you to get?"

Brit, who has been hanging back, now strolls over.

"Perg?" she speaks carefully.

"What's up, girl?"

"This is amazing. What you've built for yourself."

"I'm glad you like it. I think I still need a pop of color here and there, but it's getting there."

"I mean, I get it, right? It's nice to have power. A kingdom."

"There are worse things. Like . . . hawks. Gotta always be on the lookout for hawks, yo. But hell yeah. I am the BOSS. It's good to be the boss. There are perks: Nice parking spot. Good benefits package. But, mostly, people, you know? They . . . They *listen* to you." He nods, looking off like all he's ever wanted is someone to just listen to him. It makes me kind of sad for a second.

Brit keeps going. "Sure. But . . . they don't, do they? Not really."

Perg's moustache twitches again. "Who don't what?"

"I mean, who's actually *listening* to you, Perg?" She gestures at the attendants, who remain eerily motionless, like statues waiting for a command. "Who's questioning you? Who's challenging you? Who's arguing with you?"

Silence.

Perg sniffs. "Nobody argues with the *rey*, girlie."

"Exactly." Brit folds her arms. "Nobody argues with the *rey*. Nobody second-guesses him. Nobody disagrees." She takes a step closer, voice quieter now. "Nobody talks *to* him."

Perg shifts. "That's respect."

"No," she says. "That's obedience."

I get it. I get what she's doing. It's smart as hell. She's not trying to convince Perg to leave; she's trying to get him to see that the *thing keeping him here*—the throne, the power, the role—is *not what he thinks it is.*

"Take him, for example." She waves a hand in my direction.

I straighten, caught off guard. "Do what now?"

"Carpathian Einzgear," she scoffs like I'm not standing right here. "'World Saviour.' 'Chosen One.' The guy who carries the fate of an entire realm on his shoulders. Look at him."

He looks at me. I look at me.

"This guy"—she gestures like I'm some half-hearted museum exhibit—"has had one of the *shittiest* lives of all time."

"Well, hey now. I wouldn't say—"

"I mean, think about it. His entire life has been spent fighting battles he never got to opt into. Shouldering responsibilities he never asked for. Carrying the weight of every single person who ever looked at him and said, 'Fix it.'" She spins back to Perg, pointing now. "You think *this* is power? Sitting on a throne? Having people mist your shell and call you '*Rey*'?" She gestures at me again. "Seriously, look at this sad, sorry motherfucker. *This* pathetic shell of a human."

"Uh . . . Nightwind? I think he gets—"

"*This* is power. *This* is what being important gets you."

She makes a face of disgust.

Perg squints at me, his feelers twitching. "I mean . . . he does look kinda busted, huh?"

Brit nods. "Right? Bags under his eyes? That permanent I-regret-everything expression? The deep, existential awareness that no matter *what* he does, it'll never be enough because people are always going to want *more* from him?"

"So, listen," I interject, waving weakly. "I think we all get the—"

Perg makes a little clicking noise. "Huh. Yeah. That's a pretty rough gig."

Brit claps her hands together. "*Exactly!* And the worst part? Even when he *does* get a second to breathe, to step back, to *not* be 'The Guy,' the moment he *tries* to just exist, what happens?"

Perg raises a brow. "Somebody drags him back into it?"

Brit points at him. "Bingo."

Perg looks at me again, a little more appraising now. "Damn, fool. That's a bleak life."

I sigh. "You're telling me."

Brit leans in, her voice softer now. "That's what real power *does* to you, Perg. It's never just sitting in a chair and having people listen to you. It's never just calling the shots. It's carrying the weight of it all. Every choice. Every failure. Every life that gets crushed under the heel of a decision you had to make."

She looks at me again, then back to Perg. "And the truly awful part?" Perg blinks. "You can't ever really put it down."

Another silence.

Perg shifts, suddenly looking . . . smaller. Or maybe he actually shrinks himself deliberately. "Damn," he mutters. "That's a lot to think about."

Brit nods. "It is. But the question is . . . are you *really* willing to carry that weight? Forever?"

I rub my temples. "For my part, I would *love* for someone else to carry it for a while, just saying."

Perg exhales slowly, looking around at his perfect little kingdom. His attendants, his throne, his mist. The power he built for himself.

And the chain he might not have realized it came with.

"You wanted to be more than a sidekick," Brit says, voice lower, stroking the back of his shell. "I get it. You didn't want to just follow orders; you didn't want to be an afterthought. You wanted to be *important.* To be *the* guy." His feelers twitch. "But when you're the one in charge? When you're the *rey*? You don't get to be the wisecracking sidekick anymore. You don't get to be the fun one. You don't get to *breathe.*"

Brit sidles up next to me, nods. I give her a covert thumbs-up. Even Sumnut comes over and whispers, "That was very persuasive."

"Thanks," Brit replies. "I did debate in high school."

"Okay!" Don Esteban's voice rings out as he returns, carrying a plate of treats. He sets it down on the table by which we are gathered. "Sorry that took so long; I had to soak a new batch of biscuits. Alrighty! For this guy right here"—he moves to Jameson—"the finest fruits, sweet and succulent, to be found in Tierras de la Corona . . ."

The plate is stacked with an array of treats so appetizing to the eye that they look like they were crafted in a laboratory. Which is the goal of any good chef, to make things appear as tasty as possible, but this is pretty extra. As is to be expected, it's not just random bananas and apples and strawberries and shit. It's all very on theme. Dragon fruit. Starfruit. Something that looks like it's probably called "the fruit of the curious vine" or some bullshit.

"Mi big dragon boss! Ya gone done make above and beyond. Jah tank thee."

Don Esteban gives Jameson a clawed finger gun and glides over to Al.

"And for the gent, the *rey's* favorite: Mender's Biscuits soaked in the Elixir of the Kindly Mind."

"Let me get one of those, fool."

"Of course, *Rey*," Esteban coos as he hands one off to Almeister and then brings the tray over to Perg, whose snaily brow furrows as he munches one and contemplates his life choices, it appears.

I see the crumbs spilling down his moustache before my eye drifts to where Almeister is lifting a biscuit to his mouth and, all of a sudden . . .

There is no *ZZZZZZZZZWWWWWAAAAAAHHHHHMMMMMMM!* No actual freezing of time and space. Control can't function here as it would on

Meridia. But still. Something beyond mere Mezmer; something that isn't dependent on the vicissitude of the rules of the world. Something more intuitive, more deliberate, more innate, more organic to me . . . happens.

It's like a scene out of an action movie. A moment where the hero suddenly has clarity about the threats around him. Everything moves in slo-mo, and my eyes dart from realization to realization and back again.

The biscuit in Al's hand.

Perg chewing animalistically his biscuit.

The biscuit now at the edge of Almeister's lip, his mouth opening.

The crumbs tumbling slowly down Perg's moustache.

The way the fine, golden flecks cling to his whiskers. The way his eyes look a little too glassy, his manner a little too easy. The shift in him from the friend I knew to this smug, contented monarch lounging in his self-made paradise . . .

"Shit, Bruce! It's the biscuits! The biscuits are doing something to him!"

"Yeah, no shit, Bruce! Thanks for the update!"

"Don't yell at me, Bruce! You're the one with eyes! You shoulda seen it sooner!"

Bruce isn't wrong. Whether by accident or by some latent intentionality of his own, Perg told me what's happening, and I missed it. He sees himself as "a boss." Which makes him, technically, the final boss of this, I guess, level? Of this section of the MMP. He's accidentally turned himself into an obstacle that has to be overcome in order to move on.

Not by defeating him, per se, but by identifying and defeating the true threat.

"Yes! Sumnut! Just like in The Lion, the Witch, and the Wardrobe! Tumnus plans to betray Lucy and hand her over to the White Witch!"

"What? No. No, Bruce, it's not Sumnut."

"It . . . It's not?"

"No."

"So, I missed it again?"

"Apparently."

"Goddammit."

It's not Sumnut. He's just an observer. He's not the one twisting up Perg's head. The one doing that is . . .

. . . It's Don Esteban, the affable, half-beloved sitcom comedian, half-beloved Muppet, all dragon, who told me that he lies. Who forced me to duel to, I now realize, test my abilities, my acumen, my strength. *He* is the one who is somehow a servant of the forces of evil. (Dramatic, but that's what he appears to be.)

Son. Of. A. Bitch.

I know I've said it before, but why, oh why, couldn't I have just written a breezy, casual story about a guy strolling through meadows, picking flowers, and going to pubs? That's *the revision I should've been working on here. Just me wandering into places, wandering out of them. Eating bread. Drinking mead. All that kinda comfy shit. Eh. Probably would have gotten boring after a while. Whatever. Doesn't really matter now.*

"No!" I shout, dashing over to Almeister and knocking the biscuit out of his hand.

"What?!" he shouts.

Then, for good measure—and because I'm not one to leave any tray of fruit untoppled—I smack the plate that Jameson is holding out of his monkey paws as well.

"Bumboclaat!" Jameson shouts, recoiling as the fruit scatters across the floor. "Wah yuh a do, mi Saviour? Yuh mad or wah?"

"No, mi nah mad!" I shout, taking on Jameson's speech pattern for one unthinking, mildly mortifying moment. "He's giving you mind-control biscuits!" There is a group gasp like we're in a satire of a whodunnit film. "HE is working for the Ninth Guardian!" I point at Don Esteban.

All heads now turn in the dragon's direction. There is a moment where his eyes get big, his long neck recoils, and he puts one wing to his chest over his heart in a very clutch-the-pearls, "Moi?! Why, whatever do you mean?" kind of way.

No one speaks. I'm sorely tempted to go on explicating, but continuing with my earnest and deeply challenging desire to allow things to unfold rather than talk them into oblivion, I keep my trap shut as well, waiting until Don Esteban can no longer hold his tongue. Something my lawyer always lectures me about when we're in negotiations: *"The one who speaks first, loses."*

Finally, after what to me feels like an exceedingly long time for silence to hang in the air (which, in reality, is probably about five seconds), Don Esteban sighs, says, "Oh, fine," and then shows his hand.

Literally.

CHAPTER THIRTY-FIVE

What. In the French-fried FUCK. Is happening?!"

Brit's reaction is, for once, very nearly an understatement.

Looking all kinds of like a guy transforming into a wolf in any of the myriad movies made about people turning into wolves (*The Werewolf, An American Werewolf in London, Teen Wolf*—both the movie and the slightly darker and sexier TV version), Don Esteban begins to . . . transform.

His scaled body contracts, compresses, cracks. A ripple moves through his form, flesh unknitting and reweaving itself in the same motion, shifting from impenetrable dragon hide to something yuckily supple. His tail shrinks, retracting into his spine with a wet, oogifying *pop*. The elongated snout shortens, jaws snapping into a more humanoid approximation, though the rows of dragon-sharp teeth remain, stretching into something that can only be called a grin if you've never seen an actual grin before.

His eyes, previously reptilian and reflective, become something else entirely. No, uh, what do you call it? Oh! Sclera. That's it. Yeah, no sclera, no whites, just orbs of molten gold swirling with hypnotic malice. His horns remain, but they curve backward like polished obsidian, and dark, glistening veins pulse beneath his now nearly human skin, an unnatural glow moving sluggishly under the surface.

It's all very, very cool. Which is maybe a perverse thing to think in a moment like this, but there is beauty in tragedy sometimes. Life contains multitudes.

The former dragon turned . . . Hell if I know . . . straightens. Fluidly. Confidently. As if this shape is both alien and second nature to him at the same time. His new hands are impossibly long fingered and eerily elegant, and they gesture casually, the fingers rolling back and forth in a limbering up fashion, like a Chinese hand fan opening and closing, as if he's preparing to play the piano.

And also, as though he didn't just violently defy the natural order of things in front of us.

The air in the room has shifted. A crackling tension spreads out from Don Esteban's newly transformed figure, pressing against my whole body like a steadily tightening vise. His golden eyes flick over the group, his strange new form vibrating with barely restrained energy. I do not like the way Don Esteban—if that's still his name—rolls his shoulders and stretches his hands, testing the sinews, feeling out the dimensions of his new form. It's like watching a newborn deer stand for the first time, except this deer was probably going to try and rip my spine out through my mouth.

And when he finally speaks, his voice is . . . Well, just like the first time he spoke, it is not what I am expecting. I'm obviously anticipating that he's going to sound like some sort of demon spawn or a growling nightmare from beyond the grave. Which is, I guess, kind of the same thing? Regardless, what comes out of his mouth is sort of that? But also sort of not. Not to put too fine a point on it, but he sounds like . . . Well, he sounds like . . .

Ron Perlman.

So . . . Hellboy.

He sounds like Ron Perlman as Hellboy.

Which, if you'd given me, like, five guesses, I probably could have called.

"Well," he rumbles, voice thick, rich, disturbingly confident. "That was overdue."

Brit looks frozen, trying to decide whether she wants to fight or run. It appears as though Jameson's monkey instincts are screaming at him to bolt up to the nearest high ground, but he doesn't quite let himself. Almeister, blissfully unaware, just looks mildly disappointed that his biscuit is on the floor. And Zerastian . . . Well, Zerastian is watching with curious placidity, as if she's studying us like we're an anthropological experiment. Which, I mean, sure.

"Alright," Esteban groans. "Who's first?"

"Who's . . . ? For what?" I kind of stutter.

"I guess we'll just go with you, then."

He heads in my direction, and I back up, hand gripping . . . nothing. Because I left the Blade in the car. Because I was just hanging out with my old pal Perg and didn't figure I'd need to get jiggy with some shapeshifting figment of Perg's imagination.

"Are we . . . dueling again? Is that what this is? A duel?"

"In the sense that there are about to be two halves of you, sure," he quips in that quippy way violent quipsters do before they rip your body in half.

Don Esteban *lunges*, a blur of gold and clawed fingers, his reach extending faster than my brain can fully process. Instinct takes over, and I *drop*. Not a graceful dodge; more like my legs just *give up* on being vertical. His claws *swipe* through the air where my head had been, close enough that I feel the heat of them graze my scalp. Momentum carries him forward, his bulk crashing into the space I just abandoned, and I *roll*, twisting out from beneath him as his weight *splinters* the floor.

"Yo!" Perg yells. "That was just polished!"

And, as if they are equally offended by this disregard for their hard work keeping the place nice, the various attendants who, moments before had their weapons drawn on me, now aim their aggressions in the direction of Don Esteban.

They *move* as one, a disciplined tide of blades and precision fanning out to encircle him. But Don Esteban is *faster*. He *erupts* into motion, closing the distance to the nearest attendant in a blink, his elongated fingers *piercing* through their chest like they're made of wet parchment. There's no time for a scream, just a *wet snap* as he *hurls* the body into another, sending them both *crashing* into the mist-heavy walls.

Another swings a photon-blaster-looking thing up. Too slow. Esteban snatches the barrel, crushes it in his grip, then tears the attendant's arm from its socket in one fluid, horrific motion. The room erupts into chaos. Bodies collide, weapons flash, but it's futile. He rips through them like they're nothing, a storm of claws and raw, unchecked power, leaving only wreckage in his wake.

Limbs, shattered visors, the *sickening crack* of bone against stone. The last one standing barely has time to *breathe* before Esteban *grabs* him by the throat, *lifts* him clean off the ground, and with a *casual squeeze*, ends it. The limp body *drops* to the floor, joining the rest in a silence that feels *thick* and *final*.

It's a real scene.

"Alright," he says. "Good deal. Now I'm warmed up."

His attention is on me once more, and he thumps my way with concentrated menace.

My brain is going a mile a minute. (Which is actually a stupid expression, because that means my mind is only going sixty miles per hour, which is nothing. I'm assuming that expression came into existence back when the top speed for cars was like forty-five or something.) What I mean to say is I'm freaking out not only because I'm about to be eviscerated in what looks to be a fairly painful fashion, but because it doesn't make sense.

This doesn't feel like the Ninth Guardian's doing.

Logically, it can't be, because I feel like my theory about the Ninth Guardian only being able to access the plane through the conduit that is Almeister makes sense, and Almeister doesn't appear to be spasming or convulsing in any way. He just continues staring at his lost biscuit like a little kid who can't understand why their ice cream is on the sidewalk instead of in their mouth.

But beyond that, the Ninth Guardian's game thus far hasn't really been to make me suffer. It was never the Ninth Guardian's MO to execute violence without reason. The Ninth Guardian doesn't just want to rid the world of Carpathian—the Ninth Guardian wants to adequately crush the hope that Carpathian carries with him. And you can't do that by just offing a guy in the shadows. There has to be a spectacle involved.

So, that leaves me with the much more chaotic and slightly terrifying belief that this is happening as a result of some reckless imagining on Perg's part.

"Perg?" I lift my chin in his direction, keeping my eyes on Don Esteban as I continue retreating.

"Yeah, fool?" There's a bit of a quaver in his voice as well, which does not fill me with a lot of confidence.

"Are you doing this? Is this part of your narrative exploration? Your perfect version of life?"

"Perfect version? No! I wouldn't do something like this. Everything's super chill; I'm not about the drama!"

"Well . . ." Sumnut chimes in.

"*Well* what, fool? What well?"

"Funny thing about the Mid-Meridian Plane."

"Funny how?" Knowing it's not funny ha-ha but maybe funny you're-gonna-die that he's talking about.

Don Esteban's nearly upon me. I keep making big eyes in Brit's direction, kind of tilting my head toward Sheila in an approximation of "*Can you please go grab the Blade?*" But she's not getting it. She's just opening her eyes wide in return and nodding like, "*I know! This is crazy!*"

For his part, Sumnut just keeps kind of murmuring casually.

"As I intimated previously, the stories that take place here don't necessarily require conscious effort to be manipulated. It is just as likely that a stray impulse—a whispered fear, an unguarded thought, a deeply held belief—can cause something to manifest here as sharply as anything divined from your active imagination. Unintentional intent, if you will."

Unintentional intent! So the Mid-Meridian Plane is not only here but not here, a place of dreams and imagination, *and* the "in-between," but it's a goddamn oxymoron too?

I don't like it here anymore. It's become like a New Year's Eve party that started with high energy, glittering decorations, and the promise of fresh beginnings, but now, it's 2:47 a.m., the champagne ran out an hour ago and was replaced by flat beer and the dregs of someone's questionable homemade punch, half the guests have either left or passed out on the couch, the music is still playing, but it's a single Bluetooth speaker in the corner, barely holding a connection, someone's crying in the bathroom, and the air is thick with the scent of spilled drinks, sweaty exhaustion, and the stale, lingering regret of people who stayed too long because they thought something exciting might still happen.

Except with a dragon who has recently morphed into a murder demon and wants to pull your insides out through your butt or whatever.

"Oh, shit," Perg says as I manage another drop roll to avoid the grabby chokey killy.

"What?!" I shout.

"Okay, so you know *Fallen*?"

"The movie?!" *Swipe, roll, run.* I feel like I'm in the middle of a game for which I've only mastered one sequence of button pushes, and I just keep executing the same dodge-roll move over and over again.

"Yeah. The one where Denzel Washington finds out that the guy he's hunting is really a demon that jumps between bodies . . . ?"

"Of course I do, I've watched it like . . ."

Oh, shit. Oh shit. The moment in that movie when the demon possesses a good guy and turns them into a killer is a classic betrayal twist.

"I know, fool. Your Denzel Washington obsession is something we can talk about another time, but in the meantime . . . maybe that worked its way in somewhere? Best theory I've got at the moment."

Goddamn. He's totally right. That's exactly what's happening right now. *Swipe, roll, run.*

Shit. He's creating just like I do. He's allowed a patchwork of random thoughts and ideas and obsessions to work its way into the story that he built, and now, the story is telling itself rather than him being the one to control it. Jesus Christ. He's learned how to do this from me.

I have been an irresponsible snail father.

Swipe, dodge, roll.

At some point, I have to imagine Don Esteban 2.0 is going to realize that I'm just doing the same maneuver over and over again, get hip to it, and either squeeze my head like it's an orange and he's the juicer or turn his attention to my compatriots, all of whom are huddled behind Perg's throne, just trying to stay away from the absurdity circus.

However . . .

My last roll has put me within striking distance of Sheila. If I can just get to the door, get inside, and get my hands on the Blade, I might be able to defend myself. Or, of course, I could just flee, leaving everyone behind and becoming the absolute scummiest of bags in history. My bet is I'm gonna do the right thing? But we'll see what happens once the smell of Sheila's leather interior hits my nostrils.

"You gonna die, Saviour boy," says Don Esteban. Which is so incredibly colloquial and also remarkably pejorative at the same time.

I bound for the door handle, and I'm just about to grab it when . . .

Don Esteban *grows.*

His shoulders widen, his hands twist into something even more clawlike, his horns sharpen until they look like spires, and the molten glow in his veins pulses harder. He's coming at me hot, and it's looking extra-extraordinarily probable that this is where, as they say, "the story ends."

But then, a flash of something. Four *competing* horns that also appear to have grown.

. . . Babu Sumnut has entered the game.

CHAPTER THIRTY-SIX

What in the fresh hell?!" I shout as Sumnut comes swooping in out of nowhere, a streak of breeches and momentum, his movements so precise they might as well have been rehearsed.

For a half second, I think he's wielding a sword. But he's not. It's just him, the curve of his arm cutting an arc through the air as he intercepts Esteban with fluid grace.

"I thought you were HR!" I call to him as he pounces forward with grace like a panther.

"We are also trained in conflict resolution!" he calls back as he grips one of Esteban's newly contorted talons and flips the dude's whole body in a spinning, kung fu-like maneuver.

As Esteban goes flipping ass over shank onto the floor, Sumnut reaches into his trousers and withdraws a whip. A bullwhip. Or, I guess, in this case, a demon whip. It flows out behind him, rippling like liquid steel, flitting and slithering with a serpent's grace.

"Back!" he cautions Esteban, snapping the whip in his direction. "I don't want to hurt anyone, but I also kind of do."

Esteban rises to his full height and growls, "You're going to have to do better than that."

Sumnut sighs, his shoulders dropping, and says, "Very well."

Before I can process the physics of it, he adjusts his grip, and the whip goes rigid, snapping into a straight-edged blade in the blink of an eye. Like a metallic tail suddenly going from flaccid to dangerously sharp.

Holy murder magic.

It's insanely fast, a perfect balance of flexibility and lethality, shifting states between whip and blade as though responding to some unseen cue. Sumnut doesn't hesitate, doesn't wait for Esteban to get his bearings and make a move. Instead, he presses the attack, the weapon lashing, shifting as it meets Esteban's claws in a rapid flurry of strikes. The air sings with the motion, steel whispering against the wind as he fights, looking borderline bored by the whole affair.

"Oh, imaginations run amok. Happens all the time," he sighs.

So much about it is impressive to watch, but notably, it's how fast Sumnut is. Ridiculously fast. Faster than . . . um . . . Faster than . . .

"Faster than what, Bruce?"

"I dunno. Just. Uh."

"Come on. You can do it. Pithy metaphors are your thing."

"I . . . I don't . . . Whatever, bro! My brain right now is not . . . He's very, very fast is what I'm trying to explain."

"Alright. You don't have to be a dick about it."

The voice in my head clocks out, and Sumnut clocks in again.

He shifts, pivots, dances around Esteban's incoming strikes, his movements too smooth to be chance, too practiced to be mere instinct. He slams Esteban back a few feet, picks me up from where I remain awed on the ground, looks me in the eye, and says, "Protect your Party."

"I thought you were just a guide."

"Yes, well, I wasn't always."

"What were you before?"

"Is this a conversation you really feel you want to have right now? Look out."

As if he has eyes in the back of his head (and he may; hard to know), he spins his neck, and the newly elongated horns on his cranium clash with Esteban's long claws, head meeting fist, as Sumnut thrashes around like an angry puppy.

I dart back to rejoin my motley crew. (One good thing, I guess, about living life the way I do is that thinking "motley crew" has now implanted the Mötley Crüe song "Live Wire" in my brain, which serves as a badass soundtrack, at least making this whole thing feel kind of cooler.)

Meeting up with them behind the throne, I grab Perg, pulling him along with me. He resists.

"Perg, don't be a hero. Come on." He holds firm, tugging in the opposite direction, forcing me to look at him. There are tears—salty tears—in his snaily eyes. "Buddy? What's wrong?"

I realize I said it like a father talking to his five-year-old, but now that I realize that I have been, effectively, Perg's borderline absentee father, I'm trying to make up for it.

His moustache shakes as he cries, "I'm sorry . . . I didn't mean to . . . I'm sorry."

Son of a bitch. I may have avoided having my heart ripped out of my chest by Don Esteban, but my sapient snail just managed to finish the job that the demonic beast from his imagination couldn't accomplish.

"Dude, it's okay. Really, don't worry about it."

"But—"

"Bro, have you seen what I did? This is nothing. This is . . . This is a campfire to the towering inferno that I managed to set. Really, it's fine."

"I want to fix it."

"I get the impulse. Trust me. But—"

"I can fix this," he mutters to himself. "I just—Okay, okay. So, uh, if I accidentally made a villain, maybe I can—"

I get it. I get it more than I'd like to. Because how many times have I done this? How many times have I shaped a narrative around my wild ideas and then failed to control the fallout? How many times have I played into a role I didn't even want, only to be trapped by it?

I hear claws scraping against steel and look to see Sumnut and Esteban getting all up into it now, sending out sparks that fizzle against the mist-heavy air. Sumnut sidesteps a wild lunge, pivots smoothly, and drags the edge of his spear-whip thing across Esteban's exposed ribs, leaving a thin line of blood in its wake. Esteban snarls, twisting, wings flaring, but Sumnut is already moving again, ducking low, slashing at his legs, snake-striking under the arms, the whip-sword coiling around appendages only to snap back to a sturdy blade and jab, every motion efficient, economical, and just a little bit smug.

I really need to find out what "I wasn't always" means. What was he before he became a dandy-panted intake officer?

Looking back at Perg, I can tell he's trying, trying to come up with a way to fix this with his mind. But . . . he's got writer's block. I know it when I see it, and I see it clear as day.

And, for the first time in what feels like a very, very long time, I actually feel confident, in my element. When a story grows out of hand, when it feels like it's not going the direction you like, when you feel like you've written yourself into a corner that you'll never be able to write yourself out of . . .

The solution is simple.

"Perg," I call, quiet. "You're overcomplicating it."

"What?"

"You just need to stop *believing* in him as a villain." Perg looks at me, confused. "I'm saying . . . somehow, you imagined him into this. So . . . you just need to . . . *unimagine* it."

He stares at me like I just asked him to chew through a steel beam. I can tell he's grasping for something intangible; some existential-borne dial he can turn to reverse what he's done, but he doesn't know how. His breath is quick, shallow, and I can see the fear rising in his eyes. Not of Esteban, not of the battle in front of us, but of himself. Of the power he suddenly realizes he has, and the responsibility that comes with it.

He tries. I watch it happen. His face scrunches up, his lips moving in some silent incantation. Probably a load of curse words. The space around Esteban wavers, flickers just for a second, like a glitch in reality, like a half-finished painting being wiped away before the ink can dry.

But then . . . nothing. The image solidifies again, the glow in Esteban's veins pulsing brighter, like he's feeding off Perg's struggle. He roars, his gold eyes locking onto Perg like a predator sensing a weak spot. He pivots hard, slamming his fists into the ground.

"What the hell are you doing?!" he shouts, all Perlman-esque.

He lunges, claws raking through the air, going straight for Perg now.

I don't even think.

I grab my homie, pulling him out of the way as Esteban's claws tear through the space where he had been standing. The displaced air alone feels like it could peel the skin from my bones.

Sumnut takes the opening, appearing at Esteban's flank, his weapon a shimmering streak of silver. It lashes out, something alive in its movement. Esteban twists just in time to block, his forearm meeting steel, but instead of a clean slice, the weapon writhes. A sudden ripple through the metal, like a whip coiling mid-strike, redirects the force of impact. The edge snaps taut a half second later, biting deep into flesh. A splatter of blood hisses as it hits the ground.

The wound should slow him, should at least stagger him, but instead, he grins.

He lashes out again, moving faster than before, his claws a blur of gold and black. Sumnut sidesteps the first swipe then twists, his weapon flicking outward, the blade unraveling into its whip form. The tip curls around Esteban's wrist, a momentary snare, just long enough to force him off-balance.

Esteban snarls, tearing free, but Sumnut is already moving. He ducks the next strike, snaps his weapon back into a solid blade with a practiced flick, then vaults, flipping clean over Esteban's head. As he twists midair, the weapon snaps back into fluid form, trailing behind him like a living ribbon of metal before snapping taut just as he lands, the blade dragging a deep, vicious line down Esteban's back.

Esteban howls, the sound raw and furious.

"I'm gonna mess you up!" he shouts, going for Sumnut once more.

"I don't know that you will," Sumnut replies. Which just serves to make Esteban angrier.

I roll onto my knees, looking at Perg, who is watching all of this like a kid who just realized the monster under his bed was real.

"I can't do it, fool," Perg grits out. "It's not working."

"Because you're still *trying*," I say, stepping closer.

"Of course I'm trying!"

"No, that's not what I mean. I mean, you're trying to edit the scene instead of *scrapping* it. You can't revise your way out of this; you have to accept that it's not working. You have to *stop believing in it*. You have to kill your baby."

"Kill a baby! That's sick, homes! I'm not killing a baby! What kind of terrible, human sacrifice hoodoo did you get into just for success?! *¡Dios mío! ¡Protégenos de este mal!*"

"No! It's an expression! Sometimes, it's 'kill your darlings'! Whatever! It just means, give up if it's not working. Don't torture yourself. In this case, literally. Get into a flow state."

"I thought 'flow state' is how we got here."

"It is . . . but there's good flow state and bad flow state, and . . . Who cares, man?! You gotta blast this fool with your mind bullets, *ese*!"

There's a beat before he says, "I'm serious, fool. Please don't do that."

"Sorry. I got caught up in the moment."

Perg's eyes dart to Esteban, to the way Sumnut is carving through the air around him with precise, predatory strikes, the battle still raging, still *real*, but only because *he* still believes in it. I can see the gears turning behind his eyes. The slow, terrifying realization that none of this is happening without him.

I step closer. Shoot another shot. "Look . . . You made this. You gave him this role. And deep down, you *still* think he has to be defeated. But what happens if you stop seeing him as something that needs to be fought at all?"

Perg swallows, his breath hitching. And then, finally, he stops.

Not in a dramatic way. Not with a grand gesture or a flourish of realization. He just . . . lets go. I see it in his shoulders (or . . . the place where shoulders would be) first, in the way the tension uncoils, the panic ebbs. His moustache relaxes. His breathing evens out. His mind, his grip on the story he unknowingly created, starts to relax.

And . . . so does Esteban.

The dragon-turned-demon flickers again, but this time, it's different. His form doesn't fight against it. The gold in his eyes dims, the glow in his veins fading into nothing. His claws dull. His massive, hulking frame begins to shrink inward, collapsing under the weight of its own unreality. "I'm melting, melting! Oh, what a world! What a world!" he cries.

Perg exhales, a long, slow breath.

And, at that, Esteban simply . . . ceases to be.

No explosion. No vanishing act. No dramatic reversal of fate.

He is simply *not*.

Silence crashes over the room like a noiseless tidal wave. No one moves. No one breathes.

Perg scoots back like he's afraid of himself. His eyes are wide, staring at the empty space where his villain had been, his mouth slightly open like he's not sure if he should be relieved or absolutely horrified.

"I . . . I did that?" he whispers.

I nod. "Yeah, bud. You did."

His moustache twitches again, like he's afraid he might accidentally summon something else if he's not careful. "That was a trip, homes."

"It was something," Brit mutters from the side.

Sumnut exhales through his nose, slow and deliberate, then with a flick of his wrist, the weapon ripples. The rigid blade loosens, the metal segments collapsing into one another like a serpent coiling to rest. It slithers back, seamlessly retracting as he guides it over his shoulder, where it locks into place against his back with a soft metallic *click*, like he hadn't just been engaged in battle with a literal nightmare.

"A well-executed correction," he says, as if critiquing a student's essay. "Honestly, I bear some responsibility. I feel like that's on me for not getting in front of it all sooner."

"Yeah," I reply, squinting at him. "So I guess, if Esteban is the classic ally turned enemy, you're . . ."

"I'm just a guide," he interrupts. He tries to look as innocent as possible, but it's a real kid-who-got-caught-with-his-hand-in-the-cookie-jar face.

"Sumnut?"

"Hmm?"

"What did you do before you became a Mid-Meridian guide?"

He smiles, scratches at his horns—now returned to their normal, stubby, Mr. Tumnus size—and says, "You had mentioned another missing ally, yes?"

"Yes," Almeister answers, stepping forward and finding his voice, wiping biscuit crumbs from his hands. "My daughter. Persephone."

"Ah," Sumnut breathes. "Your daughter. Very good. Well, aligning with her intent should be easy, should it not?"

Almeister looks at the ground, guilty.

"It should be, but . . . I haven't been . . . I'm not sure I can find her."

Sumnut nods, appearing empathetic. He puts a hand on the wizard's shoulder. "I understand. Well . . . Is there anyone here who thinks they might know what her ideal . . . narrative might be? If she were given the chance to craft whatever version of her story she might wish, what might she choose?"

A beat as we all figuratively scratch our heads. For someone so important to the idea of the story when I started writing it, she did, tragically, wind up being one of the more underwritten characters in the world, as it were.

But then, suddenly, Brit perks up. "Carpathian!" she declares in a kind of revelatory way.

"What's up?" I ask.

"No," she says. "Carpathian. Carpathian is her intention."

"What? What are you saying?"

"That Carpathian—that *you* are her, like, purpose."

My hand goes immediately to my forehead in an attempt at a brain massage. ". . . Sorry?"

"Dude . . ." she whispers, glancing at Almeister. "Are you not paying attention? Persephone has daddy issues. *Of course* she's gonna be hyperfocused on Carpathian the Saviour."

"No, no. Not—Don't—That's not—"

"Oh, please," she huffs. "Like you don't have your own daddy issues."

Fair.

A small, almost unhearable growl, like the sound a skeptical puppy makes, begins in the back of my throat. I choke it off before it graduates into a full-on whine.

Sumnut claps his hands together. "Aha! Now we're getting somewhere. If Carpathian here is the keystone of her intent, then aligning with her should be relatively simple."

I look around at everyone, waiting for someone else to be as alarmed as I am. No one is. Even Perg, still trembling from his reality-warping experience, just nods sagely, like I'm the idiot for not seeing this sooner.

For cripes' sake. Just once, I'd like to not be the gravitational center of someone's entire existential crisis.

"Why don't," Sumnut starts, "you all pile into your CHRONOS, and I'll lead you?"

"Lead us?" I ask.

"Yes. Now that I see the kind of, shall we say, *enthusiastic* imaginations you and your group have, it might be wise for me to attend you all a bit more. I can help you narrow down the place you might wish to look, you see. For example, there are a handful of specific meow meow meows which one whose central thesis is for the pining of a long-awaited love might seek to make their vision become a revised reality. And, fortunately for you, I know where they are!"

I stare at the CHRONOS, then at the group, then back at the CHRONOS.

A kind of doorway that shouldn't exist, leading to a place that isn't real. Except that it is.

I think about wardrobes and rabbit holes and the way that stories usually pretend that crossing between worlds is always a choice. But maybe it never is. Maybe the moment you open the door, the moment you let yourself believe in something beyond the edges of what you know, you've already stepped through.

I take a breath. "Alright. Let's go." I wave everyone toward the car. "Let's . . . Let's go see what kind of story Persephone has been telling . . . herself."

CHAPTER THIRTY-SEVEN

Okay. Do we think *this* is it?" I ask for the fifth time, rolling down the window to ask Sumnut as he approaches the car, adjusting his trousers.

"No, no. I just needed to stop for a moment."

"I know how 'dat be, mi boss," Jameson commiserates.

"No," Sumnut continues, "she would not be here, but . . ."

"But what?" I ask.

"It is just confusing. I was certain she would be at the last one."

"The last one looked like a reverse harem."

"Yes, well, intent is a fickle thing."

And then, I feel it. More accurately, I feel . . . her. Persephone. I can feel her energy.

"She's here," I whisper, though I'm not sure if I'm speaking to the others or to myself.

"What?" Sumnut replies. "That's unlikely. This is not a meow meow meow known for loving. This one is known for . . ."

He may keep speaking, but I've stopped listening. My eyes are focused on what's ahead.

A battlefield in the distance. Actually, it's just a regular field, I suppose, but the fact that there's a battle taking place upon it makes it, technically, a battlefield.

It's surreal. The air shimmers with heat waves of distortion. Like an idea forged by fire.

But that's not what makes it surreal. That's actually just kind of par for the course in Meridia. What makes it surreal is the nature of the fighting and the fighters involved.

The Giant Serpent of the Mokeisan, but composed of flame, jostles and jockeys for a chance to strike at his foe. The foe that is Persephone, hands raised, wielding Spells with an awe-inspiring precision.

The serpent surges forward in waves, its massive, molten body radiating heat so intense it makes my skin feel like it's blistering from where we're watching. Persephone doesn't flinch. With a flick of her wrist, she sends a pulse of Mezmer through the ground, and the flames around her ripple outward, sending the snake retreating back with a horrifying scream.

"This is her ideal?" Brit asks. "The story she wants to tell?"

"I guess so."

"But how is she doing all that shit? The Mezmer here is . . ."

"She is not 'doing' anything," Sumnut offers. "She is merely articulating the story she would wish to tell."

"Shhh," I hiss. Because I am absorbed in trying to figure out exactly what it is I'm seeing.

There is someone fighting beside her. Someone at her hip, waging war as effortlessly as she is. Someone very familiar. And by "familiar," I mean . . . it's me.

I'm there. Always where she needs me, filling the gaps, finishing what she starts, our movements so fluid it's as if the pandemonium is bending to our will.

Is this . . . Am I . . . high? Did the monkey weed take a while to kick in, and now I'm just—

"Look there ye see," Jameson says. "How ye be there when ye be here?"

Oh. I guess not. Unless Jameson and I are on the same trip right now. But he doesn't ever appear to lose touch with what we call "reality," so I have to assume this is actually happening.

"I'm not," I mumble back, trying to sort out what's going on as I watch myself charge through an opening she's created in the horde, Blade of the Starfallen cutting through the nearest enemy with brutal efficiency.

"On your left," Seph calls out, her voice steady, almost playful. I can hear her as clearly as if I was standing right next to her.

"Already there," I reply without looking back, deflecting a blazing tendril aimed at her. But my voice isn't mine; it's more Carpathian. Like the way I heard him in my head.

"Of course you are." She laughs. "Call for Carpathian Einzgear, and he shall answer, as they say!"

She says it with the relieved assuredness of Jim Gordon defending his belief in Batman.

Persephone's narratively produced Mezmer flares again, a wall of light erupting in front of me just as another flame creature lunges in my direction. I don't even glance at it, seeming to trust her completely as I drive forward, cutting down the creatures in my path.

I don't know if she's even aware that we're watching. To her, nothing else exists but this fight, this partnership. It's not just about survival; it's about the way they move together, the way they rely on each other with an ease that's almost intimate. Every glance they share, every unspoken signal, is charged with a sort of . . . unshakeable loyalty.

There is an honesty to it that hurts.

Another lunge from the fire serpent springs forth from the lava, its form shifting and twisting like living flame. Persephone steps forward. The air vibrates with energy as a massive surge of pseudo-Mezmer erupts from her, tearing through the creatures like a storm, leaving glowing embers in its wake.

I don't hesitate to step into the aftermath, my Blade sweeping through the few that remain. Then, I turn to her, sweat streaming down my face but a grin tugging at the corners of my mouth.

"Show-off," I say, my tone light but my eyes full of admiration.

"You're one to talk," she shoots back.

"Oh, shit," I say. (By which I mean *I* say. Me, here, sitting in Sheila. Not the me that's over there, fighting beside Seph. That version of me probably doesn't curse. Or, if he does, it's likely more stuff like, "Great Hizzens Fickles!" Or something.)

The way she holds herself there, the way her idealized Mezmer flows so naturally, so powerfully, it's not hard to see that this is what she's always wanted. Not just to be in battle but to be in *this* battle. To stand as Carpathian's equal, his partner, not just in skill but in trust. In purpose. I can feel the intensity of her desire radiating from every movement she makes, every glance she exchanges with him.

This is her version of what they call in the romance-novel world, an "HEA." A Happily Ever After. This is the way she has always wanted her story to play out.

And, and, okay, I know this is weird, and I don't think I like it, but . . .

I'm kind of jealous of myself.

This entire Mid-Meridian Plane business is enough to scramble anyone's brain. I still don't fully understand it, even after all the explanations offered by Sumnut. Which, now that I think about it, may also be a double entendre. Yes, it's Tumnus spelled backward, but he could also just be "some nut." In which case, it's possible that everything he said is cuckoo talk.

This is the problem with thinking about things. Once you start considering anything, you have to consider everything. Down which path doth conspiracy theorizing lay. So, best just to take the little horned man I met in an insensible space at his word, I guess.

Persephone's Mezmer surges in golden arcs, cutting through the chaos, sending the serpent reeling with every flick of her wrist. There is no hesitation, no doubt. She commands the battlefield with raw power, bending it to her will. And beside her, I fight with equal mastery.

(Not *me*. Other me. Obviously. I mean, I fight *okay*, but this version of me is balling.)

This is the version of Carpathian she believes in. The version she summoned en masse to rescue Almeister from the Tower. I caught a glimpse of her idealized idea of Carpathian then, but being able to sit back and watch from a distance gives me a whole other appreciation for what it is she imagines me to be.

I'm kind of a stud.

"That's the spirit, Bruce!"

(Oh, right, there's also the sometimes-praising, sometimes-chastising version of me who lives in my head. If many more iterations of me spring into being, I'm gonna need a spreadsheet.)

Regardless, other me's sword flashes silver and blue, the movements so precise they feel inevitable. I/he does not struggle, does not falter. Every step, every strike is perfect. And together, he/I and Persephone move as though the battle was built for them/us. And for a moment, it seems like we cannot lose.

But then . . . the world shifts yet again.

There is a pulse deep beneath the battlefield, and the fire creatures freeze in place. Not retreating. Not dying. Just stopping. Like something far greater has arrived. A wave of anxiety sweeps through the car, and Brit stiffens next to me, her hand clenching the dashboard.

"The fuck is that?"

"Oh no," Zerastian mutters.

"Oh no, what?" I ask. "Why are you saying, 'oh no'? I don't like that."

The air turns suddenly thicker than it was a moment ago, pressing down like stone. Sheila revs her engine without me putting any pressure on the gas pedal. But, even more worrisome than that, the gleeful confrontation that Seph and I have been enjoying stops. It feels as though the plane is holding its breath.

"Oh no," Zerastian repeats.

And then, without warning—

They arrive.

What are "they"? Hell if I know, but they're definitely friggin' here. An army of . . . Oh, crap. I do know what they are. Brittany realizes at the same time, as does Zerastian, and as one, the three of us mutter their name at the same time.

"Ashmourn."

"Fuck." (Brittany adds that by herself.)

Yep. Ashmourn; wraiths of living smoke born out of the embers of fallen cities collapsed by Templars and others allied to the Ninth Guardian. Real nasty bastards introduced in Riftbreaker book seven as an obstacle to Carpathian retrieving the Gauntlet of Sorenthali.

And they're here.

How are they here? How have they managed to invade—?

Glancing in the rearview mirror, I see Almeister, head back, eyes rolled up into his skull like he's having a seizure. Or like he's channeling something dark and toxic.

I was right. He's a damn security breach in our firewall. Literally.

And in this moment, it dawns on me: How do you weaken a hero? How do you bring them to their knees? You attack the things they care about, the people. If you can't send them to their end by assaulting them directly—if, for example, you kill them but they remort, or if they escape your direct control by finding themselves on a plane of existence where you can't immediately hold dominion over them—then you use whatever tools you have at your disposal to start picking off the people around them that they care about. You weaken them, psychologically, emotionally. You render them hopeless.

That's what happened with Mael.

It's what's happening now.

Almeister is being used to direct dark forces to draw his daughter away from her own personal heaven and down into something akin to hell. While we all watch.

That's some nasty business.

"Oh my goodness!" Sumnut declares as the Ashmourn shift between presence and absence, bleeding through the fabric of the plane as if reality itself struggles to contain them. They are not creatures in any sense that I can define. They are voids given shape, swallowing light, erasing space.

Persephone's face drops. Her head tilts. She looks confused. Something tugs at my insides. (I would say it tugs at my Heart, but my Heart is attenuated, so I'll just go with "insides.")

"What are you doing?" Brit asks as I open the car door.

"Seph!" I call out, my voice echoing strangely in the blistering air.

She looks over, seeing us for the first time, and says, quizzically, "Carpathian?"

"I am here!" other me shouts, bounding over to her, sounding like a knight from a Disney movie, kinda. But, y'know, hardass. Because it's me.

Something has changed; something is not as she expected it to be. This heavenly version of fighting side-by-side with Carpathian has been disrupted and intruded upon. Seph's brow furrows. She nibbles at her lip. And then . . .

. . . she acts.

Her hands thrust outward, attempting to force her Mezmer into the shapeless horde. She hammers ahead with clear focus, looking as though she is attempting to send a wave of power strong enough to tear down mountains. But nothing happens. It can't. Because what we were just witnessing was the fantastical version of her reality, and now, a starker, more brutal version of reality has spawned, no longer fantasy. And it has strained her Mezmer, just like the rest of ours.

Other me, however, is still made manifest in his way, the faux reality of him unaware that he cannot intercede, for he is yet to be. The true version of him, of me, that exists now is standing beside the car, staring, jaw growing increasingly slack.

Carpathian lunges forward, sword raised. The Blade of the Starfallen should be unstoppable. It has, in its time, cut through monsters, warlords, gods. But the truth of the matter is, the actual Blade is sitting next to me, impotent, stripped of power.

And when fantasy Carpathian (call him "Cardboardpathian") strikes out with his avatar, it meets the first shadow's billowy form and shatters.

The battlefield screams.

The Blade splits like glass, shards of Carpathian's sword scattering across the ground. He stares at the broken weapon in his hand, looks at Persephone, confused, and then . . .

The shadows attack, moving upon him with a disjointed inevitability.

But I . . . Carpathian . . . fights anyway. Even without the sword, the guy dodges, parries, hands crackling with fictional Mezmer forming fabricated weapons from nothing, striking back with pure, ghostly instinct.

And what's crazy is, the dude *almost* wins.

Her belief in him—in me—is so absolute that it's like she's willing the fiction into a state of solidity that it might fight off true malevolence.

For a moment, the battle between fabricated hero and authentic villain tilts. A shadow lunges too far, overextending, and Carpathian twists and pivots. He conjures a new blade, pure light burning in his grip, and drives it forward, straight through the shadow's chest. The battlefield pauses. The enemy staggers. Carpathian smirks.

But then . . . the shadow grabs the blade.

The golden Mezmer dims. The light collapses into the void. And the shadow steps forward, punching a black blade through Carpathian's chest.

The battlefield stops. His body locks up, his lips part, but there is no sound. No last words. No legendary cry. Only the slow, inevitable collapse of a story that was never real.

"What. The fuck. Is happening?"

"I'm not sure," I mutter back to Brit.

The shadow creatures envelop Persephone, swarm her like a murder of malignant crows. She screams; she fights back, but to little avail. The ground cracks apart as she thrashes and wails.

I jump back in the car and reach for the shifter to throw Sheila into drive, but Brit grabs my hand.

"What are you doing?" she asks.

"I'm going to get her!"

"But—"

"But nothing! Get your hand out of the way!"

Brit's eyes widen, but she pulls her hand back, and I slam down on the accelerator, driving straight toward the rapidly disenchanted fantasy.

Sheila roars forward, tires skidding against the unstable ground as we tear toward Persephone and the nightmare swallowing her whole. The battlefield churns in response, like it knows we don't belong here, that this isn't our fight. But I don't care. None of that matters. Not the shifting landscape, not the unnatural shadows, not even the fact that I might be plunging headfirst into what is, I imagine, the Subplane. Which, if rumors are to be believed, is not a very nice place to plunge into at all.

"Hold on!" I yell, gripping the wheel tight.

Brit braces against the dashboard, jaw clenched. "This is a terrible idea!"

"Noted!" I shout back as we swerve past the crumbling remnants of Cardboardpathian's shattered blade. His body, a phantom now, flickers and dissolves into the nothingness from which it came. Persephone stands alone. The shadows press in.

Almeister jerks violently in the back seat, a strangled noise escaping his lips. His skin is slick with sweat, his limbs twitching like he's being electrocuted from the inside. Hell, maybe he is.

"She's going under!" Brit shouts.

"I see that!"

Oh, Christ. This is bad. Memories of watching Lonnaigh get pulled under in the Cavern of Sorrows enter my thoughts. And, very uncomfortably, it strikes me that maybe . . .

Maybe wherever Seph's being pulled is where Lonnaigh was dragged to.

Maybe what's supposed to happen right now is that I'm supposed to go chasing Persephone and, in turn, find Lonnaigh. Maybe this is my chance to rescue

Lonnaigh. It would make sense. It's exciting; it's a twist; it's yet another narrative perturbation in the story being told that feels exciting and cool.

It's exactly the kind of thing I would write, were I writing this.

Which is why . . . maybe . . . I shouldn't *do it?*

To hell with it. Maybe nothing. Enough maybes. *Maybe* I need to think less, do more, and just save Seph from whatever colossal bucket of suck is waiting for her if she gets yanked along.

I slam on the brakes just in time to keep Sheila from careening into the chaos. We skid to a stop just a few feet from the writhing mass of shadow. The moment I fling the door open, heat slams into me like a physical force, air thick with smoke and burning magic.

I don't think, I don't hesitate, I don't mull shit over. I just run.

The Blade of the Starfallen is cold in my grip, lacking potency but still a goddamn sword that I can use to hack and slash at shit. It's like it knows this isn't its fight but is willing to play along anyway. *Good sword, Blade of the Starfallen. Good sword.*

Persephone is barely visible beneath the onslaught. Her screams are ragged, raw, but she's still fighting, still clawing against the impossible. I reach her just as a shadow tendril wraps around her throat, lifting her off the ground. Her eyes find mine—wide, desperate, but also, there's something like . . . I dunno if "love" is too strong a word, but . . . Whatever!

"Get off her, you creepy smoke bitches!" I snarl, swinging the Blade in a wide arc. It's not the punchiest nickname for them, but it's the best I can conjure at the moment.

The shadow holding her shrieks as the Blade connects, and to my great surprise, it splits the shadow flunky in half. Persephone drops hard to the ground, just beside the rift that's been opened, coughing on her hands and knees.

"Carpathian?" Her voice is hoarse, and there's something unsettling about the way she says my name—like she's not entirely sure which version of me she's calling for.

I know how she feels.

"No time for an existential crisis," I tell her, jerking my head toward Sheila. "We need to move."

But before I can get her to her feet, a giant wall of black haze erupts from somewhere beneath us, and just like the Platters song, smoke gets in my eyes.

The smoke swarms, thick and suffocating. I dig my heels in, grip tightening around Persephone's wrist, but the Ashmourn are relentless, pulling, twisting, dragging her toward the rift. My blade is in my other hand, but it might as well be a stick for all the good it's doing.

A sharp snap cuts through the chaos. A silver lash scythes through the dark. Another. A third.

The air cracks as something fast, deliberate, and precise slices between the shifting shadows. A streak of motion. A figure moving forward.

"Sumnut?"

He ignores me, his coat flaring as he plants himself between us and the oncoming wraiths, his whip-blade rippling between states—solid to fluid, liquid to steel—striking out in quick, sharp arcs. He's not winning. He's not even pushing them back. But he's moving. He's fighting.

He shifts his stance, keeping his back to us, the weapon snapping in his hands like a living thing. The whip-blade snaps, lashing through the shifting darkness, carving gaps in the Ashmourn's endless tide. Then, midstrike, he turns his head just enough to shoot a look at me and Persephone.

"Run."

It's not a suggestion. It's not a plea. It's an order.

I try to protest. "But—"

"Run!" he snarls, cracking the whip hard enough that the air itself seems to split.

The Ashmourn rise up as a monolith and encircle him. I can no longer see him in the middle of the cyclone of lost souls.

But I hear him as he shouts it one last time. "Run, damn you!"

Looking Seph in the eyes, I see conflict. Sadness. Regret.

And then, I tear my eyes away from hers, pull hard on her wrist, dragging her with me, and . . . we run.

CHAPTER THIRTY-EIGHT

The smoke is behind us, but it's still everywhere. The MMP hums underfoot, like it's reacting, struggling. We're running, Persephone's breathing ragged beside me. I risk a glance back to see what's happening.

Sumnut is still fighting.

The whip-blade lashes out, cutting through the Ashmourn as they close in, his movements sharp and exact. But it's like cutting through water, the shadows reforming just as fast as he strikes.

The Ninth Guardian's forces are simply here to stay.

The sky is changing. Dark, heavy. The landscape looks as though it's starting to calcify, locking itself into something permanent, tearing away the tabula rasa, open-source opportunity for creation and invention, and bending to become the thing the Ninth Guardian wants it to be. Digging up the green Eden and turning it into a replica of the Guardian's own twisted soul.

The Mid-Meridian is breaking.

And without Mezmer, there's nothing we can do.

I never plotted it out, but this must be what it looked like when Meridia fell.

The Ninth Guardian has, once again, taken over the story.

"They're grabbing control," Brit shouts from the car. "They're locking it down!"

I skid to a stop by Sheila, shoving Persephone toward the door. "Get in!"

She hesitates. "We can't just leave him—"

"Seph, please! Get *in* the damn car!"

Her head retracts as if she's been slapped. The look in her eyes suggests that something has changed. I know the look. It's the one you give a person when you've had a dream about them and then woken up and the dream has imprinted itself on your emotions in some way.

Like, if you've had a dream that someone you love did you dirty in some way, you wake up mad at that person, and they don't understand why. Because in their reality, they didn't do anything wrong. But in yours, they totally made out with Caleb Baker even though you *admitted to them* that you always found Caleb kind of intimidating, given that he was both the captain of the football *and* debate teams, making him simultaneously more athletic and more concise with language than you were. (Just . . . as a totally hypothetical example that has no basis in historical truth at all.)

In Persephone's case, she was getting to indulge her most elaborate Carpathian battle fantasies and then the real Carpathian showed up with a literal carful of intrusion and shut the whole thing down.

"'Real' Carpathian, Bruce?"

"What?"

"You just called yourself the 'real Carpathian.'"

"I did?"

"Mm-hmm."

"I did?"

"You did."

Okay. I'll worry about that later, because right now, I can barely hear myself over the roar of *something* overhead. A rift. A jagged, seething rift tears across the horizon.

Sumnut twists in our direction midbattle, the Ashmourn shifting like a tidal wave around him. His horns glow, his coat flaring as he *moves*.

"Normally, the exit interview is less dramatic!" he calls, sidestepping another strike. "But, nonetheless, you need to take the first door out!"

"What door?!" I shout back. "I don't see—"

But then I do.

The air around us shudders. Not a casual, "oops, the plumbing's acting up" kind of tremor but a full-on cinematic, clutch-the-nearest-object-and-prepare-for-oblivion quake. The plane itself lurches like an old roller coaster hitting a turn too fast, allowing me to see cracks in its construct, a fissure in the air, like the door suddenly being visible in the wall that made up the fake world at the end of *The Truman Show*.

And then . . . the air, normally an unseeable thing, starts moving.

Not falling or shaking apart like something normal in a collapsing structure. That would be too reasonable. Instead, it peels away, like the set of a stage production being unceremoniously yanked away by a disgruntled crew of IATSE members being forced to work during their union-sanctioned smoke break.

"What the fuck is happening right now?" Brittany shouts.

"Carpathian?" Persephone asks.

"Mi, gen'ral?" Jameson inquires.

And me? I say nothing. Because I don't know why, after repeated examples of me not knowing the answers to things, anyone would think I can explain what's happening here.

Through the opening seams, closing in from all sides, is a cavalcade of semi-recognizable images from the collective consciousness. From the deep reservoir of stories told throughout time. Scenes now so real that I can taste the air, feel the shift of light, hear the voices as though I'm standing there, living inside the imaginations of those who came before me.

A great hall stretches above us, a ceiling bewitched to reflect the stormy sky outside. Floating candles hover, flickering despite a nonexistent breeze. The long tables are empty, but I know them; I *know* this place, the scent of old parchment and candle wax clinging to the air.

Holy shit. It's Harry Potter.

Then it tears past us and is gone, replaced by the sprawling dunes of a desert, twin moons hanging overhead. A figure stands atop a crest of sand, wind whipping the long folds of their robe as a massive, scaled shape begins to rise from beneath the surface. A rhythmic thrumming fills my ears, the beat of something ancient, something that moves beneath the shifting earth.

Yeah. Dune. *Got it.*

A roiling sea crashes in next, white-tipped waves undulating against blackened cliffs, the glow of a distant lighthouse cutting through the mist. A ship is breaking apart, wooden splinters soaring through the air, the cries of sailors lost in the fury of the storm.

The Tempest. *Sure.*

A market appears. Cobbled streets are lined with stalls stacked high with exotic fruits, shimmering cloth, weapons with jeweled hilts that hum with unseen power. People are laughing, bartering, weaving between the shadows cast by the awnings overhead. The scent of spiced tea and sizzling meat curls into my nose, familiar and foreign all at once.

Aladdin. *Or maybe* The Witcher. *Hard to know for certain.*

We are on a mountainside, mist curling around jagged peaks, a narrow bridge of ancient rope swaying between two crumbling stone pillars. A figure, cloaked in gray, stands at its center, staff raised, eyes burning with warning. The sound of drums, deep, guttural, growing closer, reverberates from the cavern. Shadows spill forth. Firelight catches the glint of rusted axes.

LOTR. Gandalf on the bridge of Khazad-dûm. Classic.

What is assaulting me is what I would call, I guess, "a barrage of homage."

"Why is this happening?" I ask no one.

But Zerastian answers. Almost too quietly to be heard, she says, "It is forfeit."

The weight of the sorrow in her voice nearly devours me.

And then the barrage of homage appears to cease and is replaced by something more intimate, more personal. A beach, golden with sunset. I'm wet, laughing, running from the waves. A hand, warm and soft, reaches out for me. I run toward her, and she scoops me up in a gentle embrace, wrapping me in a towel. It is a moment stolen from a lifetime ago, and yet so vivid I almost reach for it.

I don't know what the others are seeing now, but the mix of emotions on their faces—the tears and laughter and awe—lets me know that it is as profound as what's happening to me. It is so very much like the experience we had in the Cavern of Sorrows, except this time, the memories aren't designed to leave us aching; they merely . . . are.

The fact that they leave me aching anyway is no fault of the plane.

I want to grab hold of these formative recollections. Wrestle them close to me so that I might be able to redraft the way in which they have imprinted themselves upon me. But they are too fast. They are too fleeting. They are as ephemeral as the breaths we take of which we are unaware. The oxygen that feeds our souls, come and gone and always underappreciated.

And then, the quietest of once-upon-a-times: A diner booth at three in the morning, coffee gone cold, laughter spilling over a Formica tabletop. A road trip, headlights cutting through the dark, music too loud, windows down, the air electric with possibility. A bar, the delicate weight of a slender arm slung over my shoulder, the easy confidence of romance, of home, of knowing exactly where I belong.

All the chapters of my life, both literal and figurative, fleeting past too quickly to grab them up and revise them in any way at all. It is unrelenting. Punishing, almost. The flood of memory does not stop. It rushes through, relentless, a hurricane of moments both familiar and foreign.

A Drakonar, wings vast enough to blot out the sky, its scales dark as deep water, its eyes burning with the memory of a thousand years. A king, crowned in gold, seated upon a throne of bone, his expression unreadable, his court frozen in silence. A temple at the edge of the world, where the wind howls like a grieving mother and the statues weep tears of silver.

Some things resonate for me as clear as the bright summer day that washes over, and others tickle the back of my brain in some way but can't begin to recall where I know them from. The past, the future, the never-was, the could-have-been. They all blur together, folding in on themselves, a dreamscape unfurling and dissolving all at once.

And then, in the midst of it all . . .

A form.

A silhouette. An unknown figure that I do know somehow, despite the fact that we have never met. They are being carried by a giant bird. An owl, to be precise. They appear to conduct and define the wash of recollection.

It is the Ninth Guardian.

But they don't seem to be here on a mission to wreak havoc as I had suspected. They appear to be, just like all the other elements I see, carried along by the dissolution of this rapidly evaporating set of realities.

And before us, Sumnut fights on.

The Ashmourn coil and press in from every direction, relentless, their shifting forms absorbing every strike, every movement, as if his efforts are nothing more than ripples in an endless tide. His weapon arcs, splitting the dark, but it is swallowed just as fast, the shadows reforming, pressing closer.

He moves like a man who has fought in places like this before. He knows he isn't winning. He knows he isn't supposed to. But he fights anyway.

"What is he?"

"He is whatever he needs to be."

"Bruce?"

. . .

"Bruce?"

It's not Brain Bruce. It's the other voice. The one who told me before that things would be okay. That I would be all right.

I feel as though this moment is something akin to being trapped in *The Three-Body Problem* if it had been written by T.S. Eliot: Poetic but baffling as hell and a touch frustrating.

The world is coming apart, unraveling faster than it can be rewritten. I can feel the pull of it now, the way reality itself is turning brittle under the Guardian's grip.

Sumnut sees it too.

He glances at us one last time, one last sharp flick of his gaze, like he's taking a mental picture of the moment, a footnote in a book he has no time to read. Then he's moving again, diving headfirst into the fray, no hesitation, no pause. A shadow engulfs him, a wall of writhing smoke closing around his figure, swallowing him whole.

I floor the accelerator, and Sheila roars forward.

Behind us, the last thing I see is the flicker of Sumnut's weapon flashing in the consuming dark before we are portaled out of here, and the Mid-Meridian appears to collapse entirely . . .

Without me having had the opportunity to rewrite a goddamn thing.

ACT FIVE

TRUTH OR CONSEQUENCES (OR POSSIBLY BOTH)

CHAPTER THIRTY-NINE

"Once Upon a Time in Meridia." Part 6

The wind over the Obsidian Gulf carried the scent of brine and iron, thick and unrelenting. Beneath the vessel's bow, the dark water churned with the slow, deliberate pace of something lurking beneath. A presence unseen but always felt. Mael stood at the ship's prow, arms crossed over his chest, eyes fixed on the horizon.

Behind him, the Super Vizier approached, the edges of her shawl whispering across the deck. "Mael?" The giant Catarincian did not respond. "What are you looking for? Do you see something?"

Mael Anderbariach reached for the ship's railing with both hands, careful not to squeeze it too tightly and risk wrenching it from the deck. He continued staring out at the sea. "Ye told me your reach extended beyond any realm I could name. Ye told me ye had means that I did not. Yet, for all your assurances, my sister remains lost. And I'm getting tired of feckin' waiting."

He turned now to face her. To her credit, she did not shirk nor cower. The Super Vizier simply smiled, a patient, knowing expression. "I know. It's frustrating not getting what you want when you want it. Trust me; I have traveled this road many times. But, unfortunately, things take time."

"I've given ye time."

"You have given us enough time to accomplish that which is merely insurmountable for most. What you require of us is akin to the impossible. And the impossible takes slightly longer."

Mael exhaled through his nose. He could break a person's back with a flick of his wrist, tear through steel doors with his bare hands. But no amount of strength could force open the doors between realms nor pull someone back from wherever Lonnaigh had been taken. That was the promise that bound him to this ship, to these people. A promise that, so far, had yielded nothing.

The ship itself was unlike any Mael had traveled on before. Not simply a vessel of wood and sail but a construct of Mezmer and intent. It cut through the waves with uncanny smoothness, guided less by wind than by unseen forces that whispered just beneath the surface of the water. The crew was a mix of hardened sailors and those attuned to the ship's magic, each serving a role in the silent, ceaseless pursuit of something just beyond reach.

Since their departure, the journey had been marked by secrecy and evasion. There had been no clear destination, no ports of call. Only the open sea and the knowledge that somewhere, somewhere beyond knowing, Lonnaigh existed still. The faintly pulsing Tri-Venn affirmed it.

And though he had severed himself from the man, he could feel in his bones . . .

. . . that so did Carpathian.

"Remind me again," Mael said, finally, "why you fled by sea? The land holds far more power than the water does."

The Super Vizier tilted her head slightly, as if amused by the question. "The land is compromised. Too many eyes, too many seeking to claim what remains of the old order. We had to remove ourselves from the equation. Here, on the water, we are an anomaly, unseen by those who would hunt us."

"You mean you ran."

"I mean we repositioned," she corrected smoothly. "The Tower's fall was not merely a setback; it was a signal to the entire of Meridia that the balance of power has shifted. And that is not, shall we say, ideal. We need time to reconstruct our efforts. And, besides all that, the Ninth Guardian asked us to. So, you know, we're following orders."

Mael turned his gaze back to the horizon. The Obsidian Gulf stretched endlessly in every direction, its waters dark and unyielding. "And Carpathian?"

"What about him?"

"He will come."

"I should hope so. Otherwise, we have both wasted a lot of time and energy."

Mael resisted the urge to scoff. He had always known his presence on this ship was transactional, but hearing it so plainly stated only hardened his resolve. He had endured who knows how many Lunar Rotations of this, adrift, waiting, watching while the crew moved about their endless tasks as the ship's Mezmeric hum worked beneath their feet.

The ship had its own rhythm, its own rules. Food was taken in shifts, the crew eating in silence beneath the watchful eyes of Mezmer-laced lanterns that flickered with an unnatural glow. The days were long, marked only by subtle changes in the air and the occasional whispered conversation between the Super Vizier and Moridius. They spoke of movements across Meridia, of how long they had to fill the vacuum left behind by the Tower's collapse before some other or others might step into the void.

None of it concerned Mael. His concern was singular.

And yet, his mind refused to let him rest.

He did not sleep, for when he did, the nightmare came.

Nightmare.

Singular.

It was always the same.

The Cavern of Sorrows. The sound of stone grinding shut behind him, the air thick with the weeping walls, the scent of damp earth and death. He saw Lonnaigh, just out of reach, her hands slipping beneath the black water, her face twisted in anguish.

In the dream, he eschewed Carpathian. He did not attend the one he now believed to be a false Saviour, turning and racing back inside—only to be taken once more by the Plinth's tendrils wrapping around his limbs, dragging him down, the Mezmer of the cavern surging through him, filling his lungs with sorrow. He would reach for her, screaming her name, but no sound would come.

They were both taken.

Then, just before the darkness swallowed him whole, he would wake.

Each time, he jerked into consciousness with fists clenched so tight his nails cut into his palms. Sweat soaked his mattress, and his breath came in ragged, uneven bursts. More than once, he had shattered the bed frame in his thrashing, forcing the crew to replace it in tense silence the following suns rise. No one spoke of it. No one asked questions.

But the Super Vizier knew.

She always knew.

"You agreed to the terms," she reminded him now. "We provide the means to locate your sister. In return, you allow us to reintegrate you into the Heart Guard. When the time comes, you will be the tether that draws Carpathian to us."

His grip tightened. "And if he does not come?"

"He will."

There was no uncertainty in her voice, only the cool confidence of someone who understood the way of things. Carpathian could not resist a call to reunite what was broken. Mael had seen it in him before, that stubborn need to mend what had been severed. And if Mael was no longer part of his Heart Guard, well . . . that could be fixed. The reintegration process was delicate, but not impossible. A forced recalibration of the bond. A matter of Mezmeric precision.

"You do realize," Mael said, finally meeting her gaze, "that if I return to the Heart Guard, he will know something is wrong."

"That is the point."

A faint hum reverberated through the deck, the result of deep Mezmeric currents pulsing beneath them.

He distrusted the Super Vizier, but his compact with her served a purpose. Just as he did.

The process had already begun. Subtly, insidiously. He had felt it when he first arrived, an echo of something lost attempting to reattach itself to him. The Mezmer they wielded was unlike any he had encountered before—ancient, layered, entwined with things that should not exist. It reached for him, seeking to rewrite what had been severed, to return him to Carpathian's side as though nothing had changed.

Except, everything had changed.

"Your resistance is admirable," the Super Vizier said, watching him closely. "But unnecessary. You are not being made into something else. You are being returned to what you were."

"What I was?" His voice carried the weight of scorn. "What I was died in that cavern."

"And yet you stand here now."

He said nothing. She let the silence linger between them, waiting, watching. Then, with a gesture as subtle as the shifting tide, she reached out and pressed her hand against his chest.

"Soon, we will reach the heart of the Zephyrian Sea. And when we do, we will find a Pulse Well and return *your* heart to Carpathian's, and his to yours, drawing him to us and completing this part of the transaction. After which we will also be able to return your sister to you. And then everyone can go about their business, happy and carefree as children. And won't that be nice?"

Mael did not move. Did not flinch.

The Super Vizier's hand lingered against his chest for a fraction too long, her fingers pressing lightly, as if testing for a fault line. He could feel the weight of her scrutiny, the careful calculation behind every word she spoke.

"Ye speak as though the ending has already been written," he said, voice low.

The Super Vizier tilted her head, amusement glinting in her eyes. "Because it has."

She withdrew her hand, her expression unreadable. Without another word, she turned and walked away, her footsteps steady against the deck. Mael listened to the sound of her departure, the rhythmic creak of the ship filling the silence she left behind.

He exhaled sharply through his nose, his gaze returning to the black horizon. The ship drifted ever forward, an arrow loosed toward an unseen target.

Somewhere out there, lost in the vast unknown, Lonnaigh waited.

And somewhere else, somewhere equally strange, another spirit was emerging.

CHAPTER FORTY

The sensation is like being pulled through static, weightless yet stretched, consciousness unraveling and rethreading itself as the world reforms around me. I know this feeling. It's the same uneasy but somehow familiar sensation I experienced before I realized that everything had changed. That moment of waking when Meridia came into being. Because that is what happened. I did not awake in Meridia; Meridia was awakened by me.

But this time, something is different.

Hard to put a name to it, the thing that's different, but if I had to, I suppose I'd call it "Joe's."

Joe's coffee shop.

Joe's goddamn coffee shop.

It sits perched on a dusty back road that stretches to the edge of a sweeping valley. The sky is a soft, lazy blue streaked with clouds, and the valley below is an expanse of golden grass dotted with sagebrush, bordered on both sides by distant, jagged mountains. The whole scene feels like something out of a road trip Instagram post captioned "Montana, but make it aesthetic." The kind of picturesque Americana that is most likely AI assisted, yet still almost makes you forget how deeply existentially screwed you are.

Joe's coffee shop.

The place I used to go to sometimes on my lunch break, back when I worked at the bus depot. It wasn't much, just a hole-in-the-wall joint a block or two away from my stop. Not terribly originally named; I don't think there ever was an actual "Joe." But man, I loved going there. I'd treat myself to a half-caf, oat milk mocha latte with one pump of hazelnut, three pumps of caramel, extra whipped cream, and a dusting of cinnamon.

Hey, don't judge me. I worked long hours. I deserved it.

My chest tightens as I stare at the shop, the memories tugging at me like tiny threads unraveling a spool. The smell of coffee and rain. The scratch of the barista's pen as she scribbled "Bryce" onto a cardboard sleeve. I didn't care about her mistake, though. It added an element of authenticity and consistency I craved. The warmth of the cup in my hands as I sat by the window, pretending not to notice how the world rushed on without me outside.

For a moment, the noise in my head stills, and I'm just standing there, staring, feeling a weird, uncomfortable nostalgia.

It's too familiar.

"What the hell is this?" I whisper to myself. I feel like I did when I found out they canceled *Young Sheldon.*

And, yeah, I know how that sounds, but hear me out. That show had no right being as good as it was. What started as a gimmick—a throwaway spin-off of a show I wouldn't be caught dead watching—evolved into something good. Something great, even. It had heart. It had character growth. It was actually funny without relying on some smarmy, audience-baiting nerd caricature malarkey.

But did that matter? No. Of course not. Because that's how it always goes. Every time a show finally finds its footing, it gets the axe, like some kind of punishment for daring to improve. Meanwhile, *The Simpsons*—a show that peaked decades ago—just keeps shambling forward like an entertainment lich, growing ever more hollow, feeding off the nostalgia of people who remember when it used to mean something.

And don't even get me started on *Firefly.* Or *Futurama.* Our culture has been robbed from us. Yet *Grey's Anatomy* has somehow crawled its way to twenty-one seasons when it should have been left in the gutter to die after three. But *Young Sheldon*? That gets cut down before its time? Make it make sense.

The smell of espresso intensifies as I approach the weathered door, each step feeling like I'm wading through syrup. The closer I get, the more vivid the memories become. The way the sun hit the counter at just the right angle in the mornings. The awkward chime of the bell over the door that always came a half-second too late to announce your arrival.

I pause in front of the door, hand hovering over the handle. The wood is worn smooth where countless others have pushed their way inside.

The bell chimes a beat too late, exactly how I remember it.

And inside?

It's perfect.

The lighting is soft and warm, the kind that makes everything feel just a little cozier. The counter runs along one side, a row of stools lined up against it, their seats cracked and patched with duct tape. The chalkboard menu above the counter is written in the same looping scrawl that always seemed illegible but somehow made sense when you squinted hard enough.

And the smell . . . *whoa.*

Fresh coffee beans, toasted bagels, a faint hint of cinnamon and chocolate from whatever syrup concoction they keep in those little squeeze bottles.

It's the same. Exactly the same.

Except it's not.

Because it can't be.

The bus depot is miles—realities—away from here. Therefore, this could not be a few blocks away from it. And I'm no longer the guy who used to sit in the corner nursing a latte and scribbling down dumb little ideas that would eventually become the foundational building blocks of Riftbreaker.

It's empty inside. Strike that—mostly empty. I'm less surprised by the fact that there's a barista behind the counter, wiping down the espresso machine like she has all the time in the world, than I am of the existence of this place as a whole.

At this point, if I saw an alternate version of me in here—young and full of the world's oppressive maudlin—sitting in front of the corner window, I'd probably be less smacked of gob than by the entire building being perfect down to the last detail.

As if summoned by my stare, the barista looks up, expression neutral, polite, and somehow completely unimpressed by the fact that a guy in Saviour garb is standing in front of her holding a legendary Blade of ass-whoopery.

Suppose that's par for the course, though. Interplanar visitors at the equivalent of an off-ramp of reality is likely not novel.

No pun intended.

"Morning," she says, voice exactly the right amount of disinterested. "What can I get you?"

I blink at her, my throat suddenly dry.

"I . . . uh . . ."

My eyes wander to the chalkboard menu, and for just a second, I forget how to breathe.

There, written in smudged, pastel-blue-colored chalk, is the same order I used to get.

The half-caf, oat milk mocha latte with hazelnut, caramel, whipped cream, and cinnamon.

It's listed as "Bryce's Latte."

The barista just waits, tapping her nails on the counter with the kind of disinterest that suggests she's been here since time began and will remain so until infinity.

"I'll have that," I say, pointing at the words on the chalkboard.

"Figured." She smiles and winks. "Already pulled it for ya."

She pushes a steaming cup toward me. The name written on the side is . . . Carpathian.

(Actually, it's scrawled as something that looks like "Carp Nation," but I know what it means.)

Slowly, I raise the cup to my lips and take a cautious sip. The warmth spreads through me instantly, the flavors so familiar it's almost overwhelming: oat milk, hazelnut, caramel. It's perfect. Too perfect.

Then, a new memory hits.

I'm not standing in the coffee shop anymore. I'm behind the controls of a conveyance vehicle—massive, clunky, worn with age. It rattles as I guide it through a maze of broken streets under a Mezmerically lit sky. The passengers are quiet, shadows flickering in the dim glow of overhead lights. I know this scene. *I wrote this scene.* It's Carpathian's backstory. *His* days as a conveyance conductor in a dystopian sprawl.

I gasp, pulling the cup away. The coffee shop snaps back into focus. I glance around, but she doesn't seem to notice or care.

I take another sip.

This time, I'm standing in front of the Interlocutrix, Almeister's great invention. The pod looms before me, pulsing faintly with energy. I step inside, nervous.

I can feel my heart, a regular one, beating quickly as I step into the unknown. Almeister places his hands on the controls, and the world tilts as the machine hums to life, as I begin the process of leveling up in ways I don't yet understand.

The memory fades, leaving me dizzy. I lower the cup again, staring at it like it just bit me.

"Go ahead," she advises. "Drink up. You have to do it."

I take another sip.

More memories flood in, moments I don't recognize but *feel* deeply. Carpathian's memories. My memories. They blur together, indistinguishable. The room begins to fade, the edges of the shop dissolving like steam.

Finally, as I get to the last bits of the drink, the memories become more recent. Me, escaping the Templars in my PJs. Another sip, and I'm in Jeomandi's in the middle of a tavern brawl. Another sip, and I'm in the Tower of Zuria, defending the cocoon form of Persephone from an asshole onslaught. Then I take the final sip, and I freeze. Because something weird happens. I hear a voice.

"Bruce," the voice says, quiet at first, but it raises in volume and intensity without me even doing anything. *"Bruce!"* the voice calls again, louder, more insistent. I both recognize it and don't in equal measure. It's a voice I should know, I have that feeling, but I can't quite place it. Is it female? Male? Old? Young? My mind slides over the identifying qualities and causes me to forget. I just know that I feel a sense of companionship with this voice.

"Bruce . . . Silvert," the voice says. My name. My real name. Not Bruce Silver. This voice has specifically added the *t* sound at the end to indicate they are familiar with me in a way that no one else in this world (at least other than Brit and possibly Perg and, more recently, I suppose, Jameson) are.

". . . Uh, yeah?" I venture, though it feels like I'm not speaking out loud. More like I'm using my mind.

"Are you ready to get going, Bruce?" the voice responds. Simple. Unadorned. No extra statements or warnings or mysterious comments.

"I am," I say.

"Okay, so drink the last sip."

"Do what?"

"Drink the last sip. That's all. Just drink it on down."

I don't know why, but I trust this voice implicitly. So, without anything else to be done for it and because I am, and always will be, subject to the sunk cost fallacy, I finish the dregs of the drink and make an audible "Ah!" as I do. Not because it's so good but because it feels necessary to punctuate the moment.

The air distorts, pulling and stretching in a way that defies sense. I hear something like a low hum mixed with the sound of rushing wind, though it seems to come from inside my head rather than the world around me. The fading coffee shop dissipates entirely, until—

WHAM.

I'm slammed into the driver's seat of Sheila so hard it feels like I've been bodychecked by a professional wrestler. The steering wheel is suddenly in my hands, and the familiar hum of the engine surrounds me. My knuckles tighten on the wheel out of instinct. It's real. The vibrations in the seat, the soft rattle of the dashboard.

Outside is Meridia; the Meridia we left. Unchanged. The long, dry, parched earth of what appears to still be the Mokeisan Desert all around.

I hear a kind of a . . . yawn? And then . . .

Helloooooooooo! Well, what have we all been up to? I can tell you what I've been up to . . . Nothing! A whole lot of nothing! Just resting and rejuvenating and recuperating and reinvigorating . . . All the -atings. It appears that you successfully navigated your stay on the Mid-Meridian Plane! Good for you! What a wonderful thing for you to have done!

Oh, no . . . wait . . . Sorry . . . Just processing some new information from your experiences there, and, uh . . . um . . . Oooh.

I see.

Well . . .

It would appear you have retrieved a previously absent member of your Party, though! Huh? So that's good! Right? Right? Sure it is! Any-old-hoo, welcome back, and I'm around if you need me!

{COURTESY MESSAGE #35}

Everyone is here, thankfully. Still with me. Brit, Perg, Seph, Jameson, Al, and Zerastian. I'm about to call out an obligatory, "Everyone okay?" but I don't. Because I can see them. And they're not. I run a quick evaluation anyway.

Heart Guard Evaluation

Heart Guard Member [Teleri Nightwind]. Status: Present

Heart Guard Member [Pergamon Slow Bottom]. Status: Present

Heart Guard Member [Persephone Vizardsdottir]. Status: Present

Heart Guard Member [Tavrella Redacted]. Status: Deleted

(Do you wish to permanently delete member? [Yes] [No])

Heart Guard Member [Xanaraxa Caputrukahs]. Status: Missing

Heart Guard Member [Zerastian Teronia]. Status: Present

Heart Guard Member [Almeister T. Wizard]. Status: Present

A bit of okay news is that at least Al's status hasn't reverted back to "Corrupted." I suppose, if for no other reason than the Ninth Guardian may have gotten the use out of him that they need. And while he no longer seems to be in a trance, he does nibble at his bottom lip and stares out the window, a worried expression on his face, as if he knows he was used and abused.

Seph looks as sad as I've seen someone look in a long time. She looks exactly like . . . Doesn't matter. It's what she looks like.

Brit is shook, Perg is shook, Jameson is . . . Eh. Jameson looks fine, actually.

And Zerastian . . . Well, she looks . . . preoccupied.

"Hey," I whisper in her direction. She looks at me. I start to speak, but she stops me with . . .

"It is."

"What is?"

"You were going to ask if my precognition is functioning. It is."

"Yeah . . . How do you—?"

"Because."

It's clipped, so I don't push it. "Can you tell if Sumnut is okay? Or what happened to the plane?"

She shakes her head. "No. But it must now be sealed."

"Sealed?" I repeat, because I need to hear it again, need to taste the word in my mouth and see if it sits wrong when I say it. (Spoiler alert: it does.) "Why?"

"Because it's over. The Ninth Guardian has it now, and if it remains open, it's not just theirs: it's theirs to use. To spread. To rewrite in a way they control entirely. It's no longer Mid-Meridian—it's another arm of them."

"But Sumnut . . ."

"It doesn't matter."

I drive in silence for a second. Almost silence. A carful of anxious people breathing heavily makes a reasonable amount of noise.

I don't want to ask the next question because I already know the answer and so I'm only asking it on the infinitesimally small chance I'm wrong, but . . .

"And to seal it, we have to—"

"Defeat the serpents. All of them. Once and for all."

. . . But I'm not wrong.

CHAPTER FORTY-ONE

We've been driving for a little while. We wound up deposited a hundred or so kilostrydes from Elderkeep.

I've been staring at the Notification ever since it popped up.

You have been offered a Quest!
"Defeat, finally and absolutely, ALL [Giant Serpent(s) of the Mokeisan] in order to shutter access to the [Mid-Meridian Plane]."
Do you wish to accept this Quest?
[Yes] [No]

I keep hesitating on doing what I know is the right thing for a couple of reasons.

One, because I never got the chance to work on my own revision. Perg did. Seph did. Zerastian did for a really long time. I didn't. And I don't mean that in a whiny "everybody else got to go to the mall and I didn't" kind of way. I really mean that I just wanted the chance to explore what other ways things could have gone. Like, if given the opportunity, could I have played the whole Lonnaigh thing better? Could I have saved Tavrella? Hell, could I even have gone back as far as the stories that pre-date my arrival and somehow prevented Almeister from being captured?

Or, more realistically, could I have workshopped some scenarios that would allow me to see what the future holds? Not just in the precognitive way that Zerastian experiences possibility but in an actual manipulable way that would take out some of the guesswork of things.

If we shut down access to the MMP, that option is gone forever.

But, possibly more importantly . . .

Sumnut.

We left him there to fight the Ashmourn all on his own. But here's the thing . . .

I *want* to go back into the MMP for those reasons. That's what I *should* do. If I were telling the story the way I tell stories, it's what I *would* do. I wouldn't just let the Ninth Guardian take control of this fount of creative inspiration and land of invention and turn it into something fallow. I'd figure out a way to charge headlong into it and win that particular battle.

Which is why I shouldn't.

Change the narrative.

If I'm going to eventually defeat the Ninth Guardian and open up Mezmer back to the world . . . if I'm going to actually repair the damage done to Meridia . . .

I have to start operating in unexpected ways. Even if those ways, on the surface, seem ignoble or wrongheaded. I have to make choices for the greater good and not just the ones that *feel* good to me.

And so . . . I reach out . . . and press [Yes].

REALLY?! Sorry, don't mean to sound surprised. Just didn't expect you to go that route. Look at you, being all unanticipated! Excellent!

Quest: "Defeat, finally and absolutely, ALL [Giant Serpent(s) of the Mokeisan] in order to shutter access to the [Mid-Meridian Plane]." [ACCEPTED]

Quest Requirements:
Requires Artifact: [Gauntlet of Sorenthali]

Yeah . . . My hope is that we'll be able to get hands on the Gauntlet before the serpents show up again. I imagine they're going to be super pissed about having part of their collective tail cut off and then bound. I mean, they kind of slither around mad all the time, so I don't if it makes that much of a difference, but . . .

I wonder what would happen if I was able to defeat the serpents without the Gauntlet? Like, if I could somehow pull it off anyway, would that void the terms of the Quest? Is it possible to trick the stipulations of the agreement by bending the rules? Is there a Legal Skill I could acquire that would help in these matters? All good questions.

"Homie?" Perg's voice draws my attention.

"Yeah?"

"Can we stop?"

"Why? You need to go to the bathroom?"

So many small bladders in my troop. Can't really hate on Perg, though; he's a snail. I'm amazed he's made it this long.

"No, fool. I mean, can we stop? Just, like, stop. For a minute? We've been going without a break for, like, months."

"Months?"

"Yeah, fool. You think I just set up my kingdom overnight? It took a long time. I had to get all the paint approved, go over architectural plans, pick out fabric swatches, levels of mist for the throne. Feel like I haven't just hit pause in a long time."

Ah. That's what Sumnut meant when he talked about time not moving in a traditional way. Perg, invested as he was in the story he was telling, lost himself to the fantasy. Kind of like how when I would get into a groove with my writing, sometimes I'd stay up all night, absorbed by the journey, and the next thing I knew, it would be morning. The same thing happened to Perg, but in reverse.

Causes me to wonder how Zerastian must feel. She was there for what, in her mind, could be a literal epoch. Or Persephone. For how long did she imagine herself battling it out alongside Carpathian? For how long was she vanished inside a dream that was, for her, superior to any reality I might be able to provide?

The forlorn, melancholy expression she wears lets me know that however long it was, it wasn't long enough.

"I don't know where we can stop. Where's safe?"

"We could try here," Brit pipes up, holding one of the maps that, once more, shows a detailed relief of Meridia.

"Where?" I ask.

"Here." She points. "There's an inn just outside of Elderkeep. Right on the outskirts."

"There is?"

"Yes," she says in a pointed way. "It's the one where we stopped that *last* time we had to collect the Gauntlet of Sorenthali. *Remember*?"

I really don't. I—Oh, no! Wait! I do!

"Yes!" I exclaim a little too loudly, making everyone jump. "Yes. We had been battling with a whole phalanx of Templars because it was the first time we met Moridius, and we discovered that the Gauntlet exists and that we could use it as a necessary asset against them before discovering that it was also uniquely suited to battle the serpent!"

It's unnecessarily expository and overly enthusiastic, but I'm just excited that I managed to recall all the details.

"Yeah," Brit responds flatly.

"Right, right. The inn. The place where we had that good . . . shank?"

"Pie."

"Ah, yes, the good pie. I remember it well."

"Soooo," Perg says, "can we stop there? I can't be the only one who wants good pie."

"Aye, mi gen'ral, I be wantin' it too. Ain't right to pass up a fine pie when it's within grasp. Would be a sin, truly."

I turn around to look at Almeister.

"Almeister? How are you holding up?"

He looks back, slowly; nods, slowly; speaks, slowly.

"I am . . . feeling rather much more like myself, I believe."

He's still eyeing me critically, but I can feel him now as part of the Heart Guard, and he doesn't *feel* out of line. I think it's possible that whatever Richemerion did to bring him back to himself is finally settling in.

Unfortunately, Seph is now the one side-glancing on me like she's not so sure. Which is, frankly, another good reason for us to make a pit stop. There's a tugging at my Heart telling me that I need to . . . connect with her in some way beyond just adding her to a list of compatriots who have a shared goal. That whole thing Sumnut said about knowing somebody versus *knowing* them.

"Good," I say to the wizard. The mentor. My mentor. At least, I'd like him to be. The relationship he and Carpathian shared in the books is one I've always . . . I dunno if I'd say "coveted," but—No, I would. I coveted their father/son dynamic.

Honestly, not having been able to experience that has been one of the bummer-ier parts about him being corrupted. Maybe now I'll have a chance to get a little hand-on-the-shoulder, finger-guns, "you got this champ," steady wisdom from the dude. The dude I created, or very much believed I did. All the wisdom I had him impart to Carpathian was stuff that I knew, intellectually, sounded cool and helpful, but that I was never able to apply in my own life. Maybe because I just thought it was part of a fantasy world.

The idea of having a father who always had my back.

Anyway. I'm glad he seems to be doing better.

. . .

We drive in silence the rest of the way to the inn.

Night has descended. It comes on quick in Meridia. The larger of the two suns dips below the horizon first, leaving the smaller one to cast kind of a candlelight glow across the planet before winking out. A pretty, daily ritual in an otherwise violent world.

Up ahead, in Sheila's headlights, the inn appears like some misplaced relic of another age, a weary outpost standing at the edge of a dying universe.

The desert stretches around it, a sea of dust and cracked earth where the wind sculpts the land into rippling dunes and jagged ridges. The dark sky presses down, heavy and expectant, like it's holding its breath. Or maybe that's just me holding my breath as I wait to see if a giant serpent—or four, or four-in-one, or some other something that I don't even know about—leaps up from the ground or descends from the heavens to savage our souls.

But no, nothing.

This is, of course, the calm before the storm part of our story.

The structure grows larger, a thing that probably should not still be here yet persists like a stubborn myth that refuses to fade.

It's built from stone, quarried and cut, and stacked with purpose. Even from the dark distance I can see that the walls are weathered, scorched by years under unrelenting suns. A watchtower juts from one side, its top long since crumbled, leaving jagged edges that cut against the night. A wooden sign, bleached but still readable, hangs from a post out front. The lettering is elegant, old-world script. Sheila announces the name that I see written:

"Now approaching: The Wayfarer's End. Would you like to see what people are—"

I press a STOP button on the PCM before she finishes.

Light flickers in the windows, golden and inviting, at odds with the desolation around. A low wall encircles the property, built from stones held together with what was once Mezmer-infused mortar, remnants of a time when people still believed in the power of crafted protections, now just a rocky wall.

It looks like something out of LOTR. *The Prancing Pony*, where Frodo and Sam first meet Strider (soon thereafter known to be Aragon). The kind of place where a ranger would sit in a corner with his hood drawn low, where wanderers can trade coin for a bed and a meal and perhaps a warning about the path ahead. But here, in this wasted land, it feels almost absurd in its defiance.

Sheila's tires crunch over the dry Meridia as we approach, and for the first time in a long while, I feel something close to relief. A place to stop. To breathe.

"This was a good idea, Perg."

"I know, fool."

We slide into a parking spot out front. The place looks relatively unattended at the moment, not a lot of other vehicles in sight. Could be that we're here on a slow night, or could be the kind of thing where this place exists to service our journey and not for the sake of providing big obstacles or some crazy action-adventure. Wishful thinking, that, but while wishing doesn't make it so, it also doesn't hurt. Unless, of course, you wish for an anvil to fall on your head or something, but I don't know why I would do that, other than to just escape the cycle of drama in which I'm encircled. But that's not really where my head is at.

We unload from the car and make our way to the front door. I hesitate.

"What's wrong?" Brit asks.

"Just . . . Last time we went into a place, they called Templars on us."

"Well . . . Things have changed considerably, and we're kind of in the middle of nowhere. You also don't look a lot like the guy on the Wanted poster now."

Odd. She's right, but it's odd. With my new garb, the dirty hair, and the steadily growing beard, I do look more like the Carpathian of my imagination and less like the guy on the Wanted flyer in Jeomandi's. That guy looked undeniably like Bruce. The more like Carpathian I think I become, the less like Carpathian I seem to be. Or something. Whatever the case may be, I open the door, braced for anything that might be inside.

Which ain't much, as it turns out.

The interior is all honey and firelight, with heavy wooden tables and a long bar running along one wall. A massive hearth dominates the far end of the room. No fire, as it's hot and dry enough already, but the aesthetic completes the anticipated vibe. Just like the parking area forecast, despite the multiple tables, the place is empty of patrons.

There is a matronly Dwarf woman behind the bar. She's round faced and pleasant looking, with graying hair pulled back in a neat bun. When she sees us, her face breaks into a smile that's so genuinely welcoming it's almost suspicious. I think I may have PTSD from that overly friendly Grubble who tried to dime us out.

"Well now," the Dwarf says, wiping her hands on her apron. "Bless my britches! You're here!"

"*We* are?" I ask, hand automatically finding itself on the hilt of the Blade.

"Yes! Someone is! Haven't had visitors in a good long while; starting to think we'd never see any customers ever again. Come in, come in! Look like you've been through the mill and back. Take any seat ya like. Kitchen's still hot, and I've got a stew that's been simmerin' since dawn."

She hustles back to the kitchen, and I'm about to caution everyone to sit but stay alert, but the smell that hits me when she opens the kitchen door is overwhelming. Whatever's cooking, it smells like home, like comfort, like something I haven't had in a very, very long time. Longer than I've been here.

We plop ourselves at one of the tables, and she comes scurrying out, carrying a huge tray that, appropriately, dwarfs her. Seven bowls and seven mugs. Or tankards. Or . . . cups. Whatever. They're vessels that carry liquid, which, technically, is also what a bowl does. But in any case . . .

"Here ye are! Eat! Enjoy! And . . ." She pauses, eyeing me. I get nervous. "Ye do have money?"

"Oh. Uh . . ."

"I do," Persephone says, pulling a slim black wallet from her cloak and thumbing through a few wafer-thin hexagonal discs.

Oh, yes. Tallychips. Each one coded to a specific deed, craft, or service, etched with a filigree that flickers when active. They're not exactly currency so much as proof of contribution to the world. Every chip carries the residue of a story: a song sung, a battle fought, a choice made. It's less "money" in the traditional sense and more "receipts from the plot," I suppose. It was Brit's idea; she had gotten kind of heavy into crypto for a moment, and while she lost a bundle on some very sketchy pump-and-dump meme coins, it did provide inspiration for how money works on Meridia, so I gave her a raise. Everyone wins.

Seph drops a tallychip into a ceramic bowl on the counter. It flares blue, burns green, then settles into a soft amber glow. The glyph hovering above it pulses once, and the transaction is verified.

"Thanks." I nod to her. She nods back, politely but less enthusiastically than I have come to expect from her.

Her time with idealized Carpathian has really done a number on her.

"Alright! Enjoy!" The Dwarf beams and trundles off.

Perg, currently house-cat size, takes a slurp of the stew and moans in an uncomfortable-to-listen-to ecstasy.

"*Ay, por la madre de todos los moluscos* . . . This is better than governance, fool."

Putting aside that I don't really know what either of those sentences mean for different reasons, I'm glad he's happy.

"Good," I reply, pushing a hand through my hair. "Gauntlet?"

I don't want to be a killjoy, but I can't allow myself to get mission unfocused. If I don't get anything else out of this whole saga, teaching myself to maintain focus is one thing I can will into being. I glance at Brit, who pulls out the maps.

She nods, pushing her bowl aside. "Okay . . . So, assuming—like the Blade—it reverted back to its original location, it should be in Origin Pass."

"'Propriately named," Jameson notes. "Couldn't name a place better if ya was writing in down in a storybook."

Brit and I share a look. *If this macaque blows our cover, I swear . . .*

"Yeah," Brits huffs. "Anyway. It'll be hidden in an old break where the land split during the Fault of Sorenthali."

Rubbing my palms together, I say, "Right. Okay, well, so, how do we want to do this?"

"However we wish to engage with the Quest, it should be done swiftly," Zerastian warns.

"Why?" I ask. "I mean, I know why, but . . . Why?"

"Because the MMP will soon be overtaken entirely."

"You can feel that?"

She nods.

"The girl is right," Almeister says, his voice stronger, more resolved. Possibly for the first time since I've met him, he truly sounds like the Almeister of my imagining.

All heads turn toward him.

"The Mid-Meridian Plane is falling under the spell of the Guardian at an alarming rate."

"You can feel it too?"

"No. Not feel . . . Sense."

"Sense?"

"Resonance."

"Resonance?"

"Yes. To resonate means—"

"I know what it means . . ." (The whole "we all misunderstand each other" runner needs to be retired now, I think.) "Just . . . What are you saying?"

"When I was corrupted," he continues, calmly, "I was opened. My will was not my own, but my perception . . . It was, somehow, expanded. Forcibly, but still. I have seen things I was never meant to see. Patterns of convergence. Veins of power strung between the planes like latticework under the skin of the world. When Richemerion freed me, most of the control was severed, but not all the perception. The threads remain. And now, I see them still. Fainter but real."

He blinks. Like maybe saying it out loud made it more real to him too.

"What once was violation," he continues, "now grants me . . . glimpses."

"Of what? The future? You're also precognitive now?"

Zerastian almost pouts, I think.

"No, not of the future. Of . . . the flow. Of what *will* become if left unaddressed."

Ah. It's not prophecy, exactly. Not like Zerastian's clairvoyant echo-chambers of possibility. More like forecasting. He's not seeing a future; he's seeing where the threads are pulling. If Zerastian is a seer of many futures, Almeister is kind of a diagnostician of trajectory, I guess. He has a sense of inevitability? But not of choice.

Zerastian sees what *could* be. Almeister senses what *will* be if you change nothing.

Well, that seems fairly complementary, kind of dangerous, and, potentially, very helpful.

The idea that his corruption has had unintended positive consequences for our side is great. However . . . it also implies, to me, that a bit of a corrupted acorn might live inside him for good.

And if he's able to be taken hold of again, Mezmerically, while still attached to the Heart . . .

Can't think about it right now. Paralysis via analysis isn't gonna help anything.

"Alright," I declare. "Then we need a Pulse Well so we can get right before we go Gauntlet hunting. Nightwind?"

She studies the maps. "I don't see one close by."

"Really? Nowhere?"

"Not on the maps."

"Ye looking for a Pulse Well, d'ya say?"

The Dwarf is back beside us.

"Uh, yes. We've had a set of . . . adventures. We should validate ourselves."

"There's one out back," she informs. "In an old Temple of the Body. Real old. Haven't had anyone through in, oh . . . must be twenty, thirty Lunar Cycles."

Brit lifts an eyebrow. "I'm an Advanced Map Maker, and it's not marked on the map."

"Maps don't know everything," the Dwarf replies, smiling. "Sometimes, the land forgets on purpose."

"Can you show us to it?" I ask. "And then, maybe we could stay here for the night?"

The idea of sleeping in a bed, resting, actually having a real moment to resettle seems like the most fantastical part of this whole deal.

"Of course," she replies. "Ye have more chips, do ye?"

I pat the pockets of my coat and shrug *I left my billfold in my other life* at Seph.

She sighs and once more pulls out her wallet, looking ever more like she wishes she could have just stayed on the MMP with the version of Carpathian who isn't a total deadbeat.

CHAPTER FORTY-TWO

Following the Dwarf woman to the temple, I trail the group. Seph and Almeister are just ahead of me.

They're walking close—close enough that their elbows brush now and then. But it's not until she stumbles slightly on a loose stone and his hand darts out to catch her that I realize something: he doesn't let go. Not right away. Not the way someone does when they're helping you keep your balance and then disengaging politely. He keeps holding on just a beat longer than he needs to, and she lets him.

It's not terribly dramatic. Not teary or sweeping or overly sentimental in a Hallmark way. But it's real. And I've never known that kind of thing between them. Not in this world; not in the books. Almeister always had the aura of a cloistered academic: wise, aloof, vaguely distracted by the mechanics of some unseen star cycle. Fatherhood was more implied than expressed.

But now? He's trying.

And I remember what he said on the MMP. How he wished he'd been better. Done better.

It resonates with me. A lot. Like, *a lot* a lot. Because I never held on long enough either.

Mollie would've taken my hand a hundred times if I'd reached for it, but I never really did. Not when it mattered. I told myself I was busy, distracted, working, writing, surviving. But mostly, I think I was afraid of what it would mean to stay. To be known.

Seph doesn't know she's wearing Mollie's shape, but this second chance, this unearned mirror of someone I failed . . . I feel that same familiar tremor. That want to be good enough.

So I watch them, her and Almeister. I let this scene brand itself into whatever part of me is still learning. Seph asked to be here, to join the Heart Guard. And that means we hold a piece of each other now. And I gotta be true to that, or else . . . Or else I don't deserve another chance.

I slow a little more, then veer off, casually, like I'm just stretching a leg or clearing my head.

"Al?" I call, keeping my voice low, easy.

He turns. She turns. They look at me.

"Can I borrow you for a sec?" I nod away from the group. "Just need a read on something?"

He glances at her, says something quiet, then falls over beside me. We step off to the edge of the path, away from the lamplight the Dwarf carries. The wind whispers over the sand, carrying the faint scent of dust and old . . . dust. More old dust. It's very dusty. It's a desert.

"Um . . . How are you doing?" I ask, and I mean it. "You've been through more than anyone here. At least recently."

I suppose that's debatable, but he's old, so he gets extra stress points.

He considers the question; then, instead of answering directly, he folds his arms.

"There's a sensation," he says after a moment. "Like standing in a room you've known your entire life, only someone has moved the furniture by an inch. Everything is still where it ought to be, and yet . . . nothing feels quite right."

I nod, even though I'm not sure I fully understand.

"But, broadly, I'm okay." He takes a beat. The night sits. "How are you? Carpathian?"

He says the name carefully, like he's trying it on to see if he thinks it fits.

"I'm . . . okay. So, listen . . . All that, um, Brucillian stuff that you—?"

He waves his hands. "That was . . . I was compromised. DONG did quite a heroic job of inculcating me into a belief that was not mine."

"Right. Did they, uh, happen to go into any detail about Brucillian, though? Did they suggest who he might be, exactly, or where he came from or . . . anything like that? Like, what's in this Gospel?"

He stares at me, says, "They say he is borne of the Ninth Guardian's Mezmer itself. That he is neither man nor myth, but rather both at once. That he is the Creator, the Created, and the Eternal. And that it is he who shall bring salvation—through destruction. I will be honest, now that I have my wits about me again, I must admit that the whole thing feels terribly contradictory."

I let it swirl around, trying to figure it out. I can't. I'm not much of a philosopher, I'm afraid.

"May I ask you a question?" Almeister counters.

"Of course."

"How were you killed?"

"Sorry?" I heard him. I just say it as a reflex.

"I know you, Carpathian Einzgear. I trained you. There is no way you could be felled by mortal wounds alone. Was there some other reason? That you . . . expired?"

Thump-thump.

"Um, I don't . . ." I really don't. As in, I don't know what the hell to say. "I, uh . . . I suppose . . . I suppose I just grew tired of fighting. If I'm being honest."

He closes his eyes. His head drops forward.

"Well . . . I appreciate your honesty." He looks ahead at Persephone. "I feel . . . grateful."

"About what?"

"That my eyes have been opened. That I have yet another chance to be for her the father I was not before. Not in a fiction, like on the Mid-Meridian Plane, but here, now, in the living present."

He puts his hand on my shoulder, looks at me in a fatherly way, and I almost start goddamn crying. I don't even know why, exactly. There are five reasons it could be, but I'm not sure which of them it is. Then, he pats me gently and wanders back off to join the child to whom he is the actual father.

Clearing my throat, I catch up with the rest and find myself standing outside this particular Temple of the Body, which resembles a Vegas wedding chapel replete with all the same gaudy angles and pretentious architecture. Come to think of it, now that I take in the whole of where we are, it all looks kind of Vegas desert-y. A pastiche of the familiar.

The Dwarf woman whose name I have completely neglected to ask—as she has either inadvertently or deliberately chosen not to inquire after any of ours as well—takes out an ancient-looking key, slides it into an ancient-looking lock covered in dust and spiderwebs, and turns the tumbler with a noisy *clack*.

"Just twist it locked from the inside before you leave. I'll have rooms all ready for you." She smiles and starts to go, but before she does . . . "I hope ye don't think it impertinent of me to ask, but . . ."

"Yes?" I prompt.

She looks at Jameson. "Could I get maybe just a toke of that, son?" Her stubby finger is pointed at the fatty dangling from Jameson's lips.

"'Course, mi Dwarf sistren."

She smiles appreciatively, takes the joint from him, puts it between her lips, and no shit, draws in the longest, most lung-filling toke I think I've ever seen. Even Jameson's eyes go a bit wide at the sight.

"Thank you, luv," she chokes out before letting out a monumental expulsion of smoke that blankets the air above our heads in a halo of ganja residue.

Then, she claps her hands, nods once sharply, and trundles off into the night.

After a beat, I simply ask, "Temple?" and we head inside.

Stepping inside, I'm immediately hit with a new fragrance: the smell of old gymnasium; that unique blend of sweat, rubber, and industrial cleaner that somehow manages to be nostalgic rather than offensive. The interior looks like an athletic club from about seventy years ago, all polished wood floors, mirrored walls, and workout equipment that is outdated but still pristine.

There are weight benches with leather that hasn't cracked, pull-up bars that gleam like they've never been touched, and what looks like a boxing ring in marvelous condition. Everything is immaculately maintained but clearly designed for a different era.

At the back is the Pulse Well. It sits in what would normally be the area for a swimming pool, but instead of water, there's a circular depression about twenty feet across filled with what looks like liquid light. It pulses rhythmically, sending waves of soft blue luminescence up the walls with each beat, and the Pulse Well sort of floats upon it.

"Okay." I clap my hands much like a 1950s high school basketball coach who would've thought this situation to be the peak of performance optimization. "Who's first?"

No answer. They all kind of shuffle their feet and look everywhere but at me.

"What's the problem?" I ask. "Why are you all acting like you've never seen a magic box of Mezmeric power validation before?"

Brit tugs me over to the side.

"What's going on?" I ask.

"I think everyone's anxious."

"About what?"

"We were down on the MMP for a while."

"Were we?"

"I have no idea. But that's the point. Our Mezmers were attenuated for who knows how long."

"Mezmer."

"What?"

"Pretty sure the plural of Mezmer is Mezmer, not Mezmers."

"I will murder you in front of everyone here."

"Fine. What's your—?"

"What if it, like, broke something?"

"Broke what?"

"I dunno. That's the point. What if the attenuation set us back to our original software settings or something?"

"That's not how it works."

"Isn't it? The Pulse Well doesn't give you anything you don't already have inside you, right? It just validates and verifies the things that you have acquired. Well, then shouldn't the inverse also be applicable? Isn't it possible that the attenuation might've atrophied what we had already gained?"

"No."

"No?"

"I don't think so? But, even if it did, isn't that something that we need to know? We don't want to just go marching into battle thinking that we have a whole phalanx of tanks with us, only to discover that we're packing water guns instead."

"I'm not so sure about that."

"Excuse me?"

"Do you know what the Dunning-Kruger effect is?"

"Dunning-Kruger? Of course I do. It's that thing where you don't know how dumb you are because you're too dumb to know you're dumb. How do you think I've managed to get anywhere in life?"

"Exactly," Brit says. "So, let's say our Mezmer really *was* hollowed out while we were down there. Wouldn't we actually be safer if we didn't know it?"

"That is categorically the worst logic I've ever heard."

"It's protective reasoning."

"It's suicidal optimism."

"I'm just saying that I think everyone would probably feel better if they knew that we're going to be okay with what the Well is going to tell us about ourselves." She clears her throat.

"So you want me to go in first."

She shrugs. "You are the Saviour."

I look at the others; they're now all looking at me.

"Yeah, alright, fine. I'll go. I'll show you it's okay. No big deal."

I pfft at the end, just for good measure, and walk toward the platform with all the swagger of a man who just declared he's not afraid of heights and now has to climb a water tower in front of his ex. Every step feels louder than it should. Brit's words loop in my head like a cursed nursery rhyme.

What if it broke something?

What if we got reset to factory default?

The Well only confirms what's already in you . . .

I clear my throat and shake out my arms like I'm warming up for a jog I definitely don't plan to go on. I throw a wink back at the group.

"Y'all are gonna feel real silly in a second when I light this thing up like the new Lunar Festival in Strainionberg."

No one laughs. I step up—then pause. It's not that I'm scared; I'm not scared. I'm *considering.* It's different.

I examine the machine. Same as I'm used to, only this one is, actually, a little different. It has a nice ring of polished brass and is slightly raised. *Or is that my blood pressure?*

I stretch my fingers. Crack my neck. Take a deep breath.

"Here we go," I say to no one in particular, then step up into the center, and—

Nothing happens.

I wait a second.

Then another.

I shift my weight. Check the floor. Look up.

Still nothing.

A thin sheen of sweat forms behind my ears.

"Calibrating," I say casually. "You know how it is. These things take a second."

Brit crosses her arms, shakes her head, her face scrunching.

I lift one hand and flex my palm. Maybe that'll help. Maybe it needs a signal, a primer, just a *taste* of my Aura. Like sending a scent into the air to tempt a dog.

Still nothing. Not a hum. Not a blink. Not even a polite flicker.

I try a different stance. A wider one. More heroic. I raise my chin, lower my voice. "Pulse Well . . . activate."

Nothing.

Panic creeps in, steady and familiar. The kind of panic that says, *What if the magic is gone?*

What if everything Brit said was true, and I've come back hollow?

What if I'm downgraded?

What if . . . I'm no longer the Saviour?

I try again, this time with one foot off the ground, like I'm trying to summon an elevator. "Carpathian Einzgear," I declare. "Present."

Nada.

I see Jameson whisper something to Zerry. She nods, points in my direction. I hate that. I hate when people tell secrets right in front of me. I hate it when macaques and precogs do it even more. There is a beat of perfect, painful silence as Jameson walks over, calm as ever, and looks around the side of the contraption.

"Mi gen'ral," he says.

"What?"

He points toward the side of the base.

"Is nuh plug in."

I blink.

"Sorry?"

"Mi girl, Zerry. She de one who notice."

I look to where he's pointing and there, I see . . .

A long, thick cable, unplugged.

Jameson grabs it, hauls it over to an outlet, and . . .

CLICK.

The Well thrums to life. Light spills around me like I just booted up a holy mainframe. A low chord hums through my bones, and the air shimmers.

Jameson exhales a colossal cloud of herb smoke, then nods at me.

"See? Ain't de magick dat gone, mi king. Is jus' de plug." He leans back, eyes half lidded, grinning like a prophet on vacation. "Power always be in de system. Y'jus gotta flip it on."

CHAPTER FORTY-THREE

I told you not to worry!"

My haughtiness is pretty transparent, but after the time I've had lately, I feel entitled to bask in a little validated swagger; especially since the Pulse Well not only lit up for us like a game show jackpot, it verified that our time on the MMP provided us serious glow-ups to boot.

The Pulse Well practically *beeped* with delight when it recognized me. New slot unlocked. Statistics confirmed. Mechanical Heart intact. Blade of the Starfallen still extra Starfallen. My Aura's pulsing like a well-fed moon. No signs of attenuation. No hollowing. Just the familiar hum of being, somehow, *enough*.

Brit's map-making mojo continues climbing. She still can't see into the unseeable, but she can dial into granular detail like a satellite. Convocationist showed up with newly defined abs and backstories. She tried to act all casual about it, but when she summoned a miniature star to vaporize a punching dummy, I saw her smirk. I'm not saying she's OP now, but if she starts naming her summons, we may need to renegotiate the power hierarchy.

Perg's brain is now a dangerous place. Or. More. More dangerous. I overheard him muttering "peristaltic wave manipulation" under his breath. I don't know what that means, but we're all giving him space right now. Respectfully. And nervously.

Seph looked at her Stats afterward and said, "I believe I may require a second set of arms to properly channel everything." Which I would've thought was a joke if she hadn't already started talking about developing something called "*Your Pleasure.*" Also, apparently, she now leaves afterimages even when she's standing still. If she blinks just so, it feels like a backup version of her might emerge and politely offer to tag in.

Almeister was pretty businesslike. He just stepped in, stepped out, and said, "Well. That's better." He's got that old Vince Lombardi quote vibe of, "When you get into the end zone, act like you've been there before." Which he has. So, no need to make a thing out of it.

The most compelling, to me at least, was Zerastian. I couldn't even begin to recall what her sheet looked like the last time we saw it in Riftbreaker, but it's not trifling now, that's for sure.

She's Resonating at Steelshard with elevated Stats across the board and has all kinds of cool shit at her disposal like a Neural Crown, Eidolon Drones, and Pyresticks, which came in handy the first time they all—or, *we* all—had to battle the serpent, so they'll surely be useful again. She also has a raft of Spells like Tether Sync and Locus Burn. The next time we're dealing with a specifically technologically based challenge, she'll have us on *lock*.

. . . Presuming there is a next time.

I don't know what awaits us going forward. But do I know this: Whatever happens, this crew—this wild, stubborn, overpowered crew . . . We're goddamn ready.

Almost.

Maybe.

I think.

The moment we reenter the inn, the Dwarf woman is already waiting for us behind the bar, wiping down the counter with a rag that's more symbolic than useful.

"Rooms are all set," she announces cheerfully. "Six of 'em, top of the stairs, keys in the doors."

I freeze.

"Six?"

"Yeah, one for each of those five," she says, pointing at everyone but me and Seph, "and one for the two of you," she finishes, pointing at only me and Seph. Then, without pausing, she turns to Jameson. "Fellow spirit, another hit?"

He hands over the doob, and she takes another monster draw. I suppose I get it. She looks like she's here all alone most of the time. Little escape from the doldrums must be nice.

But, back to the issue at hand:

"Um, we're not . . ." I start. "Not a . . . We each need our own room, I think."

"Oh," she coughs out smoke. "I just assumed. Way she looks at you. And you her."

At that, nobody's looking at nobody. We both look at the floor.

I do sneak a glance to see if Seph is maybe peeking my way. She is. And now, we exchange glances. Hers is blank in the way a clean slate is blank. Not because it lacks meaning but because someone wiped it clean after writing something important on it.

Mine is probably just light panic.

"But, no problem!" the Dwarf continues, a little giggly now. "I can set up a seventh. Just give me a moment. Might be a slight surcharge, what with the extra linens and all."

Seph waves her assent, and the Dwarf heads up the stairs muttering something that sounds like, "My third cousin once married a lantern. Worked out better than you'd think," before vanishing up the stairs in a haze of weed and nostalgia.

Perg is the first to head up to bed.

"Okay, fools, so, what are we doing tomorrow?"

"Tomorrow, we seek the Gauntlet of Sorenthali, fight all the remaining serpents to the death, close the MMP for good, and then figure out what the next priority needs to be, presuming we have survived the prior."

"Okay." He ponders for a second. "You think we'll get breakfast first?"

"Probably."

"Chillero. *Buenas noches,* homies." He starts for the stairs, then, realizing he can't quite figure out how to navigate them, looks to Zerastian. "You think you can . . . ?"

She nods, steps over to him—allowing him to shrink down to his miniature self—then picks him up, turns to us, says, "Safe night," with a certainty that suggests she's telling us we're probable to have one as opposed to just wishing us one, and then the two of them head up.

Brit stretches, her body cracking in about fifteen different places.

"Fuck me," she groans. "You think there's hot water?"

"I dunno. I can't . . . remember . . . if we took a bath here. Last time."

She sucks at her teeth. "Yeah. Honestly? Me neither." She laughs a little. "Not like me."

The latter is said with just the slightest hint of worry, but I vibe it. The longer we stay here, the more and more probable it is that we'll forget what was and only know what is. It's more than an intimidating proposition. She clears her throat and hauls her exhausted body up the rickety stairs.

Jameson puffs a couple puffs from his joint, staring up at the ceiling.

"Ya 'tink de Dwarf have a partner?"

"A . . . You mean, like, a business partner? Or—"

"Like a Mistah Luvah Luvah. Or a Mrs. Or whatever."

"I . . . don't know. Are you . . . interested?"

"She hold dem smoke. Rare quality." Jameson nods solemnly like this is a matter of deep personal philosophy, then stubs the joint out on the rim of his tankard and pats his chest in a self-soothing gesture.

"I tink I sleep now. 'Fore I fall in love wit' a Dwarf."

He starts to amble toward the stairs, stops, looks at me.

"You tell me if she single." He lingers for a second at the foot of the stairs, scratches the back of his neck, then glances from me to Seph, and back to me. "Y'know," he says, voice light, lazy, like it's just a throwaway thought, "truth always travel faster than footsteps. Sooner or later, it catch up." He nods toward the stairs. "Gonna let it catch me up top. Night, mi people."

Which just leaves the three of us.

Almeister stands by the hearth, hands folded behind his back, gazing into the empty stone grate like he's watching the embers of some long-dead fire play out the final notes of a song only he can hear. Seph doesn't speak. Neither do I.

After a moment, Almeister turns, looks at her, me, nods. Not a deep, ponderous, wizard-y nod. Not one of those "Ah, yes, the threads of fate align" kinds of gestures, more just . . .

I don't know. It's gentle. A little sad. A little hopeful. The kind of nod that says, *I trust you both. Please don't break each other.*

Or maybe I'm just projecting.

Regardless, with a soft, delicate, "Thank you both for what you've done," he makes his way up the stairs as well, pausing just long enough to say, "Good night. My children."

And we are alone, surrounded by the flickering lamplight and the gentle creak of floorboards above.

She's not really looking at me, and I'm not looking at her, so we're doing that dance of "who will say something first" that could go on forever if left unchecked. Finally, I check it.

"You should get some rest. I'll wait for the room to be ready."

She doesn't move other than to shift her weight a little. After a few hip swishes, she sits.

"I'm not tired yet," she says.

I sit as well, opposite her at the table. It feels like we are convening at some high-level diplomatic meeting to negotiate an accord. Which isn't altogether far from the truth, probably.

There's an abandoned mug in front of me that the Dwarf forgot to collect. I sniff it, decide to try a sip. It's lukewarm. Tastes like a campfire pretending to be grog or something. I drink it anyway.

Across from me, Seph has a posture that feels familiar. It's like when a teacher or some other authority figure has posed a question they kind of know the answer to but are just waiting for you to cop to it. Like they're waiting for someone to say something hard but necessary. Shoulders a little back, eyes relaxed as though they're attempting to make it easier for you; giving the words permission to exist.

The command is clear. Not from her but from the universe. As more and more people (and monkeys) begin to ferret out the truth of what's happening here, the less and less it makes sense to withhold the truth of what my being on Meridia is all about. Especially from those who likely deserve to know it the most.

But here's the thing: I'm not sure yet what the truth of my being on Meridia is all about. Because I think it's a complicated one.

There's the simple, obvious version that Brit and I talked about: I screwed a bunch of people when I wrote about this place, and then just abandoned them to reconcile with their stories. In that scenario, my presence is penance: an opportunity—or a demand—to fix it all.

However, if that's the case, so far, I'm doing a shitty job. I'm complicating the "simple."

There's also the possibility that, as I keep seeing evidence of, I didn't create a damn thing but merely transcribed the stories of a world in chaos. As such, I am here because I chose to stop the reportage and someone, somewhere, perhaps the Ninth Guardian, is none too happy about it.

This theory might explain the Brucillian of it all. The actual architect of this narrative is pissed and forcing me to have to continue interacting whether I want to or not.

Then, there's a third option, which is that existence of all kinds on all planes and in all conceivable realities is merely a product of some other, greater, more powerful system. That nothing is anything, nothing means anything, and the only thing that matters—at all—is the moment that exists *now*. If it exists at all.

And that the point of being alive is to be here in the now because to anticipate the future or to remain consumed by the past is a way of avoiding having to live in the present.

"Y'know, Bruce, another way of avoiding having to live in the present is to overthink shit to a fare-thee-well."

"It would be great if I could catch a break right now, Bruce."

"Copy. Sorry. I was on my tough-love jam. Carry on."

Bruce isn't wrong. I just ain't able to hear that right now.

I sip the drink again. Still tastes like regret and hickory.

"So," I say slowly, trying to formulate a sentence that I'm not sure I know the direction of. "How ya doin'?"

She smiles ever so slightly. Warm and sympathetic. "I am tired, I think."

"Then you should—" I start, pointing up at the stairs.

"Who are *you*?" she asks, interrupting.

Thump—

My Heart stops. I mean it. Literally. It just kind of stops beating before picking up again.

—thump.

"Say again?"

"I asked, how are *you*? I am not entirely unwell, if a bit laden upon. How are you?"

"Oh. I thought for a second you . . . I'm okay." I attempt to pull it together and Carpathian it up a bit. "I am eager to enjoin the battle with the serpent. Er, serpents. In order for us to progress further in our goal of ending the Ninth Guardian's reign of terror, we must seal off their ability to reimagine narratives of destruction that can . . . uh . . . do . . . damage. More. I mean. More damage. To, y'know, everybody."

It's crazy. When I'm sitting in front of my keyboard, I can toss out long, floral Carpathian pontification all day, but here, now, I feel kind of tongue-tied. Probably something to do with not being able to see the words appear on the screen in front of me. Linus had a security blanket; I had a security M3 processor.

She tilts her head gently, like she's appraising me. Or maybe just waiting for the next bit of verbal slapstick to fall out of my mouth.

I try not to shift in my seat, but I probably do. It's not fear. I mean, it kind of is, but it's not exactly that. It's that strange, hollow feeling you get when you realize you might actually be safe . . . but only for a minute. And that if you let yourself feel it too deeply, you'll crack.

"May I ask you something?" I ask preemptively. She tilts her head in a *yes*. "What, uh . . . If you don't mind . . . What, uh . . . Where's your . . . You had a mom, yeah? I heard you had a mom."

She chuffs a small laugh. "Of course."

"Do you know what . . . Where she is now?"

There's a long moment.

"I don't."

I have about a dozen follow-up questions, but none of them feel appropriate to ask, so I keep them to myself and instead say . . .

"Seph?"

"Yes?"

"I'm very sorry."

"For what?"

She probably doesn't know how loaded the question is. Or maybe she does.

"For leaving you. In Bell's View. For leaving you behind. I really am."

"It's alright."

"It's kind of not? I just . . . I had reasons. Not necessarily good ones, but . . . I'm sorry."

"Thank you." A breath. Then . . . "You know, for a long time, I used to think that if I just got strong enough, I'd be able to play the role that I wanted to play."

That catches me off guard like I was watching a bird flying overhead while the opposing team was about to take a penalty kick.

"Uh . . . what?"

"In the fight. In the Rebellion. I thought if I could build my strength, progress my power, that I'd be the kind of ally who would be suitable to fight alongside the Saviour."

"I—You are. You absolutely are."

"I don't feel that way," she admits. "It's why . . ."

"It's why what?"

"It's why, on the Mid-Meridian Plane, when I was given the chance to craft a reality that might inform my true reality, I attempted to imagine what it would be like to be worthy. To . . . be your equal."

Ho-ly Mac-a-roli Poly Knolly Goalie Stoli.

Are. You. Funking. Funking with me?

Jesus. She isn't sheepish or sad because she sees me as something other than her dream version of Carpathian. She's sheepish and sad because she doesn't see herself as being adequate enough to *be* with Carpathian.

Oh. My. *Falderdash.*

I've been . . . But she's . . . And I . . .

For the love of Pete.

"Hey, hey, hey," I say, now standing and coming around the side of the table to join her. I have to keep saying it, "Hey, hey, hey, hey, hey, hey, hey," because it's a really long table and it takes me a second to get over there, but when I finally do, I plop down beside her and take her hand, which makes her jump a little.

"That's crazy talk," I tell her. "You're absolutely Car—my equal. Of course you are."

"I don't think that's true."

"It is."

"I want to believe that. I do. It's why I worked so hard protecting Bell's View and bettering myself. I thought that if I could bolster myself enough, I might reach a point where I would never lose anyone again. That if I proved myself worthy, those around me might stop leaving."

Her voice isn't bitter; it isn't even sad. Just measured. Like someone finally putting words to a feeling they've been carrying so long it lost all urgency and just became part of the fabric of their experience. My throat is tight. I hate that it's tight. I hate that this moment is real. That she's real. That she isn't just some coded character on a page but a full, breathing, thinking person who waited for someone who never came back.

That's a lie. I don't hate it. I just regret it.

I reach across the table to grab the mug. (I have to stretch. The table is not just long, it's wide. And now, I wonder why I didn't just bring it with me when I came around.) I down the last of the whatever-it-is in the cup. Not because I like it all that much but because it gives me something to do for a moment while I plot my next move.

It works. Because a realization hits me. Something I think to say that I feel might land.

"Y'know," I start, "there's another aspect to progressing Skills and strengths that doesn't have nothing to do with . . . progressing Skills and strengths."

"I don't understand."

"That's because I'm not doing a very good job of . . . Lemme try again." I take a breath. "What happens when we step into a Pulse Well? What's the point?"

She looks at me strangely. "We validate our gains. Our strengths. Skills."

"Exactly. Except *we* don't, right? The Pulse Well does it for us. We ask the Well to confirm for us the things that we already have existing inside us."

"Alright."

"But . . . that's the point. They already exist. Inside us. Even if you never got confirmation that you're a Dreamweaver, you'd still be a Dreamweaver. It's who you are. At a point, gaining levels and even having them validated is inconsequential. You must simply know it within yourself. That's the point."

I'm not sure who I'm explaining this to, but the low-key narcissist in me can't help thinking I'm not just talking about me.

She stares, so I keep talking, afraid that if I let the silence settle for too long, someone will inevitably interrupt and subvert the impact of the moment. I know how this shit works.

". . . When I was first chosen," I say, "to be the Saviour, I didn't believe it either."

That gets her attention. Not just the words but the way I say them. Like I'm not reciting some mythos she already knows but remembering something personal. Something lived.

"I kept waiting for someone else to show up. Like, clearly, there'd been some mistake. Some better candidate. Someone more . . . destined." I offer a shrug, as though maybe if I downplay it, it'll sting less. "I wasn't a great fighter. I wasn't even particularly brave. I was just . . . willing."

She tilts her head again. That little shift she does when she's listening with her whole self.

"I thought, okay, maybe I'm a placeholder. A warm body until the real Saviour arrives. And then I'd get to bow out, return to the background. Fade into grateful obscurity." I laugh once, quietly. "Still waiting."

She doesn't smile at that, not exactly. But her mouth does that thing where it considers it.

I clear my throat.

"I kept wondering what they saw in me. Richemerion, the other Wardens, your father. The System itself—Although now I'm coming to realize that perhaps the System may have just seen me as someone who can be easily duped and has manipulated everyone around me to take advantage of the situation, but putting that aside for a second . . . Why not someone stronger? Someone more certain? Someone who didn't spend half his time inside his own head building escape routes?"

I look at her. I mean really *look*. Not at her features or her expression or her posture, but at her. I see her, the way Sumnut talked about. The part of her that sat in Bell's View waiting for someone who never returned.

"I don't think I ever really stopped questioning it. I just . . . got better at pretending I didn't."

The silence now isn't awkward—it's charged. Loaded with something electric and precarious. A breath hanging on the edge of a sentence.

"I think that's why—" I pause.

There's a pressure in my chest that's not from the Heart. A tickle behind my ribs. The words are there, rising like steam, like the water's boiling and something's about to overflow.

I think about telling her.

Telling her everything.

That I'm not who she thinks I am. That I'm not Carpathian, not really. That I'm Bruce, the guy who used to sit behind a screen writing down lines for her and others like her to say. But that I quit.

That I'm the reason Carpathian died.

That I'm the one who gave up. Who made him give up.

Because I didn't want to carry the weight anymore.

But that I somehow have come back to finish the job he and I started, but I don't know what the rules are anymore, or even if there are rules, or if I'm rewriting them by just being here.

And in that silence, inside that pregnant pause that has her looking at me, eyes wide, lips barely parted, close enough to me that I can feel her warm, expectant breath on my cheek . . .

Clomp-clomp-clomp.

The sound of boots on stairs. The Dwarf reappears in a cloud of hazy light and good intentions.

"Seventh room's ready!" she chirps, voice crackling.

Of course. As I said . . . I know how this shit works.

"Okay. Thank you," I reply.

She mutters something under her breath about "prickly trees always having the sweetest sap" and disappears again.

Seph and I stare into each other's eyes. Inside hers, I see about twenty different things: possibility, hope, fear . . . Stories yet to be told. And I decide . . .

She doesn't need to know the truth. Not yet. Maybe sometime, when the moment makes sense, but for now, it gains us nothing. She needs to believe. And, honestly, so do I.

"You should get some rest," I tell her, pulling back in an invitation to stand.

"As should you."

"I will," I tell her. "I just want to sit here for a few more minutes."

"Shall I remain with you?"

"No, no. You go. Sleep. I'll be along. I just want to . . . plot out how tomorrow is likely to go. Feel like thinking it through is better than just jumping in without a plan."

She tilts her head, then . . . places her hand on my chest. Right where my Heart is.

"I am with you," she says. "And I am grateful."

She turns, steps away. I think she's going to say something else, but she doesn't. Just heads upstairs.

I watch her go.

There's a moment, one of those impossibly fragile ones, where the quiet gets loud and you can almost hear the shape of your life shifting around you. Like it's adjusting to make space for the thing you were too scared to say.

But the words are still in my mouth.

And that's where they stay. For now. Above me, the floorboards creak. Doors open. Close.

I reach for the mug in front of me, but I remember that it's now empty. No matter.

I feel full anyway.

CHAPTER FORTY-FOUR

We're already on the road when the suns make their full appearances, cresting over the jagged rim of the world. The car hums beneath us. Sheila's been holding up like a champ, I have to say. I feel like I owe her a nice, Mezmeric lube job soon, which I realize might sound dirtier than I intend. The inn is well behind us now, like a strange dream you can't decide if you were glad to wake up from.

Check out was . . . odd. No one could find the Dwarf to settle up until, finally, the door to Jameson's room swung open, emitting a wall of smoke so thick you might get knocked back onto your ass if you tried to run through it, and from within the billowing cloud, she appeared, humming a tune that sounded approximately like, "No Woman, No Cry." I asked her if we owed her anything additional before we set out and she just said, "No, me big patron. Ye just go on ye merry way, safe like de baby, ye know."

It wasn't until that moment that I realized how easily a Jamaican accent can sound kind of Scottish if you aren't being very careful.

Anyway.

Now, with our brief intermission at The Wayfarer's End now behind us, we're back on script. Onto the Quest. One more broken place to explore, one more artifact to retrieve, one more line in the shape of our fate to follow forward.

Elderkeep's ahead, folded into the desert rocks like a secret kept too long. Once we arrive there, we'll reach Origin Pass. And beneath that . . .

The Gauntlet of Sorenthali awaits.

I glance in the mirror and make eye contact with Seph. We shared something last night. Something intimate. Something far more intimate than whatever Jameson shared with the Dwarf. (Which, while I don't know exactly what it was, I am now imagining scenarios and wishing I hadn't started thinking about it.)

I feel like the only way we could have gotten any closer—really, truly more connected—is if I had been completely honest. If I had said, "So, this is funny, but . . . I'm not Carpathian. Surprise! I'm Bruce. The guy who either made or recorded the story of your world, then tried to forget it existed and kind of ruined everything! Haha! Funny!"

I know it's gonna come out sooner or later; I just need to be very, very careful about how.

"For Christ's sake, Bruce. How many times are you gonna have to learn about jinxing?"

"It seem too quiet to anyone else?" Perg asks.

"Why would you ask that?" Brit replies.

"What?"

"If it seems 'too' quiet?"

"Because it seems too quiet, girlie. I don't understand your confusion."

"That's the kind of thing people say right before chaos descends. Don't jinx us."

"See, Bruce. Other people get that jinxing is bad too."

"Everybody just . . . hold on for a second," I request-slash-demand.

Perg's not wrong; it is awfully quiet. It's like the whole of Meridia knows what we did, how we brought down the Tower, and is holding its breath.

Because the felling of the Tower—Meridia's bright, oppressive monument—didn't provide what we'd hoped. Sure, we took it down. We cracked it open like the overripe symbol it was. But at its center? No throne. No lair. No Ninth Guardian sitting in wait like a final boss clapping politely at our arrival. No clarity.

Just more layers.

Which means the Ninth Guardian's still out there. Watching. Waiting. Or worse . . . moving pieces around like a grand master. Manipulating the board behind our backs while we focus on the pawns and knights and other metaphors in front of us. Because if the Tower was just a puppet stage, that means there's still a puppeteer.

I don't know whether that makes me feel relieved or more nervous.

No, yeah, I do. Nervous, obviously, because puppet masters are never good news. But also relieved, maybe, because it means the play's not over yet. There's still time to fix the ending.

I have a saying when I write: "Complicated is good. Confusing is bad." It's not that clever of a statement, but it's succinct and true. And I need to do all I can to limit the complications of this boondoggle so that it doesn't turn into a confused mess that I can't contort my way out of.

The terrain stretches out ahead of us, glittering faintly in the morning light, dust swirling off the edges like steam lifting from a pot that's just begun to boil. The hum of Sheila beneath our feet offers just enough rhythm to keep the anxiety at bay. Just enough momentum to pretend that forward means safe.

Which, of course, as just noted, is stupid.

I tighten my grip on the wheel and shift slightly in my seat. Behind me, Jameson coughs. The kind of cough that either means "I'm nervous too, mi gen'ral" or "Mi smoke, it too much, mi hotbox too fast." Again, hard to say.

I turn my focus to Zerastian and Almeister. This feels like an excellent time to test out what her precognitive Ability and his newly instated *sense* of the future thing might be able to warn us of as we sally forth.

Zerastian's in the passenger seat, staring at the road ahead with the kind of concentration that suggests either deep foresight . . . or mild car sickness. Hard to say. Her eyes have this vacant but flickering quality, like she's tuned into a station I can't quite hear.

I turn my head to see, behind her, Almeister looking worried, holding on to Seph's hand.

"Al? You okay?"

"Yes, yes. I'm just . . . I can once more feel the Mezmer of this place. Of the Mokeisan."

The whole car goes on high alert. Because this is what flipped his switch the last time.

"And what does it feel like?" I ask.

"Like . . . Like we must make our next decisions carefully."

That would probably sound more ominous were it not for the fact that we should be making literally all of our decisions carefully, so I'm not sure that tells me much.

"Zerry . . . ? Oh, is that still cool?" She sighs a little, tilts her head. "Thanks. Zerry? What do you see? Or foretell? What's it looking like?"

She breathes deeply, focusing her eyes on something only she can see. It's not quite a trance or an eyes-roll-back-in-her-head type of deal; it's something else. I think I described it as, *"A look between wonder and fear; the face of a person who has seen the cloak of a god and known that to witness more would be too great a burden for any mind to bear."*

I kinda stole that from the thing in the Christian Bible when Moses's hair turns white after he sees God's garment for the first time. But that's just such badass storytelling, I had to bite it. Believe in that collection of stories or not, the bros who wrote them were imaginative as hell.

Ironically.

After an extended beat, Zerastian speaks. Her voice is calm, even. But not entirely steady.

"There are resonances. Strands overlapping. Futures that tangle instead of diverging. I see us reaching Elderkeep, yes. I see . . . something beneath it. Something waiting. But the closer I get to it, the harder it is to make out. Like looking through water; the shapes are there, but they shimmer and break apart the second I try to name them."

The concern in her voice resembles the kind that an old person has when they begin to realize that they no longer have the fullest of grasps on their memories. Like it's harder than it should be to simply call up a story from the past and share the details, lost in a haze of cloudy recollection. Only, for Zerastian, it's not being able to see what lies ahead.

It's evident that the length of time she spent on the Mid-Meridian Plane has scrambled her a bit. Or, more concerningly, she was there so long that she became one with the plane and it's now a part of her. Meaning that, just like Almeister, there may be a touch of evil in her Mezmer.

Which would be just so on-brand.

"Can you tell if it's a trap?" I ask.

She hesitates. Again, rare.

"No. It's . . . blurred. Like someone's moved a hand across the ink before it dried."

I glance at Almeister, who looks up as if catching the same scent of interference.

"I feel it too," he murmurs. "Something . . . muddled. But not muted. The Mezmer here isn't gone, it's just unfamiliar. Like a foreign dialect I've never had to translate before."

You'd think that with two (*two*) visionary vision-havers in the car we'd be a little more bulletproof, but . . .

"So, we're going in blind?" Brit asks.

"I mean, not entirely," I point out. "From the standpoint that we don't know exactly what's to come right now, sure."

"So, blind."

"But," I go on, "from the standpoint that we . . . did this once before . . . we *kind* of know what it is we can expect . . ."

CHAPTER FORTY-FIVE

Cataclysm's Spawn, Riftbreaker Book Seven, Chapter Twenty

The wind howled through the broken ribs of Elderkeep. Long abandoned, the town sagged under the weight of dust and time, its bones exposed to the hollow sky. Walls had collapsed inward. Towers leaned like weary sentries. Doors hung ajar, creaking softly as if still hoping for the return of those who would not come.

Beneath this ruin lay Origin Pass.

A fabled fracture. A wound said to predate even the breath of Meridia itself. Some among the Elder Wardens, those who carved truth into silence, believed Origin Pass was not merely a depth in the world but its first trembling. The place where form first gathered itself into meaning. Where stone remembered how to bear weight.

Others whispered that it was older than Sorenthali, older than even Mezmer. A buried trace of power left untamed because to tame it would be to wake it.

And a few, the truly mad or, perhaps, the truly knowing, claimed that Origin Pass was not carved by hands but by the need for hands to exist.

Whatever the truth, it was here now, and Carpathian moved first, Blade sheathed but hand near the hilt. Almeister followed, robes fluttering across the cracked stone. Teleri walked just behind, her face drawn in concentration, and Pergamon, steady as ever, brought up the rear, eyeing the shadows as if they might leap. They had not spoken since leaving the inn.

Despite the protests of Zerastian, Xanaraxa, and especially Mael, they had chosen to travel alone. Carpathian felt they would be swifter, more nimble, were it just the three of them.

Zerastian had suggested that she had seen an ill wind blowing for them on their own, and yet Carpathian had persisted. He had known the dear precog long enough by now to take her caution seriously, and had also learned it was her caution that allowed him to alter fate. Knowing that a possibility existed kept him on the highest of alerts.

The silence between the four was thick with purpose. The battle with the Templars several Rotations before, if Rotations could even be measured properly anymore, had changed them all yet again.

The new weapons this Templar, Moridius, aided by his brother and second-in-command, Charlemond, had unleashed . . . They defied explanation. Not steel, not flame, not even the conjuring of Mezmer, but something beyond all of it. A shrieking fusion of time, metal, and invocation. The kind of thing even Carpathian couldn't parry without aid.

"We'll not outlast a second encounter without it," Almeister had said then. "The Gauntlet is not a matter of advantage. It's a necessity."

Now, in the heart of ruin, they stood atop the place where legend said the world first cracked. Pergamon stopped beside a half-toppled statue, its face worn smooth by sandstorms.

"We are close," he murmured. "Stone's thin here. Air carries upward . . . something foul."

Carpathian knelt, placed his hand upon the earth. Felt it. Not warmth—a pulse. He drew his Blade and drove it down, not to strike but to open. The stone groaned beneath them and split. No light came from within, only a slow exhale of air, ancient and cold.

One by one, they descended.

The passage twisted like a wound, too narrow in places, jagged in others. At times, they were forced to crawl. Carpathian led, each footstep echoing too loudly for his liking. The walls grew darker as they dropped further, not from the absence of light but from the presence of something else; something that resisted the concept of seeing. Teleri's spells pulsed dimly at her fingertips, enough to show the next step but no more.

"It feeds on Mezmer," she whispered. "Drinks it. Foul magic."

They reached a chasm. Across it, only void. No bridge. No stone. Just emptiness.

Pergamon, sized now to human height, moved forward.

"What are you doing?" Carpathian asked urgently.

"Trust," the snail answered, sniffing the air. He then edged further onto what should have been nothing, should have sent him careening into the emptiness below, and found a pathway. "Illusion," he said.

"Strange," Almeister wondered aloud. "I did not sense it."

"It is not Mezmeric. It is other. Of the living rock borne. The same foundation that caused this great shell of mine to come into being. I did not sense it either: I am of it."

A solemnity fell over the group as Pergamon continued ahead and the others followed.

The void screamed lies in every step. False visions flickered. Mael turned to dust; Zerastian sobbing over a shattered timeline; Xanaraxa rendered mute. Carpathian's jaw clenched. He walked through them. He did not indulge their falsehoods.

Beyond the chasm waited the Hall of Echoed War. It was not a place of remembrance but of repetition. The moment they stepped within, they were there, each of them pulled into visions forged of battle and memory.

For Carpathian, it was the first ambush at Virelock Rise. Teleri relived the Siege of Paleharrow. Pergamon found himself back in the pits beneath Haldrine Keep, facing down the Fire Wyrm he had once driven out with naught but a bucket and his own will. Almeister's eyes went white, then black, then clear again. It was unknown what was shown to him, even to his own imagining.

One by one, they broke free of their trials. Not by overpowering the illusions but by owning them. Accepting the truths they'd hidden from themselves.

The hall fell quiet.

The silence did not linger.

From just ahead, there came a sound. A resonance, deep and reverent, like the groan of ancient doors straining to remember how to open.

They moved as one now, Carpathian just barely leading, the Blade remaining sheathed, but his fingers hovering near the hilt. And, shimmering into vision like a mirage, the leviathan doors that could now be spied began to unseal with an agonizing slowness. They creaked and moaned and, finally, exhaustingly, exposed a vault beyond. One carved from a rock so deep blue that it imitated blackness.

And inside . . .

A pedestal.

And on it . . .

The Gauntlet of Sorenthali.

It was larger than expected, forged of unknown metal and run across with runes that pulsed with their own rhythm. Carpathian stepped forward, cautiously reaching the plinth, his hand hovering above it.

"What is this writing?" he asked.

Teleri stepped up to look. "Vecamire script," she said. "The lost tongue of the Pale Kin."

"If it is lost, how do you know?" Carpathian asked in an equally pale attempt at a joke.

Teleri smiled and tilted her head at the Saviour. "I cannot read it, unfortunately."

"It may be an invitation," said Almeister, "or a caution."

"Or both," Pergamon added.

Carpathian, thrice warned, concluded that there was only one way to know for certain.

Reaching out, he placed his hand within the Gauntlet. But when he went to retrieve it . . .

It would not budge.

There was no expected surge of power. No anticipated light. No world-shaking tremor of revelation. Just the weight of the object, ancient and silent, coiling around his forearm like a thing long slumbering and still not quite awake.

Carpathian held still.

The others stood by in wary silence, not daring to step too close. There was a pause, as though the Gauntlet, alive in ways steel should not be, was waiting for something more.

And so, Carpathian gave it.

Not loudly. And not in any tongue the others would know. Not even in one he himself remembered learning. It rose from somewhere deeper than memory, seeded long ago, blooming now under pressure. He bowed his head.

And he spoke.

The sound barely crossed his lips, and yet it echoed. Through him. A shape of a thought, older than prayer, folded in the space between breath and heartbeat.

The Gauntlet stirred. It dimmed, then brightened. Not in response to Mezmer or will but to recognition.

Carpathian's breath caught. The Gauntlet no longer merely wore him—it knew him.

The others saw his shoulders rise and fall slowly. Saw his gaze go distant. Saw the fingers of his Gauntleted hand flex once, and in so doing, stir a faint ripple in the still air.

They did not ask what he'd said, but if they had, he could not have told them. Because some oaths are not for ears. Some are only for the world to remember.

And for the world to fear.

Carpathian pulled back, studying the magnificence encircling his arm, when a low, guttural moan echoed from deep within the walls; neither living nor mechanical, but something between. The runes flared violently, then somehow shattered like brittle glass, spraying shards of Mezmerated light in every direction. The pedestal cracked down the center. Behind them, the passage they'd entered through crumbled into a cascade of stone.

Out of the fractures in the vault's black walls came figures—armored, gaunt, burning with corrupted intent. The vague suggestion of Templar forms but twisted, boneless in their gait, and clumped together in a mass of roiling abstraction.

Ashmourn. Wraiths of living smoke, born out of the embers of fallen cities, and now here to impede the Saviour the acquisition of his long-desired right.

Almeister was the first to act, thrusting his staff into the air. "Back! I say back! These halls are sealed by sacred vow—"

But they did not heed the demand. Of course they didn't.

A passel of amorphous wraiths lunged like firelight in water. Teleri countered with a burst of energy that fractured the mass, but it kept coming, shrieking now.

Carpathian ducked a phantasm of blades aimed for his throat and raised the Gauntlet. Instinct took over. A concussive blast of force erupted from his palm, vaporizing the body of a group of Ashmourn midcharge. The remainder paused, but only for a breath.

"Form the line!" he called.

Almeister turned, planting his staff and murmuring a Spell that shimmered like cracked ice. A dome of Mezmer crystalized around them, unstable, already splintering under the weight of enemy strikes.

"They're breaking it," Teleri noted, already preparing another wave of force. Her hands moved with fierce precision, eyes glowing. "I can burn through one, maybe two, but not all."

"Then we don't hold," Carpathian said, slipping the Gauntlet fully onto his arm. "We push."

He charged, slamming the Gauntlet into the nearest passel of Ashmourn with such force that it exploded in a radius of cauterized shadow. The feedback hit him like a hammer, nearly dislocating his shoulder. The Gauntlet didn't just strike: it detonated.

Carpathian turned just in time to see a new Ashmourn phasing through the wall, lunging for Almeister. The old wizard turned too slowly as Carpathian raised the Gauntlet and called, not for wind, not for fire, but for anchorage.

The ground beneath his boots cracked outward, fissures blooming like spiderwebs. A pulse erupted from the Gauntlet, not outward in a blast but downward, inward, into the bones of the world. For a second, time seemed to hitch. The Ashmourn's lunges slowed, just slightly. And then . . . everything locked into place.

The air hardened. Shadows froze midslither. The Ashmourn trying to phase suddenly found themselves caught between planes, flickering, unable to complete passage.

Carpathian felt it in his limbs, a gravitational drag, as if he had become the center of weight in the room. Not crushed, but held, the world around him refusing to move.

The Ashmourn let out fractured shrieks, their phasing hitching in place as the Gauntlet exerted dominance over motion itself, temporarily syncing every molecule to now.

With a shout, Carpathian brought the Gauntlet down a second time, and the air shattered like brittle glass, releasing the energy all at once.

The Ashmourn vanished in a burst of displaced shadowstuff.

As dust and quiet settled, Carpathian stared at the new advantage he, quite literally, held. He thought to make another quip, some kind of joke to release the collective tension, but he did not. For he realized what had just occurred was not a battle won.

It was merely a rehearsal for the war still to come.

CHAPTER FORTY-SIX

Pulling past the faded Elderkeep sign once again, my head is on a swivel looking for giant snakes while a Notification shows up on the windshield as a reminder:

Quest: "Defeat, finally and absolutely, ALL [Giant Serpent(s) of the Mokeisan] in order to shutter access to the [Mid-Meridian Plane]."
[ACCEPTED]

Quest Requirements:
Requires Artifact: [Gauntlet of Sorenthali]

As is well documented, I don't remember many, many things from the canon of Riftbreaker, but when I write what I think is a particularly strong bit of prose, I tend to recall it. The whole "merely a rehearsal for the war still to come" bit felt as hard as Syntorian steel to me, so I logged it somewhere in my memory bank.

Of course, my understanding of that sentence at the time was that it presaged something in the books. Not something happening to *me*. But it appears to have been a foreshadowing twofer.

That said, I, like the old person who feels they can no longer trust their own memories, am justifiably skeptical of mine. Moreover . . .

I have no flippin' idea what Carpathian said to himself in the echoes of his own mind to cause the Gauntlet to become unanchored.

I'll do that from time to time. Write what I think is some mic-dropping bit of prose that implies some great, mystic secret, but have no idea what the secret is. So, I've got literally no clue what Carpathian uttered to himself when he pulled the Gauntlet free.

However, there is one person in this car who was really, actually there when it all happened.

"Hey, Al?" I twist my neck to see him in the rearview mirror. His head turns. "When we captured the Gauntlet that last time . . ."

"Yes?"

"You remember that it didn't want to come loose right away?"

"I do."

"Cool. Um, and do you remember like, at all, what I might have done or said to make it?"

"Oh, shit," I hear Brittany mutter, clearly now remembering the same thing I just did.

"What's the matter?" Seph asks.

"Well, um, as your dad can attest, I, uh . . . I muttered something to free the Gauntlet."

"An incantation?"

"Probably? Sure. That's the . . . concern, I suppose. I didn't say it, like, loudly enough for anyone to hear, and I'm not sure I'll be able to remember what it was."

"Why not?"

"A) It was a while ago. And B) I didn't really *say* it so much as kind of felt it, and it just sort of . . . worked."

There is a long moment of silence. Because at this point, there are three others in the car (in the form of Brit, Jameson, and Perg) who know *exactly* why I can't recall what I/Carpathian said; one (in the form of Al) who certainly suspects that I'm not who I'm purported to be; one (Zerastian) who surely has to have some kind of feeling on the matter, being a precog and all; and, of course, Seph, who . . . Honestly, I don't know what the hell Seph thinks at this point, but I'm holding on to the belief that outright *breaking her heart* right now is not the play.

I've kind of become like my friend Joe's uncle Brad. Uncle Brad has had a "roommate" called Jason for, like, twenty years. Both Brad and Jason are awesome dudes, and nobody gives a shit that they're not just roommates, but for whatever reason, they continue to keep up the ruse.

I suppose, at this point, they're just so entrenched in the narrative they've created around their relationship that they feel like it's easier to keep it up rather than risk any blowback that might come from telling the truth. Again, I don't think they believe anyone would have a problem with it; I think they probably just don't want to field all the, "We know! Why didn't you ever say anything?!" responses.

I'm like that. Keeping Bruce in the closet, not quite ready yet to let him out.

Out of the quiet, Zerastian finally says, "I may be able to help."

"How?" I ask her. My understanding of her talents is that she is precognitive, not post. But maybe she's both. "I didn't know you could dig into things that have already occurred."

"I can't. But you'll have to say it again to get the Gauntlet, yes? I may be able to glimpse the words before they are made manifest. Like an echo of the future."

An echo. Of the future. Bro, I seriously hope that Brit is storing all of this away in her memory bank, because these Meridians be dropping gems that would be aces in a book. If I ever write a book again. If I ever write anything again. If . . .

Doesn't matter. First things first. Get Gauntlet, defeat some snakes, shut down the entry to the MMP so Ninth Guardian funk doesn't get all up into the world.

"Okay." Breathe out. "Let's find the way into Origin Pass, and then we'll dissect how, exactly, we plan to tackle the task at hand."

I swipe away the Notification. There's no danger of me forgetting what, uh, danger I'm not in, um, danger of . . . forgetting.

I'd really like, just one time, to get a Quest to try and find ice cream or something.

You have been offered a Side Quest!
"Find Ice Cream!"
The iced cream of the wild mountain beasts of the [Insurian Snow Peaks] is well-known for its medicinal and nutritional properties.
Slay [100] beasts to acquire their icy cream!
Do you wish to accept this Side Quest?
[Yes] [No]

I actually debate pressing [Yes] for a second because I'm a little curious, but mostly because I'm considering delaying the inevitable. But Brit points out that scaling the Insurian Snow Peaks without having first validated some kind of resistance to cold would be a terrible idea, so I table it for another time. Maybe. Almeister says that you've never tasted anything as decadent as Insurian Speckleberry.

Regardless, the Insurian Snow Peaks is not where we find ourselves. We are instead standing in the middle of the parching heat of the Mokeisan, in the desiccated remains of Elderkeep, the place looking extraordinarily much like I described it in Riftbreaker.

Half the buildings have given up standing, and the ones still upright are leaning like they're too tired to finish the job. Doors hang open like mouths midsentence. No people. No sound. Just heat, dust, and the sense that whatever life was here didn't end, it just stopped.

Brit is studying maps.

"So, if . . . memory"—she clears her throat—"serves, the way into Origin Pass is beneath this old building here." She points at the husk of a who-knows-what-it-might-have-been. "Almeister? Is that what you recall?"

He considers and nods slowly. "Yes, that seems right to me. The details of life before are resuming slowly."

Yeah. Tell me about it.

"Very good," I declare. "So, I don't think we should all go."

Persephone snaps her head in my direction before the sentence is out of my mouth.

"What? Why not?"

"Because it's going to be dangerous. It's going to be crowded, and because . . . Zerry? What are the possibilities that happen if all seven of us try to navigate the Pass?"

She takes a deep breath in, lets it out, allows her head to tilt back slightly, then lowers it again. "It might actually be to our advantage." Seph gets a contented smile. "Or, it very much might not."

Seph's smile drops.

Gotta be real . . . Precognition in a world of free will where the choices you make affect the outcome in myriad different ways may not be as completely bulletproof as it sounds.

"So . . ."

"I feel I should accompany you. I can be helpful," Seph interjects.

There's a tiny yearning in it. So, of course, there's no way I'm going to say "no" now. And . . . if I can't say "no" to Seph coming along, I can't say "no" to any of the others. (I mean, I *can.* Of course I *can.* But it wouldn't feel right.)

"Of course you can." I wink at Seph, and she grins. "So, let's talk about what we're likely going to encounter and what, exactly—"

The ground gives a short, sudden tremor.

"What's that, fool?"

Then another.

"Mi tink mi know 'zactly what dat be, nah."

Of course he does. We all do.

And then—*the sound.*

It's like a rockslide swallowed by thunder. But wetter. Hungrier.

Then I see it. Part of it.

Only a glimpse in the not-far-enough-away distance. A thick, sinuous coil peeling across the ridgeline like a living fault line. Scales the size of coffins. Movement fast, heavy. Then it's gone again, submerged behind ruins, leaving behind a seismic groan and the definite sense that the combined snakes, still become one, are circling. Stalking. It's still a combined force. Four serpents in one, bigger than the biggest mountain on Earth. Paul Atreides's worst nightmare.

I look to Brit. "Quickly, where do we go?"

"Uh . . . I think . . ."

Another air-rending shriek. The serpent is closer.

"Nightwind? What's our story?"

"Um . . ."

Something I'm coming to realize about her maps: Even with her Advanced Map Maker Ability, there's only so much they can show. They can get us in the vicinity of where we need to go. They can even show us a certain amount of graphic relief. But to really give us the tight, granular detail that you could get from, say, a Google map or something like that, she'll probably have to get bumped all the way up to Legendary. But if we don't get into the Pass and get our hands on the Gauntlet, that ain't never gonna have the chance to happen.

"T. Night," I repeat. "What do we know?"

"I think . . . I think we get to Origin Pass through a door in the floor of the back room?"

"Al?" I ask for confirmation as another wail from the giant(er) serpent cracks the air.

Almeister doesn't blink. "That sounds correct."

"Wonderful," I say, already moving. "Back room it is. Let's hustle."

We sprint across the splintered floorboards, the heat inside the ruined structure somehow worse than the air outside. Brit is practically shoulder-checking debris out of the way, Seph right behind her, hand already glowing with some warm, defensive Spell, and dragging Al along.

Perg, grown to approximately my height, hurries in with appropriately terrified speed, his shell catching on a nail sticking out of the wall and ripping part of the old wood down with him.

Jameson vaults a broken chair and lands with an awkward tumble, rolls into a karate stance, takes a puff from his joint, and then points at me like he's saying, "No worries, me gen'ral."

But Zerastian . . . Zerastian lingers for a second at the doorway. Her eyes go distant, head tilted just enough for it to be ominous.

"Zerry!" I call out. "What are you doing? Come on!"

She doesn't look at me when she says, "We're not being chased."

"What?"

"We're being herded."

"Herded? What the hell does that—"

The wall to my left detonates inward; not with fire or Mezmer or anything like that, but with sheer, unstoppable mass. A whip of serpentine flesh tears through the building, reducing the corner of the room to matchsticks. Dust and heat surge inward.

"Contact!" I shout for some reason. Probably because I've heard people yell that in movies, and it feels kinda right.

The serpent doesn't fully enter. It just slams its body through like it's taste testing the environment. I catch sight of one gigantic eye, blinking with horrifying calm, feeling all kinds of like Captain Ahab.

"BACK ROOM!" I yell, already diving.

Brit spins just in time to throw up a Wall of WOW! that catches the second strike. Barely. The impact flares like a camera flash and sends her skidding back into a wall. Seph grabs her, pulls her upright, and the two of them vanish through a side archway that I *hope* leads to something resembling this supposed back room.

Perg scoots past me and bodies the remains of a doorframe, Jameson on his six, the two of them doing a momentary snail/macaque lazzi that would be delightful in an array of other circumstances.

Then, something honestly kind of cool happens. "Cool" being relative at the moment.

Almeister pulls himself away from his daughter, turns to come back into the front area that's currently under assault, and flicks his wrist.

It's just a tiny motion. Not even a full-on Peter Parker. Barely more than a flick, the kind of gesture you'd use to shoo lint from a sleeve. But what comes of it feels . . . tectonic.

The light in the room shifts, angles ever so slightly off its axis, like the laws holding it in place have been given new orders. Almeister steps forward, hand raised, and the temperature drops. Just a few degrees, but enough. Enough to wake up your skin. Enough to make the serpent hesitate.

The giant coil slithering through the ruin grinds to a halt midlash. Its momentum buckles. You can hear the weight of its drag, like a train hitting the brake too late to stop but early enough to change tracks. The serpent reels back, an arc of its body lifting from the ground as if Meridia itself became less trustworthy. Its eye swivels, enormous and wet-black, suddenly unsure.

I've seen some wild things since landing on Meridia, half of them pulled straight from the wreckage of my own imagination, but what Al just did . . . ?

That wasn't on any page I ever wrote. It wasn't flashy. It was old, foundational. Like the laws of physics stepped aside for a second because he asked nicely. I've been running around, shouting and scrambling and casting and flailing, and here comes Al, calm as glass, speaking power into the shape of the world.

And suddenly, I realize, whatever I thought I knew about power and strength, I don't. I've been playing in the sandbox version of Mezmer. Almeister is operating in the source code.

This is a glimpse at the Almeister I had expected to meet.

And it's awesome in the truest definition of the word.

The serpent holds its position. It shifts. Repositions. Reconsiders.

It keens, a sound sharp enough to crack bone if you're standing too close. The floor trembles with something halfway between panic and fury.

Al lowers his hand. And I see the tremor in his shoulder. It lasts a blink, maybe less. But it's there. But then he moves, slow and deliberate, toward the back room, breathing a little heavy.

"Come," he calls.

I stare at him, then over at the serpent. It's still there, just kind of frozen now. And I can tell what it is that's been done to it. What Al caused to happen.

The serpent didn't flee—it hesitated. Because Almeister didn't wound it. He gave it the burden of thought. And in that moment, it became something worse than dangerous.

It became *aware*.

"Come," he says again, gesturing me to follow. "It won't last long."

I shake my head up and down and then . . .

Thump-thump. Thump-thump.

The Heart registers something other than what its mechanics might suggest. Not unlike the way it registers something with Persephone. Only with her, it's more of a fluttering. This is safer. More grounded. Paternal.

This is the Almeister I wrote about. The mighty wizard who found Carpathian Einzgear the Conveyance Conductor and helped him believe that he was more than he thought himself to be. Who allowed him to trust in himself.

The man who made Carpathian . . . Carpathian.

His mouth quirks, suggesting—to me, at least—that he recognizes me recognizing it. I have about a krillion different emotions colliding inside me at once, but the one that feels dominant is certitude. (Is certitude an emotion? Whatever. It's what I feel.)

I don't wait for him to call me over a third time. Mostly because I think the serpent is about to start flailing again but also because he doesn't need to. This version of Almeister, the one I dreamed of, is with us finally. And I will follow wherever he beckons.

"Found it!" Brit shouts from the back room. "Let's go!"

I move to the kindly old wizard, pausing long enough for him to place an ancient hand on my shoulder, and he says, "Thank you."

I don't ask him *"For what?"* because I know what he means. I feel the same way.

I pat his shoulder in return, and the two of us take our leave to conquer the next Quest together.

Mentor and mentee.

Tutor and pupil.

Father and son.

Almeister T. Wizard. And Carpathian . . . Uh . . . Actually, I don't know if Carpathian has a middle name. Don't think I ever gave him one. *Eh.* When I get a chance, I'll ask Brit how to say "big swingin' dick" in High Vertraxian. That'll be cool.

CHAPTER FORTY-SEVEN

The tunnel stretches out ahead, long and gray and humming with quiet. Not a musical hum; more like tired plumbing. Steam pipes run the length of the ceiling, wrapped in insulation that flakes if you look at it too hard. The lights overhead buzz in intervals. One of them clicks twice, then goes dead. It always does that.

The floor's stained, uneven, slick in places. A low layer of moisture hangs in the air like the building's sweating from the inside. And there's always that sound, like a deep exhale from somewhere behind the wall. Not air exactly. Not water, either. Something heavier, more tired.

I walk it every day. Same pace. Same steps. I know the dips in the tile, the patch of wall someone spray-painted over ten years ago with the words "PEACE THROUGH MAINTENANCE."

I've never known if it was a joke or a warning.

I hear footsteps behind me. Reggie, pulling off a cap, wiping sweat off his head with the back of his hand even though it's cold out.

"Heard she chewed your ass out again," he says without looking.

"Yeah." I nod. "Said I stopped too far from the curb. Blocked a bike lane."

Reggie snorts. "That ain't bad. I got read out for sighing."

I look over. "Say what?"

He shrugs. "Passenger complained I sighed too loud. Actually called in to complain. Said I had an attitude."

"That's insane."

"Yeah, well. 'Don't be bringing that energy into the workplace,' she said."

I open my locker. The hinges creak. Inside are my gloves. I take one out. Leather, worn through at the palms. I study it for a second before sliding it on.

"Hey, Reg?"

"Yeah?"

"You ever think about . . . ?"

"About what?"

"Just saying to hell with it and getting out of here?"

"Every day, young blood. Every day." He closes his locker. "But what else would I do?"

He gives me a half smile, slaps me on the shoulder, and heads off.

I study the worn glove on my hand, imagining . . . I'm not sure what yet. But . . . Something.

We've been navigating our way to Origin Pass for longer than I expected.

At first, the passage beneath Elderkeep had structure: cracked stone, crumbling steps, the kind of symmetry that at least pretended someone once built it. That illusion faded five bends ago. We're in a place shaped by force now. Pressure. Collapse. Maybe even teeth.

Big, jagged, scary teeth.

Like the kind created by a thing called "the Gnarl," perhaps.

Thinking back on Carpathian's journey into Origin Pass and how pressed I was to get the book to print, I definitely did not do a particularly good job of describing it in detail. By which I mean, I don't think I described it in detail at all. So, I never got a chance to lean into this pretty terrifying architecture. Not that it makes a difference, but it would have been nice to be a little more prepared.

Eh. Why start now?

No one's spoken for a few minutes, but our breath tells the story. Shallow, timed. Everyone's conserving, it seems like. As though we're aware that we're going to need every bit of air into our lungs that we can muster when we start running. Or screaming.

Ostensibly, I'm leading this expedition, but I'm also half following Zerastian's impulses. She'll start, stop, start again. She has this habit of raising her finger in the air like she's listening for something, which is not a trait that I remember writing about. It's a unique little peculiarity that I find so much a reminder of the organic truth of the person as opposed to the conceit of her in my mind.

She stops again.

"What is it?" I ask. "Do you sense something?"

"I sense fifty somethings. Perhaps more. It's not simply about the direction we travel or the large choices we make; it's also about the small, seemingly insignificant moments."

In the stillness, I look around to see that Jameson is perched on Perg's oversize shell like some kind of mystical backpack accessory.

"Fool, stop digging your claws in. Shit tickles, yo."

For his part, Jameson is muttering a constant low stream of, "Mi feel it, mi feel it . . . Oh, mi no feel that . . . Keep movin', keep movin'." Fairly typical high-person chatter.

Brit—near the center, eyes scanning the dark, hand hovering near her side like it wants to reach for the map but knows better—watches the walls. Left, then right. Then up. Like she's trying to memorize the shape of the air.

Light plays tricks. Our shadows are misshapen.

I glance at Almeister. He holds his hands clasped behind his back, fingertips interlocked, eyes adjusting to every inch ahead of him like he's reading the tunnel itself.

Seph is just behind me—literally *just*; close enough that I can hear her breathing. It stays steady, measured, like she's pacing her own heartbeat to mine. Her hand carries a low-lit shimmer; not quite a Spell, not quite a shield, something in between. I think she called it a tether? It pulses in time with the tempo of the group, always calibrated to the quietest among us. A readiness to respond, without drawing focus.

I can feel that she's watching me, mostly. Not just the tunnel—me, eyes flickering to my shoulders, my back, like she's tracking the micromovements I don't even know I'm making. Maybe she's trying to figure out what I'm thinking. If she comes up with an answer, I hope she'll tell me.

"There," Zerastian says, quiet, pointing.

I look to where she indicates.

There's a shallow overhang just ahead, barely visible in the gloom. Seph lifts her hand, letting a dim pulse of glow ripple forward across the space. It clings to the edges of the overhang, bends around it, and that's when I see them glistening across the low ceiling, wall to wall.

Strings. Dozens of them. Gleaming like silk, but with a faint hum, like tuned wire.

"I didn't see those," Brit whispers.

"You wouldn't have," Zerastian replies. "They're laced with boundary Mezmer. Benevolent, in theory. Until provoked."

"Provoke?" Jameson asks. "What dat mean? Who provoking who?"

Almeister answers. "Movement," he says. "Certain types of breath. Boundary Mezmer registers presence as a shape, and shape as purpose."

"You're saying," I posit, "that if you walk into them, they'll kill you?"

"No," Zerastian replies. "They'll permit you to kill yourself."

"The fuck?!" Perg exclaims. "What do you mean, 'permit me to kill myself,' fool?! Why would I be asking for permission in the first place? Do they screw with your *cabeza*?"

"Not exactly," Almeister responds, still studying the glimmering threads like he's weighing an equation. "They amplify what's already there. A thought, a fear, a story you carry in your blood. Walk through them improperly, and they manifest that burden; turn it into a mirror then make you hold it."

"That's right," Zerastian confirms.

"Do you not remember passing through these before?" Seph asks.

It's a reasonable question.

I squint at the wires. They shimmer slightly, somewhere between silk and circuitry. They feel like something I *should* remember. But I don't. Which means they either weren't in the books at all, or I tossed them in during a late-night revision session and forgot about it the next morning. Could've been that stretch where I was really into metaphysical booby traps. Or maybe I just didn't describe them well the first time because I got distracted trying to make it all sound cool.

"Bits and pieces," I say. "Hard to tell; the lighting's different now."

That earns me a glance from Brit. A *glance* glance. But she doesn't say anything.

Seph, for her part, gives a small nod, takes me at my word.

Perg leans in, eyeing the wires. "So, what we do then, fool? Crawl? Snip? Burn?"

"They won't burn," Almeister says.

"Can you do something to them, Technomantically?" I ask Zerastian.

"I could try, but it's unlikely."

"Why?"

"Because they respond to choices, not Mezmer. The cleaner the decision, the more stable the passage. Hesitate, and they will adjust. They are less Mezmeric that way and more . . . sentient."

Amazing. Spend a ton of time leveling up and validating your cool, shiny Skills, and at the end of the day, getting past this obstacle just comes down to being definitive.

I mean, *this* is probably why I never wrote about them. Nothing very fantastical about making the decision to stand on business. It's just . . . standing on business.

"Okay." I clear my throat. "I'll go."

"You're sure?" Seph asks.

"I did it once, right?" I smile. She smiles back.

Brit, Perg, and now Jameson all give me a look of worry mixed with judgmental caution.

I step forward. Not a big flourish, just one foot in front of the other.

"Uh, Bruce?"

"Yeah?"

"You sure about this?"

"Not really, but I'm doing it anyway."

"Ah. Classic Bruce."

"Thanks, Bruce."

"Not sure it was a compliment, Bruce."

The wires start to shimmer a little harder; not brighter, just aware. If awareness had weight.

I plant the second foot forward. No pause. No hover. Just full send. The wires shimmer in acknowledgment, like I pressed a key on a piano that hadn't been tuned in a century and it still knew the note.

The strands nearest my shoulders vibrate. They don't move toward me. They don't move away. They hold, suspended, observing. And then . . . they part. Not wide, barely enough. But enough. The space between becomes a hallway, narrow, perfectly me sized. Like now *I'm* Charlton Heston and this is my mini Red Sea. In that story, the ocean stayed parted. So. Fingers crossed.

I breathe once through my nose, then walk.

Every step lands straight, centered. No weight to either side. No question in the joints, no indecision in the heel. The wires tingle against the edges of my field of view, like memories brushing past my skin.

Behind me, silence. Not the kind you get when people are afraid to speak; the kind that feels like someone hit record on their phone and are waiting to see if it's gonna make for good content.

Thump-thump.

Okay, so, that wasn't me. That was a vibration I could feel moving through the ground like a pulse checking *me* for a heartbeat.

"Bruce?"

"Not now, Bruce. I'm busy."

"Bruce?"

"Shit. *What?"*

"Just wondering if we have a plan for when this thing decides it's hungry and we start tasting like overcooked trauma."

"How is that helpful, Bruce?"

"I dunno. I'm sorry. I'm just tense."

Shutting out Brain Bruce, I focus and . . .

A single strand to my right lifts. Curves. Reaches.

"Oh shit, fool, it's gonna eat him!" I hear from behind me.

I maintain my focus. Not freaking. Not breaking.

The strand hovers beside my cheek, close enough to feel its vibration in the tiny hairs near my ear. It doesn't strike. It doesn't recoil. It lingers, curious, testing the space I occupy. Or maybe the way I occupy it.

Then, after a deeply filled beat . . . it drifts away.

Just like that. Like it got what it needed.

"Mi big gen'ral! Ya done faced it down, and it BUCKLED in the face of ya might!"

I am grateful to have Jameson hyping me up, but . . . he's only half right. Yeah, I did face it, and yeah, it did make room for me. But not in, like, fear or deference. More like . . . holding space. Like . . . recognition.

Whatever these threads are wired into, they read me. They weigh conviction. Certainty. Identity. I stepped forward like Carpathian Einzgear would have.

And the wires made way like they remembered.

Behind me, no one breathes. Because suddenly, this stopped being a maybe. I'm not trying to look like a badass, but the wires just treated me like one. And that's encouraging as shit, I gotta say.

The corridor constricts one more time before dropping away entirely.

The threads vanish like they were never there, and the way forward opens into something else, wider, flatter; not a chamber exactly but a kind of shelf cut into the dark. A place to catch your breath before it's maybe stolen again.

My boots hit grit; fine dust over smoother rock. The air shifts, smelling like iron and ozone.

Behind me, the others emerge, spacing out across the ledge and adjusting to the change in shape and sound. The wires don't follow, staying behind in the passage like curtains that only open one way.

Brit does a slow three-sixty, hand hovering like it wants to draw the scene but doesn't know where to start. Perg exhales with his whole body, with Jameson muttering something about "ancient bone breath." Almeister steps beside me and looks ahead, thoughtful, while Zerastian lifts her hand and makes a subtle motion, like measuring wind that isn't there.

Seph comes up beside me last. Still close. Still steady. I nod forward.

"What's ahead?" she asks.

"Uh . . . I think it's . . . um . . ."

I squint, take a step forward, then crouch down, pressing my palm flat to the rock. It's warm, which feels wrong for how far we're underground, but I don't say that out loud because I'm trying to break myself of the habit of remarking on what isn't. That's a kind of placeholder habit I'll use when I'm feeling my way through a situation—which is passive, and I'm trying to get away from that.

So, instead, I focus on what *is*: A long scrape down the stone, as wide as my thigh, shallow but deliberate, like something massive once landed here and took its time peeling itself back up. Brit would probably call it "geological compression." I call it a bad sign.

"It's a threshold," I say finally, rising.

Zerastian comes forward, tilts her head, squints. "Several futures intersect here. They bleed at the corners."

Jameson lights another joint with a flick of his thumb, the cherry blooming like a devil's eye in the low dark. "Mi say, dis place feel . . . ancient. Like somebody lock a memory in a box and toss de key down a volcano."

And, as if the monkey spoke too loudly and summoned that very memory . . .

It starts with a blink. A weird little shimmer at the edge of my vision, like the rock itself flickers.

Then the shelf shifts. A full-body lurch, like the world hiccupped.

We all struggle to stay standing like we're on a tilting floor in a fun house.

"The fuck is happening nooooooooowwwww?" Brit moans. "Isn't the eventual promise of having to deal with the goddamn Ashmourn—again—enough?"

It would appear not.

The rock behind us splits open, a seam tearing where the corridor meets the wall. No light spills through, just breath. Thick, hot, and iron rich, like someone steamed a war wound.

Then comes the sound. A scream, but drawn inward. Not exhaled—pulled in.

And then it's there.

The thing I didn't have the time to write about. The reason this place is called "Origin Pass." The original sin buried in this catacomb.

The goddamn Gnarl.

CHAPTER FORTY-EIGHT

The Gnarl?!" Brit shouts. "The goddamn Gnarl?!"

"Looks like it!" I yell back as the wall opens up like it's been waiting.

Stone peels, a seam folding outward like a mouth unclenching. The breath comes first, warm and foul. Iron thick. It pours across the shelf like a fogbank dredged from the marrow of something long asleep.

Everyone behind me stills. I can feel them recalibrate.

Then comes the shape.

It drags itself from the rupture, scraping wet across the rock. A coil—no, a fold, like tendon carved into architecture. It doesn't walk; it unfurls. Layer over layer of armored flesh, dense as bedrock, flexing in slow revolutions. There are no eyes, just a knot of limb and pressure and raw, psychic *mass*. The sound it makes doesn't come from a mouth but from the stone behind it, as if the whole cave system is its throat.

It's even worse than Nox in the Cavern of Sorrows. Partially because Nox was just a spirit, a trapped essence. And partially because I kinda knew about Nox. I wrote about Nox.

The Gnarl . . . Well, the Gnarl just *is*.

It's pretty bad. Know how I know? Jameson drops his joint. That's how I know.

"Sweet roots, mi soul," he mutters.

And then the Gnarl strikes.

The shelf heaves, a knot of it coiling like a muscle and slamming toward us. I don't think, just shove back with my hand.

"Stay behind me!"

I don't shout it. I command it. A full-bodied bark from somewhere deep.

"Why?" Brit asks.

"Why ask why, fool? You got it, Carp! Take it down, homie!"

"Carpathian!" Seph shouts, coming for me. I stick out my arm and hold her back.

"No," I say, quieter. "I got it."

"Daughter," Almeister calls, "let him."

She looks, eyes wide, at Zerastian, who simply says, "It is hard to know."

She looks flummoxed, but I don't give her a chance to say more.

Because this is mine.

I charge.

The Gnarl flexes without warning, a ripple of muscle and geology, and a length of it cracks sideways like a whip. I duck low. Roll. Feel the wind of its shear overhead, sharp enough to take a head off. My heel catches grit. I use the momentum, come up fast, elbow forward, and slam into it . . .

Which is like elbowing a cathedral.

Bouncing off, I land hard, pain blooming in my shoulder. The Gnarl turns or shifts or reconfigures . . . I can't tell which direction is its front because I don't think it has one. It's just mass, all directions at once, volume without symmetry. A riddle of matter.

At least now I know how strong I am and am not.

I push up with my bare hands, catching the raw grit beneath my palms, the coarse grind of rock against skin. It scalds hotter than it should, I feel like. But the texture triggers something.

I glance down. Fingers scraped; forearms braced.

And that's when I remember: I've got better tools for this.

Now that I have *POCKETS*, I am no longer reliant on having to call to Brittany for help. I'm becoming more and more self-sufficient by the moment! Huzzah!

I grab up the miniature Stoneheart gloves, pop them into their hand-size size, jerk them onto my mitts, and thrust a palm at the Gnarl to summon a spine of earth between us. It catches, barely, but it does slow the creature's movement for a beat, which is all I need.

I reach for the second thing I now get to keep on my person at all times, and swing the Blade in a wide arc across the nearest stretch of the Gnarl's hide.

Unfortunately, while the cut scorches, it doesn't sink. It leaves behind a glowing streak, not unlike dragging a sparkler through night air. Handsomely decorative, but useless.

The Gnarl bulges, then contracts. The space it occupies thickens, like it just absorbed the heat, metabolized it, and now wants to return the favor.

"Okay," I mutter, adjusting my grip. "So you eat fire. Noted."

I mentally inventory my battle options. I could slow things down with Control, but I'm not sure to what end. I don't want to use up the clock on something that doesn't feel like it's going to make a farthing's worth of difference. I start to glance behind me to make sure everyone is still safe and that nothing's come up behind to eat them alive or anything, but I don't wanna take my eyes off of what's in front of me. And that's when I realize . . . you can't eat what you can't see.

So, I throw on a veil of CloakRender and dash over to stand on the Gnarl's spine—or the part that feels the most like spine—and it occurs to me in a flash that I don't have to use just, like, one weapon at a time. I haven't actually combined these two before—not like this. But the logic holds. The Gloves give me grip and weight; the Blade gives me heat and hurt. Together? Let's see what happens. I don't have to be like those guys in kung fu movies who stand back and wait for their kung fu brothers and sisters to attack before they launch in with a chop. I can unleash anything I want all at once. So. I do.

Thump-thump. Thump-thump.

I combine the Stoneheart gloves and the Blade into one MacGyvered two-in-one weapon and slam my invisible arsenal down at once, adding weight and direction, driving momentum like a meteor into its coil.

This time, it feels it.

The point of contact blooms like a forge erupting midstrike, raw light and smoke bursting out in a cone. Sparks peel off the blade in trailing spirals, ember-orange at the tips, while the gloves hammer stone downward from my hands and into the impact like I've plunged my fists into the world's core. For a second, I'm fused with it. Me, the rock, the weapon, all one thing, all surging downward.

The Gnarl absorbs the blow like a redwood taking a lightning strike, a long, shuddering flex rolling out from the impact. The shelf beneath my feet ripples, buckling not so much from injury but from being touched where it thought itself untouchable.

(To be fair: That's just me guessing, but it seems valid.)

I let CloakRender drop off before it has a chance to disperse on its own. I'm getting better at manipulating the contours of my Mezmer.

You certainly are! You know what? I was just about to say that! I was just about to say, "Carpathian! Look at how good you're getting at manipulating the contours of your own Mezmer! How very proud of yourself you must feel! Swear to Richemerion, that's exactly what I was going to say. That's so funny. We really are becoming bonded. Yay, team us!
{COURTESY MESSAGE #36}

"Yeah!" I hear Perg yelling as I hold on tight. "Ride that squiggly bastard!"

I press in harder, grinding the blade through another ridge of armored sinew. The Stoneheart gloves hold me in place, anchoring me, pulsing in tandem with something beneath the surface; some frequency the Gnarl doesn't want disturbed.

It shrieks again. That same inverted scream drawn from stone, not air. My jaw clenches as it rattles straight through my teeth. A tendril snaps overhead, carving the dark with wet force.

"Above you!" I can hear Seph calling out. "Carpathian! Move!"

I dive. Land hard. Push back with a burst of stone from my palm that juts into a quick wall. The tendril slams against it, cracking through, but just wide enough.

"Keep movin', big gen'ral!" Jameson whoops. "Mi say keep that thing guessin'!"

I don't answer, vanishing again. Shifting to the left, reappearing behind a coil that's folding inward like it's shielding something. Still no face, no eyes, no real core, but I know the difference between defense and collapse. Even though I've only engaged with these Meridian beasts for a short time, I haven't.

I've written about every manner of monster and mayhem. Every kind of nightmare. And while it's obviously not the same—imagining things and writing about them is not doing them in the same way that playing a Formula One driving game is not the same as being behind the wheel of a land rocket moving at 230 mph—I've dedicated enough of myself to the concepts that I can be clear about one thing if nothing else: Every beastie has a rhythm.

And right now, I'm here to ruin this one's.

I come in low, both hands on the Blade, aiming to drive it straight into the seam I burned earlier. Like maybe if I can wedge it in far enough, I can pry something loose, tear something real that will do actual damage. But the Gnarl twists. Fast. Smarter than I gave it credit for.

One of its limbs (if you can call it that; I call it that because I don't have time for an anatomy class on the thing) hooks hard beneath me, catches my ribs like a wave catching a ship midturn, and flings me skyward. I tumble. Hard. The Blade's nearly torn from my grip as I spin through heat and shadow and distance I didn't mean to travel.

And then, quite unexpectedly, I'm off the ground.

By which I mean . . . I'm . . . flying?

Kind of. Not completely Superman-ing it, but definitely hovering.

The Blade of the Starfallen holds me in the air like it's tethered to a constellation and I'm the weight dangling beneath it. The world underneath doesn't feel heavy anymore. The Blade isn't a weapon in my hands: it's an axis, and I'm rotating around it.

"Homie! That's crazy! Does everyone see what I see?"

"That he's levitating?" Brit answers Perg.

"Yeah!"

"Yeah. Hard to miss."

I'm not steering it. That's the thing. I didn't will this, didn't summon some latent, epic-side-of-the-prophecy power move. My grip's still tight, sure, but I'm not lifting the Blade anymore. It's lifting *me*, carrying me, like it knows where it needs to go and all I have to do is hold on.

The Blade pulls me forward, slow and deliberate, like it's chosen a line through the dark and expects me to follow.

No part of this came from willpower. I didn't call it up, didn't go digging for some locked-away, Chosen-One move. My grip holds firm, but the Blade leads. It arcs with grace and purpose, weaving a path above the Gnarl's heaving body like it's mapping the trajectory of a falling star in reverse.

Below, the Gnarl coils and shifts, trying to anticipate, trying to adjust. But it can't. The charge climbs up the hilt into my arms, into my chest. My boots drag air. The shelf becomes a blur beneath me, each ripple in the rock lighting up like filaments flaring in a bulb. I fly without flapping. Transit by conviction or something.

The Gnarl rises again. One tendril lurches, thick and mean. I angle down, and the Blade answers. The strike isn't mine, exactly, but it also is. In the same way that none of this is *mine*, and yet all of it is.

The Blade dips, pivots midair, and carves through the tendril in a crescent that leaves behind a blossom of seared tissue and stuttering heat. The Gnarl recoils, like it's met the one thing in this world that wasn't carved *by* it but *for* the purpose of interrupting its shape.

I descend with the force, landing in a three-point crouch that cracks the shelf beneath me.

Man. I wish there were cell phones here so that somebody could be recording this. I bet it looks so friggin' cool.

"Homie! You look so friggin' cool right now!"

I knew it.

The instant my boots find ground again, the Blade drops slack in my hands, like it used me for what it needed and now it's letting go. The Gnarl pulls back, mass folding inward, regathering its chaos.

"Did . . . Did you win, fool?" Perg asks.

I exhale—once, twice—and grip the Blade tighter again.

"Not yet," I mutter.

Something's different.

I can feel it in the way I'm standing. In the weight of the Blade across my palm. In the silence of my body. Quiet, calibrated, no longer running to catch up with what's happening but somehow pacing ahead of it. Like I didn't transform exactly, more like stepped into the outline that was already waiting for me.

"Maybe this is what it feels like when you stop trying to play the part and start being the part, Bruce."

. . .

"Yeah. That's what I was saying, Bruce. I was just trying not to hang a damn lantern on it."

"Ohhhhhh. Got it. You don't wanna go spelling it out."

"Exactly."

"Like Faulkner."

"What?"

"Like how Faulkner used big allegories and didn't, you know, feel the need to stop and explain every little detail to everyone. You're getting more sophisticated in both thought and deed. I like it!"

"Great. Can you shut up for a second now? I've got shit to do."

"Aye, aye, Carpathian."

The Gnarl surges in a most unpleasant way, like it's adapting to what's happening.

The coils unfurl wider, legs or limbs or whatevers branching at angles that make no kind of spatial sense. A sudden sweep catches the shelf and cracks it straight down the middle. The whole ground bucks. Brit stumbles. Jameson catches her sleeve. Perg barks something that sounds like, "EVERYBODY HUG A WALL, FOOL."

I leap.

The Blade of the Starfallen thrums as I rise, angle wide, and strike across the arc of its reaching appendage, severing something that spurts marrow and then clots again before it hits the floor.

The Gnarl roars.

Or, I mean, that's what it *feels* like. It has no mouth, but still. The sound spills into everything: wall, ceiling . . . blood. It's a heavy trip.

I catch a blur out of the corner of my eye. Zerastian, half shadowed, whispering something I can't hear but feel like I can feel.

It lands behind my sternum. Not quite in my Heart, but adjacent, and my next breath clicks into place. Whatever that murmur was . . . it settles me.

I don't know how to articulate it. It wasn't, like, encouragement or instructions or anything like that, just a kind of certainty that moved my hands a half second before my brain caught up. And suddenly, I'm moving again. Sharper. Cleaner. Like a legit superhero.

Which is kinda fire.

The Gnarl rises to full height, which is not insubstantial. It's as tall as a city gate but with no center of gravity. No symmetry. It billows upward in a staggered spiral, like a fever dream trying to become real.

I have an instinct to flinch, but instead, I rush the sum'bitch.

Leaping again, I gain height and swing at what I *hope* is a central . . . node? Sure. We'll go with node. The Blade connects. The Blade flares. The Blade *burns.*

But . . . it doesn't break through.

Which is straight-up dookie.

I drop, hit stone hard, skid, twist, brace; a whole ballet of combat. I am the Black Swan.

The Gnarl turns toward me fully and compresses into a tight, dreadful ball. I can feel that it's going to strike. Probably one clean, annihilating blow.

And here's the thing: In this moment, I'm not completely sure if what comes next is about strength or power, as such. Obviously, that's always a factor. You can't knock down a mountain with a feather. However, if the feather just plants itself, stares at the goddamn mountain, and refuses to move over millennia, eventually the feather may still be there after the mountain has given way.

And while standing here for millennia isn't an option for a variety of reasons, not least of which being that I don't trust the Gnarl to play "who blinks first loses," there's still something to not showing fear. To not bowing in the face of great might. To kicking the shit out of the thing threatening to kill you and letting the world know that you getting kicked around ain't something that's gonna happen much longer.

And so . . .

I lift the Blade over my shoulder, cocked and ready; not as a gesture of defense but of dare. A challenge written in fire and silhouette. The Gnarl tenses, compressing tighter, all its awful imminence centered like it's winding up to erase me from existence.

"Carpathian!" I hear Persephone shout. I think. It might just be in my mind.

Honestly, it doesn't matter because the point of this exercise isn't really to show anyone else that I'm forged from hellfire and steel. It's to show it to myself. (I mean, look, if Seph happens to think I'm Extra Force Dynamite and is crazy impressed, cool. But that's not the primary reason I'm putting on this display.)

I take one step forward. Just a single step, like I'm closing the distance on a long overdue conversation about, I dunno, not leaving the toilet seat up or something.

The Gnarl takes a step (inasmuch as it can take a step) toward me in return.

Another step. And another. And another. And then, all at once . . . a shriek of collapsing force. I lash out with a strike that tears the air in half, peels the shelf, and rips gravity sideways, but I'm already gone.

Gone?

Gone.

The Blade drags me clear, pulling me along a line of impossible angles like it's rewriting the rules of battle midfight. And, after a moment of suspended animation, I crash back in hard enough to rupture the gallbladder of the universe.

The Gnarl stutters, because this time, I don't cut across its skin. I carve into it.

A full, clean goddamn line, straight through the thing that has no center and yet still finds itself halved. The sound that follows breaks the cave's very shape. Shards of the Pass rain down, light bleeding from everywhere like oil catching fire.

And I land once again, knees bent, back straight, smoke curling from my shoulders.

The Blade crackles in my grip like it's catching its breath, or maybe exhaling mine. Behind me, the Gnarl hangs—split but not quite slain—its body lurching in spasms of disbelief, as if the universe forgot to tell it pain was an option.

For one impossible second, everything holds still. The Pass, the echoes, the haze of ancient light. Every layer of this warped place suspends like it's waiting for someone to shout "Cut!"

I rise. Slow. Deliberate. Cinematic as balls.

My silhouette catches the ambient glow leaking from the fractured seams, casting a ten-foot shadow across a platform that probably wasn't even there a second ago. Sparks fall around me in lazy arcs. The Blade hangs low in one hand.

And I see . . .

The stares.

Every single one of them. Gawking. Even Brit, mouth hanging open like the rest of them. Which means I must look pretty seriously friggin' sweet.

"Fuck, man," she kind of whispers.

"I know, right?" I say back.

"So. What next?" Perg asks.

"Zerry?" I inquire, noticing that my voice is about half-an-octave deeper, with a little bit of that accent I used once or twice before.

She licks her lips. "The way forward has changed."

"Really? It has?" My voice has returned to its natural state of slightly confused disbelief. "Why? Because of the Gnarl?"

"No," she answers. "Because of you."

I swallow. "Oh. Uh . . . Cool." Then, I put my Carpathian cowl back on and say, "Well, good! Let's go see what else wants to get carved then, eh?" I smirk. They just continue staring. After a moment, my shoulders drop, I let the tip of the Blade touch the ground, and add, "So, just . . . This way, then?"

Zerastian nods. I sigh and start walking. Then pause. I turn back, flashing the Blade and smiling. "We should tell everyone that Carpathian Einzgear is coming! And this time, he brought backup!"

No one responds. Perg clears his throat, and Brit looks at me like she's embarrassed for me.

It's fine. I'll keep workshopping it, I say to myself as I move deeper into Origin Pass.

CHAPTER FORTY-NINE

Let's get etched!

Eh. Too dermatological.

They drew first steel.

Nobody drew steel.

Time to carve our names into myth, ye Guardians of the Heart!

Too long. Too hubristic. Too presumptuous.

Well. Looks like someone brought a Gnarl to a Blade brawl.

That doesn't make any sense at all.

This ends in ash or anthem.

Too . . .

No. No, wait. That one kind of slaps.

I file it away mentally, in case I get another hero moment.

"How we looking, Zerry?" I ask her.

"The Pass is watching."

"Isn't that a given?" Brit questions.

". . . More." Zerry replies.

Ahead, the ruin grows stranger. The layout changes. The walls no longer feel broken by time but sheared by design, like something inside Elderkeep pulled itself inward and left the rest behind. And there, recessed into the heart of the stone, framed by Mezmer runes so old they don't even flicker anymore, we find the next threshold. The entrance to the Hall of Echoed War.

Clearing my throat, I say, "Things are likely to get a little crazy once we pass through here."

"*Get*?" Perg says.

"Continue being. More. Whatever. Point is, everyone needs to be ready. How are we all doing? Anyone need a bathroom break?"

"Mi went a few minutes ago."

I kind of tilt my head at Jameson, because . . . "When?"

"When you were fighting the formless evil."

"The Gnarl."

"Dat de one." He draws deep on his smoke.

"So while I was . . . you . . . Okay. Fine. Anybody else?" Headshakes all around. "Dynamite. So, just to make everyone who hasn't been here aware," (Technically, that's everybody except Almeister, but . . .) "The Hall of Echoed War is—"

I pause.

"Carpathian?" Seeing me freeze up like an animatronic robot, Persephone steps over. "Is everything alright?"

"Yeah," I say slowly. "Richemerion."

"What about the Warden?"

"You said . . . You said they're very wise."

"Yes?"

"You were right."

It hits me like a ton of stalagmites thrown from a pair of Stoneheart gloves.

. . . Because I think I get it all of a sudden.

The gauntlet, that ridiculous mess that Richemerion forced us to go through. The Warden of Protection didn't test us for no reason; that gauntlet wasn't just a weird hazing ritual or narrative flourish. It was a warm-up. A pattern primer. A dry run.

The Hall of Echoed War, the illusions, even the Gnarl. It's *familiar* because we've done it. Smaller, stranger, and arguably funkier, but we've done it.

The gauntlet. Our time on the MMP. Hell, maybe as far back as the Cavern of Sorrows.

The way the MMP lets you try ideas on? It's the same thing. It's possible that the Warden's been prepping us this whole time for what comes next. Feeding us shapes so we'd know how to move when the real ones came swinging.

The experiences haven't been reckless. They've been a rehearsal.

I imagine the reason I didn't see it until now is because I've never been a planner. I've always been seat-of-the-pants, start at the middle and hope the end figures itself out.

But what I'm feeling now: control, cohesion, confidence . . . ?

I didn't beat the Gnarl because I'm necessarily stronger. I beat it because I recognized the rhythm. Because something in me remembered the steps before the dance began. Because someone showed me the outline before I hit the page.

"*There's power in preview.*"

"What's that?" Seph asks. "What, Carpathian?"

I didn't even know I said it aloud.

"Uh, just . . . Let's all stay alert."

She shakes her head solemnly and falls in next to me.

The frame ahead glows, fades, and glows again like it's deciding whether or not we should be allowed to keep going. Seph steps closer. She doesn't look at me but doesn't drift away either, staying angled to the same axis I'm on. Her hands are relaxed, but I can sense her pulse ticking fast enough to make her shoulders shift.

I keep walking, and Seph matches step without speaking. I don't speak or slow, glancing briefly behind me to make sure everyone else is attending.

It begins with the layering, a soft accretion of voices that don't overlap so much as compress into one another, like sedimentary thought pressed down by time, voices that maybe belonged to me once or to someone I knew or maybe to someone I invented or pretended to be during one of those long winters when I needed another skin to wear, and they come in pulses, not like echoes or refrains but like the air itself has been waiting to recite its own biography in half-heard warnings and recycled farewells, all of them crawling sideways through the Mezmer seams in the wall, like whispers wearing the shape of memory.

And still, I walk.

"That was a very William Gibson-y thought you just had, Bruce."

"I know. What do you think that's about?"

"Not sure. Maybe it means you're evolving?"

"Into what?"

"I dunno. A Canadian?"

The run-on sentence feels like a reflection of something real. My movement forward feels like who I'm becoming. What I do now. Keep walking. Keep the rhythm. Unceasing. Not letting this place know it's working on me, even though it is. Of course it is. How could it not be? The Hall was built to sift the real from the not real, the strong from the hollow, the present from the frayed, and it is very good at its job.

A page from one of my old notebooks, torn and crumpled and floating midair like it's caught in an unseen updraft, the words rearranging themselves faster than I can read them, forming stories I never wrote but still remember having told.

A sound like loose gravel skipping over sheet metal, which I realize a moment too late is the sound of Crystal's tiny monkey claws scuttling across the ceiling of a dream I'm not dreaming, and when I glance up, she's gone, but I still feel her weight on my shoulder and the warmth of her little fingers gripping my collar.

My old locker at the depot, open, the gloves still inside, one of them twitching like it wants to be worn, the light above flickering not because it's faulty but because something is tinkering with it.

Echoed wars. Wars of which I no longer fear the fighting.

Beside me, Seph keeps stride. Close. Her breath huffs with mine, and her hand lifts halfway once before settling again, like maybe she thought to touch my arm or grab my wrist or say something but decided against it and instead kept walking. It's a choice that says more about her trust in me than anything she could've said out loud, and that realization lodges in my Heart.

Behind us, I hear Almeister inhaling like he's bracing for an old verdict; one he already lived through but never quite accepted. He's been here before. The guy has fought so many battles that the Hall can have its pick of recollections to force into his gray-headed noggin.

It is vastly unlike the Cavern of Sorrows, where we were all rendered lost in torment. We are now seasoned. Tested. And ready. The echoes of war are upon us and . . . we are winning.

It's kind of weird, actually. I had expected this section to be appreciably worse, but—

"STOP!"

Zerastian's shrieking voice causes me to stumble. Literally stumble forward, like I just got hit in the back of the head by a goblin fist or some shit.

"What is it?" I ask, spinning around, scanning for threats. "What's wrong?"

She stands with one hand lifted, not in defense but like she's trying to listen through her fingers. Her eyes lock to mine—not past me, *at* me—and her jaw trembles, like something is vibrating through her bones and hasn't decided whether to settle or flee.

"I don't know," she replies, and that's the first sign that we're in trouble.

"Is it ahead?" I glance at the corridor. "Behind? Above?"

"It's here," she says slowly. "Right here. Around you."

"Around me?"

Everyone takes a step back like I have cooties.

"Yes. I saw a line close."

"A line?"

"Of sorts. Not physical. More like a . . . a shape that snapped shut like a clasp. It was around you, Carpathian. It was centered on you."

Almeister's brow tightens. "He's walked this Hall before. Perhaps it remembers him."

"No," Zerastian says. "It didn't *remember.* It *knew.*"

"What do you mean, 'it knew'?" I ask.

"I don't . . . know. Exactly."

"It knew something that you don't know what it was but you know it knew it?" Perg asks. And were it not for the fact that I know he's just nervous, I might be annoyed at the unnecessary circular thinking. Or not. Who am I to judge?

"Okay, well," I start, "Can you try and know? Or explain what you're sensing a little more . . . word forward? What kind of danger are we in? Am I in?"

She lets out a long, low breath. "It feels as though . . ." Her eyes search the stone around us, then land back on me. "Imagine a fable."

I look at Brit, who scrunches up her face, then back at Zerastian. "Yeah, I can do that."

"A fable of which you are a part. But then, suddenly, the story folds in on itself, like a page bending. But instead of creasing, it clicks. Locks. Not because something new has started but because something old has caught up. Something that was always supposed to happen."

Almeister steps forward slightly. "You're saying the Hall changed?"

"No," Zerastian says. "I'm saying it didn't have to." Her voice sounds small when she says it. "It feels as though Origin Pass has been waiting for this. For him. But not as a visitor."

"Then as . . . what?" I hesitate, but ask anyway.

"As . . ." She seems to be searching for the words. She settles on, "The origin itself."

No one speaks for a moment.

Which sucks.

Perg clears his throat. "So . . . are we, like, good to keep going? Or is he gonna explode or something?"

Zerastian shakes her head. "He's not going to explode." Her tone is firmer now, steadier. "I think the clasp wasn't a trap. It was a . . . designation. Like something falling into place."

Almeister murmurs, "A lock recognizes its key."

"Yes." Zerastian looks at me again. "Whatever this is, it's not pushing you out. It's letting you in."

Everyone seems to ease a little. Or at least no one's backing away from me anymore. And yet, the thing that crawled under my skin when she yelled "STOP" hasn't left. If anything, it's deeper now, like it crawled past the nerves and found something older to rattle.

"I'll, uh, I'll be right back." I start off in the direction we just came from.

"Where are you going?" Seph asks.

"I just . . . Now I need a bathroom break. All that Gnarl fighting got me . . . You know."

I sweep my cool coat behind me in an attempt to salvage whatever amount of aura I can after declaring that I need a pee-pee break.

To be abundantly clear: I do not actually need a pee-pee break. Or, well, I kinda do? But that's not the reason I take my leave. I'm excusing myself because I need a moment to process what I just heard. Because the forces that be, who or whatever they are, continue to do heavy work in the direction of encouraging me to own the truth. But here's the problem: I'm no longer sure what the goddamn truth is. I'm having an existential crisis that would make Kierkegaard go, "Eesh, bro."

"Hey." Brit's voice comes from behind. "What's going on?"

"Huh? Nothing."

She cocks her head. "Dude . . ."

"Okay, I'm just trying to figure out what I'm supposed to do now."

"What does that mean?"

"It means that Zerry's ability to see probabilities is predicated on the notion that she has temporal realities laid out before her, right?"

"I guess."

"But because I'm not a part of a temporal reality she has familiarity with, I'm something more of a, I dunno, a metastructural realignment; I'm obstructing her ability to be of maximal use. She can't unspool the options because she also can't tell if I'm the chicken or the egg."

"Who's a chicken?" comes Perg's voice as he approaches.

"Nobody," I tell him.

"Bruce is concerned that he's blocking Zerastian's precognition because he's both the reporter and the story."

"Bro, the reporter is never supposed to be a part of the story, fool."

"Yeah, I know."

"They're supposed to be fair and balanced."

"I know. I—"

"That's the reason people don't trust the mainstream media anymore, bro, and turn their attention to podcasts and alternative news sources to obtain their diet of information, which only compounds the problem, as then there can be no consensus on what we consider foundational truth."

"Thank you, Marshall McLuhan!" I whisper-shout. Then, seeing his blank, slack-mustachioed expression, have to explain, "He's the guy who coined the phrase 'the medium is the message.'"

"Oh, well then, thank you. Because he's right."

"Whatcha'll be talkin' 'bout over here, den?"

Jesus Christ.

"Bruce is worried that he's jamming up Zerastian somehow."

"First of all, that's reductive. I—"

"Girlie, you just called him . . . Uce-Bray in front of . . . Ameson-Jay. Are you Oco-lay?" Perg expels with urgency.

"He knows," she says.

"He what?"

"Mi know 'bout mi big boss, Bruce Silver de writer from St. Louis. Oh! Dat be like Santus Luminous! Mi get it now!"

"When did you tell Jameson, fool?" Perg accuses.

"While you were off being the *rey*. So maybe don't get on my ass about pretending to be something I'm not, 'kay?" I snap.

"I was just asking a question, homes, Jesus."

"I feel like we're getting off topic here," Brit redirects. She looks at me. "What's your damage here? What's got you worked up, exactly?"

"Richemerion said the System is kind of broken? That we shouldn't necessarily trust it?"

"Yeah?"

"What if I'm the reason?"

"What are you talking about?"

"What if the Ninth Guardian isn't the real cause? Or, at least, not directly the cause. What if, like the way they were using Almeister, they're using me?"

"Is this something you've been considering?"

"Little bit." Her fists ball up, and she breathes heavily, calming herself down. "What are you doing? Why are you mad?"

"Because . . . Goddammit. You know what I think?"

"Do I want to?"

"I don't care. I think it doesn't fucking matter. I think that I just watched you take down a shapeless, formless mass of pure whatever-the-fuck-it-was and *fly* in the process, and now you're second-guessing shit again. And I think this is your MO. That you get a little traction, you start to gain true power and ability, and then you freak the fuck out and find a dozen reasons to twist yourself into a pretzel trying to figure out how to duck it in case shit blows up so you don't have to live with the guilt. Or whatever."

There's a beat. Perg's moustache twitches. Jameson smokes, the cherry from the joint crackling in the stillness of the Pass.

"Or not. I dunno, dude. I'm fucking beat. The mattress I had at the inn kinda sucked. I just want to get the goddamn Gauntlet, beat the serpent's dick into the dirt, and close the fucking Mid-Meridian Plane so we can check off this Quest and get to the next thing. Lest you forget, our punch list still has a shitload left unpunched."

I start to respond, but before I can . . .

"Carpathian?"

"Shit. Seph's coming. Everybody cool it with the Uce-Bray stuff. Hey, what's up?"

She sidles up, her hand hovering near her belt like she thinks she might need to fight something. It's pretty hot, can't lie.

"Are you alright?" she asks.

"Huh? Yeah. I'm . . . fine?" I say, but the word tastes like a half-truth. Not because I'm lying but because I don't know what the whole truth would feel like right now.

"What are you all discussing?"

"Battle strategies," Jameson replies, nodding like it's the most obvious answer in the world. "Tactical options. De usual."

He winks at me. I think he likes being on the inside.

"Oh," she says. "Very good. Can I help? What should I know?"

I look at her, bright eyed, ready, completely in, and fully invested in what we're doing. And for half a second, I think about saying it. About letting it come out right here, in the stone silence of a Hall that already knows too much.

She's earned it, hasn't she? She deserves the whole truth. Because she's been strong and steady and kind in ways I can't always name but feel all the time. Because she looks at me like I'm someone worth following, and I want to be that someone.

Because the half-truth gets heavier the longer I carry it. Because maybe if I say it aloud, I'll stop feeling like I'm two steps removed from my own story.

Because I need, at some point (soon) to stop being such a friggin' Nancy. (No disrespect to Nancys.) I mean, shit, if I were writing this story—my story, now—I'd be acutely aware of how much I'd need to turn a corner with the character that is me. So, why can't I just do that in action? Here? Now? In real life?

The answer is because real life is more complicated than that, but . . . does it *have* to be?

Seph asks again, gently, "Is there anything that I should know?"

I look at Brit, at Perg, at Jameson, who's once again winking at me as if granting permission. Seph brought the guy back from the dead, for cripes' sake. They share a bond. If he's telling me it's time to just come clean, I should probably listen.

So, I make a choice. I take a deep, thick breath. Blow it out. Narrow my eyes at her and say . . .

"Yeah. When we get the Gauntlet . . . keep your father safe. It's likely to get hairy in there."

To say that Brit, Perg, and Jameson look disappointed would be an insult to the very concept of disappointment.

Seph squares her jaw, steels her expression, and says, "Understood."

She turns and marches back. After another moment of processing their judgmental stares, I look at my three would-be consiglieres and say, "Let's go," before heading off after the underinformed wizard's daughter.

CHAPTER FIFTY

The air holds still inside the chamber. As ever, some things kind of match how I wrote them, some don't.

For example, the chamber door opens exactly as it should, but the doors part without sound. That's different. In the book, they groaned and shuddered, announcing their own presence, but in reality, the divide is clean. No protest or pageantry to speak of, just a line split down the center that allows them to swing wide with a soft whoosh, and then, a room, waiting.

I step inside.

The walls also don't match exactly. I wrote them as an obsidian stone, darker than midnight, streaked with silver and dusted in myth and all that shit. But what surrounds us now is pale granite, smooth and flat, empty of any fantasy embellishment. Truthfully, the space doesn't feel terribly sacred. It kind of feels . . . cleared. Like something came through and scrubbed the history of whatever once was from the walls.

I glance. No one's moved in with me. I guess they're giving me room to do my thing. Or waiting to see what wild, unexpected shit happens to me first.

The light is even and silent, but it's here. Ambient like in a romantic Italian restaurant. I don't know where it comes from, and I don't bother to wonder. Like I told Brit back in the day, "Mezmer powered, I guess? I dunno."

Heh. Made her so annoyed. I miss those days.

Five steps in, the ground shifts underfoot. Not visibly, but in texture. Less stone, more compression. Like the floor was designed to remember where people stood. I didn't write that either, but it's a cool detail.

I exhale, let the moment settle.

And then, I spy it.

The pedestal. The object atop it.

It's the right size. The right shape. Overbuilt and impossible. Marked with runes I can't read but know by feel. The metal drinks in the light like it hasn't had a sip in weeks. Every inch of *it* is exactly what I imagined.

I flash back for a moment to the inspiration.

The gloves were nothing special. Standard-issue Metro transit gear. I inherited them, in fact. Thick brown leather, already creased from the driver who wore them before me. They smelled like effort. Like hours behind the wheel of the number seventy-eight bus and the heater that only worked some of the time. There was a rip at the seam of the left index finger. I never stitched it.

I used to put them on slow, like a ritual. Middle of winter, early shift, windows still dark. I'd slide in one hand, then the other, and think: This is how I begin.

It wasn't magic; it was muscle memory. It was the sound they made when I flexed my fingers, the way they felt warm even when they were cold.

That's where the idea came from.

Not from grand prophecies or epic poems or ancient legends. Just from the way I felt gripping the wheel, turning down Delmar, pretending I had somewhere heroic to be.

So yeah. I took a pair of city-issue driver gloves beat to hell by life and turned them into an artifact of unimaginable power in my mind. The story I was telling was never about grandeur; it was about transformation. About believing that something worn and ordinary could still hold purpose. Could still fit.

And here, now, made manifest, is the fruit of that imaginative labor. Waiting for me.

The Gauntlet of Soren-damn-thali.

I take a breath, then another. My hand twitches near it. Hovering, not touching.

The Vecamire runes said to be the lost tongue of the Pale Kin that Teleri famously could not read wrap across the wrist and knuckle joints, curling like they're mid-sentence. So wild to see it in front of me. Almeister had suggested it might be an invitation or a warning, and Pergamon, being Pergamon, had added, "Or both."

All of it was a narrative flourish when I wrote it. As the kids say: Vibes. But now, standing here, those old guesses feel so very right. Like two truths trying to crack their knuckles inside me. (Even though anybody paying attention knows that the shit is a big old warning, for sure.)

The funny thing is that Carpathian surely knew it too, but went ahead and touched it anyway. Just like I'm about to do, knowing full well what's almost definitely going to happen next.

The metal pulses faintly, like breath. Slow and steady and intimate, like it's syncing up with mine.

Thump.

The longer I look, the more the runes seem to squirm like they're getting impatient.

I step closer. My fingers extend.

"Bruce?"

"Yeah, Bruce?"

"You gotta say the line, remember?"

Oh, shit. That's right. The line. The thing I said before. Or . . . Carpathian said. The invocation or prayer that made it possible to release the Gauntlet from its housing.

I rack my brain, try to conjure whatever mystical half thought I muttered the first time. But it's a blank. I remember the rhythm of it, maybe. The emotion behind it. But the actual phrase? No idea. It wasn't language, anyway; not really. It was permission. A mental lean-in. An emotional click.

"Zerry?" I call her over. She steps up, hesitantly. "You said you might be able to help?" She chews at her lip. "What's wrong?"

"I thought so, but now . . ." She frowns, eyes darting between me and the Gauntlet.

"What?"

"I'm attempting to triangulate the threads, but it's like trying to trace the edge of a shadow in a windstorm."

"That sounds hard, fool," I hear from the peanut gallery.

"Your presence is distorting the timeline," she goes on. "I can't quite see what might come next because . . ."

"Because what?"

"Because you're already standing in it."

Shit.

"So . . ."

"I might be able to try another way of dislodging it."

"What's that?"

"I may be able to interact with the pedestal itself."

She extends both hands toward the Gauntlet, not touching it yet.

Ooooh, she's giving Technomancy a try. That's cool. That's something she'd do all the time in the books. If the more oblique aspects of her gifts failed, Zerastian could always fall back on manual Skills to crack a problem. It was intended to be a comment on the fact that while the nature of life is a mystery, not everything about it is always mysterious. Sometimes, you just need to roll up your sleeves and get a little grease under your fingernails. There's more than one way to untether a Gauntlet, as the old expression goes.

Zerry's fingers fan out, loose but intentional, and from her wrists, soft filaments of translucent light begin to braid outward, like threads of electric silk pulled from the Mezmer stored in her skin. They reach toward the plinth, mapping it in a matrix of pale lines, a lattice of light connecting each rune, each etched contour, with the elegant precision of a spiderweb being woven in real time. It's beautiful in the way that only concentrated effort can be.

She narrows her eyes. Her voice drops, nearly prayerful. "System access requested."

Annnnnnnnnd . . .

Nada. The room doesn't change. The Gauntlet doesn't move. The pedestal does hum in a low, guttural subsound you sorta feel in your knees before you hear it. The whole contraption pulses, reluctantly but not terribly reactively.

"Come along," she whispers. "Come along now. Let me in."

The lattice thickens. Lines double back and layer in upon themselves, forming an architectural diagram of access. Glyphs float up from the Mezmer seams and hover in a slow, looping spiral around her wrists. It's very *Minority Report* meets *Doctor Strange.*

Then . . . more resistance. One of the threads snaps. A flicker of heat rushes through the pedestal, and the light around the Gauntlet flares a dark orange, like something fending off an infection.

Zerastian jerks back. A jolt of force spits from the base like a static discharge laced with memory. It catches her square in the chest, sends her stumbling. She hits the ground hard and exhales all the air she had stored for the next thought.

Both Perg and Jameson shout and start toward her. "Homegirl!" "Mi precog princess!"

But she waves them off, coughing. "I'm okay," she says, sitting up slowly, her hair half lifted sort of adorably with residual charge. "It didn't want me."

Another thread pops. Then another. Glyphs glitch, distorted into unreadable scribble, then settle, inert.

Zerry turns to me, face a little pale but composed. "Whatever releases the Gauntlet, whatever freed it before, I fear it's the only way."

Son of a Boston cream pie.

Persephone turns to her dad. "Father? You were with Carpathian on his previous retrieval. Do you have no ideas at all what was said by him? Your connection to him as his mentor, as his guide, should allow some manner of insight, yes?"

She asks a great question. And, probably, a correct one. The reason she granted Insight to Perg back in Bell's View was only so that we'd have some sort of guiding hand until we got Almeister back. Now that he's here, restored, back to more or less his old self, the intuitive bond he and I have should be primarily restored. But it can't be because, technically, it's never been there. The Carpathian here now is not the Carpathian he once shepherded along.

"I . . ." Almeister stutters. "I suppose I should, but . . . not unlike Zerastian . . . there is something in the way. I cannot fully . . ." He gives me a deeply skeptical look. "I don't know."

Jesus Christ. This shit is getting exhausting. I have no idea why I'm maintaining the pretense anymore; it would be so much goddamn easier if I just ripped the Band-Aid off. But, for some stupid, annoying, profoundly embedded trauma in my psyche, I can't make myself do it. I feel like a gigantic asshole, but I've just been hiding behind so many different kinds of masks for so goddamn long that I don't even know which one I should be pulling off at this point.

I'm sorry, Mom. I'm not sure I'm as strong as you think I am.

Anyway—

"Don't say that, Bruce."

. . .

"Mom?"

"No. It's not Mom."

. . .

"Then . . ."

"You are strong, Bruce. You're stronger than you know. You'll be alright. Everything's going to be alright."

The voice. The other voice—or, I guess, the *other* other voice. The one I first heard in Jeomandi's, then later in Garr Haven. The one I thought was my other half and then thought was Mom and is now telling me it's definitely neither?

"Who are you?"

"You'll find out when it's time. I promise. For now . . . trust in yourself. Not a System. Not a Warden of Protection. Not anything from without. Trust yourself from within. You'll find it."

A feeling comes over me; a wash of something inexplicable. I step forward, place my hand inside the Gauntlet. My forearm slides inside, and I experience the sensation of the texture of the thing against my skin.

I look over to see six sets of eyes watching me with a kind of pregnant curiosity. Their mouths are all filled with unasked questions, but none of their lips will part to let them be asked.

Breathing deeply, I stare at the glove and interrogate my own thoughts, trying to remember the origins. Nothing comes. Not at first. Then . . .

The smell of diesel. Salt on the road. The hum of my route radio crackling nonsense. I used to wear the gloves before the heat kicked in, sometimes hours into a shift. They held the shape of my fingers, the feel of the wheel. They made me feel less breakable.

The Gauntlet spasms. Kind of. Almost like it's conforming to me. I hear a gasp but don't look to see who gasped it.

Studying the thing I'm holding (or that's holding me, maybe), I consider its truth. The Gauntlet may be born of myth, but the myth is also mine. It was birthed from me needing to feel like I could hold something steady. Like I could grip something and not let go.

That's the truth.

I try to remember what I wrote . . .

"*And so, Carpathian gave it. Not loudly. And not in any tongue the others would know. Not even in one he himself remembered learning. It rose from somewhere deeper than memory, seeded long ago, blooming now under pressure. He bowed his head.*

And he spoke.

The sound barely crossed his lips, and yet it echoed. Through him. A shape of a thought, older than prayer, folded in the space between breath and heartbeat.

The Gauntlet stirred."

What was it? What did he say? I didn't express it, but I must've had some idea. Some inkling. Somewhere inside myself, I must have had a notion about what it could have been. What kinds of things did I say to myself once upon a time? How did I will myself?

I used to whisper dumb shit to myself as I put my work gloves on. Like pep talks, but defeated. A sort of passive chiding that was the best I could summon up at the time.

Let's not screw up today.

Let's not die in traffic.

Let's just get through the morning.

None of them sound much like legendary incantations. But maybe . . .

I grip tightly.

"Let's just get through this," I say, low. Not so much to the Gauntlet as to me.

"*There was no expected surge of power. No anticipated light. No world-shaking tremor of revelation. Just the weight of the object, ancient and silent, coiling around his forearm like a thing long slumbering and still not quite awake.*

Carpathian held still."

I also hold still.

"*The others stood by in wary silence, not daring to step too close. There was a pause, as though the Gauntlet, alive in ways steel should not be, was waiting for something more.*"

The others stand by in wary silence, not daring to . . .

Whatever. I don't need to go phrase by phrase. The point is that things seem to be going in the right direction? At least as a reflection of the story.

"*It dimmed, then brightened. Not in response to Mezmer or will but to recognition.*

Carpathian's breath caught. The Gauntlet no longer merely wore him—it knew him."

It knows me too. The guy behind the wheel who sat in an idling bus in winter dawn, whispering little mantras to survive the morning without losing it. The one who thought maybe if he could *write* a better version of himself, he'd become it.

Or fake it long enough that nobody would notice he was hollow in the middle.

"*The others saw his shoulders rise and fall slowly. Saw his gaze go distant. Saw the fingers of his Gauntleted hand flex once, and in so doing, stir a faint ripple in the still air.*"

The Gauntlet tightens like a memory curling its fingers into a fist. It's not reading my thoughts; it's reading my intent.

Intent. The wellspring of creation. The foundation of what allows the Mid-Meridian Plane to exist. The place from which all stories find their genesis. The essence of what drives the story's need to be told. The thing hidden behind jokes, half-truths, and fables. I feel like . . . I feel like the Gauntlet is tracing the line between who I was when I made this whole thing up and who I am now, standing here with my hand inside an avatar made real.

It's possible that the Gauntlet, possessing more understanding of me than I even understand myself, is saying something I haven't been able to say out loud yet. Not to them. Not even to me.

The Gauntlet isn't unlocking a weapon. It's unlocking a story.

Not Carpathian's.

Mine.

A pulse ripples from the base of the Gauntlet, radiating outward. It doesn't shake the room. It doesn't blow back my hair or dim the lights. It's subtler than that. It feels like the page turning in a book no one else can see.

"*They did not ask what he'd said, but if they had, he could not have told them. Because some oaths are not for ears. Some are only for the world to remember.*"

The others shift behind me. I can sense them trying to understand what just happened, but nothing *has* "happened." Not precisely. Not on the outside, at least.

Inside, though?

Inside, something has come unlocked. Not in the pedestal. In me.

There is a soft, quiet *click*, and I step back—Gauntlet fully attached to my arm—and flex my fingers.

"Whoa, that's some real Iron Man shit, fool."

"Who is Iron Man?" Seph asks.

"Uh . . . bad dude. Had to fight him in uh . . . Poughkeepsie Berg."

Brit points a warning "shut up" finger at Perg. He dummies up.

I keep staring at my arm, remaining still, because recognition has taken the place of hesitation, and movement now belongs to something greater than impulse or fear or the long habits of concealment that have governed me for too many kilostrydes to measure.

The Gauntlet exists with the fullness of something returned to its origin, as though the metal had been waiting all this time for skin that remembered what it once meant to hold on when everything else had slipped away. Each breath I take seems drawn deeper than before, fed through a channel of intention I never fully understood until this moment, and while the others remain silent behind me, I sense the shift in the room, a quiet realignment, the hush that falls when a page prepares to turn and the ink stills long enough to become part of what's been written. The pedestal has ceased to matter, the light has ceased to perform, and the chamber itself feels less like a place and more like a promise.

I look at my hand, enclosed and certain, and I begin to understand that the story was never shaped by what I imagined; it was shaped by what I allowed myself to carry, what I brought forward even when I believed I was standing still.

I feel pretty frickin' solid, I gotta say. That is, of course, until I remember what comes next.

"*Carpathian pulled back, studying the magnificence encircling his arm, when a low, guttural moan echoed from deep within the walls; neither living nor mechanical, but something between. The runes flared violently, then somehow shattered like brittle glass, spraying shards of Mezmerated light in every direction. The pedestal cracked down the center. Behind them, the passage they'd entered through crumbled into a cascade of stone.*

Out of the fractures in the vault's black walls came figures—armored, gaunt, burning with corrupted intent. The vague suggestion of Templar forms but twisted, boneless in their gait, and clumped together in a mass of roiling abstraction."

Aw, crap.

"Ashmourn."

CHAPTER FIFTY-ONE

Oh, fuck me. I knew it! Everybody, get ready!"

Brittany shouts as the floor quivers in that particular way stone shouldn't, like it's bracing for something it already knows is coming. A hairline crack streaks through the pedestal's base, straight and mean, and the light above folds inward, sucked through some unseen aperture in the room's structure. I pull my hand back a few inches, and the glove clings with the obedience of something that has waited a long time to serve again.

I feel so much like another Bruce of legend. Bruce Campbell in The Evil Dead Part 2.

(I don't say "Groovy," but it honestly takes a lot of willpower not to.)

From the far reaches of the chamber, the first fracture appears. A rift through the granite, jagged and breathing, leaking thin streams of lightless vapor. Then a second, and a third, and then too many to damn count. They don't arrive with spectacle; they just widen, spread, reveal.

Across the chamber, matter rearranges, moving against gravity, pulled together by a force both deliberate and mindless. Fragments of armor, scorched and unfinished, drag themselves from the walls. Not so much pieces of soldiers as pieces of memories of soldiers, distorted by heat and fused by . . . I dunno. More heat. They twist and lock into each other, building shapes that do not hold shape, outlines that refuse to commit. The floor flexes. The ceiling bows.

Oh, this is so much worse than I remember describing it.

"Everybody back," I say, louder than I need to. Which is to say "at all," because they're already moving back. My voice echoes flatly, the chamber eating the sound. There's pressure building in the ceiling, in the floor, in my chest.

Thump-thump. Thump-thump.

I feel the Gauntlet tighten.

Well, well, well. Looks as though someone has a new toy! Good times, eh?! This should make the completion of the Quest, at least, achievable now! To which end—and I hate to be the bearer of bad news (which isn't explicitly true, but is the kind of thing one says)—you may want to note the other . . . series of unfortunate events that are unfolding.
{COURTESY MESSAGE #37}

A new whine rises from somewhere beneath the stone, steady and escalating. A pressure cue rather than an exact sound; the kind of frequency that warps the soft cartilage in your ear and makes your molars feel like strangers to your own mouth.

"What the fuck is that, now?" Brit moans.

Cracks ripple outward from everywhere, the rock no longer forming so much as suggesting, each segment lifting slightly as if reconsidering its agreement with gravity. But the fractures don't break. They frame a space that was never part of the original room, something older than the stone, something that predated the idea of rooms entirely. And that's when I can start to make out what's happening. Through one of the cracks, I spot it . . .

A broken rainbow.

Or, the partial one. Yellow, Red, Green, Orange, Blue. I can just make it out through a fissure. The Ashmourn aren't just coming out of the walls here, from Origin Pass. They're coming from someplace deeper, more foundational.

The rift is opening the door to the Mid-Meridian Plane itself. Meridia's rough draft and its published edition are becoming one.

"Shit!" I shout, dodging a wall of Ashmourn blades launched straight for my head.

"What's happening?" Seph yells.

"It's because we've all been there!" Zerastian responds.

"Been where?" I shout back, spinning away from another wave of Ashmourn rising from the rift.

"The MMP," she says. "Because we are now bound to both planes, and so is the Ninth Guardian's forces, retrieving the Gauntlet has not only loosed the sentries of Origin Pass, but all protectorates everywhere. Every version of all that has ever been imagined is merging!"

"Oh, come on!" I shout. Which is hardly adequate, but it's what I've got.

Then, something happens. Or . . . something else. Just like when I levitated earlier, the Blade doing whatever airborne voodoo it did to get me up there, the Gauntlet takes over on its own.

My arm lifts before I know what's happening, the Gauntlet functioning like it's already halfway through the move. I don't guide it. I don't even really give it permission. I just . . . let it do what it wants, and it does the rest.

My hand meets the floor, and I am thrown down with almost slapstick physical comedy. (I have to acknowledge it: Just like Bruce Campbell in *The Evil Dead* . . .)

Oh, my god. Oh. My. God.

I just realized something else in the middle of all this . . .

Bruce's character in the film is called . . . Ash. Ash is the hero of the *Evil Dead* movies.

For the love of . . . I know I can be derivative, but Meridia is like a damn cover band!

The Gauntlet connects with the ground, and the chamber feels it. Every surface contracts. Every outline firms. The space clenches around us like a jaw braced for impact when one can see the punch coming but can't get out of the way in time to avoid the impact.

I feel the shift in my bones, not so much as pain but more like gravity redirecting itself. The air stops being air. The Ashmourn stop moving. Their charge halts midlunge. What was formed mere seconds ago now sits anchored in the present without recourse.

The Gauntlet draws itself up, and I watch my arm lift into the air. But this time, I don't wait for it to act alone. I lean into the movement, match its rise, meet its weight with mine. My fingers flex, and the metal responds like a muscle I've always had but only now remember how to use.

A pull in my chest lines up with a pulse in the glove, and then we're synced, working together without language, the separation between tool and wielder no longer detectable.

I bring the Gauntlet down with my full weight, calling the strike as it lands, sending a declaration into the floor, into the stone, into the space beneath the shape of the world where roots of old memory still twist.

Every Ashmourn shape ripples with internal fracture, some still halfway through a charge, others locked midcrawl across the ceiling, their frames beginning to stutter. The Gauntlet flares along the knuckle ridges, feeding off the convergence of my aim and its hunger, and together, we hold the world still.

And then, with a breath I do not realize I've taken until it exits, I twist my wrist and release. The chamber cracks. The Ashmourn scatter like ash flung through an updraft, structure torn from mass, weight stripped from body, and I look down at my arm. It belongs to me. It answers to me. And I feel pretty goddamn invincible.

Until . . .

WHAM.

A length of armored smoke, blackened and jointed, swings from behind and slams into my lower back with enough force to tilt my vision thirty degrees off normal. I drop to one knee, the Gauntlet catching against the floor, and whip around fast enough to crack my neck.

It's a full . . . appendage? I guess? Sure, call it an appendage, fused from a clump of Ashmourn, all plated chests crushed and bound along a central column, ribs torn and repurposed as barbs, whole shoulders still jerking reflexively from residual determination. It doesn't slither or coil or anything like that. It stamps. It swings with engineered malice, and then swings again.

I roll as it hits where I just was, shattering a slab of Meridia open so that I can see straight down. And what I see causes my Heart to catch mid-*Thum*—

"Sumnut?" I half gasp to myself.

Through the rent in the fabric of the universe, what I see is our old pal, Sumnut, the HR ninja, still fighting, still working to defend the MMP against the Ashmourn, and doing a yeoman's job, but faltering. He looks like electrified hellfire as he fights all alone, flickering chaos all around him.

His poet blouse hangs in ribbons, one sleeve entirely gone, the other scorched to the shoulder. The scarf around his neck is blackened and unraveling, threads trailing like spider silk. One of his loose trouser legs is soaked dark to the knee with something viscous and red. His skin is mottled with burns and soot, and the four small horns on his forehead are chipped at the tips, one cracked all the way down to the base. His hair clings to his temples with sweat. His feet bleed where they've clearly torn open from too many steps across ground that was never meant for walking.

His chest rises in quick, uneven breaths, snagging in the middle. But somehow, he fights with the giddy enthusiasm of ten warriors, moving like wind funneled through steel, every slash of his whip-sword cutting with purpose. His steps drag a bloody color through the ash. Ashmourn—thousands, maybe more—fuse and lurch, limbs swallowed into bulk, and I watch as Sumnut is knocked from his stance.

I shout his name this time. "Sumnut!"

"Carpathian! Hello! Oop! One moment."

He turns and spins inward on a planted heel, ducking beneath a cleaving crescent of something neither arm nor weapon but an amalgam of both, severing it clean at the joint with a flick of his whip-sword that sends a ripple of kinetic light shearing off into the smoke. His scarf, singed and dancing with embers, trails behind him like it's trying to keep pace.

"You've returned!" he calls.

"Not exactly!"

WOW!

I snap my head, noticing that Brit has thrown up a Wall of WOW! to keep my distracted face from being chewed into by a nasty-looking cohort of Ashmourn who have assembled themselves in the shape of an Iron Maiden.

"Thanks!"

"Yep!" she calls back, straining to hold the barrier in place.

"Sumnut! I'm coming for you!" I shout to the friendliest fighter.

"No!" he calls back. "Don't do that! You must close the access to the plane! Not open it wider! Opening it wider is, in fact, the opposite of what you're supposed to be doing!"

"But—"

"Hold that thought!" He pivots, drops low, and zings his whip-sword across the ground in a loose arc that splits three rising Ashmourn clusters at the midline, carving them into melting halves that stagger, fuse, then dissolve back into the churning slate. "Listen!" he shouts, "the sooner you close the plane down, the sooner I can be done with these! Until the plane is sealed, they are likely to just keep pouring in! Once it's shut, I can bring in the cleanup crew!"

WHOA!

Damnit. Brit's Wall of WOW! has dropped out.

"Sorry!" she calls to me.

"It's okay! Perg!"

"I'm on it, big homie!"

"No, no, wait!"

He starts to grow. Like, GROW, massive big, the way he did in the Tower. Which is, in fact, not what I was going to ask him to do. I was *going* to ask him to temporarily wedge himself inside the rift until I could figure out what to do next, but unfortunately, he went the other direction. Quite literally. By which I mean . . .

. . . He bursts up and out through the very canopy of Origin Pass.

It reminds me of a time when there was a water pipe that broke in the ceiling above the tunnel at the metro station. What a mess. Water everywhere. It took almost a week to get it all cleaned up and repaired. This, however, feels like it's going to take quite a bit more effort to get sorted out than a soggy bus depot.

Because, in the case of what Perg's volumizing has exposed, it's not a torrential downpour of what I have to imagine is very likely sewage. I mean, that's pretty gross, and it would have been my preference for it not to have happened. But, on balance, I'd argue that it's still preferable to an all-in-one Giant Serpent of the Mokeisan.

Which is what is towering above us now. At least for the moment. The second it spots the hole in what was just a second ago the roof of Origin Pass, and notices the fight taking place down below, it clearly feels left out, because . . .

. . . it turns and shoots like a missile in the direction of what is, for probably only another few seconds, my head.

CHAPTER FIFTY-TWO

This is too much," Brit says as she reads through the most recently printed out pages I've handed her for review.

"What do you mean it's too much?" I ask, swiveling back and forth in my desk chair, pen between my teeth, one hand lazily dropping fish flakes into Gonzo's tank.

She pulls page after page off the top of the stack with increasing urgency.

"It's . . . It's just . . ."

"I don't even think you're really reading anymore."

"It's overwrought," she declares.

I stop spinning. "I'd call it ambitious."

"You've got them trapped in a time-locked elevator inside a skyscraper that's also a sleeping god. Meanwhile, one of them turns into a dog whenever the emergency lights flicker, and the villain keeps quoting Morrissey for some reason?"

"That's texture."

"That's therapy in disguise."

I shrug. "The transformation serves as metaphor."

"For what?"

"I haven't decided yet."

She lifts her fist before putting it back down. "Why are the elevator buttons sentient?"

"They're witnesses. Passive observers of cyclical trauma."

"You gave one of them a crush on Carpathian."

"To show how much Carpathian means to everything on Meridia!"

I toss another flake into the tank. Gonzo grabs it, then burrows away like he's embarrassed to be witness to the conversation. Brit tosses the pages down and flops onto the chaise, stares at me.

"Are you okay?"

"What? What do you mean?"

"It seems like you're getting wilder and wilder with the story ever since Mollie—"

"I'm fine," I cut her off. "I'm just . . . doing what I do. That's all."

She squints at me for just a second before letting it go. "'Kay. How do you plan on getting them out of it?"

"I'm not sure. But I'm open to ideas."

She picks up the pages, stares at them again for a second. "Maybe you just stop writing Carpathian into situations that are virtually impossible to get him out of."

I smile, tired . . . but genuine.

"Where's the fun in that?"

"This be no fun, mi gen'ral!"

Jameson ain't lying. Everywhere I look, something is trying to kill us.

Perg's half immersed in the rift, giant sized and groaning.

"Perg! Get out of there!" I shout.

"I think I'm stuck, fool! *¡Mierda! ¡Jodido gusano no se mueve!*"

The way his shell is wedged, the serpent is going to have to smash through him to get to the rest of us.

A quick scan shows mayhem at a scale that is challenging to process:

Ashmourn surge through three rift points, maybe more. They just keep building, shoulders, torsos, legs, claws, nothing in proportion. They're crawling across every surface now. Walls. Ceiling. Air.

Glancing again at Sumnut, he's being overwhelmed. The guy was able to fight the Ashmourn off on his own for who knows how long, but now that the pathway between worlds is torn asunder, there's no way he'll be able to contend.

Brit's started spinning her hands to summon . . . something. Not sure what. Which is, I guess, why it's called "Summoner of Something."

Seph appears to be trying to create the copies of herself that can serve as a distraction and battle on her behalf as avatars, but the Ashmourn keep cutting through the new images as they appear.

And Almeister . . . Oh shit. Almeister is spasming. Once more, his eyes are rolled to the back of his head. Somehow, he appears to be taken over again. I check his Heart Guard status quickly . . .

Heart Guard Member [Almeister T. Wizard]. Status:
PRE_COR_PRE_COR

His status is flickering back and forth, starting to declare him as PRESENT but then fritzing out to say that he's CORRUPTED. I can see him straining, working as hard as he can to keep from being taken hold of entirely by the Guardian's pull, but . . .

He turns. Not toward the Ashmourn. Not toward the serpent.

Toward *me*.

"Uh, what's going on there, Al?"

His eyes are bright. And not bright like, *Hey there, bright eyes, who's a cutie?* But bright like *Children of the Corn*. Lit from behind, like someone else is shining a flashlight through his skull. His mouth moves, working to make words, then—

"False Prophet!" he screams

I blink. "Um. What?"

The air cracks, and the burst from him hits me hard enough to knock me halfway across Meridia. Fortunately—or not—a wall stops me. Hard.

My shoulder crunches.

"Son of a bitch!" My vision fuzzes as I lay there, battered.

He's coming closer now, that wild light still in his eyes.

"You bear the Gauntlet but carry no name! You wield what you do not understand! You do not belong here!"

"Al!" I shout. "Hey, it's me! It's Carpathian!"

But it's no use. He's not fully gone, but he's not fully here either. The thing in him has decided I'm the threat. I try to stand, but I think I also broke something in my . . . spine? Maybe? Too? Feels like my spine. Or, actually, it doesn't feel like anything at all, which is why I think it's my spine.

"Father, no!" Seph's voice rings out, sharp and horrified, more *wound* than word. She sprints forward, vanquishing a wall of Ashmourn with a *whoosh* of her hand. "Father!" she yells again.

He whirls toward her like he doesn't recognize her. Or worse, like he does, and it doesn't matter. The strike comes fast, bright, brutal. She barely throws up a warding gesture before it lands.

CRACK. THUM. BOOM.

The blast catches her clean. She flies backward, limbs flared, cloak twisting in the air like a torn flag. Slams into stone. Drops.

"Seph!" I call for her. Or think I do. My voice box might be shattered.

Almeister's still coming, eyes lit like he's under black light. On the plus side, he's not yelling anymore. On the minus side, he's chanting. Like a Ritual.

"Unworthy bearer. Fabricated soul. Break the seal, scatter the name . . ."

I don't know what he's casting. I don't know if he knows. His hands are moving like he's pulling memories apart and throwing them at me.

"Al, Al, Al, Al, Al." It's all I can manage.

He looms above me now, arms raised above his head like Tom Berenger about to cave in Charlie Sheen's skull at the end of *Platoon*, when (kind of just like in *Platoon*) a fresh blast of pressure erupts from the northernmost fracture. A concussive wave punches the ground like an invisible fist and sends a whole corner of the chamber upward like a flipped table, which sends Almeister tumbling away from me, toward the rift where Sumnut fights.

And then . . . the serpent pivots, coiling, writhing, building even more mass. (Like it needs it.)

The rift responds to its tension, stretching like fabric caught on a zipper. Segments of its body flex and brace around the lip of the breach, circling Perg, muscles sweeping past his shell so close I can see his reflection split across its scales, cutting off the sky like a curtain being drawn.

And that's when the real problem (Ha!) shows up.

The rift splits again, but this time downward. The floor falls away in a perfect oval, revealing a chasm *beneath* the chasm, a still-deeper pocket of the MMP that shows . . .

I'm not sure.

I don't know what the hell I'm looking at. Light and shadow fall through layers that aren't organized by depth or shape or gravity. The breach shows a vast, vertical spire of something alive but unmoving, or once alive but still listening? Hard to say. There are icons carved into the air itself, turning slowly like debris caught in orbit. Pages . . . No, not pages; the *idea* of pages flutter through emptiness and dissolve before they can be read. Not blank. Too full. Overwritten.

Whole story frames drift sideways, suspended in gold-wire scaffolds like the blueprints of dreams half dismantled. I spot a staircase made of teeth leading into the base of a chapel that burns without fire. There's a city folded inward like origami collapsing, and it's whispering in every voice I've ever heard all at once.

I can't tell whether I'm looking into a memory or a forecast or the part of myself I keep locked away. All I know is this: Something down there remembers me. Or someone who came before me. Or . . . all of us.

"Who is 'us,' Bruce?"

"I'm not sure."

My eyes are wet.

The rift keeps widening, and I am stuck in a trance. Caught between before and after. Now and never. Was and will be again.

Thump-thump.

I call on Marrowmancy, and it feels like someone just lit a match inside my bones.

The break in my back starts to fuse, spine realigning itself with quiet clicks and something like guilt. My shoulder knits. The pain doesn't go away, exactly, but it does become a memory.

I spit out blood, roll my jaw, flex my fingers.

Okay.

Okay.

Quick inventory . . . ? We're boned.

I see Zerastian. Kind of, weirdly, chill.

"Zerry!" She turns her head to me, almost robotic. "How do we get out of this?!"

She sighs, heavily, and says, "We don't."

The single most frightening thing about this entire situation isn't the Ashmourn or the serpent or the combination of any of the hostile elements surrounding us. It's the cold-blooded simplicity with which she says the words.

Before I can shout back a robust, *WTF are you talking about?! What does that mean? Zerry? 'We don't' get out of this?* "Big homie!" Perg's voice draws my eyes up to see that the serpent is done building up a head of steam and is now set to take another dive-bomb which will, without question, punch straight through Perg's shell and explode his snail body into a million tiny bits of escargot.

There's only one thing I can think to do . . .

ZZZZZZZZZWWWWWAAAAAAHHHHHMMMMMMM.

Thump-thump. Thump-thump.

The impromptu battlefield freezes midcollapse, a mural of disaster in stasis. Ashmourn crawl through the air like insects caught in sap. The serpent hangs, coiled in midlunge, jaws yawning wide. Time curls sideways. Gravity reconsiders its options.

And I move.

It's starting to be more like it was for Carpathian when he became fully godlike. I'm not there yet; there's no zipping around like a cartoon superhero, but while everyone else is frozen, I'm thawed and on the go.

I launch myself toward the nearest knot of Ashmourn slinking along like predatory drapery. My arm moves before thought. The Blade of the Starfallen arcs out from my palm and cleaves through a wall of shadows, emancipating them like I'm fanning away smoke from an out-of-control bonfire. Their forms collapse in on themselves, folding into bursts of oily light.

But they don't vanish.

What the . . . ?

Their shadows smear along the stone like wet paint, writhing as if trying to reassemble.

I keep moving, shoulder-checking a twisted half-form with the Gauntlet and feeling something like vestigial bones shattering beneath the blow. The impact sends it flying across the chamber, frozen midcrash, midcrumble, but even before it lands, more are crawling up, bulging and leaking from the rift seams.

I slash through yet another, this one shaped like a hand with teeth where the fingers should be, and it splits clean down the middle. But instead of dissipating, it fragments into two smaller ones. Both still moving. My boots drag through static ash, my lungs burn, and a sound buzzes in my ears, like a needle stuck in the end groove of a record.

The Gauntlet flares, forcing fury into a wall, and stone erupts in jagged fingers, skewering six enemies in a single upward lurch. Their impalement lasts a moment, then the spiked columns begin to crack. The things impaled on them start to *pull themselves down*, chewing through the rock.

Every motion I make is clean. Efficient. Deadly.

And none of it matters.

I'm moving faster than anything else in the world, faster than sound, faster than time, and it's still not enough. This isn't a fight. It's a goddamn loop.

Which is, like, super frustrating.

I reach Zerastian, standing with her head tilted slightly toward me, her movements glacially slow, like her spine is resisting the angle. Her hands hover in front of her, fingers twitching along invisible wires.

"Zerry . . . What did you mean?"

No response. Her eyes flick toward me, dragging across the space like she's underwater.

Thump-thump. Thuuuuuump-thump.

The effect of Control is draining color from the Heart icon in my vision faster than I expected. I assume it's because of the sheer force and weight of what it's holding at bay. The pressure of keeping all these elements slowed down is straining my resources.

I grab Zerry by her shoulders.

"What did you mean, we don't get out of this?!"

"Ssssomething chaaaaaanged."

Thump-thump.

"What?! What changed?! Why can't I seem to make any progress against these assholes? What was the point of me getting the damn Gauntlet?!"

"When the riiiiftsss tooooooorrrrreeeeee . . ."

Thump-thump.

Oh, Jesus Christ. Why can't Synchron work in the other direction? I need to be able to make the people I want to move as fast as I can in Control . . . *move as fast as I can.*

"Yooooouuuu musssst speeeak."

"*I* must speak? What do you mean, *I* must speak?"

Another voice from behind.

"IIIIIII thiiiink sheee meeeeans yooooou."

I turn. Brittany.

"Me?"

"Yoooooouuuu. Bruuuuuuuuce."

"Meeeee 'tiiiiiink sheee riiiiight, miiiii geeeeen'raaaaal."

Thump-thuuuuuuuump.

This is, without question, the worst acid trip I've ever been on.

I grab Brit and Jameson, their molasses-like bodies loping as if they're rag dolls under my grip, and pull them over so that they're facing me, limp and lethargic, like two sleepy kids who just got told they need to get out of bed quickly because the garage is on fire.

"What do you mean *me*, Bruce? What are you on about?!"

"Yoooooooou have to be the one who answers the call."

I worry for half a second that Control has just dropped off without me paying attention because I hear the end of the sentence in real time, clear as a crystal bell. But, looking around, things are still in semi-slow motion.

Thump-thuuuuuummmmmmmp.

But not for long.

That phrase. The one who answers the call.

I first wrote that in a scene between Carpathian and Almeister, and then Richemerion said it when we visited with them; Persephone said it when she was fighting alongside me on the MMP.

And now, Brit's suggesting that, possibly . . . the reason the Blade isn't extinguishing the Ashmourn, that they're looping on themselves . . . the reason Zerastian can't see what possible realities we may face . . . it's because she can't see past the mess I've made of things by an unwillingness to just come correct. To be up front and forthright about who and what I am.

Goddammit. The road to Meridia is just paved with dumb intentions, ain't it?

The blood in the Heart icon is almost fully drained. Not long now. In less than thirty seconds, shit's going to pick back up again.

I had to retrieve the Gauntlet to complete this Quest. To defeat the serpent and close the rift.

But that's not the real point of this Quest, is it?

No, it is the point. You do have to do those things. It's just that, sometimes, Quests are more nuanced than they initially appear. Anyway, you'd better decide how you want to play things soon. It looks as though some Ashmourn are about to devour your girlfriend. {COURTESY MESSAGE #38}

She's not my—Oh, shit!

Seph, curled on her side by a column of broken stone, her fingers still twitching with the echo of the powerful Mezmer that threw her, does not see two of the Ashmourn, tangled into each other like nerves without skin, descending slowly, mouths wide, limbs splitting into . . . well . . . sharper limbs. They're still mid-crawl, but I can see their trajectory. They're going to land teeth first.

I run, hitting their slow-ass asses with the Blade, and it carves them midair, scattering black sinew like exploded ink. They dissolve into static midlunge, and I drop to my knees beside her.

She's breathing. Eyes closed. Brow creased. She looks inappropriately cute for the moment.

"Seph, Seph? Wake up. Seph? You okay?"

Her eyes flutter. Then open.

"What . . ." she says, blinking, ". . . happened?"

I hesitate. The real answer is complicated, so I shrug. "Bit of everything."

Just like when we were in Sheila in the desert, when the rest of the world is under the effect of Control, for whatever reason, she isn't. She's with me. At my pace. It wasn't like that the first time, at Bell's View. But . . . she wasn't yet in the Heart Guard then. So . . .

Another contemplation for another time.

I help her to her feet. "Seph, come on, we don't have long to—"

SHWOOOOOOOOOOOOOOMMMMMMMPPP.

And by "not long," I mean Control is now at its end. The world kicks back into motion like a rubber band snapping to full tension. Time returns in a roar. The Ashmourn scream. The serpent speeds. The blast wave of reengaged chaos sends a shock down my spine.

And this time, it's not metaphysical.

I'm saying that my back gives a real shudder of warning that no Marrowmancy can repair.

Zerastian is screaming something I can't hear. Her hands are up, weaving a line of light, but a bolt of shadow clips her from the side, and she crumples behind a shattered pillar.

Brit's holding her own, but it appears her Summoning is kind of stuttering in and out, unreliable. This field of battle is too unstable. She calls for something large, something named: "Get 'em, Geraldine!" and a Tentasaurian comes hurtling out of nowhere toward the serpent to try and intercept it, but before it can achieve its end, it . . . turns and flies the other way.

"What the fuck?!" Brit screams.

She and I make eye contact, but no words are exchanged. I can simply feel her urging me to *do something.*

I'm trying, Brit! I'm trying!

Jameson is hurling rocks at the Ashmourn because that's, quite literally, all he knows to do, and I am regretting very much that I have not forced the little dude into a Pulse Well so he could find out if there's more to him than he realizes. The Ashmourn swallow him up like a giant fish gobbling up smaller, more stoned fish.

"I can help!" Persephone exclaims as she turns toward the spiral of Ashmourn swallowing up Jame. But even with all her new levels, she's also swamped. Three of them break off, clawing down toward her like tangled wasps. She flares and splits, and two more of her appear beside her like flanking dancers midstrike. Still, it's not enough.

And then . . .

"*¡Ay, ay, ay!*" I hear Perg bellow. The serpent has crashed into him like a John Mayer song. Not full impact. Not yet. Perg has shifted slightly, wedged deeper. But the serpent's head smashes the stone around him like a divine hammer, sending shock waves through his shell, cracks spiraling out like spiderwebs in glass.

He groans. Loud. Deep. Like tectonic plates grinding.

Then . . . he goes silent.

"Perg!" I shout, stumbling through the chaos toward his giant frame, but then—

Another blast.

And another voice.

"BLASPHEMER!"

I look back. Almeister's hand is open, and the light around it ripples, warps, snaps.

I feel it before I see it. The Spell is old, deep, pulled from the Mezmer of something that predates civilization. His eyes are locked on mine. Not confused. Not controlled. Not this time.

Chosen.

"You think you can lie your way into prophecy?" he howls. "You think you can wear divinity like a borrowed coat?"

A blast shoots from his palm and hits me center mass.

I don't fly this time.

I collapse. My legs give, like scaffolding collapsing inward, joints and ankles giving up at once. The Gauntlet flickers. The Blade clatters from my hand and skids across the stone.

"You are not Carpathian Einzgear," he says, stalking forward now, eyes on fire. "You are not the World Saviour. You are an Interloper. A Pretender. A False Witness of the Written Age."

And even though I want to scream back that he's wrong, that he's just been corrupted again, I can't. Because he's not. Not entirely.

Abandoning her attempt to save Jameson, Seph is up once more, dashing after him. "Father, please!" she calls, voice breaking. "Stop! Carpathian is not the enemy!"

But he doesn't stop. He raises one hand, trembling now, as if gathering everything he has left. He's going to end me.

He can end me.

And I know . . . I *know* . . . that if I don't do it now, I never will. Probably because we'll all just die here, but also because I know me. Like . . . I do. I *know* me. And everyone else should know me too. It's the only way.

"Wait!" I croak.

Almeister hesitates.

It feels like everything does. Like even the serpent seems to lean back slightly.

"You're right! Okay? You're right!"

"Carpathian?" Persephone's worried, haunted expression is too much to look at, so I turn my head away.

"I'm not who I have claimed to be. You're right. I'm not the Saviour."

Almeister narrows his eyes.

"I'm not Carpathian Einzgear."

The words burn. In my chest, in my throat. I take a breath. Maybe my last, but to hell with it.

"My name is . . ." It wedges in my voice box. I try again. "My name is . . ."

The entire known universe freezes just long enough for me to get it out.

"Bruce. I'm Bruce. My name is Bruce Silver."

Which is, for some reason, the first time I've realized how much it *really* does sound like . . .

CHAPTER FIFTY-THREE

"Once Upon a Time in Meridia." Part 7

Brucillian?"

Moridius said the name like it was a mistake. Like the syllables had slipped from his tongue unbidden, an error of thought more than speech.

He and the Super Vizier moved quickly along the starboard corridor of the vessel, wind hissing between the slats as lanterns swung above them. Mael stood at the prow, silhouetted in gold, watching the horizon.

They kept their voices low.

"So it would seem," the Super Vizier said.

"How did you—?"

"The Guardian passed along word."

"But . . . Brucillian . . . is not *real*."

"That had been the assumption, yes."

They passed a deckhand, who glanced up, then looked away just as fast. The Super Vizier didn't pause. Her robe whipped in the salt air as they turned sharply toward the underdeck stair.

"No. The name was introduced," Moridius continued, voice still low but tight, "as . . . as a fiction, I thought. A narrative virus meant to dilute the legend of Einzgear."

"That was the story."

They stopped beneath the overhang by the cargo rig. The shadows there thickened the lines on her face. Wood creaked beneath their feet. Somewhere above, Driftclaws shrieked like an omen on loop.

"But now?"

She didn't answer until the wind lulled. Then:

"Now . . . he has arrived."

Moridius stared at her. "So the Guardian lied to us?"

"No," she said, voice calm. "They simply failed to inform us of everything."

"Semantics."

"Agreed. And is that really an argument you believe yourself in a position to win?"

His jaw tightened. She stepped toward the hold where the scrying basin had been mounted into an old barrel of Brineback glass, pulsing now with recent signals.

"The distinction is this: We never *needed* Brucillian to be real. We needed only the world to *believe* he was. That he turns out to be is a happy advantage we now hold. The Resistance has spent generations defending the *idea* of a Saviour; now, they must question whether such a thing really, truly even exists. That kind of fracture is harder to heal than any wound."

Moridius hovered near the hatch. "And what of the Heart Guard? They were to remain united under Carpathian. Now this Brucillian steps forward, midbattle no less, and declares himself the bearer of the Gauntlet?"

"Yes. As I say . . . To. Our. Advantage.

Moridius paused. "And Mael? He was supposed to signal for reattachment so we could trap Carpathian. Use his sentiment against him."

"He still will."

"But—"

"Mael needn't know a thing. Yet."

"But he—"

"When the time comes, we will still use him to draw Carpathian. Or Brucillian. Or whoever this impostor claims to be. He could call himself the Weeping Moon or Harold the Benevolent for all I care." She smiled a sickly sweet smile. "A Saviour by any other name, as they say."

"How can you be sure this won't disrupt everything?"

"Because he is not a man. He is a symbol. When a man breaks, you destroy the man. But when a symbol breaks, you destroy everything it represents. It's like tearing the spine out of a book. Once you're rid of the thing holding the pages together, they drift away . . . and the story is forgotten."

Moridius's brow furrowed as he contemplated the notion. She laughed to herself, amused at the loyal, lumber-headed Templar in front of her, then she stroked his cheek and set off to plan the next chapter in the story of the Saviour's unraveling.

CHAPTER FIFTY-FOUR

"Br . . . Bru . . . Bru . . ."

Seph looks like someone who just got clocked with an aluminum bat and she's still trying to remember how vowels work. Her eyes are locked on me, not blinking, not moving, trying to sort a name from a wound.

"Bruce. Silver. From St. Louis."

"Saint . . . Lew-is?"

The expression on her face isn't one of anger. Not exactly. It's something harder to place. Like her mind is trying to glue two halves of a myth together and realizing the seam won't hold.

And in this split second, I wonder if I just did the right thing.

Not morally, maybe. Morally, I feel pretty sure I did.

But tactically. Strategically. The way you sometimes do the wrong thing because you know it's the only card that keeps you in the game long enough to matter.

Hell, maybe this was ever the only way forward. Maybe it always had to come to this: The inevitable moment when the story turns itself around and demands of the author rather than the author demanding of it.

I try to tell myself it wouldn't have changed much. That the Guardian still would've shuffled the board. That reality would've cracked somewhere anyway. That the walls would've split open all the same, and everything sharp would've come pouring out.

Still, the part of me that loves fantasies wonders if all of this could've been avoided. If the splintering, the shock, the fallout breaking through the seams . . . If it all goes back to one moment. One single, solitary instant.

If I should've just come clean way back when Almeister said . . .

"You're not Carpathian?"

Her voice is small. In fact, I can barely hear her over the—

"Look out!" The column above us ruptures as a slick-jointed Ashmourn unfurls from the upper scaffolding like a thrown net of limbs and bone. "We can talk about it later!"

I grab Seph by the waist, dragging her down beside the base of the fractured stone pillar just as the thing hits the ground like a spat curse. It rolls once, reorganizes itself midspin, and comes lunging again. But I don't give it the chance to reach its destination.

The Blade roars to life as if the syllables of my name have turned some kind of key inside it. I pivot low and slash upward, the edge cutting the Ashmourn clean across the torso. There's a delay, maybe half a breath, before the upper half slides away, vaporizing before it hits the stone.

Seph scrambles backward, hand braced against the floor, eyes wide. "But—"

"Seriously, I like you so much, and I really wanna talk about it, but we gotta make moves!"

I yank her upright and push her toward where Brit's signal fire flickers low against the exposed, swirling sky. Seph doesn't argue. Which means the shock hasn't worn off.

Good.

The chamber is chaos incarnate.

To our right, the serpent rears up and coils again, half wrapped around Perg's shell like a constrictor trying to make a snail into soup. His frame remains wedged sideways into the opening, body pulsing with the strain of keeping the stone from collapsing under him. Cracks spiral across his surface like striations of light beneath glass.

He's not groaning or cracking wise. Which is profoundly worrying.

Straight ahead, Ashmourn are everywhere. They spill from every break in the rift, crawling on ceilings, clinging to broken arches, leaping in sick spirals toward anything breathing. Jameson is surrounded near a shattered column, still hurling debris with both hands and shouting things like, "Come den, you dry-bone sket! Tek de whole bloodclaat puzzle!"

Brit has scrambled up to a collapsed mezzanine-like something to try and get her Summons to hold. Her gestures are jerky, wild. She's lost control of whatever she was trying to call next.

Zerastian is gone from sight, last spied by me behind a sloped slab of fractured obsidian with one hand raised, light crawling up her arm like it was trying to decide whether to stay or leave her body. I don't know if she's—

"He must be exposed!" Almeister has stopped casting at me, but is now knelt down by the center dais, one knee on the stone, head bowed, the Guardian's imposed glow still radiating off his shoulders. "He must be KNOWN!"

Ashmourn turn and swoop in my direction. And like a defensive lineman's twitch reaction responding to an oncoming offensive assault, the Gauntlet tightens on my arm like it finally recognizes the wearer. My fingers twitch, and the world responds. The stone at my feet shifts. My boots seem to hold firmer. The raging torment doesn't tear at me the same, doesn't generate the same kind of fear. I feel . . .

I feel like the best version of myself.

I raise the Blade again and sprint directly toward the foe. Or . . . foes. Not sure about the singular/plural thing when it comes to Ashmourn.

Seph follows a half beat behind me. She's stopped seeking clarification, but I can almost feel the shape of her questions forming inside her like teeth growing beneath the gum.

A separated Ashmourn, tall and skeletal, with hands like scythes and a mask of molten iron instead of a face, steps in my way. Which is the last thing it will ever do.

The Blade splits it from crown to crotch, and the pieces of ash waft away, each turning to pure vapor and shrieking into evermore.

Seph vaults the wreckage behind me and lands lightly just ahead of me. She turns her head. The Mezmer at her fingertips hasn't flared yet, but her hands are up now, eyes sharper.

We reach the junction where the ridge splits; upward toward Brit's perch or down toward the column where Jameson's being swallowed whole.

Seph glances toward the monkey. Then back to me.

I nod toward the mezzanine. "Go help her. Stabilize the high ground." Seph hesitates. "Please."

Her eyes narrow, and she peels away without a word, cloak snapping as she leaps to the upper incline, scattering a cluster of winged Ashmourn midflight. Her ascent is clean, furious, precise. I watch her with a moment's regret before I cast off to reach Jameson.

He's become pinned flat against the base of a collapsed shrine, one foot jammed into the ribs of an Ashmourn that's halfway through turning itself inside out to devour him. Another's clambering over the rubble, bent backward at the waist, head dragging behind it like a bag of broken glass. A third shrieks as it closes from above, teeth blooming like petals in a mouth not meant to open.

I land between the lot of them.

The Gauntlet slams downward and sends a burst of energy and rock up from the floor. If the Stoneheart gloves were a nice hotel room, the Gauntlet is like getting upgraded eleven room classes to an executive suite with an ocean view.

Spikes of light and disengaged rock spear the shrieker through its maw, pinning it to a broken shelf. I pivot and drive my shoulder into the torso of the second, flipping it into the shrine wall. Curiously, it splinters apart with the noise of rotting lumber, like being impacted by the force of the Gauntlet crystalized its ashen form into something more permanent. And easily destructed.

The third rears to pounce, but I swing low and wide, dragging the Blade across the earth. When it arcs upward, it detonates in an eruption of stone, smoke, and starfire that blasts upward through its core, spine unraveling like wet rope. Its halves slam the ceiling so hard they paint the stone with what's left of its scream.

Jameson blinks. "Mi tink ya done gon' evolve, mi big boss, Bruce."

"Can you walk?"

He nods, leaps to his feet, and scrambles up, favoring his left side as he bolts back into the fray. I whirl back into motion, eyes scanning for the next threat, but the Ashmourn are already reacting to the shift.

I can see it. The way they hesitate before charging, the way their malformed heads tilt, not toward me but toward the weapons I carry. They recognize something.

I feel a grin spreading across my lips. I have a feeling I look like Pennywise, but I'll confront my probable psychosis later. I move now like I haven't ever before. Not as Carpathian, not even as Bruce on his best day. I move like someone who stopped asking for permission and started answering for himself.

It's like I can breathe for the first time in a long time.

Another Ashmourn drops from above. Too many limbs. None of them useful, so I remove them all. The Blade carves. The Gauntlet follows, shattering a trio of stragglers as they sprint from the far wall. Light punches through them like fists from the earth. No fanfare. No mercy.

I pivot again and leap, landing hard in a circle of five converging attackers, and I simply . . . *do not stop swinging.* The air feels thinner, sharper. Like I've moved up a tier of reality, and gravity's still catching up with me.

I look to see that Seph has reached Brit. They're back-to-back, a cyclone of light and wild Summons, a kind of fire tearing through one side of the open ridge while threads of golden Mezmer streak across the other. It appears that Brit has control of her Summoning once more, because Geraldine has returned, shrieking and lashing onto the serpent's midsection with talons of pure force, wrenching at its scales like a fever dream made of rope and rage. Seph flares beside, both hands raised, launching a twin helix of flame-bound Mezmer that strikes the serpent's brow and sends it lurching off Perg's shell with a guttural hiss.

"Don't burn Perg!"

"Worry about yourself!" Brit shouts back at me.

I spin and unleash on the Ashmourn. The Blade of the Starfallen doesn't just sing—it screams. With every swing, it rends through the Guardian's shadow minions like a black Damascus cleaver cutting through raw meat, trailing streamers of white flame that linger in the air like afterimages of salvation. The Gauntlet pulses with rhythm now, its weight thrumming a drumbeat in concert with my Heart that tells me when to move, when to strike, when to end.

THUMP-THUMP. THUMP-THUMP.

A half-formed Ashmourn, its rib cage still stitching itself from shadow, rises ahead. The Gauntlet flexes. Stone answers. A spire bursts from the floor, skewering it midrise, and the rib cage collapses around the spike like broken scaffolding.

To the left, another one. Loping. Grinning. I don't dodge; I command. The Gauntlet flares, and the ground beneath it liquefies for a heartbeat, then hardens midstride, trapping its legs like amber. A swipe with the Blade takes its calcified head clean off.

A shriek pulls my gaze to the mezzanine above. Brit and Seph are about to be overrun.

"You okay?" I yell.

"Fuck does it look like?!"

The air above them is a smear of velocity and shrieking light, as if the sky itself forgot how to hold dimension. Brit's arm moves like a metronome wired to a faulting power line. Geraldine the Tentasaurian barrels into a cluster of incoming Ashmourn, but the impact barely slows the tide. They keep coming, climbing over her body like ants on a dying predator. She screeches, throwing them off with a whip of her longest limb, but she's staggering, being overpowered in all possible ways.

Beside her, Seph is twisting ribbons of Mezmer fire through the air like she's a next-gen Matador. *God, I hope they can keep Perg . . .*

Just as I start to think it, the Ashmourn change tactics.

They're sacrificing, hurling themselves toward the serpent's assaulted midsection. The essences of the forfeit fuse into its scales like they're crafting a new directive: Drag it. Pull it through. And the only way through . . .

Is through Perg.

The Ashmourn clamber over his shell, driving spectral chains into the stone around him, trying to wedge open the rift just enough to draw the serpent along. I see Perg's body shudder, the cracks in his plating now running deeper than he can likely bear.

Brit sees it too.

"They're trying to use him as a fucking drawbridge!" she yells, yanking Geraldine's Summon line tight in a desperate redirect.

Geraldine lurches, swatting two away, but the gesture costs her. An Ashmourn spears through her wing, snapping her from the air and sending her spiraling away.

"Geraldine!" Brit wails.

The same Ashmourn figure that just took out Geraldine now turns its attention to Brit, aiming to keep her from interfering further.

I fling the Blade. Not a throw—a hurl of will. It spins, end over end, searing a path through the air before it catches the leaper in the chest and explodes into a burst of light so sharp I think my retinas are burned away for a moment, until the Blade ricochets back to my hand before I can miss it, and I see it land there.

I'm Iron Man AND Thor? This is so fancy!

While my attention is focused on how impressive I have now become, the ashborne echo of something terrible lurches for me from the side. A wide, six-limbed brute lurches toward me, shoulder first, carrying some strange hooked weapon made of fused bones and talons.

Serves me right for stopping to feel myself instead of keeping eyes on the goal.

I sidestep the thing. Spin. The Blade catches its midsection and tears a seam through it like a zipper undone. Its body pulls apart like it was never solid to begin with, but this time . . . the light that escapes spreads. It spreads out, catching hold of a passel of other Ashmourn and burning them away as well. The Blade has a transitive property of asshole-obliterating that I appear to have now unlocked.

God, it is really hard not to pause and gloat, but . . .

CRAAAAAAAAACK!

Oh shit. That's the sound of a shell no longer holding its shape.

I whip my head around and see . . .

Perg.

His massive frame seizes, every part of him drawn tight before collapsing inward like a slow implosion. The deep cracks running across his carapace shatter, and he falls. Straight down. Like the weight of Meridia itself pressed a thumb into the center of his back and drove him free from the stone. His impact shakes the world, fanning debris out in all directions.

And when the dust clears, he's smaller, about the size of a large dog, limbs curled, head tucked, streaked with ruptured lines of sacrifice.

"Mi little big Perg!" Jameson bellows from across the fray. He sprints, barreling through two Ashmourn, striking them aside with his improvised boom stick as he goes. "Mi bredda!" He puts his ear near Perg's mouth. "Him alive, but we need hurry!"

Taking advantage of the now unimpeded opening, the serpent heaves forward. Its body flows through the rupture, unspooling with malicious intent, each scale catching the now abundant light like a drawn blade, its eyes fixed on me.

I draw back the Blade with one hand and the Gauntlet with the other, and ready myself to . . . I don't know. Something awesome or awful. Doesn't feel like there's an in-between.

Then, from seemingly out of nowhere, Seph lands beside me, red hair stuck to her face, one hand smudged with ash, the other crackling with Mezmer still hot from the last strike.

Less than an eyeblink passes before she speaks words I've never heard and couldn't begin to replicate (sounds kind of like throat singing), and light pours from her hand in a line, arcing upward in a curve like a scythe.

It bends midair, shimmering with a kaleidoscopic burn. It splits into four, then eight, forming its own countervailing spectral serpents of flame that lash forward in a spinning helix. Each strikes a different point of the serpent's body. The creature reels, flailing against the tethers, but Seph's not done.

Her second hand lifts, palm outward, and a pulse detonates from her chest like a second heartbeat. One of her Pyreheart Spells. It fans forward in concentric rings, burning away everything in a ten-foot radius. The Ashmourn in the path crumble to cinders midlunge.

Seph screams in what sounds like invocation, and the rings tighten, pulling the tethers taut. The serpent shrieks as it's yanked back, spine twisting violently.

That's my cue.

I launch forward, Blade in one hand, Gauntlet on the other. The Blade flashes once, twice, carving clean across the serpent's snout, while the Gauntlet follows with a seismic slam to its body, so long that I can barely see the end of it trailing somewhere in the great distance beyond.

Then . . . Seph splits.

Three of her. Then four. And then . . .

I split too.

It's not imaginary this time. Not her Mezmer. It's mine. The Synchron flares like a spark catching dry hay. Two copies of me, three, each one real enough to draw blood.

One Bruce spins forward with the Blade, carving down a column of Ashmourn before kicking off the wall and vanishing in smoke. Another hurls a stone through a vortex of Mezmer, shattering a shrieker midpounce. The third ducks low, slides across the ash, and launches upward through a wave of writhing limbs with the Gauntlet raised, punching through a rib cage and out the other side.

We don't coordinate; we harmonize. I look to see that Seph has a smile on her face. (A kind of maniacal smile, but still . . . Smile's a smile.)

Of course she does. This is the fight she's dreamed of. The moment she rehearsed in her bones. Side by side with the man she thought was Carpathian. Her story, finally made flesh.

Even if I'm not him.

As they say: If you can't kill with the one you love, kill with the one you're with.

Across the chamber, one of the Sephs lifts a hand, and a whip of fire lashes toward the serpent's flank. The real Seph spins and strikes in tandem, igniting the ground beneath it.

Another points toward Jameson and Perg, huddled on the ground, and a ripple of light clears the Ashmourn bearing down on him like they were never there.

Brit is still on the mezzanine, clinging to a fractured strut with one hand while flinging down bursts of Triple R with the other. It's only marginally helpful, but she's giving it her all.

Behind a shattered archway near the rift's lip, Zerastian finally stirs. Her hand twitches once, then again. She's still slumped, but I catch the subtle shift in her posture, the straightening of her back, the turn of her head. Her fingers trail up into the air and begin sketching shapes. Not fast, but deliberate. Measured. She's still in it.

Sparked by her will, an Eidolon Drone flares to life on the stone beside her and zips up toward the rift in a sharp arc. Another lifts and hovers nearby, flickering with telemetry.

One of the drones zips wide, light strobing in a tight pattern as it scans for weak points. The other snaps into position above her shoulder, its core lens rotating through spectrums as data floods her Neural Crown. Zerastian's lips move, silent commands routing through the circlet's filament array. The drone near the rift flares brighter, then bolts forward. A third disk rises; smaller, sleeker. This one dives straight into the mouth of the breach.

She's mapping the serpent, who never sees it coming.

And neither do the Ashmourn.

Zerastian's hand flicks again. The drones flare brighter, and she throws something small and wand-shaped from her belt.

A Pyrestick.

It tumbles end over end, and the moment it hits one of the Ashmourn, it detonates in a flare-burst of searing light. The rift pulses. Once. Twice.

The serpent feels it too.

A flash of white-hot energy cascades outward, and the serpent *recoils, disoriented.* The remaining Ashmourn scatter, screeching in distorted keys as they sputter and spark, unable to absorb or translate the new trajectory Zerastian's tether has carved.

We're winning. We're actually doing it. We're going to win. We're going to complete the Quest.

The victory lap I'm taking in my mind is, however, cut short by a sound like teeth grinding through granite.

The dais where Almeister remains bowed shatters beneath him. It ignites into something like a white fire and . . .

. . . the solid ground upon which he is knelt appears no longer solid, and he is pulled down into the rift exposing the Mid-Meridian Plane like a dirty tissue being sucked down a drainpipe.

CHAPTER FIFTY-FIVE

FATHER!" Seph's voice cracks like glass underfoot.

She lunges forward, but I'm already moving, Gauntlet raised, Blade humming with the heat of what's to come. The rift's pull is stronger now, less a tear in the world and more a mouth, wide and widening, chewing through stone and light and anything that stands too near.

I look down, but I can't see him through the haze of dispersing Ashmourn and the intense pull of stories yet untold that seem to want to rise up and enter the world.

A tower in a snowfield, crowned with crows. A woman in a red cloak with a boy holding a wooden sword. A door carved in bone. A child with antlers riding a stag. A knight made of mirrors. A figure lighting a pipe on a ship made of beetle shells. Each one thrashing to be loose from its . . . gestation.

"Save him!" Seph lurches forward, her hand seizing my forearm, dragging at me like she can pull both of us across the void with willpower alone.

I would if I could. Would help save him. Would help save Sumnut. Would help salvage all the lost souls who yearn to have their voices heard, their realities restored.

But I have a Quest to complete.

The serpent surges one last time.

I raise the Blade.

The Gauntlet flares.

I leap.

Swing.

Once.

Twice.

The first hit severs scale.

The second splits the jaw.

The third . . .

The third is the end.

The serpent comes apart in stages. Spine first. Then everything.

Monumental. More, even, than the collapse of some great structure—the fall of the Colossus of Rhodes, maybe. Like the collapsing of a dying star.

Kilostryde after kilostryde, a chain of failure unspooling from the wound in the world. Segments of gleaming black roll across the wretched expanse of Meridia, each segment as long as a city block, slapping down in waves like a coastline of nightmares giving way to gravity.

Honestly, there aren't enough similes to do it justice.

It just . . . keeps going until the last of it lands, twitching, then folding still; a ruin stitched from time and wrong intent.

I take a breath to gather myself, because . . . holy shit. And then I step toward the rift.

"Zerry!" I call out. "You still good?"

"Yes?" comes the small, exhausted, battered voice from behind me.

"Do you have something to help close this up?"

A sigh. "Yes. One moment."

"Fast moment, please?"

"Wait," Seph says behind me. Her voice isn't loud, but it stops me cold. "You're going to close it?"

I turn. "Yeah. I have to. That's the Quest, and . . . y'know . . . Ninth Guardian can't be allowed to rewrite—"

"But Father is there!"

"I know, but—"

"You're not even going to try to get him back?!"

"Seph—"

"Don't call me that!"

The still roiling sound of the open rift fades into the background for a moment. Everything turns muddy, like it's being drowned.

"Persephone," I start. "Please, we can—"

"Bruce? Silver?"

"Well . . . Silvert, actually, but—"

"Bruce Silver isn't even your name?! How are you here?! Why are you here?! Why do you look like Carpathian?! *What did you do to him?!*"

That last one hits somewhere deeper in my Heart, behind the part of me that still believes in hiding. It's not a question. It's a wound voiced aloud. And for a second, I forget about the rift, the Quest, the serpent.

I can feel her waiting for an answer I don't know how to give.

I killed him? Maybe?

Or maybe I just stole his skin.

My throat tightens. Words pile up and fall over each other before they can make it out.

"I didn't . . . I didn't do it to him," I say, but my voice sounds far away. Smaller than it should. "Or, I did, but—"

That's all I get out.

WHAM.

Mezmer fire slams me square in the chest, a corkscrew of golden pressure that lifts me an inch off the ground and drops me like a sack of bowling balls thrown from a three-story building.

I hit the stone, gasp, and lift my eyes to see Seph—cloak torn, hair wild, arms burning with the full force of her will—coming right at me. Mezmer curls off her like smoke from a battlefield, each step launching another Spell, rings, lashes, jagged streaks of flame and golden force aimed square at my chest.

I brace.

BLAM.

I cough. Like, hard. "Seph, what are you—?"

The next strike hits harder still. A radiating burst, wide, concussive. I'm sent skidding across broken stone, my shoulder catching on a jag of obsidian that tears the sleeve of my swell duds and exposes skin beneath.

She doesn't let up. Her feet churn dust and ash as she moves, and then . . . she splits.

One Seph becomes two. Then four. Then six. They fan out. One rushes for the rift. Another spirals wide, casting with both hands, Mezmer flaring into the shape of a blade. Two more lift their arms and fire twin beams of light that rake the stone in crisscrossing arcs, each of them real enough to wound. Each of them fighting against the same thing.

Me.

I grunt, roll, come up low.

"Seph—Please—"

The twin beams converge. I pivot, deflect them with a flick of the Blade. One copy closes the gap, tries to bind me in Mezmer thread. I cut it midstride, the Blade severing its reality clean.

"Seph, listen to me—"

"That is NOT MY NAME!" The bellow echoes off the heavens. "JUST LIKE YOURS IS NOT CARPATHIAN EINZGEAR!"

Her cloak whips outward in a gust that doesn't belong to the wind. Light fractures along her arms, Mezmer pulsing wild and loose, no longer tethered to formal pattern or rite. Spears of energy form in her hand. She hurls them; I sidestep (barely), and they explode behind me, sending a spiral of stone shards upward like a reverse avalanche.

Reluctantly, I raise the Gauntlet. But . . .

Too slow.

She crashes into me with a second Spell, something like a hammer made of mirrored force and echoing pain. It hits my sternum; I don't feel the crack until I'm airborne. I land on my back.

Again.

No breath. Just faint ringing.

Goddamn, she's strong. But not just with the kind of strength you get from training. This isn't strength born of simply discipline or technique. This is strength that has been forged in waiting. In the unknown stretches of time where Persephone wandered the empty streets of Bell's View, no one beside her. No hand in hers. No answer from the sky. Waiting for the man who she believed would return. Who wrote himself into legend and left her behind to live beneath it.

She worked. She trained. She spun Spells in the dark, pushed every boundary. Not to impress him but to match him. To be his equal when he came back. To be perfect. To be worthy.

And now, here she is.

Perfect.

Worthy.

And utterly furious.

The next copy hurls a bolt the size of a ballista shaft at my head. I duck, and the stone behind me erupts. Two more dive from opposite angles, spinning rings of Mezmer in their hands. I swipe the Blade. Hit one. The other crashes into my shoulder and sends me sprawling again.

There is no pause, no space between these attacks. Just her, everywhere, a war born of heartbreak and expectation.

And when I look up through the haze of my own pain, there is a platoon of her. All of them real enough to kill.

"Please, please, Persephone, just—"

WHAM.

Not a blast from her this time. A blast at her.

A beam of Randolf's Radiant Ray slices into the Persephones from above. It punches through the nearest copies like a blade through brittle glass, shattering them midformation. I spot Brit, one arm braced against stone, the other still outstretched, palm smoking faintly from the cast.

"NO!" I scream and tear forward. "DON'T!"

Seph stumbles, drops to a knee, but before I reach her, she whirls once more, eyes burning, one hand already flaring. She throws a concussive blast point-blank, hitting me full force, lifting me clean off my feet, and hurling me back yet again.

I crash into the stone, coughing blood. I push off it. She moves.

Running for the rift.

I haul up, sprinting through the pain. "Persephone!"

I catch her at the edge, putting arms around her waist in the last instant. She fights with everything she has, arms and elbows slamming into my chest, jaw, temple, like a banshee.

"Let me go! Let me go! False Prophet!"

I grip her tighter, wrench her away from the brink. We tumble, scrape, roll. She winds up on top of me, pounding at my face. I try to deflect without doing her harm, but then . . .

She picks up a rock. Nothing magical, nothing special, just a good, old-fashioned stone that she can bash my head in with and . . . I do the hardest thing I've ever done.

"I'm sorry."

Fire pours through me. Force follows. Pure, unfiltered Mezmer fills my every molecule, pouring strength into my spine, tightening every muscle with sacred finality. It floods my shoulder, braces my stance.

It breaks everything soft inside me to do what comes next.

Grabbing her with my Gauntleted hand . . . I hurl her away.

A full-bodied, thunderous, Mezmerically assisted throw, like the fire in my arm decides the anguish is its own and pours itself into the act. She sails across the chamber in a blur of undampened heartache, crashing into a fractured archway with a sound that feels like ripping loose the last stitch holding my soul together.

"**ZERRY!**" I roar, voice stripped to the bone. "**CLOSE IT! NOW!**"

Zerastian doesn't hesitate.

The drones above flicker once, then twice. The smallest dives toward the rift like a hummingbird streaking toward the sun. It hits the edge and detonates. The aperture stutters.

Another drone follows, slamming into the opposite arc of the breach.

Lines begin to trace themselves in the air. Lines of intent; glowing calligraphy etched into the fabric of the rift itself, as if Zerastian is signing her name across an open wound in space and telling it, firmly, that it is time to heal.

The rift groans. The air begins to twist inward. Not like a vacuum, like a disappointed sigh. A third drone fires past my ear, a blur, planting itself like a piton just above the lip of the rift.

Zerastian staggers upright, arms raised, Neural Crown fully lit, Tether Sync crackling down the length of her wrist in fitful pulses of white.

"*FATHER!*" Persephone wails.

I turn back to the breach.

And . . . I can see them. Can I? I think I can.

Almeister, limping and scorched, shoulder dislocated, blood caking his beard. Sumnut, one arm wrapped around him, the other spinning his whip-blade in wide, defensive arcs as the remaining Ashmourn pour upon them like locusts with too many legs.

Sumnut looks up.

He sees me.

"Go!" he bellows, voice carrying through dimensional strain like a shot from a celestial cannon. "I will see to his safety until we meet again!"

The rift begins to contract.

The images on the other side stretch. Elongate. Like I'm watching them through a dilating iris. Sumnut's shape narrows, his whip flicking in one final blur. Al's eyes—those ragged, bright, haunted eyes—lock with mine.

And the rift seals.

No explosion. No scream. No burst of light. It simply ends. A soundless blink. The wound closes, and the silence that follows . . .

Is total.

CHAPTER FIFTY-SIX

I don't hear her walk in. Not until she's already in the room, standing right behind me, hand on the back of my chair, eyes tracing what I've got pulled up on my laptop screen.

"How's it going?"

I jolt, slap the laptop closed, and spin, finally realizing she's there.

"Jesus. I didn't hear you come in."

"I noticed. How's it going?"

"Um, okay." It's then that I notice what she has on. Black sweater, boots, delicate earrings that catch the glow from the desk lamp. Hair pulled back. Casual, but the kind of casual you do on purpose. "Is it time to go?"

"Not exactly."

I glance at the clock. 8:51 p.m.

"What . . . I thought we were supposed to be there at 8:00."

"We were."

"Why didn't you come interrupt me?"

"I didn't want to . . . You looked like you were really into it. I kept peeking in to see if you were at a stopping place, but until now, you didn't look like you were. I only came in now because you were just kind of staring at the screen and not typing."

"Well . . . Jesus, Mol. Now I feel—"

"Don't. It's okay. I made the choice not to bother you."

"Yeah, but we missed it. I didn't even realize . . . Christ." I rub my eyes. My chest tightens with something uglier.

She shrugs a little. "It's really not a big deal."

"It kind of is!" I don't mean to snap, but it comes out sharper than I want.

She takes a breath. "Why don't I—?" she starts out, but I spin in the chair, stop her.

"No, look, I just . . . I'm sorry."

"It's fine."

"But it's not, though. You got dressed. You were waiting. Why didn't you interrupt me?"

"Because . . ."

"Because what?"

"Because I didn't want to fight tonight."

It hits me like a sack of bowling balls thrown from a three-story building.

"Yeah," I say. "Okay."

She breathes in and out through her nose, strokes my head.

"But," she says, "now that you've . . . taken a break. Do you wanna go out? Just you and me? Get something to eat? Talk?"

"About . . . what?"

"No, not like that. I mean just . . . talk. I feel like . . . I feel like we haven't just talked in a while, and I just wanna . . . hear how you're doing."

She's so pretty. The freckles beneath her eyes make her look like . . . I dunno. Like herself. Which is maybe more than I deserve sometimes.

"Yeah," I reply finally. "Yeah, I'd like that." I glance down at my closed laptop. "I just . . ."

". . . What?"

"I was just . . . I feel like I'm this close to something really cool happening in the chapter I'm writing right now, and—"

"I get it," she cuts me off. She leans down and kisses me on the head. "I get it."

She turns and heads for the door.

"Just, like, fifteen minutes," I say to her back.

She stops, turns to face me, and smiles.

". . . Okay."

There is a kind of . . . resolve? In it? Or no, not resolve. What's the . . . ?

Defeat.

That's what it is.

"Promise," I promise.

". . . Okay," she says again, her toothless smile widening, causing her eyes to crinkle.

She turns back to the door, opens it, steps out, and closes it quietly behind her. I stare at the closed door for a few seconds . . . before opening the laptop again and proceeding to write once more for what will turn out to be the rest of the night . . .

Stillness clings to the air like ash after a fire.

The rift is gone. No trace left but the warped edge of the stone where it once chewed its way through the chamber. The quiet isn't relief; it's anxiety. Like the world itself has paused to process what just happened and is nervous about what happens next.

Or maybe that's just me.

I'm hunched on one knee, Gauntlet smoking faintly, which I didn't know it could do. The Blade is slack in my grip. Every joint in my body groans like they're holding in screams.

Behind me, a dry croak rises from the rubble.

". . . *Ay, mis huevos.*"

My head jerks toward the sound. Perg's voice, hoarse but audible.

I sheathe the Blade and crawl toward him. Jameson is attempting to force a blunt into his snail lips.

"Ye need med'cine, mi big little snail. Puffin up now."

"Perg? You gonna make it?" I ask him.

"I dunno, homie. I feel like what's his name."

"Humpty Dumpty?" I guess.

"No, Wutzitzname. Was another snail I knew back before I met you. Homie got run over by a golf cart trying to cross the road."

"Okay, lemme try something."

I get right up next to him and wrap him in a hug.

"Whoa, fool! What are you doing? This feels like an unwelcome escalation in our relationship!"

"I'm not . . . Just . . . I need to stitch myself back together too. I think . . ."

I feel like, now that I've unlatched something, I might be able to funnel Synchron *from* me, rather than just to me. At least with members of my Heart Guard. It's the quality I wish I could have had when Lonnaigh was injured after our battle at Garr Haven. I just have an instinct . . .

I close my eyes and breathe in. Not deep—my ribs won't allow it—but enough to feel the inside of me slosh. There's damage: Muscle torn. Hairline-fractured bone. My chest's a war zone, and my limbs are worse. But under all that, something else.

Marrowmancy kicks on like an engine on low idle. Threads of color and light begin weaving through my bones, finding the breaks, knitting the cracks, cinching the strain. And this time, it doesn't stop inside me.

It spills over into Perg.

His shell warms beneath my grip. His deep fractures cinch tighter, the edges losing their crumble. Grit becomes plate. Hairlines smooth. One of the broken ridges reasserts itself with a soft *snap*.

Perg wheezes. "Yo, are you giving me a back massage from the inside?"

"Sort of."

"That feels inappropriate, yet I don't want you to stop. I feel very conflicted."

I lean into it; feel our hearts tug together. Not a metaphor—actual tempo. His beat finds mine. My pulse answers back.

Thump. Thump. Thump.

Then . . . *POP.*

He's back to his original snail size again, fully restored. Then, again . . . *POP.* He embiggens to about the size of a grizzly bear.

"What are you doing?" I ask.

"Flexing. Like wiggling my fingers, but I don't have fingers, so I'm doing this."

POP.

He is my size. Looks me dead in the eyes.

"Thanks, homie."

"I got you, bro."

This would be where we'd give each other a dap and hug it out, but, as noted, no hands, so . . .

"Is he part of it?" Seph's voice. I turn. "Pergamon? Whatever lie this is? Is that even his name?"

I turn to face her. She looks sallow. Sunken. Like she wants desperately to be rageful but isn't sure about what anymore. There's a thin streak of dried blood along her temple. Her lip is split. She looks painfully human in the most agonizing way.

I breathe out. "He, um—"

"And her? Teleri?" She points at Brit, who is making her way over like she's approaching a rabid animal. Which is approximately the case.

"Persephone . . ." she starts.

"What is your name? Your real name?"

Brit clears her throat. "My name is Brittany McAfee."

"What kind of insane name is that?!"

"Listen," I say, hoping to . . . Hell if I know. "I can explain what's going on if you'll just—"

But she doesn't want an explanation. She just wants to rage again.

"And that one?" She points at Jameson. "The one I risked my very life bringing back with a forbidden Ritual? What is he called?!"

"Mi Jameson. Me de Jameson you know. Me always jus' Jameson. Mi only found out 'bout de deception recent. Jus' like you."

I widen my eyes at him to suggest, *Deception?! Not helping!*

"And you." She points an accusing finger at Zerastian. "Who are you?"

"I am Zerastian Teronia, daughter of Hemree and Bondelia Teronia. Exactly who I have always been. I had no idea either, but it does explain why I have been unable to project cognitive probabilities."

"Why?" Seph asks, seemingly reflexively. I don't think she really gives a shit. It's just one of those things you say when you're pissed and the whole world goes white around you.

"I was trying to calculate a timeline that didn't exist," Zerastian replies.

"What in the *skarnadoonkadrella* does that mean?!"

I see Brit wince. I don't know what language Seph is swearing in, but by the look on Brittany's face, whatever Persephone just said appears to be all the worst swear words I can think of rolled into one.

"It means," Zerry goes on, "everything was bending toward him, but I couldn't chart it because he wasn't part of the timeline . . . He *was* the change to it."

"Fool is a one-man Mid-Meridian Plane," Perg posits. "He has the power to reframe things by virtue of his own identity." A beat as everyone stares at him. "I'm just guessing. I think some of that Insight you gave me to tide us over until we found your dad is still hanging around."

Oh, Jesus. I really wish he hadn't—

Seph lifts her arms, fierce energy crackling once again at her fingertips. All of us duck for some reason, as if whatever she's about to do won't just incinerate the whole zone. But then . . .

She lowers her arms, her shoulders sag, her lip begins to quiver, and she starts marching up the fallen carcass of the serpent like it's a gangplank to where the suns above the Mokeisan are shining down. I race after to try and stop her.

"Persephone. Persephone. Please. Please, please, let me explain."

She stops walking but doesn't turn. I wait. Finally, when it's clear that this is all I'm going to get, I speak to her back.

"I don't know how to explain, fully, how it happened. How I'm here. How I got here. How I came to be Carpathian. I could try, but . . ." I trail off because even in a world where Tentasaurians dot the sky and Mezmer fuels the engine of existence, it sounds too outlandish to believe. So, instead, I opt for something that I think she might be able to understand.

"Look, I don't think that matters. What matters is that . . . for a long time, well before I even knew this place existed, that you existed, I've fantasized. I've dreamt of a life that isn't like the one I was living."

I see her shoulder blades tighten through her cloak, because I know she knows what that is.

"And, y'know, the reason I didn't just tell you the truth sooner . . . Well, I thought it was because I didn't want to hurt you more. Or disappoint you. That's a thing I have. I hate . . . Anyway, I was trying to avoid, well, exactly what's happening. Breaking *your* fantasy. Tearing down the dream that kept you going. The belief that I . . . that Carpathian would return. I didn't want to do that to you because . . . Because I didn't want to do that to you."

She shakes. I don't know if she's crying or if she's just trying to keep from turning around and murdering me, but it's maybe both.

"But, look . . . if I'm telling the truth—and at this point, that certainly seems like what I'm doing—I also didn't tell you because I thought that if I believed it hard enough, I could *become* Carpathian. That I could grow into him. But that isn't . . . I can't. No one can. The only way to really, honestly, I guess . . . progress . . . in your life, in your . . . story . . . is to show up to what's real. To be present to what *is*. That's the true path to power. Actual power."

She doesn't respond, and I hate awkward silences, so . . .

"I mean, obviously capital-P Power too, that's the whole reason Pulse Wells exist, and whether I created them or they exist here anyway and Meridia has just been feeding me the details is really beside the point. The point is—"

"Father," she says, back still to me.

"Sorry, what?"

Finally, she faces me again. It's wild. I saw her no more than a minute ago, looking right at me, but I don't recognize her now. Not just in an emotional, abstract way. In a very literal way. I don't recognize the person looking me in the eye.

It's like the Persephone I knew is gone, and some resurrected replica of her is here now.

Which is, obviously, more than a little bit ironic.

"Father," she repeats.

"I know," I say. "But . . . listen. We're gonna get him out of there. You saw Sumnut. He's a bad man, especially for an HR specialist. He'll protect your father. I don't know if you heard him, but he said—"

"You lied to Father. He could see it. I thought it was the corruption causing him to misinterpret, but it wasn't. He saw who you were *despite* his infirmities. Do you have any idea how strong he must be for that to happen?"

"I . . ."

"Everything I have believed is a lie."

"Not—"

"You were not just dishonest with me. You have infected everything I have ever placed my hope in . . ."

"No, no, please—"

". . . And you sought to build a throne on the ruins of my trust."

It feels like my head falls back in slow motion as the virtual bullet she just put through my brain sends me reeling, the remains of my fractured mind spilling out of the back of my skull.

I blink, searching for literally anything I can say, do, or imagine.

There's nothing.

When she realizes that I'm just going to stay here, saying nothing, searching frantically inside myself for some way to apologize, she decides to put the button on the conversation.

"You should have allowed me to jump in after."

And, with that, she rotates her body around slowly like one of those dancing, ceramic ballerina music boxes and marches up and out into the blazing suns light as I watch her silhouette disappear into the distance, hoping that the rays will burn my eyes blind forever.

But then, I blink, because of course I friggin' do, and . . .

Quest: "Defeat, finally and absolutely, ALL [Giant Serpent(s) of the Mokeisan] in order to shutter access to the [Mid-Meridian Plane]." [COMPLETE]

. . . appears before me.

Yay. We did it.

"Don't be so cynical, Bruce. A win is a win."

"Yeah, Bruce . . . It's really f'ing not."

I hear the remaining four come up behind me.

"Mi gen'ral?"

I turn. Jameson offers me the spliff. I appreciate the gesture, but I don't deserve to feel anything but terrible right now. I wave him off.

"So . . ." Brit hazards.

"I don't know," I tell her.

"Do you wanna go find, like, what's her name? Xanaraxa?" Perg asks.

The question is so absurd, I can't even begin to think how to answer.

"I'm not sure we should try and find anyone else," I say. "I think, maybe, we should consider wandering in the desert until I fall over. Or I should. You all can do what you want."

"You mean like *Jesus*," Perg says, pronouncing it *Hay-soos*.

"Excuse me?"

"Isn't that how the story goes? Jesus—of Nazareth; that's the one I'm talking about, not Jesus of des Moines or whoever—spent, like, forty days or something wandering, being tempted by the devil, all that shit, in order for him to prove he was the true Messiah. I think. I didn't really read about it. I think you just left the TV on one time, and some dude in a shiny suit asking for money started talking about it."

"What's a tee-vee?" Zerastian asks.

"I'll explain . . . later," Brit answers.

I take a look at the precog.

"How about you?" I ask. "Do you—?"

"I think so."

"You know what I was going to—?"

"I think so."

"So are your precog Abilities now fully—"

"I think so."

I pause. "Can you help us plot a path forward that avoids the Ninth Guardian anticipating our every move and that helps us avoid these kinds of calamities?"

"Perhaps."

"But perhaps not?"

"That is how it works. But I can now see a strand. Just one. A sliver among ruin and ruin and ruin, but it *is* there. A possible story where the Guardian falls, where the Rebellion holds. But . . ."

"But what?"

"But it will come at a cost."

Almost immediately, a scene from one of the books shows up in my memory. Almeister and Carpathian sitting around a fire, discussing Richemerion and Carpathian's burden. Regarding the Warden, Almeister had said . . .

"They choose those who have never asked for it but will bear it nonetheless. They guard those who would carry the weight of a responsibility they did not ask for. Those willing to, as they say . . . answer the call."

The fire snapped, sending a spray of sparks spiraling upward. Carpathian's fingers moved absently, tracing the line of his collarbone, the pulse of the Heart beneath yet unchanging.

"Then it is not power," he said. "It is a burden."

Almeister inclined his head, a slow gesture. "It is both. Protection always is."

Carpathian's eyes remained on the fire. "And what is the cost?" he asked.

"To endure," Almeister said. "Without reprieve. Without end. To guard others even when they do not ask to be guarded."

I'm unsure what's going on lately that I seem to be able to remember sections, whole passages of things I wrote, but since the MMP, a lot has changed.

Which was, I suppose, the whole point of having been there.

I look back at the destruction we wrought. The place where the rift to the plane opened. The slain Ashmourn, the overwhelming serpent cadaver upon which we stand.

I look at Brit, Jameson, and Perg. They all shrug. I get it. What else do any of us have left?

And then, finally, I look back at Zerastian.

"A cost?" I repeat. She nods.

I feel the Gauntlet on my palm . . .

"Yeah, well."

. . . rest my other hand on the hilt of the Blade . . .

"That's the gig, right?"

. . . stretch my neck . . .

"Doing what must be done."

. . . and, after a long stare in the direction where Persephone has faded from vision, say . . .

"Regardless of the cost."

EPILOGUE

Richemerion is folding what looks like an iridescent zip-front hoodie into a duffel that appears to be made out of pure energy. It expands as needed before contracting back down to a carriable size once they've got it tucked in. It's like the luggage version of Perg. They smooth the items flat with the back of their knuckles and reach for a pair of sandals that may or may not be alive, as I hear something go, "Oof," when they're stuffed inside.

"Glad y'all got up with me before I headed out on my Season of Boundless Wonder holiday. It's been a mental-ass Lunar Cycle, for real. The Warden needs to kick back."

"Can I ask you a question?" I lob out there.

"What's up?"

"Like . . . where do you go? The whole planet is under constant threat thanks to DONG. Seriously, where can you 'kick back'?"

They eye me cautiously, then say, "If you ever get to be a Warden, I'll tell you."

"What are the odds of that happening?"

They stare at me. "Nonzero. But in which direction is debatable. The difference between one percent and negative one percent isn't just two, ya heard?"

"Actually, I think that's literally what it is," Brit offers up.

"Maybe literally," Richemerion says. "Spiritual math be mathing different."

"What are you talking about?" Brit retorts.

"I dunno, Sistah Soulja, what are you talking about?"

She looks confused. "I—"

"Regardless," I jump in, in an attempt to keep this already barely navigable ship on course. "We're here because we're hoping for some steer."

"Some steer."

"Yes. Zerastian . . ."

She waves at the Warden.

"Oh, what's up, little one? Forgot you were there."

I continue. "She says she can see a path forward for us where things work out the way that we want them to, but it's a narrow eye of a needle that we'll have to thread, and we're hoping that you can offer some guidance."

The Warden stops packing, turns, rubs their hands together, sucks their teeth, sighs.

"What happened with my homeboy?"

"Your homeboy?

"The Maestro. What happened there?"

"Um . . ."

My palms get sweaty.

Knees weak.

Arms are heavy.

There's vom—

Nope, nope. That's . . . Something about being in the Warden's presence just makes me wanna spit hot fire.

"Uh," I continue. "What do you mean?"

"I mean, I *know* what happened. I'm the Warden of Protection. I see all that shit. I mean, *why* did it happen?"

"Because . . ." I swallow. "I had to make a choice," I reply.

Richemerion doesn't flinch. Doesn't nod. Doesn't even blink. They just let the words hang in the air like a chocolate-covered mint on a silk pillow.

"Between what and what?" they finally prompt.

"Between closing the rift and going after him."

"Word."

They shrug, casual as ever, hands having returned to smoothing the seams of a tasty-looking pair of traveling pants that's folded so crisply it probably insults lesser fabrics just by existing.

"And why did you make the choice you made?" they ask in a low-key singsong way, like they're just waiting on the dumb kid in the back of the class to figure out the obvious answer to the grammar question on their own.

My tongue feels thick. I kinda want to sit down, but I don't. "Because . . . Because going after Al was the thing *I* wanted to do. The choice *I* would have preferred to make."

Richemerion stops packing again. Looks at me, eyelids half closed.

"Mm-hmm. Buuuuut . . . ?"

"But closing access to the plane . . ." I breathe out through my teeth, ". . . was the choice I *had* to make."

"Why?"

"Because I don't know what was still trying to come through. I don't know if the Ninth Guardian had something worse lined up. Some way of not only affecting the now but the before and the after. All possible versions of the story, as it were. If I left it open, I would be guaranteed the suffering of millions, maybe billions. Maybe forever. I had to shut it down."

They stand straight, lean back, arms folded lightly across their chest. Their voice is low.

"That's what's up. The part folks never like to admit. Doing what's right don't always equal doing what feels good. Don't always equal what *looks* good."

They pause, rub one thumb along the edge of the necklace they wear; five interlocking multicolored rings that pulse faintly. I would say they look like Olympic rings (because they do), but their colors are the same as the partial rainbow I've been seeing.

"Protection ain't always about standing in front of a blade," they continue. "Sometimes, it's about stepping back so the blow never lands in the first place. Sometimes, it's keeping the door closed, even if it means someone you love is on the other side. Sometimes, it's knowing the fire is gonna burn you and jumping in anyway, because it keeps the rest from catching."

Their eyes lock with mine, and I feel a warmth run up my spine.

"You made a sacrifice, B. A real one. Not the kind that makes you seem noble. The kind that leaves a hole. And you made it for the right reasons. That's what protection is, B. It's about doing what's needed, even when no one claps."

They return to the bag. Snap it shut.

"Now, that said, good intentions only get you so far. You still fucked my man up, and that shit's whack. Ideally, you'd figure out a way to do all the shits at once. But you're still learning. You'll get there, Bruce."

My head, Brit's head, and Zerastian's all snap to the Warden at once.

"You know?" I ask.

"Dog, are you for real? I been knowing the shit since you showed up."

"Oh my . . ." My mouth hangs open as I realize . . . "The voice. The one I've heard in my head telling me everything's going to be alright . . . That's you?"

Richemerion smiles. Shrugs.

"Why didn't you just tell me?" I ask.

"My whole vibe is mystery, B. I can't just be announcing that shit willy-nilly. But now that everybody gonna know, it don't really matter. Besides . . . you got enough mysteries you still gotta unravel. Seems excessive just leaving another one hanging over your head."

"So . . ." Brittany starts, eyes wide. "Do you know who the Ninth Guardian is?"

Richemerion shakes their head. "I don't." The duffel contracts down into a tidy shape. One last soft *clack* as the fastener cinches. "I wish I did, but I don't watch the cradles, fam. I watch the gates."

"What does that—?"

"Yo, Warden? Homie? We're out of snacks again."

Perg trundles in, bits of some kind of jam on his moustache.

"I got you," Richemerion replies, heading out into the other room. "We should get y'all inside the Well anyway, before you bounce. Bet that serpent joint built up some large gains."

Brit, Zerastian, and I start to follow when . . .

Alert!
[Former] Heart Guard Member: [Mael Anderbariach] is requesting [Reinstatement] to your Heart Guard.
Do you wish to allow this reinstatement?
[Yes] [No]

"Oh shit!" I cry out.

"What's wrong? What is it?" Brit asks.

"Mael. He's asking to rejoin the Heart Guard."

"What? Why?"

"I dunno."

"Do you think he found Lonnaigh? Maybe she explained everything?"

"Yeah, I dunno."

"Do you—"

"Brit, I don't know! Zerry? Do you have anything?"

She tilts her head forward, stares at the floor.

"I'm . . . not sure."

"Well, does it seem more likely to be to our benefit to let him back in or not right now?"

"I can see . . . I can see paths that . . . There are roads leading ahead that support both options."

I look to the Warden. "Thoughts?"

"I gave you the Heart, B. Well, I didn't give it to *you*. But you're the one who's got it now. Look at it. Make the decision you think is right. You'll know what to do."

Thump-thump. Thump-thump.

I stare at the Notification, thinking about what Richemerion just said. Ideally, the goal is to do the right thing without having to do the wrong thing to get there. Mael's offering a second chance to make things right.

Thump-thump. Thump-thump.

There's no question what the correct response needs to be.

I press [Yes] and feel like I've taken the first real breath I've breathed in a very long time.

"Okay," I say. "That's done. So . . . let's get into the Pulse Well to lock it in, and then we *should* be able to seek his whereabouts in the same way Persephone— AHHHHHHH!"

THUMP-THUMP. THUMP-THUMP.

Just like how it happened when Mael tried to pull himself free, suddenly, it feels like the Heart is being ripped completely out of my chest.

"What's happening?" Brit shrieks, running to my side as I fall to the floor.

"I. Don't. Know," I grit out.

"Do you think it was a trick? Was it a trick, you think?" she shouts to Richemerion.

"I mean, shit"—the Warden shrugs—"anything's possible. Ask your precog. She knows."

"Goddammit! It hurts worse than the first time!" I wail. And then . . . a new Notification helps me to understand why.

ALERT!
Heart Guard Member [Persephone Vizardsdottir] is attempting to extract herself from your Heart Guard.
Do you wish to allow this extraction?
[Yes] [No]

What? WHAT?! NO! NO, she can't—

"Of course she can, Bruce. Why wouldn't she? Don't act so shocked."

"But . . ."

"Bruce, come on. Be real."

"Bruce! What's going on??"

"Ahhhhh . . . Seph. She's . . . trying . . . to . . . get . . . out . . . Heart Guard."

"Fuck me."

I don't know what to do. I don't know what to do. I mean, obviously, the right thing to do is to let her go. That's *obviously* the right thing to do. The whole lecture about serving the greater good and . . . Forcing someone to stay somewhere they don't want to be is the exact opposite of that.

It's why I let Mollie go. Why I let her just walk out of my life when she decided it was time without even trying to put up a fight. It was the right thing to do.

Right?

Or should I have fought harder? Should I have worked against my natural instincts to avoid confrontation? Would it have meant not losing her if I had only just *tried* to get her to stay? Would she have? Could she have? Should—

"AHHHHHH!"

Another jolt surges through my Heart. It feels like my body is about to rip in two.

"Well, then, let her go!" Brit commands. She turns to the Warden. "What happens if he doesn't? What'll happen to his Heart?"

"I mean . . . he might live? But he'll feel that shit later. So will she, for that matter. But there'll definitely be some scars. Maybe even reduced function. Might go haywire. Honestly, if I'm being real? Death would probably be preferable. But, you know, tomato/heart attack."

"Goddammit! It hurts!"

"Bruce, Bruce, listen to me . . ." Brit's holding my shoulders, staring me in the face. "Listen. You have to let her go. It's too dangerous not to. I know it sucks but . . . you've got to, Bruce!"

I'm biting my bottom lip, trying to breathe and failing. Tears are forming in my eyes, mostly from the physical pain, but also not just.

"Bruce! Let her go!"

I nod. Gulp for air. Look at the Notification burning in front of me . . .

ALERT!

Heart Guard Member [Persephone Vizardsdottir] is attempting to extract herself from your Heart Guard.

Do you wish to allow this extraction?

[Yes] [No]

A couple of tears that have been building finally fall as I gather all the strength I have inside me—whatever reservoir of determination I can summon—reach my trembling, groping hand forward, and—with no idea what will happen now, and forcing aside the fear that accompanies that particular brand of uncertainty—press . . .

[No].

ABOUT THE AUTHORS

Johnathan McClain is an award-winning actor, screenwriter, novelist, and audiobook narrator who did not set out to have such a diverse set of careers but has embraced life's unpredictabilities.

As an actor, his extensive resumé includes a notable turn as Megan Draper's agent, Alan Silver, on the final season of AMC's critically acclaimed drama *Mad Men* as well as appearing as the lead of the TV Land comedy series, *Retired at 35*—starring alongside late Hollywood icons George Segal and Jessica Walter—among dozens of other TV series, films, and plays.

As a writer and producer, Johnathan's feature film debut, *The Outfit*, cowritten with Oscar winner Graham Moore and starring Mark Rylance, Zoey Deutch, Dylan O'Brien, and Johnny Flynn, was produced by FilmNation and distributed internationally by Focus Features in the spring of 2022. He has also created, written, and produced two television series which, unlike his film, have yet to be captured on camera.

As an audiobook narrator, Johnathan has recorded approximately 200 titles ranging from sci-fi, to romance, to non-fiction, to fantasy, to LitRPG, and everything in between. He is the recipient of multiple Audiofile Earphone Awards, SOVAS nominations, and an Audie for his narration of Amie Kaufman and Jay Kristoff's #1 *New York Times*–bestselling sci-fi novel, *Illuminae*, which won the Audie Award for audiobook of the year for multivoiced narration in 2016.

He lives in Los Angeles with his wife, Laura.

Seth McDuffee is the literary equivalent of a mullet: business in the front, party in the back. When he's not penning bestsellers like *Good Boy* and the Big Sneaky Barbarian series, he fancies himself a musician, a marketer, and moonlights as the host and dungeon master of the wildly popular podcast, *The d20 Syndicate*.

A towering giant with hair long enough to give Rapunzel a complex, Seth began his writing career shortly after his crushing defeat in the first round of a third-grade spelling bee. (The word was "bologna," and he's been trying to prove it's a made-up word ever since.)

When not busy disappointing elementary school spelling judges or annoying his neighbors with his ten-hour renditions of "Wagon Wheel" on the theremin, Seth can be found in his kitchen, where he uses his classical culinary training to perfect the art of microwaving Hot Pockets.

Critics have called his work "mostly readable" and "probably not plagiarized." His mother thinks he's very handsome. He lives in the Midwest with his tiny, irritating dog, and bombshell fiancée, Michaela.